Praise for Jess Everlee
and the Lucky Lovers of London series

"Everlee crafts a scorching affair...
Their romance is a combustible one."
—*Entertainment Weekly* on *The Gentleman's Book of Vices*

"This is a joyful, spicy romance; but with an emotional upheaval
of pain and trauma you feel for both of the lovers."
—*BuzzFeed* on *The Gentleman's Book of Vices*

"Everlee creates an intriguing cast of found family for Charlie
and truly thorny obstacles for the lovers to overcome. Fans of
Cat Sebastian and Olivia Waite will enjoy this queer Victorian romance."
—*Library Journal* on *The Gentleman's Book of Vices*

"Everlee's fabulous second Lucky Lovers of London Victorian romance
(after *The Gentleman's Book of Vices*) takes the series to new heights...
Equally sweet and steamy, this will delight Everlee's fans
while enticing many new ones."
—*Publishers Weekly*, starred review, on *A Rulebook for Restless Rogues*

"After wowing readers with *The Gentleman's Book of Vices* (2022), the
first in her Victorian-era Lucky Lovers of London series, Everlee returns
with a stunningly romantic, superbly sensual friends-to-lovers story
that brilliantly makes use of the book's thoughtfully rendered characters
and their search for love and acceptance."
—*Booklist* on *A Rulebook for Restless Rogues*

JESS EVERLEE

If you purchased this book without a cover you should be aware that this book is stolen property. It was reported as "unsold and destroyed" to the publisher, and neither the author nor the publisher has received any payment for this "stripped book."

carina press®

Recycling programs for this product may not exist in your area.

ISBN-13: 978-1-335-47399-8

To Sketch a Scandal

Copyright © 2025 by Jess Everlee

All rights reserved. No part of this book may be used or reproduced in any manner whatsoever without written permission.

Without limiting the author's and publisher's exclusive rights, any unauthorized use of this publication to train generative artificial intelligence (AI) technologies is expressly prohibited.

This is a work of fiction. Names, characters, places and incidents are either the product of the author's imagination or are used fictitiously. Any resemblance to actual persons, living or dead, businesses, companies, events or locales is entirely coincidental.

For questions and comments about the quality of this book, please contact us at CustomerService@Harlequin.com.

® is a trademark of Harlequin Enterprises ULC.

Carina Press
22 Adelaide St. West, 41st Floor
Toronto, Ontario M5H 4E3, Canada
www.Harlequin.com

Printed in U.S.A.

In memory of N. You weren't lucky, but you are remembered.

The emotional well-being of my readers is important to me.
If you would like to see specific content warnings before you dive in,
please visit www.jesseverlee.com/cw.

Chapter One

Warren

When it came to such concepts as "following rules," Warren Bakshi was a hit-or-miss sort of chap.

Take market day, for instance, which was Warren's responsibility in his family of two.

Rule 1: Stick fast to the household budget. *Hit.*

Rule 2: Stick fast to the household budget without shamelessly flirting up the stall keepers. *Utter miss.*

"Thank you *so* much, Mr. Singh," he sighed as he loaded his basket. This cheerful, round-cheeked stall owner was about the same height as him, but Warren angled himself so he was looking up, appreciative, loyal, *willing* even, should it come to that. It wouldn't with Mr. Singh—Warren knew his audience—but the bloke was receptive in his own quiet way. He blushed and waved a hand like the low price Warren had negotiated was more than standard, perfectly normal, nothing he wouldn't give to any fellow with an old mum to care for back home, smoldering eyes and smile aside.

It was best to leave this sort of exchange quickly with deals in hand. This was the market, after all, not the molly bar where

8 *To Sketch a Scandal*

he worked in the evenings when his domestic duties were exhausted. There he could smolder and seduce and then carry on for as long as it was fun for all parties, through a drink and a chat and maybe all the way into one of the back rooms if they felt like it. It was risky, though, to push chaps like this—ones who might not even understand why they liked Warren so much—too far too often. Rules of the game.

But today, Warren had one more rule to break before he went home, and he'd do it most affordably with a little help.

He leaned over the stall like he did over his bar, avoiding the baskets of vegetables as best he could and looking up like the two of them were conspirators. Everyone liked to feel like they were in on something naughty. Though the ability to feel that way himself had dulled after years of debauched living, he sure knew how to whip it up in others.

"Say, do you happen to know the best place to buy…" Warren rolled his eyes demonstrably. "A cheap sort of a sari? It's for someone who won't, ah…" He jerked his head to a couple of white women at the other end of Mr. Singh's stall who were eyeing an obviously overpriced, premixed curry powder instead of simply asking him about his well-sourced collection of proper spices. "Someone who won't know the difference, and I don't want to spend too much."

Not precisely an earth-shattering concern, but it didn't matter what the subject was when Warren pulled out all the stops like that. Mr. Singh swelled with the happiness of helpfulness, laughing and pointing past stalls overflowing with baskets of early-autumn produce, barrels of oysters, and fat towers of dusty flour sacks, to a stall that fluttered ostentatiously with bright fabrics and cheap incense holders. Though it was run by a family on Warren and Mr. Singh's side of the neighborhood, it was getting more traction from fashion-hungry wives like the ones with the curry powder than savvy shoppers like Warren.

"Thanks, mate." At the bar, he'd call the bloke *love*, but from the blush his words elicited, he might as well have. He added a friendly wink, setting himself up for another good price next week. "You really are the best."

If Mr. Singh suspected that Warren had implicitly lied about whom the sari was for, he did not show it. But was it really much of a lie, in the end? As he went to the cart to secure a piece of the mass-produced "Oriental" garbage that English socialites were positively manic for these days, he wasn't convinced and didn't trouble himself over it. After all, when he showed up draped in the sari himself for the upcoming drag party at The Curious Fox, most of his friends were no different from these housewives: they wouldn't know the difference between a beautiful, hand-woven piece and a cheap knockoff. Dress-up wasn't his passion—he was more interested in how to get clothes *off.* Thus, while he'd happily break society's rule about whether he ought to attend such parties, he wasn't about to break his budgetary rules over anything he had to put *on.*

"Will you hold it for me?" he asked after he'd charmed the woman at the next market stall (he only bedded in one direction, but could flirt with anyone) and selected a sari that was decidedly low-quality, but still boasted pretty colors. "Just till tomorrow? I get paid tonight."

The seller agreed, and Warren went on to finish his shopping and other errands. The postbox was his last stop on the way home. Once he got the box unlocked, he followed the rules: keep his eyes slightly averted to the rows of other boxes and the harried commuters in their bank collars and work boots so he could not see the return addresses. He felt, rather than saw, that there were three pieces of mail in the Bakshi box. Bills, he figured, but he did not check, practiced at the art of slipping the post into his market basket without looking even once.

That was the rule. And it was one he dared not miss.

He went home to the little house he shared with his mother and two other widows who'd gone in with them on the rent.

10 *To Sketch a Scandal*

Warren was strictly dedicated to the budget, but no amount of frugality could have allowed a then-sixteen-year-old Warren to keep the house he'd grown up in once his father died and his older brother, Harry, ran off to "make the family fortune." With prudence and cleverness, though, they'd at least not had to leave their tidy neighborhood entirely, nor put themselves in the hands of Christian missionaries who offered food and shelter for prices far more existential than anything you could find at the market.

Pleasantly mechanical with habit, Warren went to the kitchen and unloaded his shopping on the well-organized pantry shelves. Its sections for everything from flours and cheeses to oils and spices were labeled and marked by name with swirling doodles of different animals creeping through the letters. Bored one day while Mother was recovering from one of her fainting spells and frustrated when he could not find what he was looking for in the pantry, he'd organized the shelves and put up the silly labels in a whim so childish, he'd certainly have destroyed them by now if not for how pleased the women had been when they found them. So now, half a decade on, flour remained arbitrarily associated with a monkey perched atop the stacks, spices with an elephant spraying flavor from her trunk, oil with the turtle who balanced the bottle on his back, and so on.

Mother and the other widows in the house were seamstresses. The other two worked the sweatshops, but Mother could not, so it was as common a sight as anything to find her stooped sturdily at the foot of her fabric-draped dummy in the downstairs sitting room, fingers nimble on the custom order, and talking in bright, rapid Punjabi to Mrs. Ahuja, one of their neighbors. It seemed impossible to imagine that mother needed the neighbor here, not just to sew, but to keep an eye on her. Mother was always bright and nimble and sturdy. Until the moment she wasn't.

After finding a stopping point in work and talk, she sprang

upright to greet him, slim but not frail, aging but not stooped, with still more black than gray in her pinned-up braid. Though her status was lesser than it once had been, she had always remained as tidily groomed and fashionably dressed as life and work allowed. She fussed over some imperceptible imperfection in the fall of his jacket, trying similarly to fix something about his rakishly-long hair. The jacket he permitted, but he leaned out of the way when she came for the hair. She smiled and rolled her eyes toward Mrs. Ahuja.

"Always so vain," Mother said.

"He has every right to be." Mrs. Ahuja winked. "And my granddaughter very much agrees."

"Is that so?" Warren said lightly, as if he'd not heard that one before, not from her nor from any other of the myriad neighbors with marriageable daughters and granddaughters who were always eyeing him with secondhand interest. He didn't have much money, but neither did they, so appearing charming and responsible made him a decent catch anyway. In theory. "Well, tell her I'm flattered, but that there's only room for one woman in my life."

He put a hand to his heart and smiled winningly at his mother, who pursed her lips at this too-true joke he'd told perhaps once too often. Still, she didn't argue. Hearty complaint and begrudging acceptance seemed to go in cycles, but this week, she was resigned to the idea that he might follow through with his threat to stay a bachelor forever.

"Do you have the post?" she asked, changing the subject before Mrs. Ahuja could go on and embarrass them further.

Warren handed her the letters with a dutiful flourish. They sat together on the sofa, Mother resting the letters face down upon the skirts of her day dress.

This habit, born of Mother's difficulties in crowded spaces like post offices, had begun back when there was still hope of news about Father's lost ship, one of the last the East India

To Sketch a Scandal

Company sent out from London. She had not wanted him to have news before she did. It was silly now that Father's death was long-confirmed and their box contained mostly advertisements, bills, and the very occasional letter from Warren's wayward older brother, but they maintained the ritual nonetheless.

They did not count aloud anymore, but on the third heartbeat, she turned the letters over.

"So, what have we got?" Mother held up the first piece of mail. A bill from the druggist, for her medicines. Not unexpected or extravagant. It was set aside to be dealt with.

Then she picked up the second piece, a little postcard without an envelope.

"Oh, Warren!" she said. "You should look into this."

Warren grimaced when she passed it to him. Not again...

Buttersnipe's School for Artistic Enrichment. Pursue your passion and be part of the aesthetic revolution. The advertisement made its claims in swirling letters, complete with an overwrought sketch of a man standing at an easel and a new-and-reduced price for a season's worth of "premier instruction."

"You know he's such a good artist," she said wistfully to Mrs. Ahuja, nodding at one of the paintings that hung near the doorway, a bright and busy rendition of London Bridge done up in shades of turmeric yellow. "Like his father was."

Warren rolled his eyes, not kidding himself for a second. While his father had indeed possessed artistic talent cut short by the practicalities of earning a living, doodles like the ones Warren made when he had nothing better to do made an artist only in the eyes of said doodler's mother.

"It's probably a scam anyway," he said, not daring to disagree with her assessment of his "talent," but not wanting to get her hopes up, either. "What proper school sends tripe like this through the mail willy-nilly?"

He tried tossing it aside with the bill, but Mother took it from him with a glare. She got up and went to the many-drawered

Jess Everlee 13

desk where household papers were kept. From one of the drawers, she procured nearly half an inch of other advertisements. "If you don't like this one," she said, "I've got plenty of others. Take your pick."

"Mother, where are you getting all those?" he asked. She brought this subject up often, but when had she made a whole bloody collection out of it?

"Here and there," she said mysteriously. Very mysteriously, since she rarely left the house, and never left it alone. He narrowed his eyes at Mrs. Ahuja. Was she bringing these things around as part of some conspiracy to see him paint-stained and married off? She did not, suspiciously enough, meet his eyes, very busy all of a sudden finding a bead that had rolled off under the dress. Meanwhile, Mother added the Buttersnipe's advertisement to her stack before spreading the lot of them on top of the desk for easy perusal.

He avoided rolling his eyes through sheer force of filial will.

"One more to go." He waved the final piece of mail. Mother took her time coming back, but something changed in her eyes when she spotted the return address, and the rest of the journey became a rush. She all but threw herself back onto the sofa beside him.

Warren peered over as she held the letter out in a state of shock, blinking at the name of the sender. Perhaps a few too many late nights at The Curious Fox had left him permanently bleary.

Hari Bakshi. New South Wales.

"It's been months!" Mother clutched the letter to her heart before holding it back out. "I was starting to worry."

Warren didn't mention that he'd already passed through worry and into a solid assumption that another set of Bakshi bones was decorating the sea floor. His brother, Harry (*Hari* formally on letters and documents, but called *Harry* from the start to ease his London upbringing, same as *Varun* on birth

14 *To Sketch a Scandal*

records had become *Warren* in practice), did not write often enough to keep Mother happy, but this last stretch had been quite a bit longer than usual. Warren was, of course, always pleased to know his brother wasn't dead. Beyond that, however, he found Harry's letters insufferable, self-indulgent, and filled to the brim with useless promises.

"Well," he said. "Open it. Let's hear his excuse."

Dearest Mother and Brother,
I know that pleasantries would be most polite here, but I find myself at present too enthusiastic about the point of this letter to do anything but get straight to it.

Warren had to roll his eyes before using them to read further.

It has been years now since I left England in hopes of bettering our family's fortunes after Father's misplaced dedication to a company that cared nothing for those of us left so desperate in his tragic absence.

As if Warren and Mother did not know this, needed yet another retelling of how Harry would save them all by chasing treasure halfway across the world. Warren suspected Harry added these prologues so that strangers would know of his chivalry if the letter were intercepted.

While the temptation of despair and defeat has been ever with me on this journey, my sense of duty to the two of you has spurred me on—

God, what a prick.

—to success at last. I am thrilled to—

Mother, perhaps slowed less by rolled eyes, must have read faster. Before he could see what Harry was thrilled by, she pulled the letter to her heart again, eyes very wide.

"Mother?"

"Married?" she whispered to the floor, eyes shining with tears. Not happy ones. "My son is *married*?" She sprang up to show her friend, nimbler than ever, suddenly vibrating with so much nervous energy that Warren's whole body tensed, preparing to catch her if she suddenly went the other direction just as dramatically.

Somewhere under his fear that heartbreak might send Mother into a nasty spell, an ungenerous thrill ran through Warren at the news. Harry had gotten married? Abroad? Without any input from Mother on the match or involvement in the wedding, telling her through a *letter*? Harry had done a lot of dodgy things—he'd been dodgy to the core from day one, so far as Warren could tell—but *this*? This was bloody scandalous. Finally, Warren's "generous" brother, who had so "generously" abandoned them, was about to be seen for what he really was at last—someone who spoke a lot about how he cared for his family, but was really only devoted to himself.

"Married," Mother said again. Her voice was shaking. She clearly wasn't happy, but seemed to be trussing her disappointment up tight. If Father were alive, Harry would never hear another word from the family after this, no question. Yet his mother, on her own in a country where, legally speaking, she was at the mercy of her sons, was clearly tempering her reaction.

Tears were slipping down her cheeks, but as she met Warren's eye across the room, she did something very unexpected. Though her lips trembled through it, she managed to smile.

"Married," she repeated. "And rich."

Rich?

Now Warren got up, somehow managing to get the letter out of Mother's grip so he could catch up to what the women were suddenly gushing about beside the sewing that was apparently as forgotten as Harry's most severe transgression.

As he so insufferably reiterated in all his letters, Harry had run off to chase treasure in New Zealand and Japan, an absurd abandonment that he justified by saying it was for the ultimate care of his family. Complete bollocks. Harry wanted adventure and freedom that could not be had eking out a living here as the oldest son of a moderately successful sailor and part-time painter. So he'd taken what little they had to spare and run off, claiming he'd make it back a hundred times over before he was done. Warren had figured he'd never see his brother again. He certainly didn't expect to ever see a significant amount of money.

But as Warren read the rest of the letter, he found Harry claiming to have made a genuine fortune investing in various enterprises and properties across the south and east. Enough of a fortune that he was coming back to England, to settle down and enjoy the fruits of success with his beloved family. A family that now included a rather hastily acquired new wife named Anjali.

"We must get things ready," Mother insisted.

"You're going to have them?" Mrs. Ahuja asked, like she wouldn't herself but was amused by Mother's choice.

Mother wiped her eyes and nodded. "The circumstances at sea are different," she said, determined. "I'm sure he had his reasons, and will explain them to me when he gets here. He's a good boy."

If he weren't afraid of getting caught at it, Warren would have rolled his eyes again, right into next week this time.

Harry, it seemed, really could do no wrong.

Mother started moving to make the house fit immediately, scooping up the mail and piling it with some other papers that had been left out beside the now-forgotten splay of art school advertisements.

"Mum," Warren said, trying to be noticed above her sudden

bustling. His anxiety built with her momentum, eyes drawn to every table corner and windowsill her head could reach on the way down if she took faint. "Mum, he's not coming in this evening from the next town over. He's on a boat from New Zealand." He checked the letter's date. "Can't be here for at least two more weeks, and you know how these ships are. Could be a month. Could be two."

Or not at all, he did not add.

"And they ain't going to fit in the house anyway," he added, unable to stop himself once he had her attention. He had to take the omnibus into Soho this weekend where he'd stay through a few shifts at The Curious Fox before returning home, tension eased and pockets padded. While the other women kept an eye on her while he was gone, he hated the thought of her bustling about rearranging furniture for a son who still had plenty of time to drown on his way here. "Have him use his new 'fortune' to take a nice room. Sounds like he can afford it."

Mother glared like he'd suggested drilling holes in the bottom of his brother's boat.

"You'd have your own family sleep in some strange bed?"

That was something Warren did frequently, and it wasn't so bad. But he faltered under the fire in her stare.

"Just wait till I get home to start rearranging things, yeah?" he huffed. "You shouldn't go outside your usual routine when I'm gone."

"I'm stronger than you think."

"Please. For the sake of my nerves."

She clucked her tongue, but he'd won this small victory. She picked her thread back up.

"No extra shifts, then," she said. "I won't rearrange furniture, but only if you don't work extra. I want you back Monday night to help me figure out the sleeping arrangements. You won't be needing the money anyway, will you?"

The notion that he would not need his position at the club

18 *To Sketch a Scandal*

anymore was briefly chilling, until he remembered it was Harry they were talking about here.

He'd believe in this so-called fortune when he saw it.

Until then?

Bawdy business as usual.

The Curious Fox was much like Warren, in that it had two distinct modes. At night, the crystal chandelier was lit up like stars against a fabric-draped ceiling; the lamps were shaded in devilish pinks and reds; the tables were filled with friends in all manner of unseemly dress, gambling and drinking; while the curtained alcoves were occupied by illicit lovers awaiting their turn in one of the four back rooms. There were paintings on the walls that might each be passable as a one-off, but that gave a distinct impression of a Greek way of thinking when taken as a collection. It was not technically a brothel as there was no staff of that sort, but that nuance might be lost on an outsider if they saw the place dressed in its nighttime best.

Now, though, as Warren hung up his coat and hat and approached the bar, the Fox was in its other state. Its respectable daytime state. Lit with glowy gas lamps and cautiously cracked curtains, it was all much as a theater set might seem to those preparing the evening's show. The chaises and rugs were a little worn; the artwork was not comprised of pricy originals—the sketch of a satyr above the keg being no more than a doodle Warren had done and tacked up as an in-joke with Forester. While the wide variety of liquor bottles gleamed by night, by day you'd see that a few of them were nearly empty and likely to stay that way—since practically everyone drank the same two gins or whiskeys, there was no point paying to keep up with the level of variety they projected.

While Warren would tend the bar later, first it was his job to transition the place from one mode to the next.

After the events of the afternoon, he was half-starved. Fortunately, the manager—no, owner, he was the owner now, thanks to a little leeway from some renegade copper last year—was the sort to have thought of that. Warren let himself into the quiet club to find that David Forester had procured a nice little tea for them and spread it out on the bar, spinach pies and lemony bean salads, the signature fare of a club member who gave fellow Foxes a discount at his Berwick Street food cart.

Warren looked over the food that had been laid out so nicely on the bar. It wasn't the first time he'd come in to a spread like this, but he couldn't say it was an everyday occurrence, either. He eyed it hopefully but a little suspiciously.

"You're here already. Brilliant." David Forester came out of the kitchen carrying a pot of tea. "And may I say, you are looking especially sharp. That waistcoat is divine on you."

Forester was a tall bloke with a tidy beard and fine watch chain he'd hung on to from the better life he'd led before Warren knew him. He was protective and kindhearted, but inclined to flattery when he needed something. A meal was one thing, but a perfectly timed pot of tea and a compliment on a waistcoat he'd worn as recently as last week? Warren eyed his friendly smile sideways.

"What's all this?" he asked.

Forester put the teapot down and sat on one of the stools. "A little sustenance for the party-planning party, of course." He filled two mugs and patted the stool beside him. Warren reluctantly obliged. Forester seemed to sense Warren's suspicion, and added, "We're planning the drag ball today, aren't we?"

"Yes," said Warren slowly.

"Well, the party planners rarely get to enjoy the festivities as much as the partygoers," he said, full of false pep. "I wanted to make this part of the process a little extra enjoyable for us, while we put something together for the others. I got your favorites."

He pointed them out, gently nudging one of the teacups toward Warren. Warren was too peckish to argue with food put

20   *To Sketch a Scandal*

out in front of him, but he clocked the martyr talk nonetheless. That sort of thing was Forester all over—to be fair, a taste for self-sacrifice was good for the owner of a place like this—but it was less appealing to Warren. Particularly when the subject at hand was a drag ball that Warren himself had suggested and already half-bought an outfit for.

"Are we still having the party, then?" Warren asked.

"Certainly, yes," Forester said adamantly. "Noah's got his dress nearly done. Not to mention the wedding we've got planned—the pair is pretending to be reluctant about it, but you can tell they're nearly as excited as…well, as I am." Forester chuckled. He was an incorrigible matchmaker, and got a real kick out of enabling—or, occasionally, half-forcing—rowdy little "molly house weddings" on matches that had gone particularly well. Part genuine celebration, part bawdy hazing ritual, it was certainly good fun so long as one was on the right side of the makeshift altar.

"So what's with the party planners not having any fun, then?" said Warren. "Enough with the buttering up. What's the bad news?"

Forester sighed, running a hand down his face. "It's the security plan, mate," he said with a little thread of defeat in his voice, not unlike the streaks of gray that had cropped up in his beard after a year dealing with new laws that substantially increased the risk of their work. "We can't just have a party without considering that anymore, you know that. Things that were nothing or a slap on the wrist last year are good for two years' hard labor now, hardly any evidence needed to prove it, and it's twice as easy to justify a raid in the meantime. If we want to have a good time of it, we're going to have to take it to the back rooms and the upstairs parlor, get some layers between the gowns and the doors."

"Gowns, I think, are still a slap on the wrist."

"In and of themselves, yes. But they'll count as evidence for the rest, I'm sure. And anyway, how many blokes do you know who are on their best behavior once the petticoats go on?"

There was no arguing with that. Forester's own lover, Noah Clarke, became a menace in his drags, which was probably the impetus for Forester's nerves in the first place.

"Fair enough," Warren said. "Bit snugger than if we did it out here, but I doubt snugness is going to be high on anyone's list of complaints. What's the real bad news?"

"Well," Forester began carefully. "If the party is back there." He pointed to the door to the hall and staircase in question. "And the front door is out here." He gestured again, to the front entrance this time, like he hoped these unneeded movements would buy him time. "Then the best way to deter nosy eyes from seeing what's happening *back there* is to make sure the space *out here* looks like a perfectly normal night at a perfectly normal club. Meaning we stay open to patrons who aren't interested in the party. Which would entail…well…" He winced. "Having my very best, most capable, most loyal employee behind the bar."

"That so?" Warren asked slowly. "And who, may I ask, might that be?"

"It would be…you." He lifted the pot with a forced smile. "More tea?"

Warren slapped a hand down so hard the cups rattled. "Forester!"

"Look—"

"This whole thing was *my* idea!"

"I know." Forester topped off Warren's cup like that could fix everything, throwing a little extra sugar in there while he was at it. "A brilliant idea. And because you are the brilliant soul behind the brilliant idea, I know you want to see it done right, even if it means taking a different role than you'd have preferred."

He pushed the cup a little closer to Warren.

To Sketch a Scandal

Warren ignored it. "So, I'll just be down here with the sad saps who'd rather mope around with some gin than have an actual good time?"

"Miles Montague will keep you company," Forester said with as much brightness as he could muster. "He's not a sad sap, eh? And you get on well with him." When that didn't help, he said, "Look. You can pop up now and again. I'll cover for you when I can. But I need someone I can trust to look out for signs of trouble down here, so you can warn everyone early if we need to cut it short."

"Then why pick me?" Warren snapped. "You know I ain't trustworthy."

"You may have fooled some of the patrons into thinking that, Warren, with the way you sneak off to the back rooms with them halfway through the night. But I know better. You're my right-hand man in this place. If we want this to work, I need your help. Please?"

"Oh, bugger off," Warren muttered, finally picking up the tea. He shot it back, wishing it was something else entirely.

"So you'll do it?"

"Fine. I'll do it. But I won't like it." He took up the last of the little triangular pies and pointed one of its sharp ends at Forester. "And you owe me the cost of the sari I already bought."

He hadn't bought it yet, strictly. But he wasn't about to promise money to a neighbor and never come back with it. He had a reputation at the markets. It was different than the one he cultivated here, but until such time as his brother's "fortune" was proven, it mattered just as much.

Forester sighed. "Of course. How much?"

Angry as he was, Warren opted to report the price charged to the socialites so he could pocket the difference.

Chapter Two

Matty

When all was said and done, the thing Matty Shaw was most looking forward to about his promotion was the mustache he would grow.

"The mustache?" Inspector Barrows laughed. The two of them shared a cramped and paper-strewn office at the very end of the Special Investigations hallway of the London Metropolitan Police Station at Scotland Yard. They made an odd pair, Matty and Barrows; the former appearing too young and fresh-faced for the position he was in, the latter so gray and erect it was a wonder his impending retirement hadn't happened a decade ago.

The light had gone orange with evening as it slanted through their single second-story window, specks of dust in the air lit up to look like unseasonable indoor snow—they did their own housekeeping when there was sensitive material around, doing about as well in the cluttered office as one might expect from an aging husband who'd never had to clean a thing and the confirmed bachelor he'd all but raised himself in a detective's office. Matty and Barrows, after a day of witness interviews and strategizing their new case, had settled into their respective desks, positioned across from each other in this office they'd shared since before Matty's facial hair preferences were even worth talking about. The locked filing cabinets were behind Matty, and their case visualization board was behind Barrows. Matty sometimes imagined, as they sat together like this at the end of a shift—Matty slouched with ink-stained fingers before his files, Barrows forcing his posture to remain ever-straight even through obvious end-of-day weariness—that they might look like grandfather and grandson after a long day of flying kites or other such quaint bonding.

"You are too much, really," Barrows said, incredulous. "I retire and get my old bones out of your way; you replace me at last, take control of your own cases, gain the respect of the unit, and it's the *mustache* you're salivating over?"

"I wouldn't say salivating *over*," Matty corrected dryly. He met Barrows's eyes, but it was short-lived, gaze drifting to the latest case notes on the wall over his shoulder as he spoke. Because they were not, in fact, a quaint familial pair, but detectives with both their minds always half-immersed in whatever they were working. "That stuff typically flows the other direction, doesn't it? I'm sorry, but your position isn't high enough to justify a beard. This is Scotland Yard, man. Those of us who aren't actively trying to look like whores are supposed to don mustaches, and I am thrilled to soon count myself among the latter at last."

Barrows didn't laugh this time, his amusement at Matty's straight-faced humor confined to his eyes and a little quirk of his own steel-gray, Scotland Yard–approved facial decoration. "Well, keep your razor sharp for now, Matthew. We need you to give off that *willing youth* aura of yours one last time. Play it well and your upper lip will be cozy before Christmas."

Barrows glanced at the tackboard behind him, the one Matty was already perusing. Over the past few weeks, it had accumulated the news clippings, suspect photos, and various relevant paraphernalia for an art forgery case that seemed almost laughably quaint compared with Matty's usual fare. Blessed or cursed with the sort of pretty, innocent countenance that humanity's dregs seemed compelled to exploit, Matty's plainclothes work usually revolved around disturbing and dangerous trafficking operations. That tack board was more often filled with photographs and newspaper clippings so grim that nightmares were a job quirk he hardly thought more of than he did of putting his coat on in the morning.

Matty got up and joined Barrows under the board. He ought to be getting ready to leave, or at least encouraging Barrows to do so, but ever since the old man had announced his retirement, the end of each day had come with an increasingly tight squeezing sensation around the center of Matty's chest. The only thing that alleviated it was engaging in excuses to linger.

So linger he did, this time over the board they'd rearranged just this afternoon. A wave of fraudulent art pieces had been making its way through society, causing massive loss of money and no little embarrassment for London's aesthetically inclined. Headlines screamed for justice from where Matty had cut them out and pinned them up in chronological order. Beside them were photographs of the suspects they'd narrowed it down to. One was a large-scale Continental operation, foreign and therefore outside their department. The other was a portrait-painting academy right here in London, owned by an eccentric married couple with some dubious monetary records and a questionable reputation in the London art scene. Ruling out or proving that academy's involvement was their focus. Not too tough, not too violent—such a decent way for Barrows to conclude his career that it might seem purposeful, if those sorts of things were ever taken into account in a place like this.

Matty took down the academy advertisement that had been making its way into postboxes all over the West End this week,

26

To Sketch a Scandal

perusing it for the dozenth time for anything that hinted at untowardness. *Buttersnipe's School for Artistic Enrichment. Pursue your passion and be part of the aesthetic revolution.* Whatever the devil that meant. He suspected it meant they were training up forgers, rather than legitimate portraitists, though it still remained to be seen.

"Are we certain Buttersnipe is even a real name?" Matty asked. "Like guttersnipe? It just *sounds* fake."

"Even if it's fake, there are other reasons for a fake name."

Matty's eyes flicked from the advertisement to the single photograph they had of the suspects. The couple posed mournfully in their studio with a little dog between them—their acquaintances confirmed in today's interviews that the artists reported distrusting photography, which seemed like a convenient excuse not to have a lot of photographs floating around. Matty looked to the note beside the picture, written in his own handwriting from another of today's tip-offs: *"possible they bring figure models into their bed—either sex."* He read that one over a few times. He'd been excited to get the information because it offered a great way in, but by now was vaguely nauseous about what he might be subjecting himself to at their hands, when he went undercover as one of these figure models.

After a moment, he felt a heavy warmth on his arm. Barrows's hand.

"Alright, Matthew?"

"I'm glad to be getting old, Barrows," Matty admitted. *Without you, I wouldn't have.* Those words were on his tongue as he looked at the old man who'd certainly saved him from being a grim data point on a case board himself. But that was too sentimental. "Just glad for it. That's all."

"Twenty-five is hardly old."

Matty did not correct him that twenty-five was practically ancient in the sort of cases he had made his career investigating. He'd been successfully posing as a potential or active prostitute for years, and it was Barrows himself who'd pointed out at the beginning that, statistically, lads in that particular profession rarely lasted past twenty, for one reason or another (and some of those reasons pretty terrible indeed). In his last case—the Lord Belleville case, the big one—he hadn't even managed to pull it off, unable to seduce any closer to the center of the ring than playing valet for some harmless sodomite who ran an irrelevant side operation called The Curious Fox. The bloke had clearly liked the look of him well enough, but never even hinted at anything usefully untoward. Might have been insulting if it hadn't been so nice to be treated like a human being for once during the course of a case. His own fond feelings for the chap aside, however, the near-propriety made things difficult. Matty was still astounded he'd gotten intelligence at all in that position, much less bust the case open as successfully as he had.

So it was clearly coming to an end, this angle of his. Given the danger and degradation it required, he ought to be happy about that. Barrows, at least, seemed confident he'd be able to manage the transition, that his mind would eventually prove at least as good as the rest of him.

All Matty was confident in, though, was that he could look the part of a detective chief. He'd always been skilled at looking the part, after all.

Thus, the mustache: the only part of the job he might prove suited for, in the end.

"Well, one last case like this probably won't kill me," Matty sighed, trying to reason those worries from his mind. "Easier than the others, I'd say. These figure models are presumably willing, at least. That's better than I usually get."

"You've done well, these years," Barrows said with a very serious nod. "I've rarely met a detective so willing to do what needs to be done. It's a shame I can't be here to watch what you accomplish next."

His voice held the undeniable note of impending goodbye.

28   *To Sketch a Scandal*

Not the day's goodbye, but the other one, the one Matty could not delay by spending a few extra minutes staring at the board. It made Matty itch, like his comfortable plain clothes had been swapped for the heavy uniform that detectives only donned for Met events, or that lacy frock that had gotten him access to a certain illicit soiree… He tugged at his collar and said nothing but, "Thank you, sir."

"I have something for you."

No. God, no. He really couldn't bear this sort of thing. "Sir, I don't—"

But Barrows was reaching into his desk drawer, paying Matty's feeble protest no mind. He took out a small blue box with ribbon on it.

Matty took it reluctantly. "Sir, this isn't—"

"I know I ought to wait the few weeks, until I leave and your promotion is official," said Barrows. "But I admit, I'm impatient. And it's all in the bag anyway. So open it now. Let it keep you company through our last case together."

With hands that suddenly felt stiff and dry, Matty undid the wrapping and opened the box. It was a modest but well-made gold ring set with an inky onyx stone.

"Th-thank you, sir," said Matty, throat squeezed. He shut the box and held it back out. "Once it's all official—"

"Make sure it fits," Barrows scolded, pushing it back.

He opened the box again and slipped on the ring. A perfect fit.

"As I say," Barrows said. "You've done well, these years. I didn't want to leave without a bit of recognition for that. I know you don't get much of it around here. But I have appreciated your work immensely."

"Thank you, sir," Matty nearly whispered. "Um. It's… I like it a lot."

There was an awkward silence. The shorter-term goodbye became inevitable when it stretched too long, brought about

Jess Everlee 29

by his own unwillingness to fully engage with the other. Barrows stood, tacked the advertisement back on the board, and gave Matty a pat on the back.

"Well, Matthew, we have plenty of long nights ahead of us as it is, and these old bones are ready for a rest," he said. "Are yours? Those terribly ancient, twenty-five-year-old bones of yours?"

They were, actually, but his mind was not ready to disengage from this dusty little office. The room he rented was objectively more comfortable, but what was there for him aside from a lonely bed? A landlady and other tenants he could not talk to about his high-security days? A cold plate of the supper he'd long-since missed? He was certainly no expert in the mysterious concept of "home," but he assumed what he felt in this office was closer to it than what he felt at his boardinghouse. It was better when Barrows was sitting across from him, admittedly, but even alone, it was something.

"Not yet." Matty tapped one of the tacked-up notes with the back of a finger. "There's a little more I'd like to sort through, I think."

"The character profiles of your suspiciously-surnamed would-be lovers?" Barrows teased. When Matty didn't smile back, his own faded rapidly. He gave another pat on the back, this one firm with the unspoken weight of where Matty'd been found, what he'd been through, what he'd made of himself with the face that might otherwise have been his ruin before the age of twenty. Statistically. "You'll have earned that mustache when all is said and done, lad. More than earned it."

Barrows left, and Matty returned to his desk with his case file and the single photograph of the Buttersnipes and their dog. As usual, they were not exactly the sort he'd choose to seduce if given the option—it had only happened the other way once, during the investigation of a coffeehouse in Piccadilly Circus that he investigated for supposed sodomitical conspiracies. As an occasional participant in such conspiracies himself, Matty had opted not to find any proof of wrongdoing when the wrongdoing he found turned out to be the sort that wasn't hurting anyone, in his estimation. He'd done the same for David Forester, his harmless employer in the Belleville case. Having been shown mercy himself by Barrows all those years ago, he had an appetite for letting things slide that was nearly as inconvenient as the other one. So he'd cleared the place and in the process made a few...well, not friends, exactly, but chaps with whom he could pass the occasional hour when he'd stayed too long at headquarters but could not stomach the thought of going back to his lonely room.

Which might prove to be the case tonight. As he tried to re-read the suspect notes, hardly a quarter of the words seemed to actually reach his brain. He leaned his elbows on the desk and ruffled his hands through his hair, chest still tight with anxiety over Barrows's retirement. It would be best for both of them, in the end, when Barrows got his pension and the promotion came for Matty. But in the meantime, he was becoming increasingly wretched about the idea, convinced he'd never cut it without his mentor at the desk across the way. The sentimentality that had overtaken him at the giving of a fairly modest and standard sort of parting gift was not helping at all. A little company might put it from his mind for a bit...

He was so wrapped up that at first, he hardly noticed the sound of steps and voices in the hall outside his office. He'd known he wasn't the only one here—there was always a good heapful of someones at headquarters—so it was no shock to hear conversation. Once he consciously noticed the voices, he tried not to hear what was being said. Years of being surrounded by secrets had made his hearing conveniently selective. But even through his closed door and his efforts at ignorance, he couldn't help but hear the words "Barrows's position" quite clearly.

Barrows's position? As in, the role that Matty's name was

Jess Everlee 31

already in for? Barrows's position, meaning, Matty's position, soon enough?

He nearly left them to it, but hardly half a moment later he was on his feet, carefully cracking his door just a little. Just enough. One could not talk about the fate of Barrows's position without talking about Matty, and curiosity about what they might say about his qualifications was too great to resist. Maybe they would say the thing Matty needed to hear to believe he could handle the phase of his career less dependent on accidents of beauty.

A peek down the dark hall showed the speakers were in the office of Detective Superintendent Frost—the man who oversaw the entire Special Investigations department.

A little thrill ran through Matty's belly. An official conversation it was, then. Not mere office gossip.

He did not dare creep closer, but both office doors were open now, and not too far from each other. All Matty had to do was be still. Focus. He knew how to hear what needed to be heard, whether or not he was strictly supposed to hear it...

"So you mean to say," came a voice Matty recognized as Detective Ashton, a man at Barrows's level, though with less experience. "That the Shaw kid—"

Alone as he was, Matty let his lips quirk upward just a tad.

"That's right," said Frost, nice and loud in the quiet hallway.

"Shocking, really," said Ashton. "I never would have expected it to go this way."

The smile faded with ire. What did he mean he *didn't expect it*? Barrows had brought him on as an "unofficial asset" when he was hardly fifteen years old, a pay-rolled Detective Constable just two years later, and an inspector instead of a statistic at the age of twenty-one. He'd practically been raised for this position like some were raised in a family trade. Whether it was a particularly good idea to give the job to Matty was perhaps debatable, but who else would it go to?

32   *To Sketch a Scandal*

"Didn't you?" Frost chuckled, and it should have been a comfort, but there was something undeniably wrong about the sound. Matty felt the first tingle of trouble start up low in his belly. It would be a very good time to go back to his desk. To shut the door. To hear no more. But his shoes felt glued to the floorboards. Against his better judgment, he leaned his head on the door frame, shut his eyes, and listened harder than ever: "Well, if you're shocked, I'm sure Barrows will have that bloody heart attack that he's overdue for when he finds out. But be honest, Ashton: how can I possibly give such an important position to Detective *Matilda*?"

The words and Ashton's responding laugh were so shocking, so baldly cruel and uncalled for, that it took Matty a moment to realize they were still talking about him.

"Don't get me wrong, he does well enough at…what he does," Frost went on. "But do you really think I can ask other self-respecting detectives to take orders from the boy bait?"

Matty's heart thudded and his fingers tingled. Gossip of all kinds was common at the Met. This was not the first time Matty had overheard words like this thrown around about him. Stupid schoolboy stuff was inevitable in such a masculine workplace. It would spell disaster on the street-policing side of things, but this was the detectives' unit, and Special Investigations to boot. They all needed to do what had to be done. Such rumors hardly mattered.

Unless, of course, it was the superintendent spreading them.

"Oh, he does seem to have other skills, though," Ashton said, friendly, amiable, like they'd disagreed on the merits of a casual cricket player neither had much of a stake in, rather than a respected junior detective who'd brought down multiple trafficking rings by playing "the boy bait" by day and working his damned arse off with the hours that remained. "Did a bang-up job on that Belleville ring, didn't he? And Barrows recommends him very highly."

Jess Everlee 33

"Oh, he's been useful enough," Frost said. "But don't you think it reflects a little funny on Barrows that he's so enthusiastic about a detective with less than a decade of official work under his belt? Don't you think it might reflect a little funny on me to promote him now, given his role in that last case, bang-up job or not?"

"What was that, again?"

"Valet and confidant to a man suspected of serious sodomitical conspiracies, Ashton."

Ashton laughed again, and not in a particularly friendly manner. "Right, right. To be fair, he did take down the whole ring from that position, though. Surely that's worth something."

"Might be, if not for the rest of it."

"What rest of it?"

"I've heard, though it's thirdhand and should be weighed as such, that he has been seen walking into a very questionable coffeehouse over in Soho at funny hours. A place that's been fined more than once for the sort of activity that would prove Shaw's roles are not really roles at all." There was a pause. "There's a good chance it's horseshit, of course; someone stirring up trouble. Wouldn't be the first time I've seen that. But it all makes you wonder. And if you wonder, you don't respect. If you don't respect, you don't follow. If you don't follow...do you see where I'm going with this?"

Did they realize Matty was here? His pulse was thundering in his ears, but under the panic, he had to wonder if this conversation was a terrible coincidence or a purposeful warning.

"Do you think there's been something..." said Ashton, a new note in his voice as he left off his role of Matty's half-hearted defender. An amused note, like he loved nothing more than a little dirt on another detective. "Something *untoward* about Shaw's handling of his cases, sir? Beyond the obvious?"

"I don't know one way or the other, Ashton. I fucking hope not, I'll tell you that much. Can you imagine the papers?"

34 *To Sketch a Scandal*

"Dear lord."

"I admit, I'm nervous about it. We don't need a scandal like that, Ashton. We've seen enough scandals round here as it is. Public opinion is still shaky after that last corruption situation. It's bad enough for people on the inside to suspect Shaw's buggered his way to the center of a case at the level he's in. If I make him detective chief with these little rumors unsettled, it will be my bloody neck if it winds up true and the public catches wind."

Matty closed his eyes, nauseous. He debated making a noise, making a fuss, storming in there and demanding they stop talking about him like this. But he could not do anything but listen and listen as his bones seemed to turn to slipping, unsteady gravel that might fail to keep him standing at any moment.

"Anyway," Frost went on with a sigh. "As I say, maybe this next case of his will prove something different, but all I know about the lad now has me feeling very wary, and I plan to break that to Barrows first thing in the morning. Which brings me to why I've brought you in to discuss the matter…"

Matty did not seek company that night. He could not risk being "seen walking into a very questionable coffeehouse" at "funny hours," now could he? Instead, he went to his room at the boardinghouse after all, where he wept, and threw things, and considered very seriously the merits of killing himself.

But when he'd calmed down, shaky and hiccuping, his room looking like some desperate animal had tried to uncover an escape from it, he decided it wouldn't do to be hasty in that regard. Though it felt otherwise, he hadn't been caught at anything, exactly. These were rumors. His reputation had always been a little dodgy, that was all, and that dodginess had come around to bite him on the arse at last. He was not under investigation. He was not being formally accused of any crimes. He was not even being sacked, at least not yet, though he wasn't sure how long he'd last at the Met once Barrows left for the green pastures of his pension.

Something far worse than tightness took over his chest at the thought of being ousted from the office that felt more like home than this room did, something sharp, something lined with gnashing teeth and tearing claws. When it came to working, he'd only known Scotland Yard or the street, and wasn't so keen on the street anymore, having seen what he'd seen in the meantime. The stress of what he'd heard made the night seem difficult and endless, keeping him awake so late that the pit of sleep he finally fell into at dawn was so deep that he slept through his landlady's wake-up knock the next morning.

By the time he put himself together and arrived late at the office, Barrows was already at his desk.

"Did Frost talk to you?" Matty said in a panicked rush before he'd even shut the door behind him. "He said he was going to talk to you."

"Come in, Matthew," said Barrows gently. He stood and coaxed Matty's hand off the doorknob, where it had welded itself in a nervous grasp.

"What did he say?" Matty insisted as Barrows led him to his own chair. There was a cup of tea already waiting for him. It made him sick to think about consuming so much as a drop. "Barrows, please. I can't take another second."

"How did you know—?"

"I overheard him talking to Ashton last night," Matty blurted. "I suppose they didn't realize I was here. I heard every bloody word, and I'll tell you what, I considered not coming back at all this morning." He drew a shuddering breath. "Considered not waking up, come to that. It's a complete disaster, it's—"

Barrows shushed him, glancing toward the now-closed door. "Let's not be overheard ourselves, shall we?"

Matty ran a hand down his face, forcing himself silent even as the hysterics raged on within. He remembered the ring that

36   *To Sketch a Scandal*

was still on his finger as it caught on his lip. Barrows's gift to celebrate the promotion that would never come. He started to wrench it off, but Barrows grabbed his hands and stopped him.

Barrows leaned over Matty's desk, face very neutral. "You've known a long time now that this is how they see you," he said reasonably. "They do not understand your work, Matthew. They never have. And you know that. You cannot go to pieces over hearing it confirmed. It will do you no good at all."

"They're passing me over," Matty said, wrenching the ring off at last. "For the promotion. Even if they don't arrest me or sack me, the rug's still being pulled out in that direction. Please, for the love of God, take this thing back."

But Barrows tucked the ring back into Matty's palm, determined.

"You're still going to get that bloody promotion if it's the last thing I do," Barrows hissed. "Frost said he was wary. That he is trying to mitigate the potential for scandal. The decision to pass you over has not been finalized."

Matty pushed the ring back toward him. "Did he mention that during all this wariness and mitigation, he called me *Detective Matilda* and insinuated that your support of me reflected *funny* on you?"

Barrows paused. "He did neglect those particular points during our conversation," he went on with complete evenness. He stepped back, out of reach of the ring. "But it doesn't matter. Because none of those rumors about you are true anyway, are they?"

Matty blinked up. Barrows's face was completely blank. It was important for a detective to keep blankness at the ready, to tame as many ticks and identifying quirks as possible, and Barrows was a master. One might think he actually believed what he'd said. But he couldn't possibly. Barrows knew Matty. Knew good and well what he was, what he'd always been.

Frost, however, did not. Not beyond a shadow of a doubt, anyway.

"No," said Matty very slowly, unblinking, desperate to know where this was headed. "They aren't, now that you mention it."

"That's what I told Frost straight off." Barrows ran a firm hand horizontally through the air, as if cutting the whole problem right in two. "I told him, I said, Frost, if Detective Shaw were some sort of ethically dubious sodomite running round at lascivious establishments he himself has investigated, don't you think I'd have figured that out by now?"

Matty's heart skipped a beat. "You said that?"

"Exactly that. No more, no less." Barrows might have winked then, it was hard to say with the rest of his face so severe. "He agreed it was likely I'd have noticed. So, I went on to tell him what you told me yesterday."

"And what was that again?" Matty asked. Slowly, he slid the ring back on his finger. Maybe it would be alright there after all.

"That the levels of depravity your plain-clothes roles have brought you to have become nearly *impossible* to stomach." Barrows made an impassioned fist and brought it down on the desk. Matty could not recall saying that, but accuracy didn't seem to be the point, here. "I said that your loyalty stops you from complaining, but that you soldier through in hopes of finally proving that you're ready for something greater, something *more*. That's why you're so eager for the promotion, why I am so passionate about seeing you fill my shoes. I told him you have become so *weary* and *soul-drained* by this work that when I suggested you gather intelligence in the art fraud case as a figure model, the shame and degradation nearly brought you to your *knees*, isn't that right, Matthew?"

"Um." Matty was startled by the intensity of Barrows's stare. A show of weary reluctance wasn't exactly the same as being brought to one's knees, but he supposed it was close enough. "If you say so."

38 *To Sketch a Scandal*

"And that's why, for this case—even before all this nonsense about *rumors* and *scandals*—we had already decided that you were going to take a completely different angle than you usually do."

"Different angle," Matty repeated, confused and a bit alarmed, but starting to feel the first bubblings of hope in his breast. "R-remind me of the angle again, sir?"

Barrows went back behind his own desk and rummaged in the bottom drawer. He returned with a large paper sack and a folded jacket with quite a lot of patterned patches on it. Tentatively, Matty dragged the sack to him and began taking items out. A case of black lead pencils. Tins of paint. Three blobs of clay. Bundles of paper. Two craft books. And a green ball of yarn that had been stabbed through with a pair of wooden knitting needles.

"What's all this for?"

"Isn't it obvious?" said Barrows, dropping his bombastic act at last. "You're not going to be the model this time, Matthew. You're going to engage with the class as an aspiring artist."

Matty gaped at the implements before him. "Sir..."

"Frost ate it up," Barrows whispered, grinning ear to ear. "If you can prove your ability to crack a case this way, instead of the other, you can ease his mind about promoting you." When Matty didn't respond, he crossed his arms, mustache twitching. "A little thanks would be appreciated, you know. I had to come up with this on the spot, and think I found a pretty good work-around, if I may say so myself."

Matty's mouth had gone very dry. "Theoretically you did, yes."

"What do you mean, theoretically?"

Matty picked up the limp end of the green yarn, grimacing. "I don't know that I'm good at this sort of thing."

"Well, that's why you need to attend a class, isn't it, my boy?"

"I suppose..."

"Look, lad, you're just going to have to read these books,

experiment with these mediums before the first class, and figure out how to make it work, because the alternatives are grim. You can't be a model—I've made too big a show of how your very soul will splinter and shrivel if you try. And to quit the case at this point would reflect so poorly on you that the rumors wouldn't even come into play when they decided to sack you. Methods aside, you've got to crack it if you want the promotion, end of story." Barrows shrugged and slapped him on the back. "On the bright side, though, I'm giving you official dispensation to leave off the razor for a bit, just like you wanted. We still can't have you looking like police, so a mustache is out, but..." He unfolded and held out the odd, patchy jacket. "I think some well-applied stubble will bring the look together nicely, don't you?"

Matty blinked it all in as Barrows waggled the ugly garment like it was something quite enticing indeed. Admittedly, Matty's dread was lessened slightly—of all the possible outcomes, this was among the better of them. But there was a problem with it that stood out to him like a goatee on a street officer.

"But, Barrows," he said, and God, he hated to say it, to admit what was coming, but what choice did he have? "You're leaving. What happens if the new angle slows me down, and the case isn't solved by then? I was expecting to get a junior partway through this, not to start taking direction from some other chief, especially if I'm trying something different, do you see what I'm saying?"

"Oh." Barrows folded the coat over his arm, very casual. Too casual. "That's been thought of and handled—"

"Handled how?"

"Just a bit of creative staffing—"

"Barrows, come off it," Matty snapped. "Who else is coming on the case?"

Barrows put on as pleasant an expression as he could clearly manage. "Detective Ashton will be working with me from

40   *To Sketch a Scandal*

headquarters. He'll be split between this and the work he's already got, so you won't even be interacting much."

"Ashton?" Matty repeated, horrified. "You mean the person Frost was gossiping with last night? That Ashton?"

"I spoke to him," Barrows said, smoothing wrinkles in the coat same as he did the conversation. "He bears you no ill will—he's a more practical-headed fellow than Frost, doesn't care how the work gets done so long as it gets done."

Matty stared at the clothes and art supplies in front of him. They were a far cry from the silk suits and soft hand creams he'd been planning on as a model, preparing for seduction-as-usual. He was very comfortable with that act by now. This other stuff was troubling.

"In that case," he said. "Are we sure I can't take the usual tack with this after all?"

"Quite," said Barrows. "But what difference does it make, really? All that will be behind you in a few short weeks anyway. You're so very old now, as you said. Might as well get the head start on the next phase of your career."

Matty squished the ball of yarn with one of his fingers, feeling like a similar sort of unpleasant, scratchy prodding was happening to his stomach.

"What if I can't?" he asked.

Barrows paused, confused. "What do you mean?"

"What if…" Matty swallowed hard. "What if I'm not cut out for all this, Barrows? What if my pony's only got one trick to work with? This seems like a high-pressure way to find out one way or another, and…and I've never worked with anyone but you. What if it's you keeping all this together? What if I'm just, you know…" He prodded the ball again. "The face of the operation?"

Before he'd even finished the thought, Barrows was reaching across the desk, patting Matty's shoulder and shaking his head. "Nonsense, Matthew," he said. "Haven't I always had complete faith in you?"

"Yes," Matty admitted. He did not add the rest of the thought. That maybe that was Barrows's mistake to begin with.

Aspiring. Multimedia. Arts and crafts. Noble poverty. These were the sorts of words that went into his personality profile. Having been too distraught to shave this morning, he was, at least, ahead of things in that regard. He'd be the son of a successful banker and a long-retired dancer, as exhausted and disgusted with a practical life of finance as the real Matty supposedly was with being bait. He was to be purposefully disheveled, but undeniably posh somewhere underneath it, simply playing at destitution. The story went that he'd thrown himself into all manner of mediums, the more esoteric and socially confusing the better, but was finally running out of money. Portraiture—though terribly basic—might keep him from having to turn to his family for help, after having made a scene at supper one evening, in which he declared he'd rather starve as an artist than feast as a banker.

"I'm insufferable," Matty muttered as he took down the notes, a swirl of dusty breeze from the open window ruffling the page. "I want to box my own ears already."

"Your desperation and defiance of order will make it more reasonable for you to ask awkward questions and insinuate yourself with the teachers."

"Oh, I know." Matty sighed. "I'm not saying it isn't brilliant. I'm saying it makes me nauseous. There's a difference."

Once the character was set, he had to get used to it before the class started. He began with the part that was easy for him: the visual. He donned the patchy jacket and a rotation of silly-looking printed neckcloths, carefully neglecting his grooming. That all went pretty well. Each morning, he looked in his mirror to find a more convincing twat than the one he'd been yesterday. And he had to admit, there was something satisfy-

42   *To Sketch a Scandal*

ing about taking things the opposite direction than he usually did. He found he actually liked how he looked with his blond hair a little disheveled and his face a little rough. He looked his own age, at least, which was novel.

He wished, however, that he could say the same about the rest of it.

Matty had never had occasion for art. His youth—cut fortunately short by Barrows's intervention—had been a rather lonely plod through surviving day to day. His schooling was ill-afforded and spottily attended; his leisure comprised of causing trouble with other semi-feral boys; his home life…well, he did not like to think about that. The most artistic thing he could remember engaging in was making faces with his finger on foggy windows or dusty floorboards. There were always plenty of dusty floorboards at home.

Fortunately, the nature of his insufferable character meant he didn't actually have to be good at anything. But unfortunately, when Matty finally got up the guts to sit down at the desk he kept in his lonely little boardinghouse room, a pot of tea on one side and his character sketch on the other, facing the assortment of materials Barrows had provided him, he found that even calling himself "not good" would be overly optimistic.

First, he read the books so he'd understand the theory, then started in on the blobs of clay. They were harder than he expected, and his attempts at humanoid shapes yielded results so horrifying, he'd have marked them down as dangerous occult items had he discovered them in a suspect's home. The following nights found him mixing paints on a little palette, ruining dozens of perfectly nice pieces of paper with hideous smears that clanged and clashed and didn't look anything like the skylines and human faces he'd been attempting. After ripping those up when they looked no happier dry than they had wet, he desperately found instructions for what to do with the yarn. He sat in his chair by the fire (tea traded in for gin at this point in the enterprise) in a desperate hope that *craft* might prove better suited than *art*. With wooden needles in hand and the green yarn flopping in a basket at his feet like it was having a seizure, he strung together what was supposed to be a scarf, but looked more like algae clinging to something dreadful that had been dragged from the Thames's most unfortunate depths.

As the first class drew nearer, and he still did not have so much as an appealing stick figure for all his efforts, it was Matty who had begun to feel quite wary indeed. This level of dreadful threatened the integrity of his story. His character was supposed to look *ridiculous*, yes, but not *out of his mind*. And that's what a man of his talents would have to be if he thought he could ever earn a living in this profession.

He finished the scarf on a moonless night. When he held it up by the light of his fire, he found that finishing had not improved its beauty in the slightest.

In a hot wave of frustration, he threw it to the ground, disappointed to see it fall short of the mantel—it would be a lot prettier if it were on fire. This stuff was all sort of funny when he was in the office with Barrows, but it was embarrassing on the days that Ashton came in, and worst of all when he was facing it alone in his room for all these hours, cooped up, working at doomed endeavors, worrying about what would become of him when he got sacked.

Because he would get sacked. He knew it fully as he stared at the languishing form of the discarded knitting on the hearth rug. He wasn't going to be able to pull this off. And it wasn't just the promotion on the line when he failed. Once Barrows was gone, and Matty had proven he could do nothing that didn't rely on his dimpled smile, Frost's suspicions would return. He'd be out on his arse, out here, in this lonely room so quiet he could hear every carriage creak from the street below. Scotland Yard was his life. It was a difficult life, and not exactly one he'd chosen, but it was his. And he'd blown it by proving unable to hide an appetite that had never even done him any good to begin with.

"Fuck it," he whispered to nobody at all, grabbing that patchy jacket and throwing it over his shoulders. He scooped up the scarf and wound it around his neck out of a pure sense of chaos. If his appetites were set to ruin him anyway, if it was as true as it seemed that everything was about to crumble for good, what point was there to sitting around with another case of pencils, loneliness and dread eating his insides away bit by bit? He did not have to sit here.

Did not have to be alone, either. Even patchy and stubbled and twenty-five to boot, he was still pretty enough that he did not have to be alone ever, if he did not want to be. It was the one thing he'd been before Scotland Yard saved him, and it was the one thing he'd continue to be for a while yet when it inevitably sent him back out.

To the coffeehouse, then. He put his shoes on and locked his door, going quietly down the staircase and out into the night. For a while, he walked quickly with his head down and his hands in his pockets, but as he neared the place, he slowed. Who had seen him coming in here anyway? A prickle of nerves dampened his determination. It was one thing to accept that he'd be sacked under suspicion. It was another to allow himself to be caught red-handed in a crime, not to mention the trouble it could bring to his not-quite-friends at the coffeehouse if he were.

He stopped in the middle of the street. The thought of going back to his room, of facing its emptiness and the pressure of learning something new and doomed, made him feel physically ill. He could not go back there. He might do something stupid, he thought, if he tried.

But where else in this city could a man with such a mismatched occupation and inclination *go*?

Chapter Three

Warren

Over the past two weeks, Warren had spent every extra moment at the club decking out the upstairs parlor for the drag party and consulting on his friends' gowns and wigs. By the time the party came round, he could well imagine the wicked and delightful sight going on above his head. This sense of knowing exactly what he was missing was intensified by the piano music, shrieks of laughter, and joyous footsteps that no informer would miss even in the unlikely occurrence of Warren catching one.

While Warren was typically pleased to stick to the club's security protocols, they challenged him tonight. At home, everything was in service to Harry and his new wife's supposedly imminent arrival, Mother going so far as to rally the women to start the cooking in her certainty that they would arrive on the exact date she'd calculated. Miraculously, she'd had only one spell through all of it, but leaving her while she was in this state made him sick. And leaving her for this? Serving some dozen blokes too scared to step upstairs but too stuck in their habits to go anywhere else? It was nearly intolerable.

At least, as Forester had promised, Miles Montague was

46   *To Sketch a Scandal*

there to keep him company. A gruff, wild-haired erotic novelist, Miles wasn't one for snug crowds or inordinate amounts of risk. Though he was as scared and stuck in his habits as the rest of Warren's charges tonight, he was at least fun to talk to, and even to flirt with, because he always got flustered. It never went anywhere, though. The fellow was bafflingly faithful to Warren's old chum Charlie, whose bright laughter was recognizable even through the floorboards this evening.

"He's having far too much fun without you." Knowing Miles preferred wine and they'd both be down here tonight, he'd broken out a better bottle than he normally bothered with. He topped off the glass and winked. "You ought to get back at him."

"Is that so?" Miles braced for this old song and dance of theirs with a scolding half-smile. "Got any ideas?"

"A few." Warren put his chin in his hands on the bar and batted eyelashes up at his old friend.

Miles shook his head. "You've got a real way about you, Warren."

"What way?"

"The way of a bloke who wants nothing more than to see me in trouble."

"Oh, but, Miles, that's not true at all. I want to see you in trouble, sure, but there are at least a dozen other ways I'd like to see you too, if you know what I'm saying."

Miles's little smile cracked into a quiet laugh. "God, I walked right into that one, didn't I?"

"Waltzed, even."

As if summoned by even the least serious threat to his lover's fidelity, Charlie Price emerged from the back door with Noah Clarke—Forester's darling—hanging on his arm. They were quite a sight. Charlie's face was done up, frock coat ruffled and flowered, top hat feathered halfway to hell. Noah was in his full drag costume, Miss Penelope, with butterflies pinned to his bonnet, swirls painted on his face, and a feathery fan in his hand.

"Are you supposed to be down here, lookin' like that?" Warren said as Charlie swiped a sip of Miles's wine. "Thought you was supposed to stay upstairs if you dressed up."

"Don't panic," said Charlie over the snatched glass. "Forester said I pass as an actor and gave me the go-ahead to come down."

Warren looked Noah over. "What's your excuse?"

"That I'm so terribly convincing it hardly matters," he said in the high, brash voice he used in character before adding in his normal register, "Also: I love him to the ends of the earth, but he can't tell me what to do all the time. The world's not going to end if I'm down here for two minutes. He's being a touch paranoid, in case you haven't noticed." He took Charlie's arm again and looked mournfully at Miles, who'd loosened up substantially over the years but was still known for a thick streak of overcaution. "We've been bonding over this shared trial of ours."

"That's why she came to help me scoop you up." Charlie tugged at Miles's arm. "The wedding's about to start. Forester's got everything all set up—you'd think it was his own matrimony, the attention to detail—he's got Mr. Gray in an antique veil and everything."

"He always thinks the pairs he set up belong to him," Warren muttered. "Bloody romantic fool. It's nothing special."

"Perhaps not," Charlie admitted. "But it's shaping up to be a riot. You should come, Miles."

Miles looked torn between adoration and security. "It's not my scene, Charlie."

"Just for a bit. I promise, you won't regret it."

When Miles waffled, Noah swooped in. Rather expectedly, his "help" in this matter revealed itself to be a well-used pack of playing cards that he dug out from his padded bosom and shuffled expertly on the bar in front of Miles.

"Let's draw for it, *amore*," he suggested. "If your card's higher, you stay snug down here. If *mine's* high, on the other hand…"

To Sketch a Scandal

He smiled and flapped the fan toward the door that would lead them all upstairs to the wedding.

Warren's regret at being left out spiked terribly. At this point, he wouldn't even mind losing all his pay at Noah's card table if only he could join in the game. And now they were taking Miles from him?

Noah was examining Warren's expression from behind the fluttering fan. He seemed to misread it as suspicion. "Miles can go ahead and cut the deck if he doesn't trust me."

"Sure, he can," said Warren, resentment tightening his voice. "And just how many aces have you got up that lacy sleeve of yours to make up for it if he does?"

Noah's eyes brightened devilishly. "Well, it only takes one, doesn't it?"

Though Miles pushed the cards away and put on a little more show of hesitation, his resolve began to break once Charlie rested his chin on Miles's shoulder and presumably began whispering some creative and personal promises. Enough was enough. Warren scoffed and moved on down the bar to find someone else to talk to.

"Where are you going?" Miles asked. "Aren't you going to save me?"

Warren turned back, looking him over. "You're a lost cause once Charlie is in the room, mate," he said. "There's no saving you at this point."

Noah laughed, scooping up his cards (including the aforementioned ace) and tucking the lot back into his bosom. "He really is, isn't he?"

"Don't you act like you're any different," Warren snapped. "They may act like newlyweds, but you and Forester have been an old married couple since before I even met you."

"Offensive," said Noah testily, swatting at the air with his fan and eventually settling on Miles, since he couldn't reach Warren. "Isn't he terribly offensive?"

"He's just scared he'll wind up like us someday," said Charlie smugly, stealing another nip of wine. "That's the only reason he pokes fun. Thinks it will save him. But one of these days, the right chap's going to walk through these doors, Mr. Forester will introduce the two of them with that way he's got, and that will be that."

To Warren's satisfaction, Miles and Noah both shot Charlie looks nearly as skeptical as Warren's own.

"Warren?" Miles asked, like Charlie must have been talking about someone else. "*This* Warren? In love?"

"I think you might do well to sneak a tea in before your next gin, *amore*. Your wits are flagging." Noah laughed, taking Charlie's arm again. "Warren's immune to romance in all forms."

"Yeah, I'm not exactly worried about that, Charlie," said Warren. "I worry about a lot of things, but turning into a sappy little lovebird isn't one of them."

"I was like you not that long ago," said Charlie with a wistful air.

"You think so?" Warren came back down the bar, turning his infamous charm back on as he leaned over it and looked Charlie right in the eyes. "You're the accountant here, Price. Why don't you go run the numbers on that, see how things stack up? I've got the raw data scratched on the bedpost for you. Last room on the right."

He blew Charlie a kiss as the others laughed, fully on his side. Charlie Price, bless him, had always been jealous of Warren's charm. It served him to think they were the same. But while Charlie used to drown his substantial sorrows in the arms of whatever stranger would have him, Warren had never been drowning. He was floating. He was living. He was *Warren Bakshi the barkeep*, and anyone who'd so much as poked a head into The Curious Fox knew exactly what that meant. It meant hungry eyes, flirty touches, and cold drinks. It meant pleasure over duty and possibility over plans.

50 *To Sketch a Scandal*

It meant his friends would be as shocked to learn who he was at home as home would be to learn who he was here.

"Go on, lovebirds." He gathered Miles's glass up and gestured with it to the back door. "Go join the rest. In a sense, this is my night off, if you know what I'm saying. Not going to waste my time getting overly cozy with anyone who'd rather sulk around down here. At least, not now that Miles is abandoning me," he added with a pout and a wink that Charlie failed to pretend did not bother him in the slightest. "So leave me to it, and go enjoy your wedding. I'll be here. Forester's made very sure of that."

The others still teasing Charlie for suggesting that *Warren Bakshi the barkeep* had it in him to be smitten for more than an hour, they left. And though the fun of the jokes had added momentary joy to the dullness of his evening, the bar was dull all over again in the absence of an actual friend among a throng of customers.

"Be a dear, pretty thing. I could use another fizz."

Well, there it was. For better or worse, one of those customers was thirsty. Warren went over to him, turning on his trademark charm to get his order. The external motions were the same, whether he was joking with a friend, courting a tip, or trying for actual trade. The difference was how much fun he was having while he did it. And this fellow? A regular, sure, but not a friend in any sense of the word, though his eyes always drifted up and down Warren's body in a way that surpassed friendship significantly. He'd given the fellow a try once. He'd give pretty much anyone a try once (even Charlie, against all odds, though they had a pact not to speak of it). This one was firmly in tip-courting territory, and would remain there until he could muster up even the slightest interest in anything Warren had to add to his interminable monologues.

A rustling tinkle came from the belled curtains in the entryway just as he was pushing the bloke's refill back across the bar. Busy as he was trying to secure his money by feigning interest in his current customer's boring babble—he *was* a good tipper, if not a good tupper—he hated to break eye contact just now. Still. He was supposed to keep an eye out for trouble; if he was going to be stuck down here, he really ought to do the job right. He flicked his eyes toward the entrance to see who'd come in, just for a moment...

Or it would have been a moment, if his eyes hadn't gotten quite stuck on the newcomer.

He didn't recognize the chap. Strange. New blood wasn't allowed at the drag party, and those down here would find it an odd night to bring a guest along to check the place out. Not forbidden. But curious indeed. He glanced around the room, trying to spot the fellow's escort, but no one made any moves to greet him.

Warren did his best to watch the new chap while still making the old one think he had some ounce of Warren's continued attention. It was too dark in here to make out much of the newcomer's appearance, aside from a slim build beneath a pathetic, patchy coat, the pockets of which were straining under the force of his fists shoved deep within them. He'd kept his hat on—many did—and was wandering into the club step by careful step, head tilted to look round at the various nooks of décor. He stopped here and there to admire pieces of furniture or artwork, but didn't appear to be seeking out any particular companion. Very odd. He couldn't have gotten in without a reference on the inside.

Warren was interested. Whether this interest stemmed from suspicion or attraction remained to be seen.

All smiles and eyelashes, he finished up serving the bloke at the bar. Suspicion or attraction—either way, Warren had to go see what had come into his club on this night of all nights. He was too bloody bored to ignore anything interesting, after all.

He crossed the parlor, that thrill of disobedience that so often lured him from his post taking charge. He had no interest in

52 *To Sketch a Scandal*

the crowd who'd balked at the idea of a little upstairs fun, but a newcomer still had a chance at being novel. If the fellow passed muster, maybe Warren would end the night with a little more data on the bedpost for his accountant after all. He said he'd be on the lookout for trouble tonight. He had not, strictly speaking, promised not to cause any himself.

As Warren approached, the new man turned to meet him. Though he didn't show much outward sign of interest, Warren fancied he could sense the heartbeat the chap missed when his eyes fell unblinking on Warren's. Determined to win a better response from him, Warren pretended to brush a little something off the man's patchy shoulder and let his voice go flirty.

"Good evening," he said. "Haven't seen you here before."

The newcomer did not flinch, nor did he lean in. Rather, he went on peering at Warren very mildly from beneath a simple cloth cap. He had a youthful, handsome face set with light eyes—blue maybe? Hard to tell in red club lighting—and a scraggle of scruff that looked out of place on him, like some imp had taken a pen to one of the smooth images of Grecian beauty depicted in the painting he had been admiring.

"First time," the man said, very polite, very quiet. He didn't seem nervous or itchy or new to the whole business of a club like this, but he wasn't projecting a lot of confidence, either. Warren had seen the varying responses to a first night here, and this one didn't quite fit the models.

Interest, or suspicion? The thrill of feeling in Warren's belly tipped decidedly toward suspicion. Still, he smiled. Welcoming. Willing, if it came to that. And maybe it would. "Who are you here with tonight, gorgeous? Who's speaking for you? Maybe I can help you find him, if you're a little lost. You are here with someone, aren't you?"

"Old friend of David and Noah," the man said calmly. That casual use of first names calmed Warren's suspicion somewhat. It was a standard impropriety at the Fox, and those first names were very good ones for him to have on hand. "I got the knock and passwords off David a while back—that's how I got in, if you're worrying about my lack of an escort—but I'm afraid I never did get around to checking the place out."

The hands went even deeper into his pockets, bringing his shoulders up higher. Something in the movement shifted the way the dim light caught his face, deepening a set of obvious circles under his eyes. The suspicion receded further—the chap wasn't as young as he first appeared. Though he had that particular blond-and-blue look that the bobbies assumed every molly was helpless against, Warren had yet to encounter an entrapper sporting dark circles who had not even bothered to shave. Of course, an entrapper was the most miserable sort of creature on the planet, but they at least tried not to look it until their job was done. The man seemed legitimate enough, for now.

"Is he here?" the fellow asked, again very mild, hard to read. "David Forester?"

Before Warren could answer, the world answered for him, a whole wave of laughter drifting down through the ceiling, along with bit of stamping, the shatter of a dropped glass, all the signs and sounds of a lot of people having a lot of fun without them upstairs.

"Sure is," Warren said dryly, pointing upward. "Busy, though."

For a second, it seemed the man would grant him a smile, but the turn of his lips was so slight it was hard to call it that. It struck Warren low in his belly, like the full smile was some explosive pleasure that the fellow was teasing.

Suspicion was gone. Attraction, however, remained in full force.

"My name's Warren Bakshi," he said. "The barkeep."

"I had a feeling." The fellow got even closer to a smile, as he looked Warren up and down obviously. "Mr. Forester speaks highly of your...sense of hospitality."

Warren couldn't help but grin. His reputation, it seemed, had preceded him.

54   *To Sketch a Scandal*

"He'd better. So, love, shall I fix you a drink while you're waiting?" Warren asked, sweeping a bit more imaginary dust from the fellow's coat. "On the house?"

"That," said the chap, "would be the best thing to happen to me all week."

Warren learned that the chap's name was Matty and that he went for ale over liquor, even though the brighter light near the bar further revealed that he was as frayed up around the edges as his clothes. The scarf he unwound from his neck and placed on the seat beside him was a particularly pathetic thing, lumpy and irregular.

"Girlfriend make that for you?" Warren asked with a smirk.

"Oh, yes," Matty said without missing a beat. "You can see the steadfastness of her love in every stitch, can't you?" He got closer to smiling this time, the lips lifting, eyes brightening. But again, he backed off before Warren could get his prize. "Actually, I made it."

Matty might not have been ready to smile, but Warren couldn't help a bark of laughter. "You?"

"I'm in a highly irregular position at the moment. Trying a lot of new things, let's say. Hard to explain." He wiggled his fingers, showing Warren a bit of staining on a few of them. "But if you think the scarf is bad, you should see the painting I did. And the sculptures… I've yet to find my new calling, I'm afraid."

Warren nodded, a bit solemnly in spite of the bitter joke. He knew, by now, how to read the undercurrents in the words blokes chose to share with their bartender. "Lose your job?"

"Not quite yet," he said carefully.

"But it's coming?"

"Considering it's based largely on whether I can manage to make something look halfway decent?" He prodded the scarf

Jess Everlee 55

as if worried it might spring to cursed life. "It's hard to say for sure, but the end is definitely a bit too close for comfort."

Warren leaned over the bar, hoping to cheer the fellow up. "You've made yourself look more than halfway decent, love. So no worries there." When Matty didn't even hint at a smile, Warren dropped the cheer for genuine pity. "Is that why you're here tonight?" he asked. "To ask Forester for work?"

"Hadn't occurred to me," Matty admitted, looking around the bar like he was considering it for the first time. "No, I just… It's been a rough couple of weeks. I needed somewhere to *be*, somewhere other than my own stupid room and my own stupid head. He used to tell me how beautiful it was, this club, back when I was…seeing him more regularly. When I found myself with an itch to go and no idea of where exactly I ought to be going, I remembered him telling me. I became, let's call it curious."

"Yes," Warren said with another smile. "Let's."

"It is beautiful, actually. More so than I was expecting. I didn't think there'd be so much artwork. It's a bit taunting, honestly, given how dreadful my own pursuits have been."

"Oh yeah," Warren said. "Lost a lot of the art last year, actually. A shame, but not too bad an outcome, given we were nearly shut down entirely. Legal trouble, you know. Place like this."

Matty nodded. "Oh. I know."

"Anyway, a couple of people here are good at sourcing that kind of stuff. I think it looks better than it did before. You're lucky to have come now, if it's atmosphere you're after."

"I like that one."

Matty pointed over Warren's shoulder, past the liquor bottles, to the sketch over the keg that had been there so long, Warren had nearly stopped seeing it. Not a painting, not even a real piece of art, but that silly little doodle Warren had thrown together, much like the doodles in the pantry at home. He'd tacked it up over the beer tap in response to some nearly-forgotten in-joke with Forester—a satyr with laurels round his

56   *To Sketch a Scandal*

head and pile of orchids obscenely situated over his lap, lifting a goblet into the air.

"That?" Warren chuckled. "That's not art. It's a joke."

"It puts me at ease." Matty shrugged. "Can't say why."

Warren glowed a little at the compliment in spite of himself. This chap was really too alluring to be allowed, wasn't he? If Forester were the sneaky sort, he might wonder whether his boss had sent Matty along to see if he'd behave.

But Forester wasn't sneaky.

And so Warren wasn't sure what benefit there was to behaving.

He leaned farther, more suggestively, over the bar like he had earlier—in jest with Miles and for tips with his customer—but this time, it was for the third reason. His favorite reason.

"If you like that silly old thing," he murmured, doodling with his finger on the bar hardly a hair's breadth from Matty's wrist, "then you ought to see the pieces we keep in the back. We've got a very nice one of Apollo over the mantel in the big room I think you'd like. I could show it to you, maybe."

Matty's hand went very still upon his pint glass, and he appeared to be holding his breath. Most importantly, though, his eyes did not leave Warren's. Did not even blink as the meaning passed between them. He was new to this club, but clearly not to everything. "In the back, you say?"

"Indeed I do," Warren confirmed. "I can't leave my post for long tonight, admittedly. But…maybe long enough for a brief tour."

Those lips curved slightly upward, teasing the possibility of a real smile again. Warren hung on the sight, more desperate to watch that grim, measured façade crack wide open than he was to get the bloke alone. He flashed one of his own, a wolfish one, hoping to see it mirrored—

"What the devil are you doing here?"

Matty remained steady, but Warren nearly jumped straight to the moon as David Forester's voice slashed through the moment.

Jess Everlee 57

Surprise quickly turned to jealousy as Warren awaited the embraces, handshakes, and who knew what else would happen now that these two old friends were reunited. Forester here to ruin more of his fun. Figured.

But it took only the span of a breath and one look at the horror on Forester's face to realize that Matty—if that was his real name—had lied.

He might know Forester, but they were far from friends.

"You promised," Forester whispered, harsh, alarmed, not toned for anything resembling friendship. "You promised you wouldn't bother us."

"I'm not." Matty spread his hands in a show of innocence. "I simply wanted a drink."

"Why here?"

"I didn't have anywhere else to go."

Warren prickled, confused. "Who is this bloke?"

Forester glanced around to ensure the others were occupied, before whispering quietly: "Warren, may I introduce you to my former valet, Detective Inspector Matthew Shaw."

Oh. *Bollocks*.

Last year, Forester (and Warren by extension) had avoided prison due to the benevolent meddling of some pretty detective who'd posed as Forester's valet while seeking the prosecution of the Fox's former owner, a nobleman with enterprises far more destructive than this little bar. Of all the close calls the Fox had seen, that had been the closest by far.

Matty—Matthew Shaw—must be that pretty detective. How else would he know the knock and passwords, the names of Forester's lover and his barkeep? Warren felt like a fool, but impressed in spite of himself. Matty was convincing. He blamed Forester a little less for falling for the chap's tricks during the case. He had fallen just the same. Hard not to, with a face like that. Made one want to believe anything he said.

Which, Warren figured, was probably the whole point of him.

58   *To Sketch a Scandal*

"I swear to God, Mr. Forester," Matty piped up before the potential nastiness of the situation could fully sink in. "I'm not here to cause you trouble."

"Then what are you here for?" Forester asked, running a troubled hand down his own face. "It's not to warn us of anything, is it?"

"No. Nothing like that."

"What, then?"

Matty's gaze darted a bit, not with anything dodgy, but with what might have been embarrassment.

"Why does any fellow come into your club, Mr. Forester?" he said. "I was alone, and didn't want to be. So I came to the only place in the city where I might encounter a friendly face, a pretty bartender, and one discreet drink before I went back to spending my every waking hour trying to pretend worse than ever that I'm something I'm not."

Forester caught Warren's eye. Understanding passed between them. The reason sounded good, but how could they trust someone who lied for a living?

And yet how could they suspect someone who'd gone so far out of his way to save their arses?

"You're really just here for a drink?" Forester said carefully.

"I figured you owed me one." Matty lifted his glass, the whole thing so dry it was hard to tell if it was supposed to be a joke. "However, I understand that this is very awkward. That perhaps..." He faltered. "Perhaps the fond feelings I still hold for my time in your employment are not reciprocated. Given that I was being false at the time and you were not, I suppose that's more than reasonable. I shouldn't have come here tonight. I apologize; it's been a very trying week. Say the word, and I'm gone."

After a pause, he started to get up. Forester put his hand out.

"Just give us a minute, will you?"

Forester nodded toward the open door to the kitchen. Warren followed him, the two of them standing tilted like stage actors so they could talk to each other while still peeking out the doorway at Matty, now alone at the bar.

"Bang-up job keeping the cops out, Warren."

"Oh, piss off." He watched Matty drink his ale. If he avoided Forester's eyes, perhaps his sheepishness would be missed. "Do you believe him?"

"That depends. How's he been since he came in? Anything suspicious?"

"Not really. He's an odd bloke for sure, but hasn't caused any trouble."

"Tried to lure you into anything you shouldn't do with a detective?"

"No." Warren gave Matty another lingering once-over. He managed to look an absolute treat even slouched at a bar in a patched jacket. "Unfortunately."

Forester watched the fellow with something between guilt and admiration. "It's very likely I owe that man my life," he said. "We both owe him our freedom. And the rest of the patrons owe him their peace—he had the club ledger in his possession, at the end. He burned it when he could have used it to justify mass arrests. If he wanted to hurt us, he's had much better opportunities than this."

Warren smirked. "He can have his drink, then? No harm in it?"

Forester tensed, catching the undercurrent, the exchange of energies he'd interrupted with his untimely arrival downstairs. He turned from the doorway, an actor no more, to look Warren square in the eye.

"He is a detective, Warren," he said seriously. "He may be other things as well, but he's too close to the mechanism of our potential ruin to take risks. Even if he's not planning to cause trouble, he's in league with the troublemakers in a very dangerous way."

60 *To Sketch a Scandal*

"Meaning...?

"Give the poor bloke his pint, Warren," Forester went on. "But keep the *drink* to yourself, for once."

Warren envied Matty his blank face as he felt his own go obviously sulky.

"I mean it," Forester reiterated. "You've had your pick in this place since you got here, even when you're supposed to be working. All good fun. But there is a line here that you cannot cross. No back room. No upstairs. I can take enough pity on him to give one night at the bar—I do owe him that much—but he needs to find somewhere else to hang his hat next time. I hate to be like this, but I don't see another option."

He fell silent at last. Sounds from the party Warren had been banished from creaked and cackled above their heads.

"You're no fun anymore, you know," Warren snapped.

Forester smiled, then clapped Warren on the shoulder. "That's the ticket, mate. Thank you."

The words were as friendly, casual, and equal as ever they were with Forester, but as he went back upstairs and Warren returned to the bar, the truth of it sat heavy—he was playing the boss card, and while Warren could technically appreciate why, it still rankled. His resentment at having been left out of the party festered in the heat of being told what to do yet again. At least with the party, he reluctantly agreed with the necessity; in this, though, Forester was being cold toward someone who was clearly having a hard time of it. Such stringent rules didn't seem necessary. This club wouldn't even exist without Matty's involvement.

Not to mention, it wasn't every day someone complimented Warren's sketches. It made Matty...of unique interest.

Not that it mattered, because when he got back to the bar, the pint was abandoned, two tuppence gleamed, and Matty Shaw was gone.

"Figures, anyway," Warren muttered to the satyr that Matty

had shown a liking for. He took up Matty's empty glass, looking at the spot where his lips had touched it. With an angry thrill, Warren took a sip, the vague perversity the best fuck-you to Forester as he could manage. *See? You think you can keep me from tasting him tonight, but you can't. Not really.*

But as he pulled the glass from his lips and was about to go clean it, he spotted a shadow trailing from the bar stool toward the door. Matty had left his bedraggled scarf. Left it rolled out like a carpet to lead Warren to the door, to the alley, back to him.

The idea that he might have done it on purpose had Warren's baser instincts waking back up. But to follow him...now that would be a lot of rules smashed at once. Too many, maybe.

He might not have done it if Miles Montague had not chosen that moment to retreat back to the quiet safety of the downstairs parlor. Before he even made it to the bar, Warren took up the scarf and grabbed him by the arm.

"Watch the bar for me, yeah?" he said. "I've got to return this."

Miles, who only begrudgingly spoke to strangers and eyed anything but snooty wine with disdain, blinked wildly. "What?"

"The bar. I bequeath it to you." He couldn't help the grin that spread over his face as responsibility and rules fell away and something more fun took its place. "Our safety, freedom, and drunkenness are in your hands till I get back."

"Are you fucking kidding me?"

Warren pecked him on the cheek to soften the blow before he went for the door. "Have I ever told you you're my favorite?"

Chapter Four

Matty

Nearly paralyzed with embarrassment, Matty leaned against the alley wall once he'd escaped the place. How could he have been so foolish? What did he think would happen?

He'd gone into Mr. Forester's home last year, posing as a valet with instructions to tolerate anything nonfatal that might come his way. Due to the nature of the kingpin Mr. Forester had been working under, a nasty trafficker and manipulative letch with hired killers in his pocket, Matty had essentially agreed to be harassed and abused for months until he and Barrows could scrape together enough evidence to crack the case at last.

But he'd not had to tolerate anything of the sort at Mr. Forester's hand. In fact, some days had been so pleasant compared with the desperate scrambling that comprised the actual detective work that Matty had taken to dreaming he could forget the case and just become a pretty, mediocre valet for real. While Mr. Forester had an obvious weak spot when it came to weighing the worth of a valet's skills versus that of his countenance, the fellow hadn't subjected him to anything worse than small talk, friendly compliments, and, most novel of all, a whole slew of barely-coded "club gossip." The bloke was almost delusionally devoted to The Curious Fox, this little club that, though technically illegal, had proved to be the very least of Lord Belleville's crimes by such a wide margin that Matty had gotten away with sparing the place. It would be impossible to hear Mr. Forester chatter on about the intricacies of his club without becoming curious indeed. Sentimental too, what with the way he described his care of friends and enablement of lovers that he so charmingly called "matchmaking" when the rest of the world would call it something very different indeed. He spoke of safety. Community. Scandal too, of course; scenes and spats. If there was anything Matty took away from those mostly one-sided conversations, it was that Forester did not necessarily like everyone who came through his doors, but he took interest in and shielded them all the same.

Somewhere along the line, Matty must have gotten the mistaken impression that there might be a place for him there too.

But no. He was a misfit among misfits.

He ought to have known better. Just because he had a fuzzy feeling about a place or a person didn't mean it was reciprocated. In fact, it almost never was. Hard to believe he'd fooled himself into thinking otherwise. Must be the exhaustion and stress, making him forget how the world really worked.

At last he gathered up enough stability to walk on. This ousting, in retrospect, was inevitable, but he couldn't help being disappointed that it had happened so early in the evening. He'd heard plenty of stories about the handsome, naughty "Warren the barkeep" and his exploits. Mr. Forester hadn't explained them *explicitly* to his valet, but Matty'd been able to catch the gist. Though he'd not gone in tonight certain that exploits were on the table, he'd been enjoying the one that was just being made of him when Mr. Forester found him.

It was hard to keep Warren out of his mind as he went back along the increasingly misty alley toward Soho Square. He was different than Matty had expected from the stories. Handsomer, even, than described, hair glossy black and impolitely long in the front, a well-shaped chin, and big dark eyes with long lashes that he knew how to use, clearly communicating he was up to no good without a single incriminating word or gesture.

But he'd also been kind, hospitable, funny, and his sketch of the satyr really had been lovely. Mr. Forester had never mentioned Warren's artistic abilities, nor, in fact, any of the gorgeous paintings he'd hung on the walls. Matty had a sense, though, that if he were actually the aspiring artist he needed to be, he could have enjoyed the place as a gallery, devoid of all company…except, perhaps, for a handsome guide who didn't even realize he was one of the most interesting artists featured in the place. One who might show him the special collection behind closed doors…

"Mr. Shaw!"

The Curious Fox was tucked back in a dirty Soho alleyway. It was deserted at this time of night, though Matty knew there were more eyes on the place than its shadow-denizens realized until it was too late. Still, it was dark and the fog had come thick tonight, so when he turned, he didn't see anyone right away. It made him nervous. He hated the thought that some of those quiet eyes—ones that could potentially recognize him—might find him here alone. He'd been spotted at the coffeehouse. He knew the Fox was not under suspicion, but that was only on his and Barrows's decreasingly respected word.

It was not a coworker who finally emerged from the mist, however.

It was Warren Bakshi.

Matty was nearly knocked sideways by the deep hunger that rolled through him at the man's approach. It was different from the attraction in the bar, which had been slower and softer. This feeling was the automatic, opportunistic arousal of a man who had to make the most of sparse, speedy encounters. It was a feeling he knew well; Warren probably did too.

It was a shame, considering the more lingering, maybe even more personal moment they might have shared back at the bar. Those moments were rarer. More precious.

But this, he supposed, would be better than nothing.

As Warren closed the distance between them, the chorus of sounds—voices and hooves and the occasional clatter—from the more populous streets beyond their dark little alley seemed to fade to nothing.

"You forgot something." Warren sent something soft and scratchy over Matty's head, where it landed against the back of his neck. That lumpy scarf, the ugly fruit of his first forays into artistic passion. What had felt like a dreadful waste of time suddenly seemed like hours well spent indeed.

"Thank you," Matty said. "Don't know how I could have lived without seeing it again."

Warren tugged on the scarf, drawing him closer. The flirtation between them at the bar was clearly not forgotten; in fact, it seemed it was the fellow's primary purpose. Matty positively burned at the deft, brazen movement—as an expert in the calculus of seduction, he could appreciate skill when he saw it. Seductive and gorgeous and kind and funny...

And completely off-limits, of course, no matter how badly he wanted to ignore that fact.

"You should go back," Matty whispered even as they were stepping in like the toes of their shoes contained magnets. "You'll get in trouble."

Warren shrugged like he enjoyed trouble well enough, his handsome smirk just visible in what little moon and thoroughfare lamplight had strayed down this alley along with the fog. The air was damp, cold, and stinking, but Warren was warm as he pressed Matty against the wall, smelling of the smoke and incense of his club. The look in his eyes was absolutely unmistakable.

There wasn't much time in places like this, and Warren clearly

To Sketch a Scandal

knew better than to waste what they had. Their purpose, at this point, was straightforward. Moving the ends of the scarf to one hand like they were reins, he used his other to cup Matty's face. For a breathtaking second, he thought Warren would kiss him right on the mouth—he was staring at Matty's lips, his own parted. But of course he didn't, it's not what one did out here on the street. At the last second, he tipped Matty's head back against the brick to take advantage of his bared throat, kissing and nipping there instead, all that stupid-looking stubble Matty had grown making it a more sensitive enterprise than the last time he'd taken company, and he clenched his teeth and dug in his heels to keep from making a fuss that might see them found out.

Warren's kisses trailed up to his ear, filling Matty's awareness with hot breath and naughty teeth.

"Tell me the truth before I take this further, Detective," he whispered, flicking his tongue so Matty gasped. "Did you really come to the club for a drink? Or have I made a dreadful mistake coming after you?"

"No mistake." Matty's eyes dropped closed. Warren was still doing something to his ear that would be hard to explain, something soft and welcoming, interspersed with bursts of perfect, nippy pain. He struggled to speak, but knew if he didn't, the touch would stop and he would perish with wanting right here in the alley. "I promise you, the idiocy I displayed in coming here tonight was one-hundred-percent genuine. Though I confess…" He noticed he was holding Warren by the hips already, and dragged him deliciously closer, pulsing his palms in the rhythm he wanted more than anything. "I was hoping for, perhaps, a bit more than a drink if I could find it."

"You're a real devil, then, aren't you?" Warren whispered. "You like that? Everyone out there thinking you're a respectable lawman, only to come back here and just fucking melt when some bloke does this to you?"

All the heavy fears that had dogged Matty for weeks finally

receded as Warren dragged a practiced hand down Matty's neck, his chest, his belly....

"God, yes." Matty caught himself halfway through, changing from groan to hiss as quickly as he could manage. "I mean... not yes. I don't... What I mean is..."

"What are you saying, Matty?" Warren asked, his lips shaped in near-laughter against Matty's neck as his hand explored the contours of Matty's excitement. "I'm afraid you're not being entirely clear for some reason."

Matty squeezed his eyes shut. "I'm saying I'm not sure anyone's convinced I'm respectable, actually."

Matty vaguely heard some arguing and clatters from the street beyond them as Warren finally did laugh, warm and dark against his skin, but it all seemed too far to hurt them in these sweet, misty shadows. Even if it could, it's not like he had much to lose that wasn't on the chopping block already.

"Not surprising," Warren whispered. "I think anyone could look in those eyes and see what you need."

Within moments, Matty was tensing on the edge of his crisis. He batted Warren's hand away and turned to face the wall. They'd lingered too long in this teasing—if they didn't get down to business, no business would happen. Warren pressed in tight, close and hot and as ready as Matty was, but after a little pulsing with his hips and tickling with his tongue at the nape of Matty's neck, there was an echo of laughter from somewhere beyond their alley, and he paused.

"You sure you don't want to go back to the club?" Warren whispered in his ear as he traced the curve of Matty's arse. His words were considerate, but the panting in his breath and the hard insistence of his arousal belied any true desire to put this off. "I could sneak you in the back door, I bet. He'd never be any the wiser."

Matty shook his head, bracing himself against the brick. The words brought back the thought of something cozy and drawn out, something they could not have and probably should not have even if they could.

"I like it like this," he said, which was true enough to be getting on with.

And Warren, for all his suggesting something else, was clearly no stranger to this pastime, either. He unfastened Matty's falls so efficiently Matty wondered if he'd missed a few buttons when he'd done them up, moving Matty's drawers out of the way with one hand while the other went up to Matty's mouth.

"Do yourself a favor, love," Warren whispered, ragged, knuckles brushing Matty's arse as he worked at his own buttons. "I didn't bring anything."

The deft filthiness of that nearly had Matty adding heartily to the scum of the brick before he could comply with the dizzying request...

But another of those nearby sounds brought him woozily back from that edge.

The sound had seemed closer, this time. He felt Warren go very still as they listened. Indeed, the little thump was followed up by things that didn't carry very far: the rustling of clothes, footsteps, a cough...

"Fuck." Warren jumped back and straightened his clothes. Matty hastily tucked himself back away, but by the time he'd turned it was too late.

The man was in plain clothes, but there was nothing plain about the whistle he'd pulled out, ready to summon whoever else was patrolling tonight.

"Come quiet," he said, in a low, authoritative voice. "Come quiet, and it goes easier."

A few heartbeats passed in which Matty recognized two things very clearly.

One: The officer. A constable outside Matty's department, but possessing such a big mouth and so little experience to back it up that he was well-known around the Met and not much better liked than Matty was. There were rumors about him too. Different ones, but no friendlier.

Two: While perhaps Matty was confident he was going to lose all either way, the horror on Warren's face seemed to indicate that his momentary reluctance to see this through in the alley was not due to comfort or vague concerns. Unlike Matty, Warren *did* have something to lose. Something important. And, worse yet, he looked like he might try to save whatever it was by going quietly as requested. As if he believed it would really be easier that way.

It wouldn't.

Matty started backing up, shielding Warren as best he could while nudging him in the direction he needed to go.

"Run," he hissed. When Warren hesitated, he spoke louder, desperately, hoping to gain the fellow at least a second. "I said *run*, mate. This fuckster can't catch you! He's..." Wild amusement suddenly lit Matty up as the inspiration came. "I heard his hemorrhoids are the devil; he won't get far."

Between the new stubble, the patchy clothes, and the dark, foggy location, the constable didn't seem to have realized who Matty was. The blatant shock of hearing his personal business come out the mouth of a back-alley sodomite granted the second Warren needed.

He bolted.

And while Matty intended to stay and absorb the trouble, Warren grabbed his hand at the last moment and tugged him along.

"This way!" he said.

The officer roared with rage, blew hard on his piercing whistle, and started after them. Warren pulled him out of that alley and into another, then another, their feet pounding and chests heaving as they twisted and doubled back and tried to lose the officer who, fortunately, did seem slowed by his notorious affliction.

70 *To Sketch a Scandal*

But he was whistling like mad. He'd be joined by his comrades any second, probably faster ones.

"In here."

Warren dragged Matty into a gap between buildings so tight he felt one of his coat patches catch and rip on the rough walls. He could hardly get a full breath.

"Why are you doing this?" whispered Matty.

"Hiding? I know you're the brilliant detective here, but I should think that's not much of a mystery."

"But why bring me?" Matty hissed. "What if I'm setting you up?"

"Are you?"

"No."

Warren smacked his arse. "Then shut up before he hears you."

The spot was close and uncomfortable, but so pitch-black and impossible that when the officer passed, swearing to himself and followed by two other similarly single-minded pursuers in full uniform, none of them even thought to peer into the cranny they'd crammed themselves into. Their footsteps receded into the distance.

Matty and Warren stood still a moment, hardly breathing, until the silence seeped in and their muscles began to unknot with their trust that the coast was clear.

"Back where we started, eh?" said Warren, laughing with the release of fear and yanking on Matty's hips. He was pressed up tight to his cheeky conspirator in not so different a configuration as they'd been caught in.

They squeezed themselves back out of the gap, staring wildly at each other.

"Forester was right," Warren said with resigned good humor. "You're nothing but trouble, are you?"

"I'm so sorry," said Matty. "I shouldn't have put you in a situation like that."

"I told you we should go back to the club."

"You were right."

He peeked over his shoulder. "Does the poor wanker really have hemorrhoids that bad?"

Of all the things Warren could have said, that one caught Matty the most by surprise. Before he could stop himself, he was grinning.

"I wish I could say I didn't know," he chuckled. "But I think Scotland Yard gossip might give you lot a run for your money." They both laughed, and something changed on Warren's face. Not necessarily a bad change, but it gave Matty pause. "What?"

Warren shook himself. "Nothing. Just…"

Abashed, Matty shoved his hands in his pockets and cut him off before things could grow awkward. "I should go."

Some foolish part of him hoped for an argument, but there was none to be made. They both knew this encounter had been a mistake from the second Matty knocked that secret knock on The Curious Fox's door.

Matty turned and started off.

"Hey!" Warren called gently. Matty turned back to see that bewildered look still there, making Warren look more beautiful than even his reputation had indicated.

"What?" Matty asked.

"You've got a lovely smile," Warren said. "I hope life gives you more occasions to use it."

Matty had nothing to say to parting words like that, but as he walked back to his room, he felt them nestling into some cold empty space within him, much as the two of them had filled that dark gap and turned it from inhospitable cavern to safe refuge.

The ordeal had been foolish for sure, but maybe it hadn't been a mistake after all.

Chapter Five

Warren

Warren returned to the Fox with a sense of unreality clinging like the mist. He was shaky from the brush with disaster, hardly daring to believe they'd both gotten away.

He tried to muster up some indignance. That fool should have gone back to the club when Warren suggested it. While a raid was worse than a brush with patrol—harder to run like that—they were far less common. Matty should have known that even better than Warren did.

Of course, Warren couldn't kid himself for very long. He hadn't exactly followed Matty out to coax him home for a cuppa and a sweet chat by the fire. He'd gone for exactly what he almost got. Sure, he'd briefly rethought the idea, but not very emphatically. They were both fools in the end, and they'd both nearly paid for it.

But they hadn't paid. In fact, shockingly, Warren suffered no ill consequence at all. When he got back to the Fox, he found everything exactly as he'd left it. Miles, it turned out, had managed to keep the bar going in his absence with no trouble.

"I've played stranger roles," he said cryptically as he handed over a paltry collection of tips proportionate to his own stores of congeniality.

Warren pushed the pittance back; he'd feel like a miser if he accepted such a sad little sum. "Forester been looking for me?"

Miles shook his head. "No, he was busy. One of the newer chaps took faint. Not used to the corset."

And so Forester never found out about Warren's escapade at all. In fact, once the drama with the corset was done, Forester came down to take a turn at the bar himself, so Warren could go upstairs and catch the last hour of the party.

Against all odds, there was only one lingering problem.

Matty Shaw's smile.

The thought of it, given so suddenly right at the end of their adventure, was haunting. It would not leave Warren alone. Matty looked so different when he was lit up in amusement— the mild eyes brightened, the scruffy face glowed, the perfect contours cracked into a set of charmingly crooked dimples. And it was probably just the thrill of escape that did it, but the sight was recorded in Warren's memory as the most beautiful thing he'd ever seen.

Very annoying, really, considering he would never see it again. Forester made *that* perfectly clear while they were cleaning up the next morning.

"I do feel bad, not being more hospitable," he said. "He's a good chap, I think. But keeping him at arm's length is definitely for the best."

"Do you think he'll come back?" Warren asked, casually as he could so as not to give away which answer he was hoping for.

"Nah," said Forester. "He's too savvy to make the same mistake twice."

Fortunately, while the weekend's work did nothing to save Warren from the pathetic condition of wondering how *he* might get lucky enough to make the same mistake twice, once he got home, the distractions became plentiful. He got to the house

74   *To Sketch a Scandal*

to find cheerful voices pouring out of the parlor before he'd even opened the door.

Harry, it seemed, had made it home in one piece after all.

Warren's brother was neither Sikh, nor pirate, though he'd kept company with both and it showed in the way he'd snatched the righteousness of the former and the swagger of the latter for himself. Time and travel had added lines to his face and gray to his temples, but Warren would know that self-aggrandizing, roguish grin anywhere.

When they all noticed Warren come into common room, there was a general shout of surprise and happiness so loud it might have come from a group twice as large as the one actually present: Harry and Mother, along with two neighbor women and another younger one whom Warren did not know, but surmised must be Harry's new wife, Anjali.

Harry himself wasted no time. Dressed in an eccentric combination of a tidy kurta, a peacockish silk coat from who-knew-where, and clompy boots that had either seen better days or a lot of adventure, he sprang up like he was still seventeen and yanked Warren into a real collision of an embrace.

"My brother!" Harry clutched Warren's shoulder and looked him over in amazement. "Bloody hell, when I left, you were…" He broke off with a laugh, turning to the young woman. "Anjali, can you believe this? Every time I tell you about him, I talk like he's some little boy, only to get here and find I'm introducing you to a proper man."

The woman—who was eccentrically dressed in men's trousers and sailing boots, same as her husband—smiled. And Harry, seemingly driven by forces greater than himself, dragged Warren into another overly-enthusiastic hug and kiss on the forehead. He looked Warren joyfully but seriously in the eyes.

"You've done brilliantly, Warren," he said. "In between scolding me for getting married a world away, Mother's been telling me how well you've managed things all these years. I thank you from the very bottom of my heart. I truly could not be more thrilled to tell you that your reward is here, and your toil ends now."

If the world started lurching on its axis, Warren could not have been more upended than he was now, staring into the face of the brother he had assumed as good as dead. The Harry he remembered was a self-destructive bullshitter, propelled this way and that by mad dreams, hot air, and a bizarre notion that it was merely their father's devotion to a particular company that had made sailing miserable for him, rather than the fact that it was not his passion in the first place. Determined to right this supposed ancestral wrong, he left Warren—sixteen years old, forced to become man of the house and half the woman too, considering how poorly Mother's health was at the time—and while he'd talked of coming back someday with riches for all of them, every word had rung false. It had been nothing more than a socially acceptable excuse to run away and explore the world without feeling bad about what he'd left behind.

And maybe it had been just that, back then. Warren didn't think he'd misjudged his brother at that time.

But today?

Neither the light in his eye nor the sparkle of the gold rings he'd put in his ears seemed false in the slightest.

As Harry draped an arm around his shoulders and brought him to meet his wife, Warren's instincts told him it was all true even before Harry got into the details. He'd done it. He'd secured a good amount of money. Was it a fortune by London standards? Not quite, it seemed. He would not, for instance, be getting a house in Grosvenor Square and a seat in the Commons with it, that was certain. But it was enough. And, more shocking still, he would share it with his family, just as he'd promised in his self-important letters.

It should have made Warren happy. Mother seemed happy—

76 *To Sketch a Scandal*

though she eyed her new daughter-in-law with grave suspicion. The neighbors were happy—eyeing Warren more favorably than ever for their granddaughters. Anyone would be happy, wouldn't they?

But even as Harry discussed his investments and properties and deals ("not just one company, never one company"); even as he told them of the accounts and annuities that would take care of all the Bakshis in England (and a few others back in India), Warren could not seem to dig up any happiness through the thick layer of dread.

Everything he'd built for himself and his mother was about to go right out the window for good.

Harry did do one thing right: he agreed with Warren that their room was too small for four adults.

Unfortunately, he took it a step further, claiming it was too small for two adults as well. He'd see to it that they rented the best house the neighborhood had to offer.

"Nothing that nice over here," said one of the neighbor women. "You should go to Westminster, lots of beautiful homes there. New built."

"And raise our children up knowing only English bankers?" Harry laughed softly. "I see no need to uproot my family from where they've grown comfortable and have community, just for the sake of a finer house. They're fine enough for our purposes right here, I think."

Warren appreciated that. The women, however, seemed skeptical.

"Westminster would be closer to the gentleman's club where your brother has been working," one of them pointed out. "Your mother says he does very well for himself over there."

"I forgot that's what you were doing." Harry's brows scrunched up as he clearly struggled to remember all the bor-

Jess Everlee   77

ing things other people got up to while he was adventuring. "Which club is it again?"

"White's," Mother said proudly at the same time as Warren sputtered "Brooks's."

An uncomfortable silence fell thick upon the room.

"I thought it was White's?" she said.

Damn. Warren could have sworn he'd told her it was Brooks's. That said, all he'd cared about at the beginning was making sure the club name he dropped was nice enough to explain the amount of tips he brought home, and ensure it was somewhere too exclusive for the neighbors to ever check up on whether he actually worked there. After the first couple of months, though, he'd softened the blatant lie in conversation, referring to his place of employment only as *the club*.

"Did you?" said Warren carefully. "Sorry, Mother. What I think I was trying to say is that it's very much like White's."

"You said it was White's," she repeated darkly.

"Either way," Harry interrupted cheerfully, clearly hoping to make this tension between them vanish and get the attention back where it belonged: on himself. "It hardly matters, does it? You won't be needing a serving job anymore, will you?"

The casual waving off of that half of Warren's life struck him silent. Harry seemed to think it was a happy shock, and went on to decimate the other half: "Won't be the only one helping Mother at home, either."

He patted Anjali's hand. She'd been quiet thus far, her strange attire the only thing speaking for her as she let the rest of the family engage in their long-awaited reunion. When she finally smiled, though, Warren noticed it was nearly as roguish around the edges as her husband's.

"That's right," she said in a full, slightly rasped voice, stretching a bit and causing a lock to fall from her braid and into her face. She swept it back with an air of ease. "That sort of thing will fall to me."

78 *To Sketch a Scandal*

There was another of those awkward silences at her pronouncement, which Anjali ignored and Harry seemed not to notice.

"She's looking forward to the change," said Harry with an amused sort of pride. "Raised on the sea, she was."

"It's a hard life," Anjali said. "I could use the ease of women's work for once, I think."

The ease of women's work? Horrified, Warren tried to meet Mother's eye, but she was too busy staring open-mouthed at Anjali's assertion that there was anything easy about keeping a house to spare him a glance. And he couldn't blame her. His sister-in-law was in for a bit of a shock, if this was her attitude.

But that wasn't his problem, and his problem was big enough that he couldn't ignore it.

Warren forced a laugh into the awkwardness, hoping it didn't come across as anxious as it felt. "What am I supposed to do, then?" He turned to Harry. "I assume you don't want me to become idle."

"Of course not! You can marry."

The neighbor jumped right on that. "Oh, my granddaughter—"

"I don't want to marry," Warren said as politely as possible.

Harry looked bewildered. "Why not?"

There were a hundred reasons why not, and Warren heard another of them at least once a week. The bloke whose family was brought to shame when he became one of the first arrested under the new act. The one whose baby was born blind when he brought the pox from an alley to his wife. Charlie Price, the accountant, who'd nearly drowned himself in gin on the eve of his own engagement even as he told himself he was having fun. Warren was careful enough for his own sake, but as his ill-fated tryst with Matty Shaw had shown, he was not careful enough to bring that risk to a household.

"Bachelorhood suits me," he said simply.

Harry looked like he wanted to delve deeper, but Mother waved a hand to indicate it was a lost cause.

"Well, we'll figure something out, I'm sure," Harry said. "For now, though, let's focus on getting all of us settled in, shall we?"

A suitable house was found not too far from where they were living. Harry made sure they all knew it was well beneath what he could afford, but it was charming and clean and everyone liked it, even Warren, though he would miss the widows they'd been living with (the widows, at least, would not miss his share of the rent, that entire sum now being paid from Harry's coffers indefinitely). The most important rooms were on the lower level, which was good for Mother, and while it was close enough to the familiar neighbors and markets they'd grown to love, on the other side were some more fashionable new neighbors and tidier shops like the ones Warren had originally grown up with.

"It's a bit on the smaller side compared to what I was hoping for," Harry admitted as he pointed to where the deliverers should put the old couch, the only bit of furniture that was not newly acquired. "But I think that might be for the best."

He glanced over his shoulder. It was just him and Warren overseeing the furniture delivery, but the empty walls and floors magnified every scrape of a chair leg or moving-man's throat clearing. Harry lowered his voice against the effect as he went on.

"Anjali...as excited as she is to try something new, she's genuinely never kept a house." He grimaced. "I'd like to bring in some help, of course. That's the normal thing to do, and I certainly will to some extent, but Mother..."

Warren nodded, understanding immediately. "Already calling her a spoiled princess, is she?"

"*Useless pirate* is actually the phrase she opted for, if you want

80   *To Sketch a Scandal*

to get specific. Her father sailed with me, as he's been sailing all his life. Most of hers as well. And it shows."

"Were they pirates?" Warren asked. He was joking, of course, but Harry paused just long enough that he wondered whether he ought to have asked more genuinely. "Harry." He couldn't seem to keep a straight face; after the wedding fiasco, nothing could surprise him. "You weren't sailing with pirates again, were you, mate? Once is an accident. Twice is a habit."

Harry rolled his eyes, but still looked a little uncomfortable. "I acquired this fortune legally, if that's what you're asking."

"That's actually not quite what I'm asking—"

Harry cleared his throat quite loudly. "*Anyway*," he said. "Keeping house is going to be a massive adjustment for Anjali, and I worry they won't get on if she proves...untalented. You and Mother have been industrious in my absence."

"You could say that again," said Warren. "And without looting a single ship or asking for a single ransom."

Harry glared, and Warren came very close to not grinning.

"You've made your living entirely aboveboard, then?" Harry said with an accusing edge. "Over at Brooks's...or, goodness, was it White's? Dear me, it can be so hard to remember, sometimes, where one actually works—"

Warren gave his brother a sharp elbow to the ribs. "Point taken."

"I just hope Anjali can settle in and play lady of the house at least long enough to show Mother she's capable," Harry went on. "I think it would smooth things over quite a bit."

"She could stand to put a skirt on, too," Warren suggested. "Might help."

Harry didn't seem to appreciate that. "She is what she is, and I'd think you of all people would understand that."

"What's that supposed to mean?"

But Harry's attention was gone as one of the movers waved him over for his opinion on the placement of a curio cabinet.

Jess Everlee

★ ★ ★

It was a less than smooth operation, settling in together as a proper family after all this time apart. Warren didn't know what he was supposed to do with himself, what with a new housekeeper and Anjali suddenly taking over the tasks that had kept him busy for years on end. One or the other of them seemed to always be in his way when he made tea. Or they'd have taken the shopping baskets from under his nose when he'd planned to go to the market himself. Anjali was there to bring Mother her medicine before Warren had even realized she'd had a faint in this bloody big house Harry kept complaining was too small.

Meanwhile, the worried-about wariness of Mother in regard to her new daughter-in-law proved entirely justified. She seemed to think Anjali—who'd been caught swearing twice and continued dressing in snug trousers and sometimes even unbound hair—was good for very little. The stronger that implication became, the harder Anjali worked at proving she could function in a normal house, taking on a calm, wifeish attitude that did not suit her one bit. The more she tried to prove herself, the more annoyingly *everywhere* she was, stoking fires that smoked, tucking the wrong sheets on the wrong beds, making enemies of vendors Warren had charmed for years, and burning the bloody rice night after night until one day, Warren snapped when he smelled the unmistakable smoke, and went into the kitchen himself to fix it.

He found her in there with an apron on and her hair put up very inexpertly, so the fluffy black strands fell all over her sweaty face again anyway. She was mixing up something inscrutable and likely inedible in a helpless crock of once-innocent yogurt, humming as the stove behind her smoked and crackled.

"Your rice is burning," Warren snapped. He could have been kinder, but he was frankly sick of her incompetence when he could have been doing all this work happily enough himself (sick of eating burnt rice, too, if he was being honest).

82 *To Sketch a Scandal*

"Oh bugger!" she said, housewifely dignity slipping instantly. She rushed toward him just as he was trying to rescue the damned pot from the stove before she did further harm to the cookware itself, and when he turned, it was to find her an inch from a painful collision.

Split-second maneuvering spared her the clash with hot metal, but only because he darted back, bent against the stove, pot of rice clattering between them upside down.

They stood silently for a moment, shocked. Then bent down at so exactly the same moment that they banged heads.

A few more sailor-like curses escaped both of them as Warren got a little distance from the stove at last, rubbing his aching forehead, while Anjali flopped fully back to sit on the floor by the wreckage and nurse her own lump.

"Would you please just get out of my way?" she said.

"Me? In your way?" Warren scoffed. "Look, I smelled burning, yeah? I was just trying to help."

"No, you weren't," Anjali snapped. "Not *just* anyway."

Alright, so maybe she had a point there. "I wanted to make sure it was done right."

"How will I ever do anything right if you never let me try?" Her glare was harsh. "You're always there."

Hearing the same accusation leveled at him that he wanted to throw at her was highly disorienting. "Forgive me," he said when he'd gathered his wits back up, "but unlike you, I've been *there* for ten bloody years. Tough habit to break."

"You're the boy who grew up in the kitchen. I understand that." She'd lifted her knees in a posture that would have been obscene in a skirt, resting her arms on them and sulking as she tried to blow a bit of damp hair out of her eyes. "But I'm the girl who grew up in the shipyard. These were necessary aberrations, but they won't serve us well forever."

Her candidness was shocking. Well. If she could speak her mind, he would too.

Jess Everlee 83

"Seeing as my 'aberrations' have always served me just fine, I'm afraid I've developed bolder opinions on the subject," he said. "I'd have thought, when we first met, that you might have too."

"Perhaps I have," she said coldly. "But mere philosophy, bold or otherwise, won't make your mum accept me as a daughter, will it? Or does she have some bold opinions of her own that I've not been made privy to?"

Warren had opened his mouth to argue already, but what he'd been ready to say paled in comparison to the point she'd made.

"I want a good relationship with her," Anjali went on. "I don't have family in London, Warren. If I cannot get on with my husband's family, I will have a lonely existence indeed. I'm already starting at a disadvantage, you know."

"The wedding," Warren said with a nod of understanding. "If you can even call it that out in the middle of nowhere, with no one involved."

"It had to be done," Anjali said very seriously. "Things at sea can be dangerous, complicated, and time-sensitive."

Warren, with his own history of shameful bedpost notching, didn't have to stretch his imagination much to understand what she actually meant by that and didn't ask any questions.

"Anyway," she went on. "I'm pleading the none-too-bold idea that I practice the household work she expects of me, while you, perhaps, do what your brother expects of you."

"And what's that, exactly?" He raised a skeptical brow. "Everything's abstract with him. Ideas and notions and promises. What am I meant to actually *do*?"

"Find something meaningful to do with your hours."

"My hours have always been meaningful, until the two of you came back and changed everything."

Her expression softened. "Look, Warren. I just want the time and space to get settled in here with your mother and learn what

I need to learn. She thinks I need to master the practical tasks before I can properly manage staff, and I suppose that sounds right. I can see that it's a difficult transition, but we will all be happier in the long run for it. Or am I completely misreading the situation? You tell me. You are, as you point out, the expert in matters of your mother's household. What do you think?"

Ugh, bugger her for being right. While Mother had allowed for Warren to take on so much domesticity out of necessity, he couldn't kid himself. If she'd had a daughter in the first place, either of her own or if Warren had married one of those granddaughters after all, things would not have happened the way they did. Mother was a vibrant woman, but while Father had been a bit more flexible, she had never been especially modern in her thinking. Anjali's lack of household skills did not have the mystique of Warren's necessity in her eyes. Harry was right. She would always look sideways at Anjali, if Warren didn't give these women the opportunity to find their rhythm.

"I don't know what to do," he admitted. "I've been launched into higher status without warning. Second sons of status are supposed go into the military or religious life, or so I'm told. Can't say I'm inspired by those options."

"Get educated, then," Anjali suggested. "Go to university. He'll pay for it."

"I've spent the past decade caring for my mother and pouring drinks. I don't think Victoria herself could pay a university to take an interest in me."

"Then get yourself to a point where they will."

"How?"

"Study something," she shrugged. "Pick a topic. Some starting point. You're in the most exciting city in the world. There are libraries, schools, societies, teachers all around you. What captures your bold mind?"

So certain he'd been that his life would never change, he'd never let his mind be captured overmuch. The last thing to really get his attention and shake up his patterns had been a certain detective who continued showing up in his dreams even now.

While Matty Shaw was not, sadly, an official course of study, thoughts of him led down a path. He wasn't sure how he felt about the path, or whether it was an especially good one, but the fact that it existed made it the best he had. He put a finger up for Anjali to wait, then went to the new desk in the new study that still held all his and Mother's old papers. It was a bit of a stretch, but maybe…he tried one drawer and then another, and was about to give up hope when he found them. It had always been hard to shake her of an idea once it got into her head, and this was no exception: she'd bothered bringing along that whole stack of art class advertisements she'd been saving for who knew how long. He riffled through the stack until he found the one that had come in the post along with Harry's last letter. He gathered it up and brought it back into the kitchen, where Anjali had gone cross-legged, seeming to have taken up the floor itself as her new captain's chair.

"I've been told," he said, as he joined her down there, passing over the ad, "that a few of my drawings are alright."

Anjali examined the postcard, both sides. "Art," she said, looking pensive. "I think that sounds lovely, but will your family find it frivolous?"

"If they do, they'd be fools to say it," he said. "My father was an artist."

Anjali raised a brow. "Harry said he was an inventory manager and a sailor."

"What?" Warren couldn't keep the disgust off his face. "That's what he did for money, sure, but it wasn't the whole story. Didn't he tell you those are our father's paintings in the sitting room?"

Clearly, he had not, though Anjali didn't verbally confirm her husband's misrepresentation.

86 *To Sketch a Scandal*

"Well," she said carefully, "in that case, I think it's a noble enough pursuit. And I assume your mother would be happy with it."

"Who do you think has been saving every art school brochure for me since eighteen eighty-four, or so it would appear?"

"I do wonder, though...."

"If Harry will approve?" Warren filled in.

"Will he argue with your mother, if he doesn't like it and she does?"

"He'd better not, but considering what else he's gotten away with, nothing would surprise me at this point." He shrugged a little apology. "No offense."

"None taken. But if he does argue with her," she said with a sly smile, "I'll take her side."

Warren grinned back. "She'll like that."

Looking much happier, Anjali passed the postcard back. "It's settled, then. The best thing for both of us. Though you could probably do better than this little school. Not the royal school, as you said, but surely there's something in between..."

"I told you some people said my drawings are alright, but to be honest, I'm far from convinced." He thought of his father's paintings, their skill and beauty. How different they were from the silly sketches Warren did in moments of idleness. "If it turns out I'm dreadful, I'd hate to have wasted resources. This might get me out of your way, without causing too much embarrassment if it doesn't work out."

She nodded. "Why don't we all talk it over at supper? I think you're onto something."

He tried to imagine himself as the artist at the easel printed upon the postcard. Not an easy feat, but the fact was, he had no other ideas, and if he didn't take the idea that he had, it could cause rifts in his family that would be hard to heal later.

"Alright," he said. "In that case, I suppose I'll get started with the 'getting out of your way' bit, then."

He started out, but she stopped him. "Wait!"

He looked back to find she'd turned over the pot. She'd somehow managed to burn half of the rice to the bottom, while the rest remained so soggy it had spilled all over the floor in a sticky, gloppy mess.

"How did you even do that?" he laughed.

"Will you help me clean it up?"

"I thought you wanted to do everything yourself."

"I do," she said. "Right after this one."

They shared a smile and started cleaning up the mess.

Chapter Six

Matty

Matty's professional life had been spent mostly in the shadows. Ten years ago, Barrows had led him from a small, dark cell into a small, dark room and said, "I'd like to make a deal with you, lad." It was all shifty alleys and midnight whorehouses after that.

His arrival at Buttersnipe's School for Artistic Enrichment couldn't have been more different. There was still bite to the air, but it was an oddly sunny day for the time of year. He might have enjoyed the change if he trusted his new character, but as he went up the saggy steps that led to the door, feigning impoverished artist rather than confident model, he felt frighteningly visible. It felt like every person on the street below knew precisely what he was. Even the door seemed to be staring back at him, its grimy window like a massive eye glaring right through his ruse.

Oh, he'd done the visual right, because that's what he did best. He wore his patched jacket and a neckcloth printed with loud, flopping poppy flowers, the green scarf wound loose over his shoulders with pride in the handmade life. He'd put the ring from Barrows on a chain around his neck so it did not

Jess Everlee 89

get in the way of his creative fingers. His informal cap was squished upon hair that had missed a trim, that stubble he'd been promised hinting that he'd just been *too busy creating* to bother with upkeep. With his sketchbook tucked under his arm, he cut a fine enough aesthetic figure. Nothing external would give him away.

But as the door's window peered judgingly at him, he could simultaneously peer judgingly right back at his own reflection. His face was all wrong. People wanted their playthings docile, dim-witted. He'd played that part so long, he could see himself slipping into it even now. There was no spark of the headstrong creativity that he'd written up in his character profile. Even under the quirky accessories and stubble, he looked tame, accommodating, unlikely to make a fuss about anything. He was not sure whether his real self possessed the bold qualities he needed—maybe, maybe not, his own nature was not his concern—but the undercover self he'd built up over the years certainly did not.

He steeled himself against the cruel convictions of the door, grabbing its handle firmly, preparing to do battle with it. The handle was smooth and cool even through his glove. He turned it with the determination he so desperately needed, but had hardly heard the click of its release before that determination wavered and wobbled and then finally expired on the spot. He took his hand back like it'd been burned, roiling with anxiety.

He couldn't pull this off.

There was so much uncertainty inside this building. So many things that could go wrong. So little he felt equipped to handle. To be found out could spoil a case completely, could prove dangerous or even fatal depending on the circumstance. While he saw potential art fraud as less grim than the usual crimes he investigated, the consequences the Buttersnipes would face if they were caught in a scheme of this magnitude were still grievous. People could become desperate when their freedom

90 *To Sketch a Scandal*

was on the line. He did not have enough information about this couple yet to ascertain how badly his discovery might spiral if they caught on to his ruse. Surely that risk was worse than the unprovable rumors he was facing back at headquarters?

He couldn't go in there. It would be the end of him more certainly than anything else. He needed to talk to Barrows. Needed to go back to the old plan, to risk it, because suddenly it seemed the lesser risk by far. He spun round, head down.

His escape was thwarted as he crashed headlong into a man who had gotten up behind him while he was buried in his ruminations.

"Oy!"

There was an instant of off balance, right on the edge of the steps. Matty found his footing first, and grasped for the flailing arm of his hapless victim, steadying him at the top of the stoop.

"I'm sorry, I—" Matty tipped his brim and raised his eyes to a sight he'd assumed doomed to lonely fantasies. He'd yet to see that face in the light of day, but even if he'd not recognized it, its beauty would have caught him just as off guard as its familiarity.

"War—" *Manners, Matty, you're not bum-out in an alley.* "Mr. Bakshi?"

Warren looked round like he expected someone to jump out of the bushes and tell him this was some big joke. "What are you doing here?"

"I told you I needed to study art," he said vaguely.

Warren's eyes narrowed. "Why would a det—"

"Shh!"

Matty took him by the arm again, pulling him in close on the corner of the stoop to speak in an ear he found devilishly adorned with a delicious-looking yellow gem. He took a steadying breath. "It would be best," he whispered, "if we kept my occupation between us."

Perhaps the prettiest brown eyes Matty'd ever seen met his

Jess Everlee 91

own, having an inconvenient effect on his pulse's tempo. Still, he did not look away. Warren examined him for a long moment, the curiosity on his face finally cracking to reveal excitement instead.

"Are you investigating this place?" he asked in a rather feeble attempt at whispering. He looked up at the building like he'd uncovered some satisfyingly nasty dirt on it. "Ha! I knew it. I told my mum the advertisement looked like a bloody scam!"

"Shh!" Matty squeezed his arm in hopes it might quiet him down. Dear Lord, had he really been fretting about having his cover blown by his own lack of creative spirit, when it was about to be blown far more explicitly by the very last person Matty had expected to meet on this stoop? He could not let Warren know he was investigating the instructors—that would ruin everything—but he could not allow open discussion of his detective-hood, either. He cast about for a reason to inspire Warren's discretion.

"I'm...not on a case just yet," he lied desperately. He didn't like doing that, but what choice did he have? "I'm training for one. I'll have to play an artist, but since I have no skills, my supervisor made me sign up for this class. I need to get better before it's too late." As the falsehood slipped from his lips, he wished it were true. Wouldn't that have been nice? To not be thrown in the deep end with an ugly coat and a ball of yarn? To have had a chance to get to know a way of being *before* he was expected to fit seamlessly into it?

"If you're not investigating them," Warren asked, "then why can't they know who you are?"

"It's a small community, the artistic one," Matty said wildly, not sure how true that was. Sounded true. Probably true. "I don't know who these, ah—" he pretended not to remember the name, checking his pocket for the ad "—these *Buttersnipes* might know, and I don't want it getting around that there's some junior detective taking art classes in London if I can help

92   *To Sketch a Scandal*

it. It would be poor timing. With the, you know. The actual case. Which is coming later. And has nothing to do with these folks, who I assume are, you know, perfectly fine."

Damn, where was all this babbling coming from? Matty was suddenly thankful he'd rarely worked around attractive suspects; seemed his ability to remain convincing faltered under such pressure. Warren looked him in the eye for another moment, as if suspecting there was a crack in this story. Or maybe that was Matty's own paranoia, because it wasn't long before he snorted a laugh.

"If you say so, Mr. Shaw," he paused. "If I may call you Mr. Shaw, and not some pseudonym you're taking on for the class's duration."

There was a devilish note of friendly conspiracy in his voice, not unlike the last time they'd met. Poor Matty forgot not his own name—at least—but the one he'd intended to use.

"It's a common enough name," Matty said, deciding to let the pseudonym go rather than inspire more suspicion in this chap. "Have at it."

"One more question."

Matty swallowed hard. He realized that after all this time he was still, quite inappropriately, clutching Warren's arm. He let go, straightening the lumpy scarf about his neck and trying to forget all the wonderful ways Warren had used it to his advantage last time they'd met. "What question?"

"Why were you leaving?" Warren asked. "When I got here, you were starting down the steps and you had, if I may be so bold as to say so, quite a lot of momentum behind you. If I didn't know any better, I'd say you were in the process of bolting."

"I, uh…" Matty faltered. "I just… I wasn't sure if—"

"Are you really so bad at drawing that you considered not going in at all? Not even when you needed to?" With that judging tone, he might as well have said, *Tell me, Matty, darling, are you some sort of bleeding coward?*

Warren's skeptically-raised brow changed everything. Matty was not a bleeding coward. He was plenty of dreadful things, but that had never been one of them. Witnessed now, not just by the eye of the door, but by someone he wanted the approval of, he could not follow through with the act of cowardice he'd so nearly committed.

"I was," he admitted. "But I think I might stay after all."

Warren grinned, briefly wolfish but settling quickly into something more suited to the daylight they'd so unexpectedly found themselves in.

"Good." He reached past Matty for the door handle. "Then maybe this won't be a complete waste of my time and my brother's money."

Matty had never been in a proper academy of art, and he suspected that the owners of Buttersnipe's School for Artistic Enrichment had not, either.

"What the devil is that?" Warren whispered as they took in the enormous portrait that was the focal point of a small, dusty foyer. A stately man and a buxom woman stood stiffly side by side, holding paintbrushes in a field of purple lines that might have been lavender. Between them sat a patchy little dog with its own paintbrush between its teeth. Their faces were all oddly similar—even the dog's—uncannily round and staring straight ahead. It was one of the ugliest things Warren had ever seen. "Bloody hell, you may not be...you know." He nodded to Matty, keeping the word *investigating* from passing his lips. "But that doesn't mean we haven't walked in on a scam after all."

Matty prepared himself to go. If Warren walked out, there would be less shame in him doing the same. But Warren was striding up the carpeted stairs like the idea that this might be terrible had increased his enthusiasm considerably.

94   *To Sketch a Scandal*

"Come on," he coaxed. "From what you've told me, even that's a good step up from what you've been making, isn't it?"

"That's..." Matty reexamined the painting, where its subjects seemed to stare straight through him. Ugly or not, they were at least recognizable as human and canine. He self-consciously adjusted his scarf. "That's hard to argue with."

It was even harder to argue with the perfection of Warren's teasing grin, beckoning him along. He had been attractive enough in red club light and thin moonbeams, but was something else entirely in the full light of day. An edge he'd had in the darkness was softened here, less styled and cunning. Both he and the topaz earring he wore still twinkled, but more with mischief than seduction. The effect was irresistible. He followed Warren up the stairs, hoping (but still unconvinced) that it would end better than the last time one of them followed the other somewhere.

Led by the sound of cheerful voices, they wound up in a large salon. Matty began his mental notes immediately—undercover, he could not write them down until he was alone, so by now, his memory was like a slate on the wall of his mind. Some two dozen mismatched stations of school desks, easels, and uncomfortable-looking stools were set facing a collection of sketches and paintings in various states of completion. (*Note: they're as shabby as the rest. A genius cover, if indeed it is a cover.*) There was no figure model yet, though a stool off to the side indicated that there would be eventually. (*Note: they're not in a rush to replace the model, calling into question the seriousness of the class. I formally quit that position several days ago.*) The other students were a ramshackle bunch, men and women both in unusually equal number claiming the choicest stations and chatting nervously about the weather. (*Note: who would suspect a female forger? Brilliant choice, potentially.*)

Cool autumn air wafted through the open windows, but the stink of oil paint and turpentine was so heavy that Matty hated to think how unpleasant it would be if they were closed more effectively against the chill. The walls were crammed so tightly with portraits that the frames knocked shoulders. Each one featured the same eerily round faces as the one downstairs, in spite of differences in sex, race, age, and—occasionally— species of the subject.

"Is that budgie related to the dog in the foyer?" Warren whispered, his warm breath an indecent tickle against Matty's ear. He nodded at a painting where said budgie was painted nearly as large as his human companion's head, his eyes identical to the aforementioned dog, and off-puttingly situated in the center of the bird's face as it stared directly at the viewer.

The best thing would be to brush off that sort of comradery. Matty had work to do. But a chuckle bubbled in his throat as their eyes met against his will.

Distracted by each other, they drifted to neighboring easels, nearer to the fire and farther from the window, where the odors and warmth combined and Matty felt like he'd downed some gin. Given the distraction of Warren settling in on his right, he wasn't thrilled about having his head made foggier by the mantel on his left.

That said, perhaps the proximity to flame would prove a boon. If he created something so cursed that the subjects of uncanny paintings demanded its instant destruction, he'd have fire at the ready. Seeing as there were no other options left, he opened his sketchbook to a fresh, unwitting page and propped it on his easel.

Out of the milling throng of students, a familiar woman with hair frizzing out of its bun made her way to the front of the room where she stood between two of the displayed canvases. She clapped her small hands together to get everyone's attention. She was followed by a man with spectacles, one Matty also recognized from the single photograph on his case board. As the couple stood there, waiting for the buzz and ruffle of

96 *To Sketch a Scandal*

the room to settle, a little dog poked its head right out of the woman's skirts, staring around at the students.

It was always a sober moment, seeing his suspects in person for the first time, and Matty—

"Is that the couple from the painting downstairs?"

The moment shattered before it could fully settle. Warren was leaning toward him, his whisper and the smile that shaped it still lingering on his pretty lips.

Matty was supposed to be assessing these people for hints of serious transgression, but once more he was holding his breath to keep from laughing. Warren was right. Though he'd known what the Buttersnipes looked like from his photograph, the painting was such a creative rendition of their forms that he hadn't even recognized them. The real woman was built straight as a rail from top to bottom, the man plump and shorter than his wife by a good inch that had been generously inverted in the portrait. But the color of her hair, the perch of the specs on his hawkish nose, and—most saliently—the way their little dog emerged from its tent to settle between them was enough to give the gist.

If they were secretly skilled forgers, they'd sure done an impressive job building a cover of questionable artistry to hide their guilt.

"Welcome, welcome," the woman said. "We are ever so pleased to have you with us for our tenth session of Artistic Enrichment."

"I'm Frederick Buttersnipe," piped up the fellow. "I teach this class right alongside my talented wife, Priscilla, and our greatest treasure, Miss Martha Buttersnipe."

While there had still been a certain amount of mutters and rustling during this introduction, a silence impressively thick settled on the room at this last pronouncement. All eyes moved to those of Miss Martha Buttersnipe. The little lady gave a panting smile, tail wagging so hard it became tangled in her mother's skirts.

"Each of you is here," Mr. Buttersnipe went on, "to participate in a most endangered art form. The incessant proliferation of *the photograph*—" he spoke of it much as Superintendent Frost had recently spoken of Matty "—threatens one of humanity's greatest gifts: that of one human immortalizing another through the work of his *hands*."

All three Buttersnipes looked round at their students as if daring one to admit he'd once granted immortality using some less desirable part.

"We offer these lessons," Mrs. Buttersnipe went on, "at a considerable discount, for it is our own common peers who are most tempted by the cheap tricks of the *photography studio*. Our proprietary methods of portraiture, however, are learnable by all and will produce a beautiful piece of lasting memory in a fraction of the time typically expected of the portrait artist."

"This," Mr. Buttersnipe said, "allows for those of lesser means to afford to learn the art—nay, the ministry!—of portraiture. Then members of their own communities can commission meaningful records of their visages for their descendants without bankrupting said descendants in the process nor resorting to the *lesser means* previously mentioned."

He shuddered. A few others in the room half-heartedly tried to muster up some disgust of their own, kissing arse before the pencils had even come out. That was a good idea, for anyone looking to make friends with the teachers. Matty followed the sycophantic students' lead, wrinkling his nose at the very *idea* of photography.

As suspected, Mrs. Buttersnipe spared Matty and these others special nods before she continued. "Some of our students have gone on to make lucrative careers for themselves serving families who might otherwise have been lost in obscurity. Others have moved on into other forms of artistic expression. We

98   *To Sketch a Scandal*

ourselves offer individual, specialized instruction to students who show particular promise in these open classes. We will be assessing each of you to ascertain whether you might warrant an invitation, and fervently hope this class is simply brimming with such talent."

Those words went right on the mental slate: *discount*, *proprietary*, *lucrative*. Specialized instruction was of particular interest. That went along with Matty's hunch about their methods, and also gave him a path to the deeper rings of the potential operation.

Though he really shouldn't have taken his eyes off the suspects, the warm chemical fog of the room made the temptation beside him too great to resist. He glanced at Warren, curious about his response to all this. The bloke was biting his lip hard, brows up in incredulous amusement. They caught each other's eye just long enough to realize that was a terrible idea if they didn't want to be tossed out on account of laughing. While Matty had to assume the possibility that the Buttersnipes' ridiculousness was an act, there was a chance that they were genuinely this batty. And that idea tickled something inconvenient behind his navel—what if he really was not in a room with clever criminals at all, but just seated beside the man who'd nearly been his downfall, about to follow the artistic instructions of some mediocre eccentrics who were not covering for anything, but were like this all day, every day? It would be bloody preposterous.

When Matty trained his gaze back to the front, holding his breath until the chuckles died in his chest, it was to find that Mr. Buttersnipe was in league to make him laugh. No longer upright, he was now stooped down, tying a basket to the front of his precious dog.

"Miss Martha will be around to collect your payments," he said. "In full, if you please."

Never had a creature looked so proud as Miss Martha did,

trotting up to each student in turn. Her tail wagged happily as she accepted what probably amounted to a quite a bit of money, though a pittance, of course, compared with what might be lining their pockets if this was not actually the bulk of their income.

"Worth every bloody penny," Warren muttered to Matty as he dropped in his envelope.

"Easy for you to say," Matty whispered back as he came face-to-face with Miss Martha. "It's your brother's money."

Warren looked surprised that his offhand comment on the stairs had been tucked away in Matty's head for later.

"You don't miss a trick, do you?"

"Only at the Fox," Matty quipped very quietly. "I try to miss your lot's tricks whenever possible."

Matty was so consistently deadpan that he never really expected a joke to be taken as such. But Warren's dark eyes immediately danced, lingering on Matty's face for two heart-stopping seconds too long before Mrs. Buttersnipe started clapping for attention again and this odd new chapter of their lives began.

Chapter Seven

Warren

For someone who had supposedly used his good looks more often under cover of night, Matty Shaw was downright distracting in the sunlit classroom. As suspected, his eyes were blue—such an obnoxious and unlikely blue that Warren would have expected the shade more readily upon one of the Buttersnipes' canvases than on an actual person. Though Matty was still using stubble and patchy clothes to hide the impression that he'd been dreamed up and brought to life Pygmalion-style, it was a futile effort.

The nearly mathematical beauty of him lent a sense of unreality to this entire reunion. Warren wasn't in the habit of bumping into blokes he'd fucked (or nearly so). If ever he did, the right response was to feign complete ignorance that they'd ever even met. Though they both should have known better, they'd bungled that one from the beginning, already acknowledging each other, climbing the stairs together, and choosing seats beside each other. Matty'd shared a secret, and Warren had shared a laugh. They were already in a lot deeper than they should be, and Warren didn't have a script for this one.

"We shall start," Mr. Buttersnipe said as his wife collected the payments from her little helper, "by identifying and copying basic shapes. Our proprietary portraiture method centers around identifying the shapes that are unique to your subject, and applying them to the shapes that are universal in the human form. We will do this by finding shapes around the room to start with; our figure model had to pull out at the last minute, but I'm sure we will find another by the next class."

Warren glanced over at Matty, poised to make a quip about volunteering, but found the bloke looking very busy resetting his sketchbook on the easel. Warren had to wonder if the clumsiness with which he adjusted it was part of his act. In fact, maybe all this talk of being dreadful at art was an act too...

Warren shook himself and got back to setting up his own station before he got caught staring. There were an awful lot of reasons not to speculate about Matty Shaw. He was specifically trying to avoid notice, after all; seemed rude for Warren to over-examine someone who needed to blend in. Not to mention, even if he were receptive to Warren's attention, he was decidedly off-limits. Joking and watching might not be the best way to remind himself of that. The coincidence of the class was not Warren's fault, but Forester wouldn't be happy if he heard they'd gotten friendly, whatever the context.

Mr. Buttersnipe started in with a lecture on identifying the "basic shapes" of people's heads and facial features, a process that was as overcomplicated as it was potentially offensive. That said, Warren found it easy enough. The instructors themselves were full of shapes—the shallow triangle of his chin, the long rectangle of her torso, the perfect circles of both their spectacles. Warren applied them casually to his paper until he grew bored and started looking for other sources of inspiration.

Matty was sitting right beside him. Sure, he ought not pay too much attention to the bloke, but it was the assignment to look around a bit, wasn't it? He found the pretty detective

To Sketch a Scandal

sketching out his oblong faces, triangular noses, and rounded eyes with impeccable posture and some sense of resignation. Like he knew perfectly well that the instruction was garbage, but considering his own ability was at the bottom of the bin, it might provide him with a way out if he could grasp and scale it. He meticulously etched each marking with a slow deliberation, his brow furrowed and his tongue between his teeth in utter concentration.

So distracting was that tongue in particular—it looked so innocent, but Warren knew better—that he did not notice Mrs. Buttersnipe coming up behind him until he felt Miss Martha lie down atop his own shoe. Up close, the smell of turpentine that hung around her was stronger, which probably explained a lot.

"Good," she said at last, nodding slowly as she examined his paper. "But don't stop now! Keep going, fill these pages to their very limits! The more shapes you can see in your subjects, the more individualized your portraits can be. You're off to a very good start, Mr. Bakshi. Too soon to tell, but I have a good feeling about your chances at a certain invitation."

Before he could even thank her for the compliment, the weight of the dog was gone and the instructor was too, moving on to Matty.

"Oh." She froze as she laid eyes upon his paper. "Oh my dear. I…" She broke off, looking down at Miss Martha for a moment of deliberation before going on in a pinched voice. "Have you ever done anything like this before, dear?"

Warren tried to ignore this conversation. It was not his business.

"I have not, ma'am," Matty said in an even voice that cut right through Warren's defenses. "That's why I'm here. To learn from geniuses like yourselves."

Warren snorted quietly at the completely straight-faced way Matty managed that one. Against his better judgment, he took

Jess Everlee 103

a peek and found Mrs. Buttersnipe's face had gone as pinched as her voice.

"Well…carry on, then," she said airily, turning to go.

"Do you have any tips?" Matty went on before she could abandon him. "For me particularly? What do you think I'm doing wron—"

"Just be sure to practice at home," said Mrs. Buttersnipe with a dismissive wave. "You'll need to catch up to the other students before the figure model arrives next week, or…" She shrugged. "It's not for everyone, dear."

"But, ma'am—"

She went on to the next without another word. Matty stared after her for a moment, sort of blankly bewildered, then turned back to his paper, looking lost.

Warren returned to his own collection of shapes, determined first off to pretend he'd heard nothing, and second to choose a different seat next week. Matty was a distraction and a temptation too great to resist. Of course, he wasn't about to follow him into another alley, but even the friendliness he felt compelled to start up was all wrong. Their respective jobs simply didn't allow for it. Matty wasn't here for friendship, and Warren couldn't be friends with someone in law enforcement, not even one who was determined to miss all his tricks. Forester was right about that. Trouble for their sort could move swifter than a pox if you weren't careful who you let in.

As he worked on his shapes, though, trying not to glance over, he felt Matty's gaze find him instead. Those ridiculous eyes of his were like the hottest of little blue flames. Warren tried to ignore the burning of attention, but eventually succumbed to meeting it head-on.

"What?"

Matty grimaced, caught. "I'm sorry, I was just… I was trying to capture the shape of your ear. Like she said to do." He turned his sketchbook to point out something that looked uncannily

104   *To Sketch a Scandal*

like a horrid lump of bread Anjali had baked last week. "Hold still, will you? Can't you see I've nearly got an exact replica?"

Something warmer and sweeter even than desire swept through Warren at the self-deprecation.

He shouldn't. He really shouldn't.

But the rule of avoidance he'd been trying to talk himself into all morning could not stand against the memory of those artistically deficient hands running up the back of his coat.

He stepped over to Matty's station. The paper was filled with darkly penciled, tortured-looking shapes. The problem was instantly obvious to Warren—the lines were childish, a function of grip. He couldn't fix everything—that scarf was a really sobering reminder of just what Matty was working with—but he did have a tip. He could share it, probably. What harm was there in that? He liked being helpful, and with opportunities to do so at home waning, he couldn't seem to help the chance that appeared before him now.

"Here." Going against every limit he'd tried to convince himself mattered, he took Matty's hand and helped him to adjust his stiff, awkward fingers. Matty didn't react much, but Warren heard how his next breath came very even, deep, and nerve-settling.

"I should think," he muttered as close to Matty's ear as he dared, so no one else would hear, "from our last encounter, that you have sufficient experience to know you don't need this sort of death grip to get the job done."

Matty looked up at him, still sitting on his stool whilst Warren stood. The angle destroyed any last bit of resolve Warren had.

"Relax a little," Warren went on, shaking Matty's arm out and guiding him back to the paper with its more suitable grip. He lingered only for the split second that Matty would notice and anyone looking on would not, though his own fingers went on tingling after he let go.

Matty took another of those steadying breaths and tried again on the kidney shape he was attempting for an ear.

"That's it," Warren said.

"No, it's not," said Matty. But his second try, while still too heavily drawn and pinched at the bottom, was a bit better. "Thank you. How did you learn that, anyway?"

The question poked at a soft spot that produced a protective shell of sarcasm: "Don't take much learning to realize you shouldn't hold a pencil like you hold a bobby bat, mate."

Matty didn't blink. "Natural ability, then?"

Warren would have preferred to leave it there, but it felt too dishonest. "My father was an artist," he said grudgingly. He glanced around self-consciously, but they weren't the only pairs quietly chatting as they worked. He went on. "That's why he and my mum came to London in the first place. He never got to do it full-time. The work he took to support the family was too demanding. We'd doodle together when he was home, though. Silly stuff."

It was actually a relief to talk to someone clearly accustomed to sucking every drop of information from a sentence. It was quite the opposite of what Warren usually experienced, chatting up some man from behind the bar. He was lucky if those fellows let him get a word in, luckier still if they heard the words he spoke. Matty, on the other hand, was obviously listening, considering, and remembering. He took Warren's words in slowly, nodded like he really understood, and then did not ask a single stupid question before returning quietly to his work.

Warren supposed he ought to do the same. He tried to look about the room at the other would-be artists, attempting to break their forms up into the constituent shapes they'd be working with to make these cheap, cookie-cutter portraits. Every fiber of him wanted to look only at Matty—he was, by far, both the loveliest and the most interesting person in this room. But he brought his reluctant attention instead to a stocky bloke

106   *To Sketch a Scandal*

with longish hair, one who looked like he'd taken some of Oscar Wilde's old anti-fashion advice a bit too much to heart. In terms of shapes, he was comprised largely of wide rectangles. Head and shoulders, and...

The bloke turned and caught Warren looking at him. His eyes went to very oblong slits and his mouth to an upside-down crescent. Not so easily intimidated, Warren held up his pencil, swirling it around a little. *I'm doing what I'm supposed to be doing*, he communicated as best he could without words. *So bugger off, will you?*

The bloke did just that, going back to his work with a moody little huff and a toss of his long curls.

"Making friends already?" came the pleasant, dry voice from his left that was becoming alarmingly familiar. Matty's eyes were on his own paper, but his mouth was doing that tantalizing thing again. Almost smiling.

Warren shrugged, face heating as he returned to his rectangles.

"Maybe I am."

Chapter Eight

Matty

When he held the pencil like Warren had shown him, Matty figured out how to draw simple shapes of passable quality—when he copied other shapes. When he tried to draw them from life, however, to disassemble entire human beings into simplistic parts like some abstract, artistic serial killer, his ability went similarly to pieces again.

And that was dreadful, because the amount of useful intelligence he'd gotten by the end of class was basically zero. Well, not quite zero. They did pick students out for individualized instruction, but that might only prove Warren's small suspicion that they knew how to suck money out of artistic dreamers. It was not remotely unique to a forgery operation. Either way, though, he was likely never going to find out: not only had he attracted no special interest from the instructors, but had already been flagged as a hopeless case who might do well to quit while he was ahead.

Matty lay flat on his bed the next morning after waking. Necessity had made him a disciplined fellow, and he rarely lingered among his pillows very long. Today, though, for the first

108 *To Sketch a Scandal*

time in a long time, he could muster up no motivation to move. He wouldn't have minded another undercover day so much—in spite of his misgivings, it had proved a fairly pleasant change to his routine, if not especially fruitful. But having not impressed the Buttersnipes yet, he would be back at headquarters until he could try again in the next class. He was filled with dread, doom, and a feeling that had never plagued him before:

He didn't want to go into headquarters.

It was easy to blame the nature of the case, but that wasn't really the problem. He'd been dreading his days for a while now, ever since Barrows had announced his retirement. Add to that the nasty rumors, the change in his methods, the pressure to perform, and the presence of fucking Detective Ashton on the case and headquarters had become near-intolerable when compared with the pleasant work and pleasanter company at his easel yesterday.

He briefly wished he really was some foolish rich boy who'd convinced himself he could abandon everything else for a life of artistic ease, spending his days discussing truth instead of secrets and his nights somewhere like The Curious Fox with only the usual worries to bother him. Reaching across the small expanse between bed and desk, he gathered up his sketchbook and flipped through it. He rather liked some of the pages he'd done. A real class and a bit of help from Warren had improved him more than he'd thought possible...

Or maybe it was his imagination. Yes, surely that was all. It was delusional, to think he could actually learn a new trade at this point. He couldn't even manage a new undercover role without losing his way.

It felt better to believe that the rent boy roles he'd taken on before this had been as fabricated as this one, but they hadn't been nearly so big a stretch. Though he'd only been angling for his second trick when he was arrested at fifteen, the intent had been there. The desperation. The damage. Until Scotland Yard, he'd been just as beautiful, just as friendless, just as undereducated as the lads he pretended to be when he was undercover. He knew what it was, to charm from a place of need, whether it be for bread or for evidence. And it had made the roles easy.

He had no such experience to draw on now. This character, this aspiring artist... He snapped the sketchbook shut with a loud clap. This artist thing had nothing to do with Matty whatsoever. And it never would.

Unless...

He opened the sketchbook again, tracing his fingers over the pencil lines until they were fit to leave all manner of smudgy gray prints behind him. He'd long since learned to be suspicious of ideas that seemed too convenient to be true, conclusions that were temptingly tidy and satisfying. No crime was that simple, and that went for other aspects of life as well. The notion that crossed his mind now, though, had that sort of convenient allure. He ought to put it aside, but so snug in his bed with so little to look forward to at headquarters, he couldn't shake it.

Matty could smash clay and dull pencils at his desk all day long—even if he mastered the mechanical aspects of drawing, he would never convince these Buttersnipes that he was worthy of a moment alone with them if he could not drive out the cultivated dimness in his eyes and set off a spark of creativity there instead.

He made a good whore because he'd been a whore. If he wanted to make a good artist, didn't it make sense to be an artist? Even if just for a little while? If he made the investigative aspects his secondary concern for a time, giving in to his curiosity of what this false life would feel like if it were real, it might counterintuitively put him in the very position he needed to gather the intelligence that was otherwise barred from him.

Brilliant.

Or brilliant-seeming, anyway.

110   *To Sketch a Scandal*

Far too brilliant-seeming to actually *be* brilliant. And the detective in him knew that.

But the detective in him was no match for something else that was rising up in him this morning. Something tired and protesting that simply could not stand going in there and watching Ashton smirk and say *Shaw* with his mouth while he flashed *Matilda* with his eyes.

He threw his sketchbook on the ground, then rolled over and shut his eyes to go back to sleep.

Artists, he felt, didn't worry overmuch about getting to the office on time.

That afternoon, he packed up all hints that his room had ever belonged to a detective, replacing legal books, grim memo pads, and tidy black inkwells with an ale mug of sharpened pencils, a fresh stack of wide drawing paper, a bowl of erasers that didn't know what toil they were in for, and a small bottle of absinthe that he hadn't gotten up the nerve to consume yet, but figured was an important thing for any real artist to have on hand. He put his patched coat and lumpy scarf back on— his uniform—and began practicing the most useful shapes he'd learned in class yesterday, one by one, like little armies marching across his paper. He would cultivate obsession. He would draw by choice, on his own time, until Matty Shaw could say he was indeed an aspiring artist in all the ways that mattered.

He never went into the office at all. Why should he? He went on until the encroaching evening had him lighting candles— not lamps, lamps were not as aesthetically pleasing—and just as he was settling back in to continue identifying and marking down the shapes he found in the untouched absinthe bottle before him, the landlady banged on his door.

"Oy, Detective. Comp'ny for you."

Matty covered his work with a stray piece of paper so no one could witness his hideous disassembly of the innocent bottle in too violent of detail.

When he opened the door, Mrs. Wooster was standing with Detective Barrows, who did not look pleased with him at all. Barrows took his hat off his mostly bald head and held it to his chest.

"I apologize for coming so late," he said with barely-contained irritation. "I hope it's not too much trouble."

"Not at all," Matty said, very tense. "It's…it's lovely to see you, sir. Mrs. Wooster, could you ask Gretta to put the tea on?"

"Of course," the landlady said. "Will you take it in the sitting room?"

Barrows shook his head before Matty could answer. "If it's alright, I think I should like to speak with Mr. Shaw privately."

Matty grimaced. "If she could bring it up here, then, please."

Once she left, Barrows rounded on him. "Where the devil were you today?"

"I can explain, sir." Now in the presence of his higher-up, that artsy defiance he'd been cultivating all day vanished. His posture went straight as a goddamned board. "Come in."

Matty helped Barrows out of his long overcoat, finding a hook for it and his hat. When he turned back, Barrows was taking in Matty's transformed room: the open art books, piles of crumpled papers, and the now-prominently-displayed absinthe bottle posed right in the center of his desk.

"Does it always look like this?" Barrows asked with concern.

"No, sir!" Matty threw open his wardrobe to show the more suitable objects he'd replaced today. "After the first class went rather poorly, I decided that I need to really, *really* get into this particular character, or it will all be lost."

Barrows lifted a skeptical brow. "By not showing up at headquarters?"

Matty cringed inwardly, but tried to keep it from showing. "Yes, actually. Come…come sit, sir, we'll—"

112 *To Sketch a Scandal*

But Barrows did not sit. Instead, he paced, sharp gaze dusting every surface as if expecting to pick up fingerprints with his eyeballs. It was his first time seeing this room since the day he'd secured it and paid the first year's rent for Matty's eighteenth birthday, moving him out of Barrows's own spare room in a move far too generous to have upset Matty as much as it did at the time. Figured it would be today of all days that Barrows would come—when he'd made his bed up only lazily, all evidence of his mostly-upright life hidden away in favor of excess and absinthe. Matty squirmed as Barrows went around, brow cocked in judgment. He traced the new spines on the bookshelf. Eyed the box of obnoxious neckcloths that had been procured from a pawnshop and left sitting out after dressing. At last, he got to the desk, where he moved the paper Matty'd used to cover his recent crime against beauty. Barrows stared at Matty's efforts, then covered them back up the way he'd found them, as quick and respectful as with any tragic and unsightly victim.

"Is this really what you've been doing all day?" Barrows said at last. "Leaving me worrying and Ashton making snide remarks so you could turn your own private quarters into an artist's den?"

Matty took a deep breath. "Yes, sir."

"And why, exactly, did that seem like a good idea to you, lad?"

"Because," Matty said, unable to fully meet his eye, "I believe I've swum out rather grievously over my head on this one, sir."

Just then, Gretta the kitchen girl arrived with their tea. Buttery crumpets had been added to the tray unasked—Mrs. Wooster liked to stay in the good graces of officers. Barrows thanked the girl with a very convincing smile, one which vanished impressively fast when he was alone with Matty once more.

Not having much occasion for private company, Matty's room was set up for one, with a single chair he moved a few feet between desk and fireplace as needed. Presently, he moved it from the desk toward the fireplace, partly because it seemed more hospitable, and partly to get Barrows facing away from the absinthe bottle, which glowed like an eerie beacon in the candlelight. He gestured for Barrows to take the chair. Matty perched on the mantel, elbows on knees and fingers tapping against each other in a frantic rhythm.

He drew breath to explain himself, but was cut off very gruffly.

"You've gone to pieces," declared Barrows. "After all this time, after all you've done, you've gone to pieces at the last moment, haven't you?"

Maybe it was that he'd already gone against his orders once this morning. Or maybe there was a sense of having been cornered, a sense that had not seemed possible between them until Frost's suspicions and Ashton's presence ruined everything. Either way, Matty could not find any appropriate words with which to respond. All he could find was an anger so large and so violent that it must have been growing since long before now.

"At the last moment," he said, tapping his fingers faster as the words hissed out of him like a slow, controlled leak from an overfilled balloon. "In case you've forgotten, sir, *I* am not retiring. This is not *my* last moment. I have to live with the consequences of this disaster, and I am doing the best I can."

"Not showing up is your best?"

"Yes." This time, Matty did snap. "The plan isn't going to work, sir. I have no talent—I will never get good enough to get the time of day out of these people. And I'm not an actor. I can't convince them I'm something I'm not, so I must become—"

"What the devil do you mean you can't convince them you're something you're not?" said Barrows. "You do it all the time."

"I do not," Matty insisted, the intensity coming faster as his control over it lessened. "I convince people I'm a little more stupid, sure. That I'm an independent entity. That I'm harm-

114 *To Sketch a Scandal*

less. These are details, though; they're not what I am. I have never actually pretended to be something so different from what I am. And, at least on such short notice, it's proving fairly impossible. If it were just that I had the wrong disposition, or just the poor artistry, it might be different, but lacking both, I will never get the suspects alone. They already hinted they might kick me out. I can't let that happen, sir. Not under any circumstances."

Barrows was staring at him like a puzzle to crack. Like he couldn't understand a word of what Matty was saying. "You're not a valet," he said at last. "You were a valet for the last big one."

"Not quite. I was a pretty young man pretending to be a better valet than I really was," said Matty. "In case you've forgotten, it wasn't my skill with a Windsor knot that got me hired by Mr. Forester."

"You're not a whore, either—"

"I was."

The silence that followed was uncomfortable for Matty, but Barrows seemed more annoyed than anything. "For one night of your life, Matthew, versus ten years of detective work. If what you were saying were true, you'd be fit for nothing but pretending you're bloody Sherlock Holmes."

"Eight years."

Barrows blinked. "What do you mean eight?"

"Well, the first two, you just had me going to school by day and entrapping when you needed me," said Matty. "I wasn't working on cases, so there was no real difference on my part aside from when the night ended, and who paid me when it did."

Barrows looked so much like he'd been slapped across the face that Matty's anger turned rapidly into regret. Maybe he shouldn't have put it so harshly. To make up for his honesty, he got up to pour a cup of conciliatory tea for Barrows.

Barrows took the full cup carefully in hand, but did not move to drink it. "That's how you saw it?"

Matty busied his hands fixing his own cup, suddenly feeling very awkward indeed. "Did you see it differently?"

He stared at Matty over the teacup, sipping at last as if debating whether to call him out for turning the question around. Once he'd pulled the cup from his lips, he said, "You weren't a whore. You were reformed."

"*Reformed?*" Matty realized with a jolt that he was missing his teacup and jerked the pot upright. "Sir, we wouldn't be having this conversation if I were reformed. I don't take money, sure, but if I were truly reformed in all the ways that matter, there would be no suspicions to worry about in the first place. No rumors that carried any weight—"

"A few indiscretions do not define a man, Matthew—"

"Easy for you to say." He hated how petulant, even childish the words sounded. He swallowed guiltily. "Um. Sir."

"Nice save," said Barrows wryly. "Look. I see that Frost's words have shaken you; I understand. But Matthew, you are not a whore. You are not an unskilled valet. You are not an artist. You are a detective, and I expect to see you at the office tomorrow morning." He finished his tea, then got up and gathered his hat. "We only have so many of those mornings together, you know, before it's you and Ashton finishing things up."

"Bugger Ashton," Matty muttered before he could stop himself.

"I've told you already—he means you no ill will."

"Means me no particular goodwill either, sir. That much was perfectly clear when I heard how fast he changed his tune with Frost."

Barrows put his hat on, the shadow of it lending a severity to his expression. "This is Scotland Yard, Matthew. We're here to serve our city. Not make friends," he said bluntly. "I will see you in the morning."

116 *To Sketch a Scandal*

As the door slammed shut behind him, it was with all Matty's hopes that he'd been more than a tool to this man on the other side of it. The lonely room took on a new echo in his absence, like all the furniture had been moved out of it and now Matty was just standing alone on the empty floorboards.

Barrows was partially right about him.

He wasn't a whore. He wasn't a valet. He wasn't an artist.

But quite frankly, he wasn't a detective, either. He was an unwanted boy saved from one bad decision, grown to a man who'd never managed to make another one for himself.

He was determined to make one now, though. He didn't have a lot to choose from at this point, his world having been so narrowly guided by one old man who'd clearly never noticed or cared what a vital figure he was in Matty's imagination. But he had the sketchbook, all his pencils, and however many classes it took to figure out what the Buttersnipes were up to.

In the week that followed, he could not, as he'd wanted, give off mornings at headquarters to cultivate some sense of new identity. He had to go in, had to please Barrows by getting back to business and deal with Ashton's intermittent, smirking presence in their crowded office. But he still believed that cultivating an artistic mindset would help with the case, a notion that now took on the weight of desire to do it for his own sake as well.

He did not discuss it with Barrows and Ashton, but before the next class, he spent his free time very differently. He visited galleries and asked questions of the artists there. He went to bookshops in Fleet Street, perusing art books but not buying them, until the shopkeeps kicked him out. He wandered museums, daring himself to feel rather than catalog what he was seeing, trying to keep his heart open and the slate of his mind clean of practical thought. He sat in parks drinking paper cups of coffee, trying to identify the shapes of strangers' eyes and noses. He slept later than usual, wasted money in cafés, and tried the

Jess Everlee 117

absinthe (though, regrettably, he would need a little more adjustment to the artist's life before he could do more than try it).

It was all so drastically different that it took only a few days for an odd change to take hold. He started to feel like the Met was where he was undercover—nodding politely, saying all the right things, remaining steady and predictable—while his off-hours took on a new allure. Though he'd stumbled into these habits as surly as he'd stumbled into his old ones, they proved a balm to the sense of upheaval he was facing at work, and he threw himself in as completely as he could.

With one exception: the ring Barrows had given him. He was still wearing it on a chain around his neck. He'd tried to shut it in a drawer a few times, but it made him too sad. Barrows did not care for him, perhaps, but Matty could not shut his own foolhardy attachment off so easily. So round his neck it stayed, and would remain, he supposed, until he either succeeded or failed to get the promotion it was meant for. Then he would wear it as a reminder never to lose track of who was friend and who was coworker again—that the promotion was a promotion, not a succession—or else give it back to Barrows in a final farewell.

When class came back around the next week, Matty put on his patchy coat and dragged his sketchbook, his lumpy scarf, and the ring talisman back to Buttersnipe's School for Artistic Enrichment, where, in all the enthusiasm he'd cultivated during the week, he had nearly forgotten the trials that awaited him there.

Trials like, for instance, Warren Bakshi's smile at seeing him. His friendly wave. The way he hesitated before returning to the spot beside him again, saying, "D'you mind?"

Matty ought to tell him yes, but he couldn't. He nodded instead, and Warren took the spot beside him. There was something uncomfortably easy about it.

"Have you gotten any better?" Warren reached quite rudely

118 *To Sketch a Scandal*

for Matty's sketchbook to flip through it. "Actually…looks like you have."

"Indeed," Matty said dryly. "And isn't the fact that *this* is an improvement the most pathetic thing you've ever heard?"

Warren laughed. He had such a lovely laugh, and so freely given. He passed the book back. "Nah."

"You're just being nice."

"Not at all." Warren opened up his own sketchbook to a clean page, rolling up his sleeves and settling his workstation much as he probably did at the bar. Not that Matty would ever get to verify that. "You know how I spend my nights. You wouldn't believe the pathetic things I hear on a daily basis. Your drawing…seven out of ten pathetic. At worst."

Matty was grinning before he could stop himself. "You've got a real biting sense of humor on you."

"Certain way of life will do that to you. You mind?"

"No," Matty said. "I think it's brilliant."

Warren looked like he wanted to say something, but their attention was taken before he could manage it, as someone unfamiliar came before the class with the instructors. Matty's figure modeling replacement had been found. The class being focused on the face, it was not nearly so salacious a position as Matty had expected, the fellow full-dressed and settled down upon a stool to look straight ahead and not move too much. He thought he might feel wistful at seeing just how easy this case might have been in other circumstances, but strangely, he did not. He was, in fact, more relieved than he would have expected that there were no strange artists prodding and posing him, that he could do something with his own hands and chat amiably with Warren here and there while he kept an eye out for evidence and built up his inroads by doing something, *anything*, but sitting there looking nice.

Aside from the live model, class was very similar. They were still in the line-drawing phase, though Mr. Buttersnipe hinted that shading would be introduced sooner than Matty was comfortable with. Once they'd taken some time to find the shapes of the model, assembling them into the basic outline that could eventually comprise a portrait, they were told to pair up and do the same thing with a partner.

"Portraiture is about capturing *individuality*, those little things that make a person unique," said Mrs. Buttersnipe languorously. "Those differences are in the details, yes, but also in the larger shapes of a person. If your two proto-portraits look the same, you have failed this exercise."

Matty couldn't help but think she eyed him particularly skeptically, but before he could ascertain for sure, a few loud claps (and a matching yip from Miss Martha) told them to get drawing.

Nervously, Matty glanced up at Warren, half-hoping the fellow would go off in search of a better partner. But he was looking right at Matty like he hadn't even considered looking elsewhere. A confident, automatic selection that warmed Matty straight down to his toes.

While he knew his picture would embarrass them both in the end, he didn't mind having an excuse to stare at Warren as much as he liked. The bloke was devilishly handsome, the sort of effortless handsomeness that made one wonder how much effort the effortlessness had really taken. In a world of specialized hair oils and manicured mustaches, his warm brown face was clean shaven, his hair falling soft and lightly processed, worn just long enough to give an *impression* to the right people without raising the hackles of the wrong ones.

"Done." Warren lifted his pencil with a flourish and gave Matty a look of playful challenge. "Want to see?"

"Done?" Matty repeated. His face heated up. There'd been a lot more staring than drawing so far and he wasn't even close to finished. "Um. Sure, let's see it."

Warren turned his sketch pad around. Matty's immediate

120   *To Sketch a Scandal*

impulse was to call him out for going beyond the assignment to make himself look good, but in truth, he really had just done the shapes. Still, it didn't look anything like Matty's or even the better examples the Buttersnipes had shown at the beginning of class. Sure, Warren's page was circles and rectangles and a few lines to connect them, but there was also enough sense of poor posture, awkward movement, and the silly patches on his jacket that it made Matty self-conscious.

"Do I really look like that?"

Warren examined his work. "Sometimes," he said. "When you're giving me that blank look, anyway." Warren tapped the empty, oval head. Matty felt himself collapse into the blank look in defense. "See? Spitting image. Let's see yours."

"It's not done."

"Come on."

To be fair, everyone else in the room seemed to be finishing up, examining their partner's work with compliments or laughter and comparing them with the sketches they'd done of the model. Reluctantly, Matty turned his sketch pad around.

Warren nodded solemnly. "Brilliant."

Matty raised a skeptical brow.

"I mean it." Warren said. "If Scotland Yard ever starts you drawing the wanted posters, I hope you do mine."

The joke could have been cruel, but there was something so oddly soft about the way Warren teased him. It made him happier than he could remember being in a very long time. A smile crossed his face before he could help himself.

When it did, Warren's eyes lit up.

It occurred to Matty, then, something that he'd been missing this week. An artist's work could be solitary, but they generally ran in packs anyway. It would be dull and limiting indeed to browse galleries alone forever. The art community wasn't Scotland Yard—a real artist had real artist friends, and frankly, it wouldn't hurt if those friends were especially good with a pencil.

It was a risk, the idea he had. A massive one.

Though, perhaps, not quite so bad as the risks he'd taken with this chap already. With that in mind...

"Warren." He fidgeted anxiously with the ring, the sparkle of the moment and the looming absence of Barrows nipping his heels like Miss Martha's misbehaved cousins until he could withhold the question no longer. "Would you care to grab a pint after class today? There's something I'd like to talk to you about."

Something crossed Warren's face. Reluctance?

"Not if you don't want to," Matty added hurriedly, smile dissolving as embarrassment washed over him.

"I want to!" Warren clarified, all honesty and a shocking hint of...desperation? "It's just..." He glanced around and lowered his voice. "It's Mr. Forester. I think he'd be uncomfortable enough knowing we're in a class together. Taking it beyond that might get me in trouble. And my job. I need—" He paused, swallowing hard as he rethought his words. "Well, I suppose I don't need it, actually. But it still means something to me. What did you want to discuss, anyway?"

While it was, technically, a rejection, it was not a particularly convincing one. His question was filled with hope that whatever Matty wanted could be justified somehow. His clear desire to say yes was galvanizing.

"Well," Matty said, thinking through his next words carefully, "what I wanted to discuss is nothing scandalous. I just need more help with my shapes before we get into shading next week. I fear such an addition will take my work from shoddy-wanted-poster to site-of-a-stabbing. I meant nothing more by my invitation, of course."

"I see," said Warren slowly. "The pint would be an extension of the class itself, then, wouldn't it?"

122   *To Sketch a Scandal*

"Exactly."

"And the class, of course, was a coincidence from the start. No fault of our own."

"Not by any reasonable measure."

Warren nodded, and though he bit his lip for an anxious moment, it didn't last long. "One condition."

"Name it."

"Smile for me again." He picked his pencil back up. "For the portrait. The first one didn't last long enough for me to get it down."

Fortunately, it was pretty easy, just now, for Matty to let that particular expression stretch across his face.

Chapter Nine

Warren

Warren was unclear whether Matty's invitation was truly innocent, or if it was some kind of insinuation. The fellow was damned hard to read. But those bloody dimples simply could not be argued with; Warren was in it for a pint, like it or not.

And he found that he very much liked it.

"To the nearest pub, then?" Warren asked as he did up his coat and Matty wound his scarf about his own neck. "I passed one on my way here."

"I think I know the one you're talking about," said Matty, the ghosts of his dimples still playing upon his cheeks. "Wainwright and...something. Let's—"

"I hear you're continuing the class this afternoon," came a voice from behind Warren. He turned to find the rectangular bloke standing at his shoulder. The chap hadn't closed his sketchbook yet, and held it on his hip like a baby, so no one could miss the sketches he'd done. "At the pub?"

Warren wasn't pleased to be interrupted. Really, was his every interaction with poor Matty doomed to be barged in on by someone or other? But, seeing as they were all stuck to-

124 *To Sketch a Scandal*

gether in this heady room for eight more weeks—more if they were chosen to progress to the next level—he decided to remain civil. "I'm just going to share a few tips with Mr. Shaw, here. Nothing formal."

Interest lit up the bloke's face.

Fuckin' hell.

"My name is Sandford Binks," he said, clutching his sketchbook and rather tellingly not offering a hand along with his introduction. If he were only speaking to Matty, Warren thought he might have handled that differently. "Might I tag along with you?"

It was astounding how much Warren and Matty could communicate in a silent second of eye contact already. Matty was clearly no more interested in a third wheel than Warren was.

"Mr. Bakshi was my partner in today's lesson," Matty said, polite with just the barest hint of morning frost. "I'm afraid the tips he has to offer are specific to my own artistic deficiencies, and will be of no use to one of your skill—"

"Oh, I don't need any outside help from him." Sandford Binks dismissively waved the free hand not busy bouncing and coddling the dear little one on his hip. "I just thought I could give a few tips of my own. This isn't my first drawing class, after all." His voice pitched up as he turned the face of his sketchbook toward them. *Isn't she adorable? Just like her papa.* "It's good to get a lot of different perspectives on these things, don't you think? Rather than limiting yourself to the first one that comes along?"

Warren's temper flared at the veiled insult, but while he was flaring, Matty was frosting right over. His shoulders looked fit to shatter. When he spoke, his voice was a perfect match for his eyes.

"Mr. Bakshi's perspective is quite good enough for me," he said. "Good afternoon, Mr. Binks."

Jess Everlee 125

He turned sharply and started toward the door. Warren shrugged his non-apology to the fuming chap and followed.

"Why, Matty," he said as they took the stairs. "I'm shocked you so rudely rejected private instruction from someone who's taken at *least* one other drawing class. What a wasted opportunity."

"Arsehole didn't want to teach me anything," Matty muttered. He looked ill-tempered as he pulled the front door open. "Didn't you notice how he kept glancing at your work all through class? He's jealous of you. Wanted to learn from you himself, I think, but was embarrassed to admit it. He's a coward. At best. Trust me, I've seen his sort a thousand times; let us be grateful we're dealing in matters of shabby portraiture, and not some more lucrative enterprise." He glanced darkly over his shoulder. "That type can get ugly."

They went out onto the street, in the direction of that pub they'd both passed on their way. Though the street was filled with foot traffic, roaming sellers with their baskets, and the occasional clopping coach, Warren hardly noticed any of it as he suddenly saw what had been mostly hidden in Matty up till now—a real detective's eye for detail. He was even walking different, more clipped and efficient. It wasn't as fascinating as his smile, but it came close.

"Wants to learn from me, you think?" Warren asked as they dodged a cab. He narrowly missed getting his shoes soaked by the puddle on the other side of it in his distraction. "Awfully silly. I have no idea what I'm doing. My father never taught me shapes or shading. We just drew things. Very unofficial."

"Doesn't matter. You're still better than him," Matty said simply. "I'm probably not the only one who's noticed. I'm just the only one you've said yes to having a pint with."

"But he's taken at least one other drawing class," Warren joked, diffusing the compliment. It made him oddly uncomfortable.

126 *To Sketch a Scandal*

"Well, he's going to have to take a few more."

"Not with me," Warren said. "Bloke wants an art lesson, he'd best be willing to shake my hand and ask straight up."

"You know, now that I think about it, I don't think *I* ever did shake your hand."

"Maybe not, though to be fair, I think our earliest meetings were suitably intimate as it was."

Matty glanced sideways, enticingly scolding. Weeks later under the sunlit afternoon sky, it was hard to believe he'd been about thirty seconds from rutting this exact same Matthew Shaw in an alley. He'd been nice enough to look at that first night, but was so incredibly handsome right now that Warren almost felt jealous of his past self for getting so far with such a pretty catch.

Though, as they went into the pub together, settling in at a warm table by the well-tended fire, he felt his present self wasn't doing so badly, either. When was the last time he'd shared a moment like this with someone new and intriguing? Anyone who fit that description was usually enjoyed briefly in a back room with little conversation. Half the time they left for a fresh drink when they were done, assuming Warren was perfectly happy putting the room back together by himself. Pubs and pints and being treated fully human were the domain of his well-established chums.

"This is a nice place," Matty said. His voice was mild, but Warren was starting to catch on that the calmer and more unflinching the fellow sounded, the more nervous he was in actuality. "If the ale's good, I could see myself returning."

There was something under what he was saying. Something pleasant and hopeful that warmed Warren's cheeks.

"Well, let's find out, then." Warren raised a hand to catch the attention of a serving woman. They got beer and bread, stuffed olives, and fried oysters. Once she was on her way, Warren admitted he was always starving after these classes.

Jess Everlee 127

"Same," said Matty. "I think it's the turpentine that does it."

Warren leaned in over the table, realizing when he got there that he'd automatically slipped into flirtation even though that was decidedly not why he was there. Matty didn't fluster, though his eyes did light up. Warren opted not to correct his mistake.

"So, how's the class going for you?" Warren asked. "Do you think you'll learn what you need to learn in time?"

"Honestly?" Matty sighed, fiddling with the gold-and-black ring he kept around his neck. "No. I don't think I will. And that, um. That's sort of what I wanted to talk to you about. I wasn't... I regret very much that I have to say this, Warren, but I lied when I said I wasn't investigating the school. I am. For potential fraud. I'm sorry I couldn't tell you before, but you have to understand, I need to be very careful about things like this."

The back of Warren's neck prickled. That was, more or less, why Forester didn't want him involved with a detective, even one with good intentions. They were liars by nature. By necessity. Like Warren was, though on the opposite side of things. You never really knew what you were going to get with someone who could not speak plainly about his life. To have it confirmed by Matty himself lent a bit of legitimacy to that idea that they probably shouldn't be here together.

"I understand," Warren said, and he found he meant it in spite of his misgivings. He certainly did not give the details of his job to blokes he hardly knew. While that first part of him felt this conversation was proof that he should leave, another part started to feel very flattered that Matty was taking a risk with him like this. Another risk. "Why are you telling me this now?"

"Because I need help, and I don't have anyone else to ask."

Warren was shocked silent, wariness and interest at war within him. His first instinct was to say *fuck no* and walk out. Warren lived half his life very much on the wrong side of the law. He did not "help" people with the power to lock up him

128 *To Sketch a Scandal*

and all his friends with a snap of their fingers. Never mind that Matty had proved that he meant no harm to Warren's precious little pocket of criminals; the idea of it still sat wrong.

But there was that interest as well. Matty was investigating the art school for fraud, nothing dangerous to Warren personally or unsettlingly hypocritical on Matty's part. That made it more palatable, but also more confusing: What sort of help could Warren be, in a fraud case?

Their beers arrived, the distraction giving Warren a moment to work through his curiosities and misgivings.

"I shouldn't," he admitted, once the server was gone.

"Shouldn't help me?"

"That's right."

Matty sighed and sipped his beer. Based on his face, it must have proved pretty bitter. "I understand—"

"Though," Warren interrupted, leaning in closer, own glass in hand. "If I did, hypothetically, what would I be doing?"

Matty leaned in too. It was conspiratorial. Warren felt the way he had during his first weeks leaning over the Fox's bar, like he and every person who met his eye were in on something together. That feeling had long since fled, replaced by ease and even rote habit. He made others feel this way, but rarely got to experience it himself anymore. He'd forgotten how much he liked being in on something. How much it thrilled him to re-examine a rule he'd once held dear.

"It's like I said before," said Matty quietly. "I need help with my drawing. The only way I can learn whether or not they did it is to get more information about their private instruction. The next step of their operation. From there, I should be able to determine if they're innocent artists, standard-issue scammers, or serious fraudsters."

Warren thought about that. "Can you tell me more specifically what they're meant to have done?"

"We're trying to locate the source of a slew of forged art pieces."

"Matty, dear, I'd hate to tell you how to do your job, but have you considered looking at the skill level of your suspects before jumping to conclusions?"

That won him a flash of dimples. "If they did it, then the dreadful art is a cover. A pretty good cover, because as you say, it does seem a bit of a stretch. I've seen stranger covers, though. Public opinion is shaky after the Fenian bombings and that last corruption scandal. With the Buttersnipes being our only domestic suspects, Scotland Yard's reputation can't afford to miss something under our nose right now. I need to complete a full investigation before putting a conclusion on the record."

"Do you think they did it?" Warren asked. "Off the record, of course."

Matty paused. "I shouldn't tell you."

"I shouldn't help you."

"Fair enough. No. So far, I don't think they did it. I think the Met is hoping to save face through a quick, domestic win, rather than the hassle this will be if it's a Continental operation. I do think the Buttersnipes' advertisements might be criminally misleading, but that's outside my department. If it makes you feel better, your help might prove them innocent of anything serious."

"It does, actually." Warren considered all that, still buzzing with the thrill of getting all this insider information. "So, it's just the drawing, then? You don't need me to do anything sneaky for you?"

"Not at all. That would be…" He stopped midsentence, mouth still open, eyes suddenly unblinking as something uncomfortable seemed to occur to him. "That would be rather unethical, I think? T-to ask something sneaky of an untrained civilian?"

130 *To Sketch a Scandal*

It came as a question, and did not seem to be hypothetical because he waited expectantly for Warren to answer.

"Er, well, yeah," said Warren, bewildered. "I think it would be."

Matty took a deep breath, but then shook something off with a physical start. He took a gulp of beer and when he put the glass down, he'd gone perfectly blank again. "All I'm asking," he said with newfound steadiness. "Is for some help improving myself. As an individual. So that I can take those skills with me into the case, which I will handle by myself and also… So maybe I can develop a little hobby of my own." His face went very pink. "Something to settle my spirit, when this case is over and things at Scotland Yard become a little more complicated. I find I'm enjoying the pursuit more than expected. So there's a double edge to the request, if I'm to be truly honest with you. It's professional, yes, but also personal."

The beer here was bitter, but impressively cold. Warren doodled a pattern on the glass's frost as he considered the idea. "You know," he said slowly, "you didn't have to tell me about the case. You could have just asked for help with the hobby thing and kept the reason to yourself. I'd have done it."

"I considered that," said Matty. "But I didn't want to lie to you again."

"Why not?"

"I don't know." Matty shrugged, turning even pinker across his cheeks. "It just didn't seem the thing to do."

Warren said he needed time to think about it, but it became very clear, very quickly that something other than his brain was doing the thinking for him where Matty Shaw was concerned. That flush. That unexpected honesty. Those damned *fucking* dimples Warren was so desperate to make appear as often as possible.

Before their food even arrived, Warren agreed.

Jess Everlee 131

★ ★ ★

The following week saw them back again, same place, same ale, same order, but they took a bigger table toward the back of the dining room so there was space for their sketchbooks. They put their chairs on the same side of it, selected unsuspecting targets at other tables, and sketched.

"You live with you brother, then?" Matty asked, eyes trained on a stranger with a walrus mustache and an uncannily slow nod.

Warren looked away from his own inspiration, the hassled-looking woman behind the bar. "Feeling chatty, are we?"

Matty shrugged, pencil going slowly and stiffly along his paper. "I don't have to be."

Warren watched him for a moment, then said, "I do. Live with him. That's new, though. It was just me and my mother for years. It's just recently that Harry—that's my brother—appeared back out of nowhere with enough money and influence to start bossing us all around."

"I see." Matty paused his pencil, then turned his sketchbook to Warren. "How's this?

"You need to press even lighter still." Warren's own pencil drifted to Matty's page, whispering featherlight strokes atop Matty's dark ones. "That way you sort of build the shape up, rather than carving it in stone straight off."

"That makes sense." Matty tried to emulate what Warren was doing, the tips of their pencils bumping briefly before Warren snatched his back. "So. Did he boss you into taking the class? Your brother? Is that how you wound up in it?"

"Not exactly," Warren said. He winced internally when he remembered who he was talking to, but he did not know anyone who wanted to hear him complain about a fortune falling in his lap; Matty, however, was rather obligated to be his audience as they sketched and sipped and snacked together on the same side of the table. "But he got married while he

132 *To Sketch a Scandal*

was overseas, and now I'm caught up between my mother and sister-in-law in the household space. My mother's not always well, you see, and I was doing a lot of the domestic work."

"Ah," said Matty with a hint of a smile. "That probably made you a very able barkeep, I should think."

"Sure did," said Warren with a little spark of pride shooting through him. Matty's attention to things like that hadn't gotten old yet. "But at home, another woman around means I'm basically out on my arse. It's stupid. She's a lovely person, Harry's wife, but she's a sailor's girl. Hardly even *lived* in a house, much less kept one. She could just hire some staff and forget about getting my mother's approval, but she's as bloody determined to do this thing she's terrible at as you are. Without half your excuse to justify it." He sighed and plucked up an olive, perusing Matty's page. "That's looking a lot better, lov—" He cleared his throat. "Mate."

"You think so?" Matty gave no hint he'd caught Warren's slip, but he surely had. He missed nothing. "It seems strange."

"Keep at it. You can add the darker lines for definition when the basic shape is built."

Warren watched him as he went on, that devilish tongue between his teeth as his concentration increased. His sketch was still decidedly *wrong* in ways that were hard to articulate, but he was at least sketching now instead of smearing the black lead around like a child with a stick of chalk.

"So your sister-in-law," said Matty. "She's taken over your duties?"

"That's right," Warren admitted. "She's off the sea and settled in England now, and feels like she has to take up the women's work to keep my mum happy, and unfortunately, I think she's right about that. So I do the obvious; follow in my father's footsteps the best I can during the day by taking art classes, and head home to burnt rice every night like a proper man." He strongly debated not saying what occurred to him next, but now that he'd gotten started, he could not seem to stop. A bartender spent hours listening to the woes and joys of others—it was very rare that anyone sat quietly and did the same for Warren. "My only comfort is that I can escape all that at the Fox on the weekends. Not a proper man or woman to be found there. I don't need the money anymore, and Mr. Forester and some of the patrons drive me up the wall sometimes, but honestly, I don't know what I'd do without it."

He was surprised how the words flowed out of him. He hadn't discussed much of this with his friends yet, in part because he wasn't ready for the ribbing he'd get about the art classes. *Warren Bakshi the barkeep* had that certain reputation at the Fox, after all, the one he very much enjoyed escaping into, but that quite purposefully did not bring many details from his home life. They knew the good news that his brother was home after Warren had presumed him dead, but that was about it. It was nice to finally get the full complexity of the situation off his chest, especially when Matty spared a little laugh for the ridiculous impracticality of it, rather than indicating that Warren should be pleased about such a change to the structure of his days, upon such an arbitrary line of what sort of body should be assigned to which tasks in a household.

"Well," said Matty, "whatever the reason, I am selfishly glad you took the class."

His voice came with such gentle friendliness that Warren looked up from their sketchbooks to examine his profile. His face was blank, though, hand busy with his pencil. Maybe he'd imagined it.

"Yeah." Warren forced a chuckle. "You need all the help you can get, don't you?"

Chapter Ten

Matty

Matty had some misgivings about the agreement, but they were simply not strong enough to overcome Warren's field of gravity as the days went by. He was honest, and helpful, and so handsome it could hurt just to look at him. He somehow managed to balance sarcastic and gentle, socially comfortable yet streaked with flashes of unexpected eccentricity. He was bloody fascinating. When Matty got back to class the next week, he didn't think he could change easels or pick other partners or avoid dogging the poor fellow on the way out the door if he tried.

He wasn't sure whether this effect was coming from Warren himself, or from the change in Matty's lifestyle outside the classroom. He was spending less time at Scotland Yard than he'd ever done before, leaving the office when his work was finished rather than staying until he could put it off no longer. He found he hated his room less, now that it was filling with things that struck his fancy. It was a relief to relax his rigid adherence to schedules, to let his hands and eyes do more work than his mind did, to leave off vanity for comfort and expression.

He suspected, however, that this might be weakening his

impulse control where Warren was concerned. Thoughts of their thwarted pleasure in the alley were coming frequent and fervent, begging for a completion that could not be fooled by the late-night efforts of Matty's hand. The indulgence of his appetites had always been practical, focused more on timing and location than anything terribly personal. He could not remember desiring an individual this way before, this sort of slow torture of learning all the ways a man's smiles and spirit rendered him more tempting than any conveniently-placed stranger could ever be.

He ought to have called upon his years of order and mental strength to nip it in the bud, but he didn't want to. The desire itself felt good even if it never wound up consummated, felt free and different and piqued his curiosity. Cultivating an erotic obsession, he told himself, was probably one of the most artistically-minded things a fellow could do. Maybe it would show up in his drawings. Or in his eyes when he begged the Buttersnipes to let him join their private classes. Perhaps they'd sense the tension of all this unresolved passion, and mercifully grant him an outlet, proving their guilt or innocence at last, and then...

And then Matty would go back to Scotland Yard, perhaps with a promotion under his belt that would require more structure than ever before.

And that...surely that would be lovely. After all this nonsense.

In any case, the nonsense was still in full swing, so to the pub they went for the third time after class, without even a word of discussion about what had become a habit. The sense of a shared mission had helped their friendship—for certainly, that's what it was now—grow easy on the surface, in spite of the doubt they both had underneath. As they walked the familiar route, they chatted amiably about their days apart and hardly watched

136   *To Sketch a Scandal*

where they were going, seeming drawn to make eye contact even as they moved forward along the busy street.

Warren opened the door for him, when they arrived. They started toward the four-seat table they'd sat at last time, one that gave them space to spread out.

Not even halfway across the dining room, however, they were stopped by a man holding himself very straight and tall, arms crossed like a barricade against any soft feeling. The manager, probably. The bloke was older than them by a goodly margin, wearing green bracers on his sleeves and possessing a chest, Matty determined after all his recent observational training, the exact size and shape of the ale keg behind the bar.

"Is there a problem, sir?" The question left Matty's lips sounding surprisingly genuine—not much in the way of innocence or manipulation in it. He hardly sounded like himself. He rather liked that, but unfortunately, it did not smooth a single thing over with the chap.

"Bad for business," the manager growled, lips hardly moving beneath the droop of his mustache. "Taking up seats, lingering for an hour with nothing but specks of foam in the bottom of your glasses, staring at my customers like they're bowls of bloody fruit." He shook his head. "No. Not this time. You take a normal table, order normal food, and behave in a generally normal fashion, or you take yourselves somewhere else."

"We're not hurting anyone," snapped Warren, matching the manager's acidic tone and even bumping it up a notch. He gestured around the dining room, which was, at most, three-quarters occupied. "It's not like you've had a full house since we've been coming in. Plenty of chairs. And we do order. If you need us to refill to hold the table, we will. You could stand to ask for what you want instead of getting in a tizzy over our inability to read your mind."

It was an admirable response, but not an especially effective one. The manager hefted his chest like he intended to carry it off behind the bar and tap it. "We're not a flophouse for that Butter-bloke's strays." He pointed in the general direction of the art school down the street. "You aren't the first to come in, and won't be the last, but I'll not be overrun by the wrong sort. I'll hold those sketchbooks for you behind the bar, if you'd like to stay and enjoy a quiet meal before taking your so-called artistry elsewhere."

He held a ruddy hand out.

Warren tightened his hold on his sketchbook like he'd knife anyone who dared to touch it. Matty, on the other hand, felt a flicker of interest at the man's words.

"So-called?" said Matty, light and eager as he could manage, though his false-charm muscles felt a little rusty. "What makes you say that? I only ask, because the class is expensive and I'd hate to think I'd been led astray."

The fellow's mustache twitched. He seemed glad to have been asked.

"You lot always come in, sit around drawing or talking up-start nonsense, next thing I know you're selling portrait sessions to my customers or worse, trying to drag them off to become 'artists' themselves."

"Do we really?"

"Yes, you do," he declared. "I don't like it. I won't have it. So hand the books over, or take your leave."

Matty was hungry and didn't mind putting the sketching off—a meal with Warren sounded fine on its own. If he was lucky, maybe he'd even get a little more information about the Buttersnipes from the manager. But Warren was shaking his head.

"I ain't handing over my sketchbook," he said. "That's ridiculous. Come on, mate, we'll find another spot."

With that, he took Matty's arm and steered him out. The afternoon light felt very bright after adjusting to the darker pub.

"I wouldn't have minded," said Matty.

138 *To Sketch a Scandal*

"Yeah, well." Warren glared back the way they'd come. "You get asked so *politely* to meet some arbitrary standard or leave a place often enough, and you do start minding. Some of us have to be awfully well-behaved, you know, depending on the neighborhood."

Matty felt silly, to have not considered that perhaps a place's patience for oddness was more limited for Warren than it might be for himself. He wondered if they would even have been noticed, if Matty had been someone who looked more like Sanford Binks.

"My landlady puts meals out every day, if you want to just come along home with me," Matty said. "You won't have to behave there."

"Where, exactly, do I not need to behave?" Warren said with unrestrained amusement. "In your room, Matty? Is that what you're saying?"

Matty's face flushed hot. "That's not what I meant—"

"We can find another pub, love."

It did not escape Matty's notice that he'd gone from "mate" in front of the manager to "love" out here where no one was listening. He knew it wasn't personal. That Warren threw that word around easy as Matty could call his superiors "sir." But it didn't matter. It ruined him completely, and the next thing he knew, he was saying something very stupid:

"Sure, we can find a pub." He shrugged. "But then we'll be wasting a perfectly good excuse, won't we?"

The clop of carriages and babble of voices in the street filled the silence that followed Matty's too-honest pronouncement. He had never, not once, felt his face go so terribly hot, and without anything he could do to rein it in. The words were inelegant. Unattractive. Baldly revealing. The sort that could kill a case or even a try for trade in an instant. And now Warren was staring at him, and he had no idea what the devil was going on behind those bright eyes.

Jess Everlee 139

"Matty," he said at last, with a touch of reluctance. He lowered his voice under the sounds of the busy street and adjusted his sketchbook awkwardly. "I'm not really supposed to see you. Like, personally. I'm already pushing it, with the extra tutoring."

Matty paused. The better—or maybe just the better-trained—part of him wanted to let it go. But this new aspect of himself that he'd made or found or been cursed with was growing stronger, and that aspect wanted to get Warren alone again so desperately, it clouded out all other concerns. It would not be disappointed so easily.

"I know full well you don't always do what he says," Matty muttered, referring to Warren's boss.

"'Bout seventy percent, I'd say," Warren admitted.

"I've heard you sneak off against his wishes all the time," said Matty. "Is this really so much different?"

It was. And they both knew it. During the investigation of The Curious Fox, Matty had broken into the safe that held Mr. Forester's club ledgers. Every member was impressively well vetted, with proto-blackmail always at the ready to thwart informing or other bad behavior before it started. Matty was quite the opposite of vetted: he had, in fact, fooled Mr. Forester about his identity for a full six months. No wonder he could not trust in the safety of Matty's presence. And he shouldn't—what Mr. Forester and even Warren didn't know, was that Matty was an even bigger risk than they realized: his sullied reputation at the Met meant his personal habits could be scrutinized at any time. As of yet, Superintendent Frost did not seem anxious to uncover a scandal, but that could change. It very well might once Barrows was out of the way.

As all this grim practicality soaked into Matty's soul like spilled tea, he shook his head. "Never min—"

"It's got to be an extension of the class," Warren interrupted,

140 *To Sketch a Scandal*

quickly and quietly. "So long as we're still going to practice drawing, I'll come with you."

"That's what makes the difference? Your excuse?"

"Yes," said Warren without hesitation. Matty did not miss the hungry look in his eye as it drifted quite a bit south of Matty's face. "Some rules are for breaking. Others aren't. It's not our fault we're in the same class. So if it's an extension of the class, then it ain't my fault."

When he looked up again, Matty was surprised to find a fire lit behind his gaze. Clearly, Matty was not the only artist around here who'd been nursing a little passion on the side.

"In that case," said Matty, very careful, unblinking. "Would you give me a practical lesson in artistry, Warren? At my place?"

Chapter Eleven

Warren

Matty had a room in a boardinghouse clearly chosen more for its proximity to Scotland Yard than comfort or beauty. But the landlady treated him—and even his new friend—with surprising deference and a lack of questions. She gave them what was left of a simple boardinghouse dinner before Matty led him up a creaking stair to his room. It was in the north corner of the upstairs with a linen closet between him and the next neighbor over, rendering it uncommonly private. That was good. Lessened the chance that anyone would hear their…pencils.

God, it was stupid, being here. Neither of them had successfully pretended it was just for drawing, and the ache he had for their honest ends became almost maddening the second the door was shut behind them.

It was clear that Matty had been living here for quite a while. The runners and floorboards were comfortably softened between a bed, a desk, and a little sitting area before the now-cold fireplace. Against the backdrop of worn books and tidy shelves with plain hatboxes and a minimum of trinkets, the objects of Matty's newly invented artistic passion stood out like a com-

142   *To Sketch a Scandal*

pletely separate painter had slapped the art books, the pencils, the pawnshop paintings, the stacks of sketching paper onto a classic piece just yesterday.

It was only one room, so of course that bed took up most of it. It was made up haphazardly with intimate overnight objects on the table beside it. A candle. A water glass.

A tin of hand cream.

Dear God.

The tension in the room became nearly unbearable. Matty was clearly feeling it too, as he shuffled a thinly-cushioned chair around. There was only one, and he seemed very undecided as to where it should be.

"Sorry it's not more comfortable," Matty muttered almost to himself.

A memory of their first meeting seemed to thrum the very air. They had been in the rudest, least comfortable circumstance possible, then.

Fuck, what was he doing here? There were a thousand blokes better suited to Warren's passions. He could have his pick of them the second the sun went down. Admittedly, Matty was probably among the most attractive of them, but given he was so actively trying to diminish his own beauty with this artist thing, he probably wasn't at the tippy top. There was nothing stopping Warren from pretending he'd missed all the implications about this visit, showing the chap a few more tricks with the pencil, and easing the tension of the day later, as Matty was clearly in the habit of doing. Contrary to his reputation, Warren wasn't helpless against a pretty face or shapely form. He indulged freely under the right circumstances—namely, at the Fox, where everyone was vetted and the rooms were tucked back and secure—but he was more than capable of keeping his trousers on the rest of the time. He had a family to support, after all.

Or rather, he used to have a family to support. Nowadays,

it seemed, they were getting on alright without much effort on his part.

Matty seemed to sense his hesitation, and it clearly made him self-conscious. With foolish diligence, he arranged his things, settling the chair and putting a pillow on the fireplace to serve as a second seat; gathering a handful of pencils, recounting them, and putting two back; placing his penknife perfectly parallel with the top of his sketchbook; everything exactly so, ready for action.

It was almost like he was trying to give Warren the option of pretending their ends were innocent after all. Very inconveniently, it had the opposite effect. If he'd been more overt, diving directly into sensuality, it might have spooked Warren to his senses. But as Matty started to look despairing of his ability to fit two sketch pads perfectly side by side on the end table he'd placed between chair and mantel, acting like he didn't have half a cockstand already giving him away, Warren was so utterly charmed by the awkwardness that his resistance was erased with ease.

"I have an idea," said Warren. "Let's quit the games. We'll just sit on the bed."

"The bed." Matty froze with two pencils in his hand, blinking and blushing. "You want to teach me to draw from the bed?"

"Am I actually here to teach you drawing, then?" said Warren with a little smirk tugging at his lips.

Matty turned very red. "I did promise this was an extension of our class. You were the one who wanted that excuse."

"Kind of you," said Warren, and he meant it. The excuse had been silly—that Matty would indulge it was actually very generous. "Well, in that case, let's put it this way: the workstation you're trying so desperately to create is unnecessary."

"Unnecessary?"

"Quite." He went over to Matty and took the pencils from

his hand, taking care that their fingers brushed when he did. "You don't need all the right supplies and teachers and setups. I learned to draw all over the place—at the kitchen table, on the sofa over tea, on my bedroom floor, and yeah, right in the bed before falling asleep. Though most of those drawings I burned pretty quickly after completion."

When Matty turned red, Warren winked and snatched up one of the sketchbooks. Feeling how Matty's eyes seemed to burn a hole through his back, he removed his shoes, and welcomed himself to the top of Matty's bed. He adjusted the pillows so he could lean comfortably against the headboard, his bent legs the easel.

Most of the beds Warren fucked in were public, with fresh sheets he'd changed himself, the room perfumed and lit with generic, if beautiful, purpose. There was something almost shocking, therefore, about the intimacy of settling onto Matty's own personal bed. It did not smell like washing soap and incense, but the fruity macassar oil Matty put in his hair and the musk of his sleep, all the rumples in the quilt and dents in the pillows having been put there by his impeccably well-tended body. Warren's heart pulsed in places he hadn't realized it could reach as Matty, moving with the same deliberateness with which he'd done everything else, took his own shoes off and sat rather stiffly next to Warren, shoulder to shoulder.

"Set up your easel," Warren said. Matty bent his knees like he'd been given a direct order. It sent a thrill through Warren's belly. "Obedient, eh?"

"If you like."

Alright. Well. On that note.

"Let's ah, let's get started, then." Warren cleared his throat. "I'll draw you. You draw what I draw. We'll take it step by step."

And so they did. An extension of class, as promised. Never mind that they were in a bloody bed together, or that every time their elbows or knees bumped it sent shots of lightning through Warren's limbs. Never mind that Warren could all but hear his own heartbeat, and that his eyes kept flicking to that incriminating jar that Matty either hadn't noticed he left out or did not want to call attention to now. They were practicing. And they weren't doing too bad a job at it, either.

"That's it," Warren said. He was sketching out a rough outline of Matty's face in profile, all the better to obscure the fact that he couldn't keep his eyes off the bloke. Matty was following along, gaze trained on Warren's paper. "Loosen up just a little more, nice and light. You can always add…there. You're getting it."

His hand was gliding over the paper, that rigidity in his wrist finally softening in a way that inspired a certain part of Warren's body to do just the opposite. He adjusted the position of his sketchbook accordingly, watching Matty's focused work. The lines he put to the paper were not expert, but they were better. A little extra help and a couple of weeks' devoted practice had wrought an amazing change. It did not stand out as being especially good, but nor was it particularly poor.

"Matty, that's—"

"Shh." His hand—beautifully formed, soft but a bit ink-stained, and dusted with blond hairs—was still moving. He lowered his voice to a whisper. "Don't scare it off. It might not come back again if you do."

Warren laughed. "Skill's not a bird, love."

"Easy for you to say." He carried on another minute, then asked, "You really think it's better? That I'm getting the hang of it? I admit, I wasn't expecting that to happen, when we got into the bed."

Warren almost said yes, but stopped himself. From this angle, he couldn't really tell, now could he? He was awfully far to the side, after all. Needed a better view, he supposed. He reached over to pull Matty's sketchbook closer, fingers brushing the

146   *To Sketch a Scandal*

soft, brown corduroy of his trousers just south of his knees. He stopped the sketchbook so it rested on each of them equally, which left his hand, well, sort of right around the space between Matty's thighs. And it was chilly in the room. They hadn't lit a fire. So his hand, really without much say from him, nestled in that warm, velvety gap a little bit.

Warren found he could see the sketch quite perfectly, like that.

"Much better. I think you could probably broach the subject of private instruction at this point. They might not let you in, but talking about it wouldn't seem so ridiculous."

Matty hadn't immediately reacted to Warren's wandering, but now his legs pressed together in an unmistakable squeeze.

"Funny," he said, with a little chuckle. "I nearly forgot for a moment that's why we were doing this. For the sake of the case."

"Will you really keep up drawing? When it's done?"

"I'd like to, though it's hard to say for sure." He didn't seem especially comfortable with the turn in conversation, and changed both subject and tone quite abruptly. "I can't believe you chose to draw me again. You ought to be sick of my face by now, after all the times we paired up in class."

"Hate to break it to you, Matty, but you don't have the sort of face a fellow gets sick of." With one hand still nestled between Matty's legs, he reached the other over to gently caress the line of his jaw, examining the angle of it and absolutely ignoring the thudding pulse of Matty's lifeblood fluttering beneath his fingertips. "In any case, there's nobody else here to draw, is there?"

Flicking from the drawings up to Warren, Matty's eyes were like pools fit to wade right into, their depths perfectly cool or deliciously warm, depending on what was needed. Warren wasn't sure which he needed. Every inch of his skin seemed desperate for the heat of Matty's, while a fire burned low in his belly and begged to be quenched.

There remained a small part of Warren that wanted to resist his response to that look. Odd time for resistance, of course—it might have been more useful before he accepted a very heated invitation to the chap's house, then further invited himself into his bed. So long as they kept quiet, the chances of being caught at anything in this private corner room where the landlady believed Matty a staunch upholder of English law were slim to none. But it was not exactly a good habit to get into, cozying up to men whose circumstances barred them from membership to The Curious Fox. Matty was so sweet, so self-deprecating, so enticingly strange that it was hard to believe he was trouble sometimes, but he was.

Casually as Warren had found warmth between his knees, Matty began running light fingers over the grip Warren still had on the pencil, as if inspecting it. The light, teasing touch brought into relief the more solid points of contact at their shoulders and bent legs, not to mention Warren's hand, still nestled, plenty warm now. They were settled in together very warm and close, mere inches and a bit of gumption away from snatching back the pleasures they'd had stolen from them in the alley.

Warren tipped his head back and closed his eyes, trying to master the roiling of his desire enough that he could decide once and for all whether he intended to indulge it. That task was not helped by Matty nuzzling some scruffy almost-kisses in the sensitive space he'd opened up under his chin, the first move either of them had made without any story to excuse it. The sparkle of warm sweetness between them swelled sharply, like Matty had thrown a shot of gin on gentle flames.

"This isn't a good idea, mate," Warren managed on a tight breath. "I know I half-started it, but maybe I shouldn't have."

148 *To Sketch a Scandal*

"I know." Matty nipped gently just under the curve of Warren's jaw. "It's just…"

"Just what?" Warren asked, and there was begging in it, desperation for Matty to find some way to make it alright.

"I keep having the idea," he said in a low voice, rough and breathy enough to stoke the flames higher. "Even if it's not a good idea, I keep having it. Over and over. Do you?"

His lips were a hair's breadth from Warren's ear. Warren gripped at Matty's leg like it was his lifeline. "I do."

"So, I just wonder," he whispered, the words so quiet that Warren felt more than heard them, "if it wouldn't be better to get it out of our systems now." He flicked his tongue very lightly. "What do you think?"

Warren thought that was fucking terrible logic.

But it sure sounded good, didn't it?

Warren tipped his head a bit farther to the side, a tiny adjustment that Matty took advantage of immediately, letting his sketchbook slip to the floor and opening his mouth to better caress Warren's neck. Warren had surely notched a bedpost since that ill-fated alley meetup, but it must not have been memorable, because he suddenly felt like he'd been strictly celibate from then until now, waiting for this moment like the faithful type of lover he poked fun at.

"Just once, then?" he whispered. "Get it out of our systems."

"Just once." Matty unknotted Warren's cravat for better access. "Then it's all strictly business."

"You mean strictly art."

He felt Matty smile against him. "Warren, are you implying my scribbles can be called *art*?"

"If it will keep you doing that," Warren panted, "I'll build a bloody museum for it."

Matty sat up to look at him properly. He was still smiling. Though the curtains were closed, daylight made an appearance at the edges of them. It was day, the bed was slept in, and

Matty was smiling. He took one final moment of careful, deliberate action, putting Warren's sketchbook aside more reverently than he had his own.

Then he leaned in and pressed that beautiful smile to Warren's lips.

Warren's eyes dropped closed and a sigh escaped him. The kiss was soft, unexpected, and positively drenched in daylight. Matty, for all his quiet, orderly ways, was clearly spurred by the sweetness to become quite bold, swinging a leg to the other side of Warren's hips in a delicious straddle. Without hesitation, they met in the deep, open-mouthed kiss that Warren had craved in the alley, but had seemed too intimate for a place like that. Here, though? Here it was perfect.

The warmth and weight of Matty, the curve of his arse in Warren's instantly searching palms, was disorienting, nearly delirious. Warren was two rather distinct creatures: one of duty and daylight, and another of bars and back rooms. To receive such a charged kiss at this hour, in this place, from this man who was barred from the half of Warren's life he more readily belonged in, felt new and fresh and like something he could get used to...

His hands froze for just a second in their exploration. *Damn.* He could not get used to it, could he? This was a one-time thing.

Matty came up for air, eyes dizzily managing to focus on Warren.

"Alright?"

Warren just pulled Matty tighter to him. His hands and mouth became more forceful, but slower, really reveling in every touch and taste. Having just this one moment and no other made him greedy. He wanted it to last.

Matty, on the other hand, was well on his way to becoming an impatient blur. Warren's cravat and collar were on the floor before he knew it, Matty's attentions turned to the hollow of his throat, hands reaching desperately into Warren's clothes for

150   *To Sketch a Scandal*

the relief of skin-on-skin. When Warren took a peek at Matty's pretty face, he found his eyelids fluttering with barely-repressed want. His desperation stoked Warren's, but if this was all they had, they had to make it last. If Matty was allowed to set the pace, it was going to be over too soon.

Since Warren was perfectly happy in any configuration, and Matty'd displayed a liking for passivity in the alley, he didn't overthink his impulse to take control. The bed was too small and potentially squeaky for anything rough, but a few intense nudges and a bite on the neck got them where he wanted: flipped over, Matty flat on his back.

As suspected, Matty proved perfectly pliant. Warren took a long moment to look him over, at his kiss-reddened lips and tousled shirtwaist, half-mad with wantonness.

"You don't get out much, do you?" Warren teased.

Matty shook his head.

"I should make you wait." Warren ran slow hands down Matty's chest, undoing one waistcoat button before picking consideringly at the next like he hadn't quite decided what to do with it yet. "Maybe take the time to draw you looking like this first." He slipped the rest of the buttons out of their places, then confiscated cravat and collar while he was at it. "Or like this." He mussed Matty's linen as well, revealing flushed skin that was just begging to be tasted, which Warren did, as agonizingly slow as he could manage. "This *really* suits you. We'd make a masterpiece, if you could sit still long enough."

Matty hummed and arched his back, a nearly pained sound coming from his throat. He clearly wanted to be louder than was possible in a midday tryst such as this.

"Forgive me, Warren," he whispered, ragged. "I don't think I can take any more fucking drawing right now."

"Just the fucking, then?"

"*Please.*"

"Fine," he said between kisses. "Next time, then."

Their eyes caught for a moment, just one, before Warren distracted them both from his mistake by sliding his hand along the hard ridge and dampening velveteen that marked Matty's excitement. Matty bucked his hips and gasped at the touch, his eyes clamping shut. Something in the intensity of the reaction had Warren instinctively pressing his free hand to Matty's mouth just in time to catch the moan that escaped him.

"You've got to keep quiet," Warren scolded in a whisper, even as he purposely made the situation worse with his most expert and artistic of grips. Matty whimpered against his hand. "If you can't, I'll have to use more extreme means."

Matty tried to say something, so Warren let him, removing the relevant hand just long enough for Matty to gasp, "I can't. I can't keep quiet."

"Well, then. What am I to do with you?"

"Extreme means, I should think." He ran his hands up and down Warren's back, clearly drinking in the modest fruits that came from lugging around ale barrels and market baskets all the time. "*Please.*"

Warren became fixated on Matty's mouth. It was not what he'd planned on—the cream was right there, after all—but he couldn't resist the supplication. In fact, he'd resisted Matty's eagerness about as much as he could in his quest to stop time. He was panting and every bit of him was aching for more. He unfastened his own falls while Matty scrambled to sit up against the pillows, licking his lips and staring hungrily as Warren took out his own cock and stroked it.

"This will keep you quiet?" he whispered.

When Matty nodded, eyes wide, Warren did the obvious thing with just a touch of regret. The end of this was on its way—he wasn't going to last long.

But the regret was not as strong as the desire, and when he found Matty's mouth so warm, receptive, and skilled, he could regret nothing at all as the moment it seemed he'd been waiting for since he first set eyes on this fellow moved closer and closer. Matty took him very eagerly, very expertly, and the perfection of his slick movements overcame Warren much, much too quickly, eyes and jaw squeezed shut against the onslaught of his release.

Spent, he moved back. Before him, Matty looked absolutely debauched. Warren had mussed the man's hair past the point of recognition in his passion; his lips were bright red, eyelids heavy and chest heaving. There was nothing calm, nothing measured, nothing blank about him whatsoever. He was stroking himself like he'd lost all sense of anything else as he drank Warren in, as if the sight was the thing that would cool the fever that had pinked up his cheeks and the pale skin of his chest.

More clearheaded now, but still very much engaged, Warren took the task over for Matty, slowing the pace until he was squirming and begging quietly, almost silently, but with a desperation that Warren finally took pity on, leaning down to taste and suck. Still slow, still lingering, still insisting on this lasting just a *little bit longer* until the delay finally drove poor Matty to grasp the back of Warren's head, urging him on until at last he swelled and tensed and released the flood of his crisis into Warren's ready throat.

They lay together for a bit, Warren's head on Matty's belly as Matty stroked his hair very sweetly. Their one time was technically over, perhaps, but it occurred to Warren, as warm, midday sleepiness came upon him, that there was no need to make that final declaration right away. No one waiting for the room. No public place that could be interrupted at any moment. They'd been quiet enough to be left alone, and could linger in this haze of consummation for as long as they cared to.

And it seemed they both cared to for quite a while.

At last, though, at some silently-agreed-upon point, they sat up, smoothing hair and straightening clothes.

Jess Everlee

"Artfully done," Matty quipped quietly. "I'd say I learned a few things in your tutelage today."

"Glad to hear it."

While Warren kept his tone light, a sadness was coming over him. It was clearly time for him to leave, but he did not want to. Leaving. Always the leaving, so quickly it seemed sometimes, to return to the club or the cleanup or simply to escape the possibility of a dreaded feeling that might threaten the careful reputation he'd built.

But it was daytime. He wasn't shackled to that reputation at this hour, and the fact was, he didn't want to leave. He wanted this day to continue. The coupling had been lovely, but it did not quell his desire to draw Matty again, disheveled and loose-limbed as he was right now. To hear Matty's little jokes and odd perspectives. To learn more about who he'd been, who he was now, and what exactly was going to become of him if he could not solve this art fraud case, because Warren was suddenly worried for the chap and invested in his well-being.

But that wasn't the agreement. Warren reluctantly left the warmth of the bed, finding his jacket, his sketchbook, and hopefully his reason somewhere among the mess they'd made.

"I'll see you in class, then, I suppose," he said.

"All art from here on out?" Matty asked. It seemed to surprise him, that he'd posed it as a question.

It gave Warren pause, but not for long. Matty, after all, was not really an art class chum, but a lawman. Not a typical one, sure, but his pay came from the same pot as it did for the blokes with the bats. He was a risk. He was a hypocrite. He was no one Warren had any business lingering with further, or frankly, even liking quite as much as he did.

Warren put his hat on, waving amicably even as some foolish part of him begged to be allowed to stay just a little bit longer.

"All art," he agreed. "From here on out."

154 *To Sketch a Scandal*

★ ★ ★

"How was your class, Warren?" Harry asked over dinner that night. "Are you learning much?"

It was far from the first time Harry had asked that question, but today it startled Warren so badly he dropped his fork with an unpleasant clink against the fine new dish that had recently replaced the old mismatched ones. He awkwardly scrambled for the wayward fork, gathering it up to find the handle—and thus his hand—now covered in curry. As he reached for his napkin, he found that everyone was staring at him, everyone tonight being the three members of his family and two of their wealthier new neighbors that Mother had befriended and was trying to impress.

When he was done with the napkin, he went ahead and reached for his wine as well, face hot with embarrassment.

"Are you alright, Warren?" Mother asked.

"Fine, yes. Sorry." He smiled winningly at the neighbors, a wispy blonde woman and her ruddy husband. They softened quickly—he knew his way around a smile. "Distracted, that's all."

"Not by anything unpleasant, I hope," said the neighbor woman politely.

Unpleasant? Hardly. He was distracted by thoughts of Matty asking him to come over. The feel of them sitting side by side on the bed. That pride when Matty's drawing turned out better than expected. The heat of the moan he'd lost against Warren's palm.

"N-not unpleasant, no," he said, reaching for a dinner roll that was only slightly overcooked—with company coming over, Anjali had only been permitted to handle the bread, and even then, only an English style. Something about *not embarrassing entire continents in front of the neighbors, please.* "It was a very good class, actually. Enough so that I find I'm still thinking about it hours later."

Jess Everlee 155

"Lovely!" Harry reached over to give Warren's shoulder a friendly jostle that the proper neighbors eyed with a sort of polite confusion. "Really lovely, Warren. What was so good about it, do you think?"

"Oh. Um." Warren sipped his wine to buy himself time. "Just. Appreciation, is all. The instructors are pleased with my work, and some of the other students have taken note as well. I've been helping one of them. Some of them." He corrected, not quite honestly. "Not just one, of course. You know. Since Father gave me a nice head start in some of these skills. And my..." What was Matty, in this version of the truth? "My friend who I was helping—one of them—made some very nice progress. It's a good feeling, to be helpful, particularly after..." He locked eyes briefly with Anjali, who, thank goodness, shook her head to keep him from saying anything even more embarrassing than he already had. He lifted his glass cheerfully. "Just nice to be helpful. That's all."

"What a charming son you have, Mrs. Bakshi," said the neighbor woman, turning a bit pink.

Mother smiled graciously. "To a fault, almost."

"You know, Warren," said Harry, who thus far, with his eccentric clothing and wild tales of travel, had seemed to alarm more than charm the neighbors. Everyone was clearly a little anxious to hear what he was about to suggest. "I'm sure we'd all love to see what you've been working on. He's been dreadfully cagey about it," he muttered to the neighbor gentleman. "But tonight seems as good a night as any for the big reveal."

Warren felt his face get very hot again. "Oh, I don't know."

"I think," said Mother, looking at him seriously. "That it's a brilliant idea. After supper, let's all retire to the drawing room and have a look, shall we? Before you fellows go upstairs for your port?"

Port. Right. That whole after-supper, separate-spheres song and dance was a rather bewildering custom that Warren still was not used to even after a few of these higher-society dinner parties. His parents used to do it, back when their status was middling, but he'd been just a bit too young before their fortunes changed to have ever gone off with the men once dinner was done and polite society dictated it was time to split off. Now that he was expected in the parlor with port in hand, he found it was not nearly so interesting as he'd imagined it would be when he was younger. At this point, he had very little to discuss with proper men, growing bored quickly. So while he was very hesitant to show his work, the idea of delaying the inevitable hour of choking down port (he much preferred gin) while Harry scandalized the ears off this dull bloke with exaggerated tales was admittedly tempting.

And so, after the dessert was cleared (some part-time staff was brought in for these engagements while the Bakshis sorted out their continued domestic angst, which, for all the distress it was causing right now, would likely end with more full-time staff in the long run anyway), Warren fetched his sketchbook from his room. He flipped through it before committing.

When he got to the last picture in the book, the one he'd done of Matty earlier that day when they were side by side on the bed, he strongly considered ripping it out. There was nothing indecent about it out of context, but the moment he laid eyes on it, a sad, tight longing stretched through his chest, one he worried might be visible to an outsider. Within seconds, he could no longer even think of the task at hand, consumed with other considerations.

Like whether Matty would still want help with the drawing, now that they'd passed through their singular moment of passion.

And more importantly whether, if he did, Warren should give it.

Certainly not. His attraction to this fellow was strong, and showing no signs of weakening anytime soon. Their indulgence had done nothing but capture every inch of his mind not already consumed with thoughts of *what if*. If the desire were solely physical, it would be easier. That sort of thing came cheap enough. It was the other desire that scared him, the one that was still in fits that they'd not had more opportunity to talk, or create, or take another meal together.

As he stared at his work, though, he had to wonder why he'd felt closed off from those things. It was the physical, after all, that was the danger. There was nothing illegal or even untoward about striking up a friendship in one's art class. None of Forester's concerns applied to a pair of companions.

But the loudest concerns didn't actually seem to be coming from Forester. They came from *Warren Bakshi the barkeep*, who was determined not to get attached to any particular notch, lest he prove himself another sappy sod, give up all his rakish allure, and lose the place in the world that had meant so much to him all these years. Particularly now, when his place at home was so strange and uncertain.

But surely it wasn't *romantic* anyway. His feelings were friendly, was all. He was being helpful. And there was no bloody harm in that. None at all.

He opted to leave the picture in, and he was glad he did. It was the best thing he'd done so far. When he brought it downstairs, it garnered approval from Harry, smiles from Anjali, misty eyes from Mother, and polite noises from the neighbors.

"Is that your friend, then?" Anjali asked after she'd had a good look. "What's his name?"

"Matthew Shaw," Warren said, ignoring how sweet the syllables tasted on his tongue and determining to chase them out with a little extra port soon enough. "And yes, he's the friend I've been helping, and may continue to do so, should he need it."

Chapter Twelve

Matty

Matty didn't do as well as he might have hoped in the wake of Warren's departure, which felt odd, because they lingered far longer than Matty would have ever expected. But something about Warren's presence and then absence from his home made the room feel very empty, the week ahead of him even more so. He missed Warren immediately, a missing that spread out from his center and began to gather up other missings. He missed the days when it was just him and Barrows doing as they pleased, and preemptively missed the old man himself, who'd be gone very soon. Worse even than that, a stray thought of his mother, whom he'd not seen in years, made him wary that he might start missing her too, if he wasn't careful. And that wouldn't do at all. Unlike Warren or Barrows, she did not deserve to be missed.

He distracted himself with another gallery visit and an irresponsibly expensive supper. When he got home, he decided it was a good time to try that absinthe again, now that he had something he wanted to numb up properly. Sadly, it still proved

Jess Everlee 159

so disgusting that he could not achieve any interesting state with it before he gave up on everything and went to sleep.

The ghosts of bad decisions often followed Matty around in the wake of them, but the memory of the encounter with Warren proved far more pleasant company than most of his mistakes did. Its only ill aspect was that it could not be repeated. Warren had seemed very set on that, and Matty didn't blame him. Someone at Scotland Yard had seen him at his old haunt, after all. There was no guarantee something like that wouldn't happen again. Warren didn't know quite how close Matty was flirting with the edge of disaster right now, but it probably didn't take a genius to know that a detective with a secret was a ticking time bomb.

He would do well to forget about all of it, but he was decidedly attached to his infatuation. He justified coddling it again by calling it an artist's doomed obsession. It made for a painfully enjoyable way to pass quiet moments at home or awkward moments at the Met.

However, it also meant that when the day of the next class arrived and he found himself a few torturous feet away from the object of his new obsession, he was lost to rationality completely.

The improvement in the Bakshi family status was starting to show by this point, and he found Warren dressed in a finer jacket than he had been in before: a simple, dark velvet, nothing ostentatious, but well-fitted about the shoulders and worn with a soft, burnt-orange waistcoat that made his black hair and glittering topaz earring gleam as he set up his station like nothing had happened between the two of them at all.

"Good morning, Mr. Shaw," he said, all casual friendliness as he flipped to a fresh page in his sketchbook. "How have you been?"

It took Matty a moment to find even the simplest greeting in return. He hadn't prepared himself for such a casual exchange. He had expected to be ignored, maybe even for Warren to have

160   *To Sketch a Scandal*

found another spot across the room from him. He'd sounded so serious about keeping to one encounter that it'd seemed likely he'd want to keep his distance from any temptation.

Though, perhaps Warren was not tempted. Maybe he really had been sated by the one-and-done. Far from getting anything out of his own system, however, Matty felt more pull and heat in the space between them than ever before as Warren went on joking, settling into class like he always did, seeming unchanged aside from looking even more like some dream Matty'd pulled out of a confiscated opium pipe. Never in his life had he tasted a man's seed and then faced him in polite company. Not once. The contrasting innocence of *now* and the raw pleasure of *then* had him flustered and heated and looking about for an empty seat he could move to, to save himself the torment of sitting here all afternoon.

He had to assume that Warren—who was telling a story of his sister-in-law's unpleasantly doughy dinner rolls like it was the most interesting thing to happen all week—was doing better with the idea of simple friendship than Matty was in the wake of their tryst. And why shouldn't he be? The chap had more potential lovers than he knew what to do with. Scratching that singular itch must have worked for him, and now he was ready to do just what he'd said: keep it strictly art between the two of them from here on out.

Mrs. Buttersnipe finally saved him from further small talk, the familiar clap of her hands signaling the start of class.

Matty fumbled with his sketchbook so badly he nearly dropped it in his haste to open to the better drawings he'd done this week. That was the real reason for these mad little lessons, after all. Not pleasures. Not friendship. Simply to drum up something he could show the Buttersnipes that might get him even a few moments alone with them. He was increasingly convinced that his intuition was correct, and that whatever crimes they were committing—if any—were well beneath

Jess Everlee 161

the notice of his unit. One conversation. He was certain if he could just...

Another round of clapping drew his nose out of his pages.

"If I could have everyone's *full* attention, please! We have a guest with us today, one who warrants the setting aside of all distractions."

Matty realized he hadn't even looked at the front of the room yet, too busy flipping through his sketchbook, fidgeting with the ring round his neck, and sneaking glances at the station beside him. He finally took a more reasonable assessment of his surroundings. When he did, he found Mrs. Buttersnipe's annoyance had been for him alone. He was the only one distracted—every other face was turned in rapt attention to the instructors, who had been joined by someone new.

As Matty finally took in the sight of the newcomer, every drop of blood seemed to drain from his face, leaving it cold and tingling.

A slim, heavily-mustached bloke in a frilly coat peered around the room with a sharp, monocled eye. He'd styled his hair different and trimmed his mustache to something decidedly stylish, but Matty knew him instantly.

Detective Ashton.

Ashton, as promised, had come on to the case part-time to keep an eye on Matty and Barrows's handling of it. And while Matty had resented his intrusion from the start, he'd been generally harmless, if a bit smirky and opinionated.

Or so Matty thought, before Ashton, apparently, invited himself into the plainclothes aspect of the case without so much as mentioning it to Matty until this very moment.

"I am so pleased to introduce Mr. Rex Harris," Mrs. Buttersnipe announced, clearly unaware of whom she was truly standing beside. "While obviously our higher-level instruction is renowned, it's not every day that such a well-respected member of the Portraitists Guild takes an interest in the goings-on of

162   *To Sketch a Scandal*

our beginner's class. He got in touch to let us know he plans to attend our end-of-session gallery night, but found himself with a free day to come preview the work our students are doing. He's going to provide some advice for those who really want to shine and find further instruction or even work through that showcase."

Matty could have kicked himself. Why the devil didn't he think of that angle sooner? Or why hadn't Ashton mentioned it before Matty came in as a dreadful aspiring artist on day one? Rustling up some phony credentials would have been a good deal simpler than trying to display any skill...

But the notion fizzled as Matty thought it through. How could he manage it himself? Renown in a man his age couldn't be drummed up out of nowhere as simply as it could for an older fellow like Ashton—Matty would have been heard of around the art scene well before he could drop his name to sit in on a class. It wouldn't have worked.

The truth of that, however, did not keep Matty from seething as he stared up at the front of the room.

Through the whispers, Detective Ashton—or, rather, Mr. Harris to the others—waved a hand that quickly brought everyone back to earth. His eyes did not fall upon Matty even once.

"I would ask you to simply carry on with your class as if I am not here," he said in a casual but somewhat grim tone. "I shall be around in due time."

His presence, however, seemed nearly as big a disturbance to most of the class as it was to Matty. They all sat straighter, stayed quieter, and marked up their papers more decisively as the instruction began—shading today, now that they'd all ostensibly mastered pure shape. They did not know that impressing this man was useless. That he knew less than the worst student in this class. Less than Matty, who had finally, with Warren's help, improved himself to the level he needed for the next step in assessing the Buttersnipes on his own. Today. He'd have done it today, the better drawings his excuse, his way in, the salvation of his career...

That *fucker*.

"You alright, mate?"

Matty looked to his right, to where he'd grown so accustomed to the shape of Warren—not bloody circles and squares but something unique and astounding—that the sight of him proved a dangerous comfort. Matty had no right to have anything of comfort just now. The fact that Ashton was here without telling him meant he was clearly in trouble, deep over his head, and it was all of his own making.

But against all odds, he had a friend. For the moment, at least. And under the circumstances, he couldn't resist acting like it.

"He's no artist," Matty whispered, barely moving his lips. "Don't react."

He might as well not have added the direction; Warren's eyes went wide in spite of it, brows climbing.

There was no opportunity to talk about it further. The figure model was set upon his stool and Mr. Buttersnipe began pointing out the way the afternoon light cast certain shadows on the lad's face, his talk of shapes coming into play again along with shade. It was not long before the pencils were out and moving, clouds of self-consciousness joining the heady turpentine in the air as the so-called "master of the craft" made his rounds with hands behind his back and glasses perched on his nose that Matty knew for a fact contained false lenses. After a few quiet circles, he began approaching each student in turn, offering advice.

Matty didn't dare catch Detective Ashton's eye until it was his turn.

At that point, he did not dare avoid it.

"Hello, Mr. Harris," he said lightly, as the fellow's shadow fell heavy over his paper. "Have you come to help me?"

Ashton paused, scanning Matty's drawing, which wasn't

164   *To Sketch a Scandal*

turning out too badly. "I've just come to see how you're faring. I heard you've taken to the art more slowly than expected."

A lump of dread appeared in Matty's throat, so hard he might as well have swallowed his eraser.

"I'm working to the best of my ability."

"I see." Ashton caught Mrs. Buttersnipe's eye, shook his head a little. "Can I speak to you in the hall, Mr. Shaw?"

"You've told everyone else what you think at their stations."

"Yes," he said mildly. "But I should hate to embarrass you, is the thing."

With a last look at Warren (who was still a bit bug-eyed), Matty followed Ashton out into the hallway.

"What are you doing here?" Matty snapped once the door was shut behind them.

"As I said," whispered Ashton. "You've been moving too slowly. Frost sent me in a few days ago. I've spoken to the Buttersnipes twice now, and investigated this building top to bottom. I don't think they did it." He sneered at the door. "They're certainly doing something untoward, with these extra classes, but only because the price is steeper than the skill they can teach. Can't rule out shady dealing of some sort, but it's not the exact fraud we're concerned about. I'll remain on the case a bit longer to confirm—the international angle is shoring up their own evidence as we speak—but you're off the case as of this morning."

Matty couldn't seem to get a good breath. Off the case?

"Why didn't Frost tell me this before I bothered coming here today?" he said, voice choked.

Ashton looked annoyingly unsurprised and even pleased to see Matty crack.

"You haven't been in." He shrugged.

"Yes, I have."

"Not as often. Not as expected."

Matty paused, trying to master himself. His breath had returned, but now it was trying to come in gasps. "Does Barrows know I'm off the case?"

"Barrows was told this morning."

"When there was no time for him to inform me. Brilliant."

Ashton shrugged. "Look, Shaw. You were taking too long—"

"Because of the rules *Frost* set for my investigation!" Matty hissed. "In spite of that, I was set up to find the same conclusion you did this sodding afternoon. And if I'd been able to handle it my way from the start—"

"You mean the way that was *decimating your soul*?" Ashton smirked. Matty instantly regretted letting that slip, but it didn't seem Ashton had believed the excuse to begin with. "I got nothing personal against you, aright? But let's not play games. We all know where you came from. Your bosom buddy Barrows tried to downplay it, but it's not hard to figure out. I could have easily finished this out without coming into the class today, but Frost wanted me to make sure your efforts looked earnest and up to the moral standard you promised. Admittedly, they do, at least at first glance." Through his false glasses he looked Matty's attire up and down, going so far as to reach out and touch one of the patches on his lapel. "Unless you've gone and made a little friend in here like I heard you might have done in your last couple cases."

Matty could feel his lip curling. "Go fuck yourself, Ashton."

"Temper, Shaw." Ashton put casual hands in his pockets. No one would take him for a portraitist in that posture. "If you don't give me a lot of lip, I can return to Frost with as glowing a report as is possible for someone who's bungled his case the way you did. I can honestly say that it looks like you tried, and you're going to need that, if you plan to stick around. He's trying to get rid of you, you know, Frost is. Whereas I'm not. You should count yourself lucky, given I'll now be your direct supervisor when Barrows takes his final bow next week. If I were you, I'd remember who your friends are, Miss Matty."

Friends? Before Matty could even wrap his head around that, Ashton morphed out of his natural posture, back undercover as an artist so fast it was like he flipped a lever. He opened the door to the classroom. Considering the situation they'd painted, Matty had no choice but to return to his own character and follow.

Fortunately, Ashton did not linger. He made his rounds and gave out his useless morsels of advice, then tipped his hat and took his leave with another half-hour still left in the session.

When he was gone, Warren moved over a couple of surreptitious inches. "What did he want?"

Matty had not thought of himself as having friends at Scotland Yard aside from Barrows, who, frankly, was a friend only in the one direction. If such friends looked like Detective Ashton, however, he didn't feel like he was missing much. He liked the one that he had indeed found in this class a hell of a lot better, even if that friendship was limited and would not culminate in another intimate encounter. His loyalty, once so staunchly attached to the Met and the Met alone, had apparently found another object in Warren Bakshi. One that did not send him into dangerous situations or call him names.

"The official story is that Rex Harris thinks my lack of talent is incurable, and I should be refunded my tuition and sent packing," he muttered. There was enough distressed chatter about Ashton's criticism filling the room that it wouldn't carry far. "The real story is that I'm off the case."

Warren winced. "That sounds like a bad thing."

"It is a bad thing." Matty snorted a dark laugh at such a charmingly trite observation. "You're spot-on with that, mate. It's a bad thing indeed."

If he was lucky, it meant he'd miss the promotion. If not, if Ashton's "friendship" did not prove stronger than Frost's misgivings, he'd be out on his arse after all.

There was nothing for it, though. Nothing to do but get back to his drawing. Wouldn't it be nice if that were really all he had to fret about? If these concerns of shape and shadow, of friendship and art lessons in bed, were for their own sake, rather than a department that was beginning to show very clearly what it really thought of him?

He reached for the ring around his neck with a solemn sense of loss and uncertainty, only to find those feelings shifting into distress when he did not feel it.

He dug around in his neckcloth, but it became quickly clear that the thing wasn't just hiding out in the folds of his clothes. He reached around to the back of his neck. The chain was missing entirely.

"Everything alright, Mr. Shaw?" Warren asked.

Matty nodded. "I…yes. Don't worry yourself. Just get back to what you were doing."

"Did you lose that ring?"

"I know I had it when I came in."

"You sure?"

He was quite sure, because he'd been fidgeting with it something dreadful as he took his usual place beside Warren, overcome by attraction and awkwardness. He nodded, then stood up, trying to get a better look round their stations and the next ones over. Warren helpfully stooped down to check under the chairs as well.

"Not here," Warren said. "Sorry, mate. Was it something special?"

The question made Matty's throat tighten up in spite of himself. It felt almost horrifically metaphorical, to lose the thing right on Ashton's heels like this.

"Special? No," he lied. "Not…not particularly."

Matty knew what it looked like when someone spotted his real feelings under the veneer of placidity he'd learned to project in all circumstances. Those were dangerous moments. Deadly ones. So when Warren's whole demeanor shifted, eyes narrow-

168   *To Sketch a Scandal*

ing as they saw through to what Matty did not want to reveal, his first instinct was to be terrified.

But Warren's shift was not frightening. It wasn't even the cool casualness he'd been projecting after their encounter, nor the gossipy excitement of "Mr. Harris's" secret. In fact, it was much like the reaction he'd had in their first meeting, when he started trying to get Matty to return to the safety of the club.

"I could use a little air, really take in what Mr. Harris was saying for a minute before I start in," Warren said, a bit too loud, like he was hoping to be heard by someone. "Tag along?"

He started moving toward the door before Matty answered, so utterly casual about the whole thing that no one even glanced their way, too concerned about their own standing to care what the others were up to.

Matty followed Warren back into the hall a few paces, where they stopped, automatically standing closer than acquaintances of their sort might usually opt for. But Matty couldn't bear to be the one to create the distance, and Warren didn't, either. In fact, now that they were out of the room and alone, Warren looked like he might actually reach out and touch Matty. But no. He folded his arms in at the last second.

"You don't seem very well," Warren said. Then asked again, "It was something special, right? The ring?"

This time, Matty couldn't bring the lie to his lips. He didn't confirm it either, but he didn't need to. He was good and caught.

"Who's it from?" Warren asked. Gentle. Genuinely curious. Impossible to wave off.

"A friend at Scotland Yard," said Matty.

"Special friend?"

He wanted to say yes. But he found he couldn't, quite. He didn't like lying to Warren. In fact might have lost his ability to manage it. Still, the fact was…

"I don't know anymore," he said carefully. "More like a mentor if anything, I suppose. But he…" Fuck it all, he was already in this deep. Matty had, it seemed, no shell left to protect him in the presence of this almost-friend of his, and he blurted the truth before he could stop himself: "He's the reason I didn't go to jail when I should have. And I don't know what that makes him, but it does make him something."

Warren froze with his face set in obvious interest. Matty glanced around the upstairs hall, and satisfying himself it was as deserted as it seemed, he went on.

"He caught me trying to pick up tricks when I was fifteen and fucking poor and confused and didn't know what the devil else to do with myself," Matty explained. "There were a lot of…complicated things going on at home. But Barrows gave me another option, and he saw me through it right up until I completely blew it to pieces just now. He gave me the ring to congratulate me for a promotion he was sure I'd get. And now I won't. I won't get it.

"And I just hate to disappoint him. He is the only person who has ever been kind to me. He was other things too, less noble things for sure, but I don't know if you can understand what a big thing that was, to be treated kindly. And now, I've let him down. I blew the case, the one he arranged to save my bloody reputation before he retired. And I guess he probably won't care as much as I do," Matty admitted on a wave of bitterness. "But it was nice to have something from him, some proof that he believed I was good for something other than decking out and sending off to look pretty until the real detectives arrived. And no," he went on, in this impassioned, unstoppable whisper of a confession he'd slipped into, "I'm not typically sentimental, and honestly, if I don't get the promotion, I should give the ring back to him anyway. But I'd at least like to be able to do that much. To have something to give back to him, something I didn't manage to lose. But I did lose it. The promotion, my reputation, and the ring to boot. And when he's gone, when

170   *To Sketch a Scandal*

he's retired and living the rest of his years off happily without me, I'm starting to think I'll have lost everything that made living this particular life worth it to me as well."

It was more than Matty had said of his life...ever. To anyone. While it wasn't much, wasn't even close to the whole story or anything like that, it felt like he'd stripped himself fully naked right in the hallway. He felt sick with himself, like a complete and utter fool who was about two seconds from seeing the back of this kind and beautiful half-friend he'd just ruined everything with for good and all.

Warren uncrossed his arms. When he stepped, it was not to turn away, but to come closer, finally cracking that friendly distance they'd been keeping all day to rub Matty's back. The warmth of his touch felt like it was breaking up a hard crust that had formed across Matty's shoulders, softening and melting a tough heaviness he hadn't even realized was there.

"That's shit," he said, very calm and reasonable. "Even if you end up finding it, the whole situation kind of sounds like shit, doesn't it?"

"I'm just..." Matty hesitated. When he next spoke, it was very quiet. "It's a tough day already, is all. Even before Detective Ashton and the ring... I enjoyed our time together, Warren. I think you're really fantastic. I was wrong, actually. What I said a minute ago. I'd like to amend it: Barrows was the *first* person to be kind to me, but not the only one. Every single interaction I've had with you has left me feeling better than I did at the start. And that last one... I know we agreed to forget it, but I'm struggling a lot more than I thought I would with pretending my admiration for you is within proper bounds. Because it's not. And it never has been, not since the moment I turned around in that alley and saw that you'd bothered to bring this stupid scarf back to me when by all accounts, you should have thrown it in the bloody bin."

No answer came right away as Warren searched his face for

clues as to the truthfulness of all this. Matty held his hands out, all in now with spilling his guts and simply awaiting the outcome. The best thing, the very best, about Warren Bakshi was that even if this gush was not welcome, it was easy to trust that he would do Matty no harm.

That was a very rare thing, and Matty would always appreciate it.

Even if Warren turned around and walked away right now.

Chapter Thirteen

Warren

Well, damn. Warren was in deep. His determination to maintain a simple friendship with the fellow suddenly felt like it had missed the mark rather badly. Matty, it seemed, was harboring some more complicated feelings.

And while *Warren Bakshi the barkeep* was still nervous about that, another version of him was surfacing, and that version was full of fucking butterflies at the notion. That version, he felt, was a bloody traitor.

"I don't know what to say," he admitted, feeling his face get very hot and sarcasm creeping in to cover it. "I get a declaration of love at least once a fortnight, you know, but never one quite this—"

"Pathetic?" Matty supplied.

"Oh, no. They're always pathetic."

It might have been better if the impulsive quip had offended Matty. It would have hurt them both in the moment, but taken care of this whole sentiment problem in the long run. But instead, Matty smiled.

"Semi-public?" he tried again.

"I was going to say *genuine*." Warren's face got hotter. He almost couldn't stand the sincerity of it, so he added, "And *sober*, I suppose."

"Unfortunately. I tried to get good and sullied on absinthe a few times this week, but I can't get enough down."

Warren wanted to continue this sort of sarcastic quibbling. Maybe tell him how to mix the absinthe more effectively. Something silly like that. They both enjoyed the banter, and it was certainly safer. But he couldn't come up with anything funny. All he wanted to say was that he was very glad to hear that Matty was improved by his company—it wasn't along the usual axis of flattery he was used to, and it warmed him.

How could he say that, though? Warren the barkeep certainly didn't say things like that. Didn't sound quite right for a dutiful son, either. He lacked words for this.

But there were other options.

A quick glance about proved the utter solitude of their little corner. He stepped in close enough to be enveloped in the scent of him, cheap, standard cologne and coconut-floral hair oil combined uniquely with whatever it was that was *Matty* and made Warren's mind spin on its axis. This was a big fucking rule to break, but in the absence of the right thing to say, he didn't know what else to do.

He put his hand behind Matty's head...

And kissed him...

Very...

Very...

Softly.

He felt Matty gasp with a shock that their rougher passion had never inspired. Every atom of connection between them— lips against lips, palm against warm neck, Matty's fingers brushing tentatively at the hem of Warren's coat like he was looking for purchase but nervous to grasp it—felt hot and alive and like nothing else could possibly matter ever again.

174 *To Sketch a Scandal*

Other things did matter, though, the greatest of which being their very public location. Regretfully, Warren pulled back. Neither of them was blinking much as their eager eyes met and clasped each other's hands and threatened to run off to France together never to be seen again. His hands drifted down Matty's patched lapels (he could feel the bloke's heart pounding beneath them) before squeezing his fingers one time and placing a little respectable distance between them.

"Let's go back in, sweetheart," he whispered. *Sweetheart.* Not *mate.* Not even *love.* It surprised Warren as much as it did Matty. "I'll help you find your ring. Little bugger's got to be in there somewhere."

"That…" Matty swiped at where there might have been a hair straying on his forehead after a wilder kiss, but it hadn't been and there wasn't. They were both still put together as anything. On the outside. "That would be very kind of you, Warren. I wouldn't blame you if you felt you'd shown enough of that for the time being. Kindness, that is."

Warren was used to very big shows of love—big plans, big meals, big sacrifices. The things that Matty seemed to feel were too much were in actuality so small that it threatened to break his heart right in two.

"Being kind to you is not as difficult, Matty," he said quietly, "as maybe some arseholes have led you to believe. Come on."

Warren went back into the classroom, Matty on his heels. He felt light as a feather, about to float off. He did not know what this meant, but the concept of *all art* was clearly not going to be troubling them again anytime soon.

"Now let's see," Warren said when they'd gotten back to their spots. "It really can't have gone far."

Matty still seemed a little woozy, so Warren took point on the operation. He shuffled their stools, looking under them for a gleam of gold before ducking under the desk, peering in the various directions that the thing might have rolled off in.

Jess Everlee 175

It wasn't under their seats, so he started asking around, pestering other students and poking other stations. *Excuse me, miss* and *Pardon, but could I just check?* His investigations were mostly met with acceptance—if a bit of haughtiness—but still caused a small scandal when he could find no phrasing delicate enough to ask one of the female students across the room to *step aside for a second* so he could make sure it hadn't rolled under her voluminous skirts.

"Nothing," he reported back to Matty, carrying back a scrap of ribbon between his fingers. "Just this."

Matty choked down a horrified laugh. "Warren! You didn't get that off her, did you?"

Warren waggled his eyebrows and twirled the ribbon like maybe he had, but then he shook his head, chuckled, and shoved it into Matty's hand. "Don't get jealous. It happened to be on the floor by her feet, but she says it's not hers."

Before they strategized further, Mr. Buttersnipe materialized by Warren's side, this time with their old friend Sandford Binks in tow. The boastful chap looked very sullen just now, his shoulders slumped and his lip twitching like he was trying his damnedest to keep a sneer off his face.

"Forgive me, Mr. Bakshi," said Mr. Buttersnipe as he pointed to Warren's picture. "Now that you're back, I simply wanted to show… Mr. Binks, do you see what we're saying here? This is what Mr. Harris was trying to tell you." He circled his finger around a bit of shading under the chin of his subject. "When the marks go in many directions like this, layer after layer, the effect is smoother than even the smoothest marks going parallel. Does that make sense?"

"It does," said Binks, the words sounding like they'd been dragged out of his throat, screaming for a chance to talk to their lawyer about the injustice of this undignified removal. "Thank you."

176 *To Sketch a Scandal*

Once they were back on their way, he turned to Matty, burning with annoyance.

"We should check *his* things," Warren huffed. "If anyone would do something so petty as steal someone's ring, it's him."

"Good thought, but I'm afraid Mr. Binks is your enemy. Not mine," said Matty. He still had the pink ribbon in hand and smoothed it a few times. "I don't think we're dealing with a thief, Warren. It's a broken clasp that's the real culprit, and me for being so stupid as to wear something I might need to give back on a cheap chain instead of leaving it at home."

"It's still on the chain?" Warren asked. "Then it can't have rolled off as far as I was looking, can it? You said you had it when you came in, and we've retraced all your steps. Someone must have picked it up."

Matty shrugged, a bit cynically. "Maybe it was my dearest chum in the world, *Mr. Harris*. The fucking dog," he added in a nasty whisper.

The fucking dog.

"What?" said Matty.

"The ribbon," Warren said. He snatched it back from Matty's hand, looking it over. "It's that dog's, ain't it? That yippy thing that's always nosing around. And we know she's got a nose for coin, the little miser."

"Surely you aren't referring to our dear Miss Martha in such a crass manner, Mr. Bakshi."

"She was fucking around over here a while ago. I was worried she was about to piss on my shoes."

"That is a classy lady you're talking about, you know. I am shocked by your continued impropriety. Shocked." He said it so straight-faced that Warren wanted nothing more than to kiss those clever lips again and again. He grinned instead, since it was all he could do.

"You're going to kill me if you keep going on like that, you know."

Jess Everlee 177

"You'd deserve it," said Matty. His voice was plain, but now that it seemed they'd solved the case, his eyes had gone flirty, the answer seeming to cheer him before they'd even confirmed it.

"Oh, would I?" Warren asked. "For what?"

Matty lowered his voice. "For coming in here looking like *that*," he hissed, nodding at the flattering attire he'd chosen. "When you knew I was meant to keep things strictly art. One might think you'd done it on purpose, to test me."

"If I had, you failed miserably, didn't you?" Warren said. "Let's get your ring."

They found Miss Martha retiring on her little bed beside the supply cabinet, a gleam of something shiny sticking out under the fall of her floppy ear. She had several pencils, an eraser, a penknife cap, three shillings, and a few crumpled balls of paper in with her as well. A light snoring emanated from this small dragon upon her treasure.

"She's a right criminal," said Matty. "A serial thief. I'd never have thought it of one such as her."

"It's always the pretty ones, ain't it?"

"Why don't you grab it?" Matty said, as they eyed the drool at the corner of her mouth. "You're the brilliant detective who solved the case, after all. You deserve the final moment of glory."

"I thought you were the brilliant detective."

"Obviously not, or I wouldn't have been removed from my case, would I? Far as I know, you've never catastrophically failed at the job, and therefore are the detective in better standing."

Miss Martha let out a particularly loud snore, as if in agreement.

"Still. I wouldn't dream of taking the satisfaction of reunion from you," Warren said, clapping him on the back. "It's your beloved object."

Looking over his shoulder to make sure the Buttersnipes

178   *To Sketch a Scandal*

did not catch him bothering their precious baby, Matty leaned down to grab the chain, pulling the treasure out from under her. He put the lost ribbon in its place.

"Thank you," Matty said as they returned to their stations. They were in full company, but he went ahead and risked a flutter of lashes and a meaningful half-smile that nearly made Warren shiver. "How can I ever repay your kindness?"

An answer to that question came to Warren faster than he would have believed possible, his whole mind lighting up with something so illicitly exciting that he could hardly believe it even lived within him. "Seriously?"

Matty seemed intrigued by the response. "Fifty percent serious, I suppose," he said. "Why do you ask?"

"Because if you're really offering..." Warren cleared his throat, the turpentine and Matty's cologne near to swooning level in the cramped room. "Then I'd like to draw you again. Properly."

To be in public right now was a special sort of torture, and Matty was clearly feeling it too. He focused his attention back onto his work, adding lines that didn't matter to keep his hands busy and his exterior innocent, as if he didn't trust himself not to give them away if he didn't create a little distance.

"Meet up after class again today?" he said. "My place?"

"No," Warren said. "We can't make a habit of that. Your landlady will notice if we overdo it."

"You're a top-notch criminal, aren't you, Mr. Bakshi?"

"Me and Miss Martha. Best around."

"What do you suggest, then?"

Warren did not answer. It didn't seem wise to get too detailed, even if they'd long since found the position and register that made their conversations sound like vague muttering to the rest of the class. He had another medium, though. He picked up his pencil and drew his response instead.

Three little triangles and three little dots, making up the

crudest of fox faces. The shape was etched into the knob of The Curious Fox's front door.

"I thought I was barred?" Matty asked.

"You are," Warren said, mouth drying at the thought of what came next. "But I might be able to change that. This Friday, I'll talk Mr. Forester into letting you in. Go relax at a pub nearby—the Gull is decent—and when I've got the go-ahead, I'll send one of the serving lads round to fetch you."

"What if you can't talk him into it? How will I know?"

"If you don't hear from me by midnight," he said, "then come in the morning."

"The morning?"

"He lets me stay the nights I work since my commute's a bit inconvenient. He used to do the same, but now he's...well, he's married now, you know." Warren glanced around. They were probably still unheard, but it was a wise turn of phrase just in case. No one needed to know that Forester was "married" to a tailor named Noah Clarke. "Saturdays, he heads home around two or three in the morning, and doesn't come back until five in the evening."

"You'd go behind his back like that? Just to see me?"

Warren considered the notion more seriously. Hopefully, he wouldn't have to. But if he did? If Forester really held his ground and refused, even after his "right-hand man" proved willing to give the chap a full reference and take responsibility for the outcome, as club members did for their own friends and lovers every week?

"Yes, Mr. Shaw," he said. "Yes, I think I would."

Quite a day, overall. It was...well, he didn't really have another word for it: inspiring. He'd done up little doodles all his life, but that kiss and those smiles and those dry little jokes... Matty's unflinching *Mattiness* had him for once feeling like he

180 *To Sketch a Scandal*

had something he really wanted to depict, as the impulsive idea of drawing him properly went from fun notion to true want.

His father had not been the sort of artist who would go on at length about muses and inspiration and abstract ideas of creativity. Not with Warren, anyway. Still, even from a young age, Warren had known there was some difference between the little animals he sketched out with his son and the paintings he worked on alone in his study, the pieces sometimes waiting months at a time under a cloth for him to return from a voyage to finish them. Warren was definitely not supposed to, but he used to peek at those unfinished works in his father's absence: the Thames done up in the bright, clanging colors of his homeland's markets, or women in saris as gray as London soot. He was saying something with them, and though he never spoke those things, they left a strong impression of his experience in life, one Warren had once hoped to emulate.

Back then, he figured he would learn how to speak with his art when Father's message was finally appreciated enough that he did not have to work the trade ships anymore. When that never happened, Warren convinced himself that it had never mattered to begin with.

But his conversation with Matty in the hall today...it had shifted something. The contrasts and contradictions of Warren's life were not the same as his father's had been, but he had his own. And there was something about Matty that spoke to them, something in the way he could feel such emotion over a gift from a man who—far as Warren could tell from what little he'd heard—had tempered his "kindness" with more than a little exploitation. It all *said* something. Something Warren recognized in himself, but lacked the words for.

He didn't know yet if he would ever be good enough to capture whatever it was, but for the first time since he'd learned his father was not coming home, he had an idea that he wanted to try.

Jess Everlee 181

He got home feeling dazed by these thoughts, particularly when Anjali all but assaulted him on his way inside before he was remotely ready to be wrenched out of his own head. He'd hardly gotten over the threshold when she was right there, grabbing him by the arms and practically dragging him to the kitchen. It might have been alarming if not for the huge smile on her face.

"I did it!" she declared in a stage-whispered scream.

"What'd you do?" Warren whispered back.

The family's kitchen was still hung with the vaguely burnt-butter smell that had arrived when Anjali did, and had not fled since. She busied herself with a bundle on the table, and when she turned back, she was clutching a single piece of roti in her hands with an enormous grin on her face. With an impressively dramatic sense of timing, she let go of the top half so he could see how it flopped over properly, rather than standing upright, tough and burnt like her last few attempts.

"A few of them even puffed up!" She pointed happily to a second, smaller bundle. "Just help me make sure your mum gets first pick of those ones, eh?"

She ripped a piece of the one she was holding for him to try.

"Not bad," he said, chuckling. "Just in time for Harry to hire that cook for you and put an end to this debacle once and for all. It's been a valiant attempt on your part, but I know you're as sick of it as the rest of us are."

"Not until I figure this out, he won't," she said, pure determination. "I'm too bloody close. If a cook comes into my house, it will be because I want them here, not because I'm incapable."

Over dinner that night, they all celebrated over Anjali's success, debating the benefits and downsides of hiring a cook to join the housekeeper they'd already brought on. The most salient thing in that conversation, though, was that no matter how it resolved, the possibility of turning that work back over

182 *To Sketch a Scandal*

to Warren was not addressed, as if they'd all forgotten he'd ever even done it.

And for the first time since he could remember, the fact of that only stung a bit, rather than flaring into full-blown resentment. Those big things he'd been doing...they were not the only way to prove his worth. Or show his love.

That said, even though it didn't seem he'd be picking the cooking back up anytime soon, he was still well aware that a layer of good food went a long way if you wanted to get someone to stomach something they might otherwise have difficulty digesting.

"I'll show you how to get all the rotis to puff," he whispered to Anjali later that evening, while Mother and Harry were deep in discussion about some suspiciously-noble exploit of his from his time at sea. "If you'll do me a favor."

David Forester was as "partial to a good curry" as any lifelong Londoner. Though the improvement in Anjali's cooking was pretty marginal compared with what Warren and the widows had been putting together back at the house, it had still been made at home, and was therefore a good step better than what one could get from shops that cooked with customers like Forester in mind from the start. After a stolen moment teaching her how to use the stove's flame to her best advantage in the bread-puffing department, she agreed to pack him up some of the leftovers to bring along to the club.

"What for, exactly?" she asked.

"I've got to butter up my boss," he said with a grin. "And since you didn't burn the butter quite so badly this time—"

A flick of flour in his face cut him off. "Oh hush." They both laughed. "Butter him up for what?"

"I'm trying to help a friend get admission to the club," he said vaguely. "It's sort of exclusive, you know."

"Oh, we know that," came a low voice from the doorway

behind Warren. He turned to find Harry leaning against the jamb, changed to bright silk trousers and robe after dinner, since unlike Warren, he was not going anywhere else at this hour. Considering how far he'd gone for adventure in his youth, he was proving to have mellowed into a rather retiring sort of chap these days, even if he did not look it. "*White's* sure is known to be very exclusive."

Warren envied Matty his blankness as his own face cracked into an incriminating grimace.

"Love, don't give him a hard time," said Anjali, a sigh in her voice like this was not the first time they'd discussed Warren in the recent past.

"I'm not," said Harry. "I was actually just a little peckish, if you must know. Didn't mean to interrupt." He went about applying butter and sugar to some of the remaining rotis, a snack they used to sneak as boys that he now indulged in in his own house without an ounce of shame. He brought enough to the table to go around.

"Thanks," Warren said as politely as he could. "But I have to go."

"No, you don't," said Harry with a casual shrug. "There is nothing necessary about your weekends away, Warren, just as there's no real need for Anjali to do all this kitchen work when there's a hundred cooks who'd be more than happy to handle it for her." Anjali gave him an offended look but he just ripped a piece off his roti and stuffed it in his mouth. Once he'd got it down, he went on. "That one's a matter of pride and household harmony, of course, but when it comes to you and your club, Warren? I'm not sure we all have quite the same understanding of your charade that it's needed. I'm supporting the family, and you have a new enterprise in your art that suits you and your station better than that serving ever will. And since you let it slip to Mother that you've been lying about what you're doing—"

"I do work as a bartender at an exclusive club," Warren

snapped, nervous about the turn in the conversation. "It's not White's. Fine. I admit it—I exaggerated the status of it. But I'm not a complete liar."

"Just an incomplete one. Right." Harry busied himself with his sweet for a moment until Warren couldn't take the suspense a second longer.

"What do you want me to say?" he said. "If you wanted all the details of what I did to keep us afloat while you might as well have been on the bloody moon for a decade, you should have considered checking in occasionally. I don't owe you an explanation."

"Perhaps not," he admitted. "But you owe Mother one. She won't let you see it, but she's in a state over not knowing where you're actually going on the weekends, especially now that you don't need the money."

"Maybe I want to have a bit of my own money," he spat. "Ever think of that?"

"Please don't panic, Warren," Harry said. His smugness gave way to a misty sort of smile. "I've been on the sea a long time, remember. I'm well aware that there are more reasons a man might keep two lives than the obvious evils that a mother's mind jumps to. And I also know you shouldn't ask certain questions about those reasons once everyone's feet are on dry land. *I* won't ask you those questions. But Mother is asking them of me, and soon, she will ask them of you directly. It's fraying her nerves, not understanding what you're up to. Surely, you don't want to see her suffering over you."

Warren's shoulders slumped at the idea. "Of course I don't."

"Then if you are going to continue with whatever life you've built up on the side now that you don't have the excuse of poverty to cover it, the three of us need to get a story straight," he said. "One that is as honest as possible, but vague enough so we don't see anyone—you or Mother—hurt too badly."

There were several very unpleasant things about this, not least of which was the idea of more purposefully lying to his mother. He'd built his story up bit by bit over the years, slowly and inexorably enough that it no longer felt like deceit. But it was.

"You'd do that?" Warren said. "Help me make it all work? Why?"

Harry and Anjali met eyes very briefly.

"We saw how you drew him," Harry said very simply.

Warren froze.

"Drew who?" he asked.

"Your friend," said Harry, not unkindly. "Mr. Shaw, I believe it was?"

He knew he should have taken that bloody drawing out of his sketchbook, that it said too much somehow. He looked desperately between Harry and Anjali, hoping he'd misunderstood what was being said.

Anjali, though, was nodding her surprisingly unembarrassed agreement. "As Harry said, Warren, we've been at sea a long time. So. There's no shock in it for us. Like there might be for others." She smiled and patted his hand across the table. "Affection comes in more forms than the land is always prepared to deal with. It would be understandable, if you've had to hide."

It took Warren a moment to understand what they were saying. They thought the club was some cover for meeting Matty? That Matty was a longtime lover of his, a fixture he'd built his whole life around over years, rather than a very recently acquired and admittedly ill-advised companion that had simply stumbled into that life by chance?

And they were fine with that because such lovers were perfectly alright so long as they were confined to *boats*?

He realized very suddenly that he knew as little about sea life as Anjali did about kitchen fires. He was too stunned by their neutral assessment of such a shocking conclusion to bring himself to correct them.

"Well, ah. Thank you," he said awkwardly.

186   *To Sketch a Scandal*

"Think about how you want to explain yourself to Mother," said Harry. He grinned, annoyingly likable all of a sudden. "And please, send your friend our regards. I acknowledge that you did not have it easy. I admit, I'd prefer to see you properly married, I'm glad to know you didn't face these years all alone."

Warren had come into the house with a lot on his mind, and as he left it again, laden with the cooking that constituted his mediocre bribe for Forester and the contents of that very unexpected conversation, it seemed he had ten times as much to carry along.

Forester was delighted by Warren's offering, and showed absolutely no suspicion either of its objective quality, nor of its purpose.

Once Forester was properly buttered (and a little red-faced from spice he clearly hadn't prepared himself for) and they got started on their usual bar preparations, Warren broached the subject of admitting Matty to the club as Warren's guest. If he could get a yes early enough, he might have time to fetch Matty at the Gull himself, rather than sending a messenger.

"Funny thing happened," he said as casually as possible, hardly looking up from the lime he was zesting. "You know how I'm taking that drawing class on the off-days?"

"The one with the dog?"

"That's it."

"Of course, how's it treating you?"

"Oh, fine." He gave a short rundown of what he was learning, so as not to seem overeager for what he was really trying to discuss. Forester was very friendly and supportive about the whole thing, which was heartening as he moved on to the subject of the day. "But there's something I didn't mention at first that I probably should have. It's just that I was a little slow to put the pieces together, and by the time I did... I don't know. It just didn't seem relevant."

Forester looked up from where he was mixing one of his popular cocktail syrups, a stiff movement that was substantially less buttered than Warren might have hoped.

"You're acting strange," he said. "What happened?"

"Nothing important," Warren said quickly. "Just... I realized that you might like to know that...that M—oh, what was his first name? *Matthew*, that's it—Matthew Shaw happened to be in the same class. Isn't that a funny coincidence?" He laughed, to prove just how funny it was in spite of Forester's obvious lack of amusement. "He came in on a case..." He paused as Forester's eyebrow crept up unhappily. Warren quickly changed direction. "But was taken off of it! And was having a good time, you know, in the class. So he's continuing..." Forester's look remained dark, so he veered slightly further into truth-stretching. "He continued on with it. As a hobby, you know."

Forester glared, arms crossed and lips pursed.

"He's thinking about maybe getting into a new field," Warren said, stretching the truth until it bloody snapped. He hadn't meant to do that, but now that he'd started... "He's not much getting along with the other detectives at the moment, it seems." Now there was a lot of truth in that, too much, probably, because Forester's mouth grew grimmer still. "Might like to get out of the situation, he says, so he's taking the opportunity—"

"He's been in this class from the beginning?" Forester said, voice very dry. No butter to be found.

Warren winced. "Yes?"

"And you waited until now to say something?"

"He's not bothering anyone. Just minding his own business as he...considered maybe starting over in something new."

"An endeavor he's apparently told *you* all about?" He paused, ostensibly to give Warren a chance to explain himself. When that didn't happen, he went on. "Come off it, mate. I've known you too long. What's this really about?"

It was much easier to lie to his mother than to Forester.

188   *To Sketch a Scandal*

Mother wanted to believe the best of him; Forester, on the other hand, was perfectly comfortable with the fact that not all Warren's qualities were admirable.

Warren squared himself and took a breath, pausing until he could gather up the pieces of honesty he'd tossed to the wind and try again fresh.

"Turns out I like the fellow quite a bit," he admitted at last. "We've struck up a friendship. I want you to let him join me here tonight. I'm willing to speak for him, and take all responsibility for the outcome, same as any guest."

David Forester was a largely indulgent sort of man. He dealt with every idiosyncrasy under the sun running a place like this, and still found the generosity, night after night, to pair up as many of his beloved patrons as possible. He had a soft heart somewhere in there, and was notoriously, almost annoyingly romantic. Warren had hoped that that was the side of Forester who would hear his request.

However, everyone knew that alongside all this sentimentality, Forester had a temper on him. And just now, his face was reddening, giving away that this less admirable aspect of him was the one peeking out to meet Warren's creative truthtelling face-to-face.

Fuck. He really, really shouldn't have lied.

"And why," Forester said quietly, "would I change my mind about having him in here? I've already told you my thoughts on this matter."

"You told me he saved your life," Warren reminded him. "He saved the club. He is the reason we are both standing here right now, free to debate how best to engage with him. I understand your hesitance. His relationship to you is messy, it really is. But who isn't a little messy round here?"

Warren gave a good insiders smile and nudged Forester with his elbow.

Forester was not moved.

"*Messy*? He's a bit beyond messy, Warren," he said. "He pretended to work as my valet for nearly six months. Lying the whole bloody time without so much as a *wince*. Better liar than you are, by far, I'll say that much for him."

"Forester, I'm—"

"Shaw cleared this place of all wrongdoing, yes." Forester bowled over him. "Did he mention to you—dear friends that you are—that he achieved that feat by *burning the evidence*? Forget speaking for him here: he's on the official record as having spoken for *us*. Do you have any idea what would happen to us—or to Mr. Shaw himself—if he were caught hanging around here, after convincing a judge I was so innocent that they should sell me the bloody building after Henry Belleville shot himself over all the evidence that your friend Mr. Shaw *didn't* destroy?"

The bad temper was catching; Warren felt the acid spring up on his tongue before the words came.

"Let's not get sentimental over Lord Bellville, alright?" he sneered. "That 'other evidence' was about him doing a hell of a lot worse than what we're doing here. He was a monster in those enterprises, and he treated you like shit. If Matty's the reason I don't have to see his ugly face anymore, I like him all the better for it."

Forester blinked in disbelief. At first, Warren regretted letting loose with such a fiery admonition about a dead man, but it seemed that wasn't the worst of his mistakes.

"*Matty*?" Forester repeated.

Fuck.

"Forester—"

"I am not trying to get sentimental," interrupted Forester, half through his teeth, because if there was anything in the world to get his temper going stronger, it was bringing up the nasty old owner of this place, whose nasty death had left a very nasty mark on his mind to this day. "I am trying to get you to

190 *To Sketch a Scandal*

realize that there is a gravity to the situation between me and your *Matty* that is beyond the bounds of what I can control at the Fox. We are all on thin ice right now. We've got *two* members jailed already, Warren, and the law's been in place for less than a year. Two members, serving two years each. My only consolation is that it did not happen on my property, and I swear to God right now: it never will. I will not have him luring police interest to my doorstep, not even accidentally. I will not have *him* arrested on my watch, either—if he is ever found here, Warren, he will face a sort of trouble the rest of us will only know in nightmares. It would be irresponsible of me to take on a risk like this. For us. For him. For you. For everyone."

It was hard logic to argue with, but the injustice of it made Warren so angry, he went for it anyway. "He helped us," he said. "Helped you, especially. Risk aside, subjecting him to loneliness is a poor way to repay that, and you know it."

"I am not subjecting him to loneliness." Forester waved an arm toward the door with its bells, which seemed very silent now, not giving the slightest jangle in Warren's defense. "There is company to be had all over London."

"Well, it's my…rather, *our* company that he wants," Warren snapped. "And I think he's more than earned a shot at it."

"Why do you care so much?" Forester said. "Are you…" He paused, his anger slipping at last. "Warren, is it more than a friendship we're talking about here? Have you… Bloody hell, you have, haven't you?" Warren didn't need to answer. His reputation did it for him. Forester sighed and rubbed his hands over his face. When he removed them, he was laughing, and while it was partially bitter, it was not entirely so. "Warren, have you gone and fallen in love with the sodding detective?"

His voice, at last, had relaxed into something easier to work with. It was what Forester liked best, people falling in love. But unfortunately, the words he formed in that friendlier voice made panic shoot up Warren's spine.

"I haven't *fallen in love* with anyone," he snapped before he could decide whether it was the wisest thing to say or even whether it was true. He had no interest in examining that second one too closely just now. He folded his arms and shook his hair out of his eyes, feeling half a smirk warping his features. "Since when do I have to fall in love with someone to have a little fun after class, eh? We're friends. That's the extent of the sentiment I'm built for."

Forester met his eye questioningly, and Warren did not blink. He couldn't quite deny to himself that his feelings for Matty were beyond his usual bounds, but he was not prepared to go admitting to anything so dramatic as love. That seemed like a far greater threat to his peace at The Curious Fox than the presence of Matty Shaw.

"In that case," Forester said carefully, "I'm sorry, Warren. I do not take on patrons I cannot protect. Protection is what they pay me for. It's not the rooms. It's not the company. It's not the chandelier. It's the fact that I have my methods of keeping them out of trouble. The safeguards I have in place for the others would do nothing for someone so instantly recognizable to the rozzers as Mr. Shaw would be. Nothing." He shuddered. "I really am sorry, Warren." He stoppered up the syrup he'd made, wiped his hands, and started for the back. "I'm going to make up the beds. If you don't want to work tonight, I'll understand."

Warren stared at the front door, where he'd so hoped to bring Matty through those curtains and spend a little time together, in the only place he could think of where that would be easy. Where the company could be trusted. Where Warren spent this half of his life.

You'd go behind his back like that? Just to see me?

"Nah," he said. "I… I understand what you're saying. You're right. I'll just suck it up and get through the night."

Forester gave a grim but clearly pleased nod. "You want me

to find you some good company to sneak off with? No falling in love required, I promise."

Warren went back to his limes. This was disappointing, but as it wasn't the end, he took a deep breath and determined to wait it out.

"It's no fun sneaking away from my post if my boss orchestrates it, Forester," he said, letting a good-natured tease take over the frustration in his voice. "I'll handle my own sneaking as usual, thank you very much."

Chapter Fourteen

Matty

It was incredible just how many personal objects could wind up in an office after some ungodly number of years. Barrows brought a large valise from home on this last day of his to gather them up, though Matty had needed to find another crate in the storage cupboard to catch what would not fit. There were framed photographs of his family, doodles and stick-and-glue creations from his grandchildren, little tins or bits of silverware from a decade of meals taken at desks during long days, kerchiefs and sweaters and a sock, even, which neither of them could remember him taking off and leaving for dead in a box of other sundry at the bottom of the closet. Not to mention the office supplies, the ink bottles and notebooks and more pens than seemed proper. Paperweights and fidgety trinkets to fuss around with while thinking things through. A little of everything, it seemed, all the proof of his life and his presence and the standard-issue humanity that would eventually lead all of them to cleaning their desks out and moving on in the end.

Matty hadn't even noticed just how much of Barrows made up the office until it was gone. A lot of it had been, quite

194   *To Sketch a Scandal*

frankly, junk. While it was hard to recall which individual objects were missing from the shelves, the room looked empty without them.

He wondered what Detective Ashton would fill the place with when he took over that desk. Barrows's position had not been filled when Matty proved undesirable for it. Instead, things were merely shuffled around, so it would be Matty and his dearest Scotland Yard chum in here starting tomorrow.

"Well, Matthew."

Matty turned. Barrows was standing near the door with his hat on, the valise clutched in his hand, the crate by his feet. With his mark on the office gone and his badge already left on Superintendent Frost's desk, he looked out of place in this room he'd been such an integral part of.

"I suppose that's it," Barrows went on. "I think we've swept out every corner."

Fortunately, with all his training, Matty's eyes never wept anymore without his mind's permission. So though his belly was churning and his throat felt lumpy, he could work around all that without a single tremble in his voice. "Not quite every corner, sir."

He dug in his clothes—his Scotland Yard clothes, not the artsy ones he'd started wearing on his own time, all plain grays or browns, not exactly a uniform in this department but nearly as unchanging as one—and took out the ring on its chain. It was a shame it had to go this way, but at least Warren had found the ring to give back in the first place. They'd have this bit of closure amid this lackluster and uncelebratory parting that had replaced the exciting handover of duties they'd expected.

Matty held it out by the chain, not even daring to touch this symbol of his thwarted successes.

Barrows just stared at it.

"Take it," Matty said, when he could not stand the wait another second. "I'm not getting the promotion. I bungled things so badly, in fact, that no one is. So take it back. Please."

"Matthew, it was a gift, I don't—"

"Please," he said again, through gritted teeth this time. The intensity spurred Barrows to action. At last, he held out his palm and Matty dropped the ring in.

"It's just that I'd have thought you'd want to keep it anyway," Barrows said quietly, hand still open, giving Matty a chance to take it back.

"Well, I don't." Matty shoved his own hands in his pockets, out of reach of any attempt at return.

With a grim nod, Barrows tucked the thing away in his coat. "I'll hang on to it for you, then. For now."

Until when? Matty did not say, did not shout right in the old man's face somehow. *When you invite me for tea and pastries? Have me over to meet your grandchildren? To have supper with your wife who always resented the time I spent in your house?* These things would not happen. If they were to, Barrows would have made some indication of it by now. He was leaving. This was final.

And Matty, for his part, couldn't bear to extend it another second. He stooped and gathered up the crate, hefting it onto his hip so he could use the other hand to open the door.

"Let's get you to your coach, sir," he said as kindly as possible. "You've got a whole new world out there waiting for you."

He saw Barrows off, and when he returned to the office alone, he gave his eyes permission to do as they pleased for a good long while.

It was a very good thing Warren had given Matty something to look forward to after all that. After such a shit show of a workday, he clung to the idea that there might be somewhere else he was wanted. If Warren could convince Mr. Forester that Matty could be trusted, he would finally spend a real evening at The Curious Fox.

196   *To Sketch a Scandal*

He dutifully went to the pub Warren had suggested, drinking stout and practicing his shading while he waited for the summons that would let him know the conversation had gone well. He waited. And waited. And waited further, the agreed-upon midnight coming and going without a word.

Just in case, he gave it an extra half-hour before losing hope. Eventually, though, the absence of a messenger became just as clear as the presence of one might have been. Mr. Forester had said no. It was on to plan B, then, where Matty would meet Warren at the club come morning instead, just the two of them. Better than nothing. Better than a lot of things. He ought to be satisfied with it.

He downed his final glass thinking back to his visit to The Curious Fox, and further back, to his months in Mr. Forester's employment. After a day like today, the time he'd spent pretending to be his valet, making steady progress on the case and being treated well in the meantime, suddenly seemed like it might have been the peak of his Scotland Yard career. A downhill slide was all that awaited him now.

Focused as he was on the morning ahead, he still had to figure out what to do with himself in the meantime. He could go back to his room for the night. But his limbs were heavy from more disappointment than he could have ever expected from something that shouldn't have been a surprise at all. After having been denied the bright, debauched comradery he'd been hoping for, the last place he wanted to land was in his own bed.

He opted to take a room at the public house to save himself the trip. The stout and the supper provided were thick enough that they lulled him to sleep more thoroughly than he had expected in the circumstances.

In the morning, as he tried to get his hair to behave before a dingy little mirror, he regretted his laziness the night before. During the haze of waiting, he'd been focused on the possible night ahead of him, imagining himself introduced to Warren's friends until they were ready to sneak off into some secluded corner, as was apparently Warren's habit. He'd forgotten that what Warren wanted first and foremost was to draw him. *Properly.* That might prove easier if Matty did not look precisely like he'd freshened himself up in the meager offerings of a cheap public house.

When he'd done all he could, he spent a moment with the glass. Matty had spent a lot of time looking at himself in glasses, creating impeccable and case-appropriate visages for himself. As he failed at his task this morning, he realized something that deepened a line that was starting to develop between his eyebrows. He'd been wrong at the start of this doomed case, when he thought he'd never done anything creative. That wasn't true at all. It was simply that he himself was the creation. Or the look of him, anyway. He'd always liked the way he looked—how could he not?—but it never seemed to have much to do with *him*. With Matty's own person. What he created in the glass might have been a painting on the wall for all he related to it.

This morning though, frustrated though he was with the insufficiency of his canvas and tools, he found something very different in his reflection. He could see himself, see the little circles that had appeared after a hard day and unsatisfying night. The continued roughness of his chin; he could have requested a razor to take care of that if he'd wanted to, but he hadn't because he was used to it now. There was the interminable rumple of his clothes that gave away the night they'd spent tossed over a chair, parts of the linen simply rinsed in last night's water bowl and left to dry freshened but a little crunchy. All the flaws he was used to smoothing away bore witness to something real, some experience, some choice he'd made, some feeling he'd had.

He liked it. He liked it quite a lot.

So though it did not seem right to sit for a portrait in this state, he opted not to head back to his room to put himself together. Maybe it was foolish, and maybe he was wrong, but some little voice inside told him that Warren might just like it too.

198 *To Sketch a Scandal*

★ ★ ★

Matty did the knock at The Curious Fox's door. Figured, didn't it, that Mr. Forester was practical enough to bar Matty from the place, yet too sentimental to change his bloody secret knock after his last scrape with disaster. The pattern had significance from his and his lover Mr. Clarke's schoolboy days, and Mr. Forester, being a romantic, had of course found another use for it.

God, it would be bloody embarrassing to run into him after all this. He hoped he hadn't come too early. Or too late. He was not prepared to deal with such an awkward encounter after seeing Barrows off yesterday...

Last time Matty was here, he'd been met with a ledger, a doorman, and a lot of questions about his references and identity.

But when the door opened this time, it was the welcoming figure of Warren on the other side of it.

"You came," he said happily.

Matty felt a wide smile cross his face before he could stop it. "You doubted?"

"Of-fucking-course I doubted." Warren laughed. "It was a mad enough scheme."

"Guess I was mad enough to go along with it." Matty peered behind him into the darkness of the entryway. "Anyone else here?"

"Just me, as promised."

"I can't believe you're doing this."

Warren took a measured breath. "Me, neither."

Matty crossed the threshold with a sense of danger. The sense melted, though, when Warren—much fresher than Matty was, warm and sparkling and clean-smelling—tugged him in by the hips without delay and kissed him warmly before they'd even come through the belled curtains. The kiss made him feel awaited and wanted and dissolved all concern for what might be happening elsewhere. As Matty's hands framed Warren's face, he realized his gloves were still on. The lack of real contact frustrated his fingers, but increased the delight of his lips—the only lucky part of him that got to revel in what they'd ached for all night.

"Take your coat?" Warren whispered when he came up for air.

"That will be a decent enough start." The core of him trembled as Warren slipped his coat off, his hat, his gloves. "So. I take it Mr. Forester said no."

"He did," Warren confirmed tersely as they hung up Matty's things. "For your own good, supposedly. Said he won't bring in a patron he can't save in the event of a raid."

"Smart man," Matty admitted. "He's right about that, you know. If I were recognized by the wrong person somewhere like this…"

Matty couldn't bring himself to continue. Warren still did not know that Matty was plagued by rumors at Scotland Yard, ones that had not been helped by his bungling of the fraud case. In spite of all Ashton's warm "friendship," the promotion was a lost cause, the memory of the ring haunting him as his fingers searched unthinkingly for it against his chest. Whether he'd go from detective to suspect himself now that Barrows was gone still remained to be seen. Being here was a bloody terrible idea, and if that was Mr. Forester's reasoning, Matty couldn't blame him.

"You want to leave?" Warren asked.

Matty shook his head. "Nothing will happen in the daylight. But he has a point about the nights, much as I hate to admit it. Does he know I'm here?"

Warren swallowed so hard, Matty could see his throat move above the points of his collar. "No."

"Will he ever?"

"Not if I can help it."

"What happens if he finds out?"

200   *To Sketch a Scandal*

But Warren was shaking his head, clearly too agitated by this line of conversation to continue. "Forget him," Warren snapped. "He owes us both better than he's giving us, so forget all about him." He came back to Matty, touching his face, tracing fingers over his lips and neck until the protective bubble of good feeling returned to block out the risks they were taking. When they came up for air, Warren took Matty's hand and led him to the parlor, which was deserted and in disarray.

"Looks like everyone had fun last night," said Matty. Lots of fun. Without him.

"Some more than others," Warren quipped bitterly.

"It looks a lot different, during the day."

Warren laughed. "Yeah. Looks like what it really is, don't it? It's not as rich an enterprise as it could be—everything's pawned or scrounged or has been here for years. It's all lights and smoke and a shot of gin making it pretty when it needs to be."

"Relatable, that is." Matty ran a hand down his face, wondering if he'd made the right choice to come here looking like a certified beast. "You might need some of those things, to pretty me up today. Especially if you're still planning to draw me."

"Nah." Warren grabbed him again, this time by the scarf he'd left behind when he took the rest of Matty's outdoor things. The purpose of the supposed oversight was suddenly clear. He pulled Matty in until their noses touched, then ran a thumb down both his lips. "You look incredible."

"I look like I spent the night in a moderately seedy pub after staying up past midnight waiting on news that never came, put the same clothes back on, didn't shave, and was able to brush my teeth only due to the generosity of a probable prostitute after buying a toothbrush off her that she swears was never used."

Warren stopped the story with a playful kiss. "It's nice to see you fitting into the neighborhood."

Before Matty knew what happened, one kiss had turned into two, into three, into a whirlwind of them. This compulsion was

Jess Everlee 201

seriously slowing their progress, and Matty started to wonder if they'd ever make it across the parlor. But after some indefinite span of hazy time, Warren took him by the scarf again and led him to the back of the room, across a threshold that no officer of the law was supposed to cross under any circumstance.

The doorway that led to the Fox's private rooms.

More belled curtains hung spaced at intervals through the hall. Clever. The curtains seemed pretty and whimsical, but were clearly more than décor. Rough movement through them would serve a subtle warning, and sneaking around would be out of the question. The deceptively innocent twinkle of the bells surrounded Matty as Warren tugged him impatiently along to the last door on the right. If there were anyone around to hear them, their tryst would be over by now. It was comforting that the bells' cry for caution merely dissipated into the air to join the mellowed mist of last night's incense and pipe smoke.

Unlike the rest of the club, which was clearly in its shabby-morning-coat phase of the day, the private room was in its pearl-encrusted midnight drags, the four-poster sporting piles of silken pillows, the lamps shaded in red and pink, and a cone of incense lit in a dish before the vanity mirror, its fragrant line of smoke doubled in the glass. Someone had put effort into making this one room into a haven set apart from the rest of the club. The rest of the world, even.

Warren scratched the back of his neck as their eyes adjusted to the dimmer light. He looked uncharacteristically sheepish.

"Too much?" he said. "I dunno, I was just here alone this morning, and I knew the rest of the place was going to look fucking beastly at this hour, so I thought..." He trailed off, trying to read Matty's face. "It's too much. You want to go back out?"

Matty shook his head, trying to drag himself out of the shock. "No, it's gorgeous, it's just..." He touched the crystalline decanter of some shining liqueur that had been left on the low table. "No one's ever done anything like this for me before."

Warren did a double take. "No one?"

"No one *real*," Matty corrected, his voice rasped with regret. "No one who knew who I was when they did it."

He preferred not to get into the details of that. Fortunately, Warren seemed to get what he meant on the first go.

"About time, then," he said. Then he laughed with relief. "Thank God. I thought you hated it. I'm no romantic, really. I honestly don't know why—"

Matty cut him off with a kiss on the cheek. "It's wonderful, Warren. Thank you."

"Well, let's get started, then, shall we?" he said, uneasiness melting. "First though, I have a request."

"What's that?" said Matty.

"Will you do as I say?" He gently unwound the scarf from Matty's neck. "I meant what I said at the end of class. I want to draw you. Properly. I've had a surge of inspiration, but the vision is specific, and I need to you do exactly as I say if we're going to get it right."

Matty very much hoped Warren was planning to draw him with a most furious cockstand if he was going to keep talking like that. Like they weren't just randy art-class friends who could never be more, but like he was a real artist and Matty was his muse.

"Anything." Matty's mind raced with thoughts of what might be asked of him, heart keeping perfectly in step as it thumped faster in his chest. "Tell me what to do, and I'll do it. Whatever you say."

"That's what I like to hear," Warren rasped with a little smile that sent a pleasant shiver down Matty's spine. In the suggestive light of this room built for one thing, Warren threw Matty's swiped scarf around his own neck like the lumpy thing was some fabulous feather boa. The movement was so natural, so genuine and beautiful, that Matty nearly had to close his eyes to recover from it. The full force of exactly who he was here with—this stunningly gorgeous creature with a devilishly feminine edge and a dangerous secret, one-in-the-same with an obvious mama's boy who loved his family and told silly jokes in an art class he was too talented for by far—was suddenly overwhelming.

"Now," Warren said. "Hold still."

With almost painfully deliberate movements, Warren started mussing up Matty's clothes, pocketing his tie and unbuttoning his shirt. When he opened his eyes, he found Warren focused on him. But he was not, as Matty might have thought, putting him back together or trying to smooth out all the wrinkles of his appearance. In fact, he seemed to be doing quite the opposite, moving bits of his hair around so they fell into his face, stripping his jacket, rumpling his collar, and then...

"Very still," he whispered against Matty's mouth. Matty froze as he was pressed with a breathtakingly hard kiss, Warren biting and sucking on his bottom lip. They stood so close Matty could feel the fabric of their trousers whispering to each other, and *very still* proved torturous as every instinct urged his hips forward, just a little, just enough...

"There." Warren pulled back, inspecting his handiwork on Matty's lips with gaze and gentle fingers. "Nice and plump."

"Are you trying to kill me?"

"Can you think of a better way to go?"

"Not really."

"Well, then." He squeezed Matty's arse and gave it a pat. "On the bed with you."

That was not an instruction Matty resented in the slightest until he realized that Warren was not joining him. Instead, he dragged a chair over to the bedside, adjusted the pillows so Matty could recline comfortably on his side, and took up his sketchbook.

To Sketch a Scandal

"Really?" Matty groaned. "You're really going to do this now? I confess, I've been half-hoping it was all just foreplay."

"Hush, you're a model, you're not supposed to talk."

"And what if I do?" Matty licked his lips, hoping to entice Warren over with memories of what he'd done the last time he had to keep Matty quiet.

Warren's eyes flashed, sweeping up and down Matty's body with obvious temptation. But he resisted, turning back to his work. His hand moved expertly over the page. "Then I'll have to draw you with a gag in," he said simply. "But if I do that, I worry it won't be suitable for the gallery night. At the end of the class, you know."

"The gallery night?" What Matty could see of his own body was half-done clothing and his cock straining his buttons something dreadful. "Warren, if you draw me like this for the gallery night, with or without a gag, we'll be carrying our certificates behind our backs on the way out."

"Why?"

"Handcuff joke."

Warren didn't laugh, but went on drawing, unconcerned. "You ever used those off the clock, love?"

"Can't say I have."

"Good fun." He nodded to a well-notched bedpost. "Got stuck to that one once, though. Idiot lost the key in the pillows and was too drunk to find it. Had to go for help. Not my finest hour."

"Is there anything you haven't done in these rooms?"

Warren paused. He smiled to himself, as if surveying half a life of debauchery, before the smile softened. He may even have blushed, through it was hard to tell in here.

"This," he said, not looking up from his paper. Though they'd been quipping back and forth, there was something very vulnerable in his voice. "I've never done anything like this. No one but Forester even knows I like drawing, much less seen me do it."

The confession sobered Matty's wit, though had the opposite effect on his wanting. He fell silent at last, burning quietly and steadily with no outlet as he watched Warren watch him. Matty hadn't done anything like this, either. Oh, he'd sat pretty dozens of times, was stared at, treated like an object under such dehumanizing circumstances that no guilt remained by the time the other officers relieved him of the role.

But Warren wasn't doing that. He wasn't looking at Matty like he was an inanimate work of beauty put there for his enjoyment. Instead, he was studying like he wanted to preserve something fleeting and alive. At first, Matty was nervous to move too much, but his adjustments were met with interest and more furious sketching. After some number of minutes or hours (things had gone disconcertingly timeless), Warren got him a little glass of that liqueur and adjusted something on him that seemed more an excuse to touch him than anything else. When he got back to it, Matty stopped trying to stay so still, and the more natural he behaved, the more focused Warren seemed to get.

He was clearly seeing *something*. Something that interested him more than mere looks. Something Matty himself was ignorant of, but grew unbearably curious about the longer it went on. At a certain point, he no longer knew what he was looking forward to more: Warren climbing into this bed with him at last, or turning that sketchbook around so Matty might see what he'd seen.

Warren finally slowed his pace, doing little bits here and there before putting the pad face down on his lap.

"Finished?" said Matty.

"For now." He glanced at the work one more time, then put it back down. "I've got enough of what I needed. I should be able to finish the rest from memory. You can relax."

206   *To Sketch a Scandal*

"Can I see it?"

Warren hesitated, then shook his head. "Not yet."

Matty was surprised. He hadn't been shy about any of his drawings at all so far. The change was charming enough to dampen the disappointment Matty might have felt.

"Come here, then," he said, moving over on the bed.

He half-expected some new excuse, but Warren stood up. How long, precisely, he'd been sporting that cockstand while he sketched, Matty did not know, but it was instantly apparent that he'd found this whole enterprise as erotic as Matty had. Though he'd been playing it cool again up until now, a distinctly hot eagerness took over as he got right on top of Matty without any hesitation, pressing their bodies tight together and sighing with obvious relief.

They were lost to it within seconds. The teasing and the looking and the wanting had gone on so long that to finally touch like this was pure heaven. Once they started, it was wildfire, tearing at clothes, rubbing against each other, coaxing moans out of the other's mouths. Matty wanted this man like he could not recall wanting anyone before, and the most disorienting thing was how much Warren seemed to want him back. His hands were eager; his tongue was desperate. So suave, so clever, so put together he'd been, even that last time when he'd taken Matty's mouth. But the delay or the drawing or something had changed in him. By the time they'd banished their clothes and half the pillows to the floor and slipped under the sheets, he looked nearly undone with desire. If Matty could draw, it was this he would immortalize.

"Please," Warren whispered, just under Matty's ear, teasing the lobe with his tongue and panting. Matty could feel that first promise of Warren's spend cooling on his thigh. "Please, sweetheart. I can't wait another second."

Sweetheart again. Matty tried not to be too overcome. It was a pet name and a lark and the sort of thing one said in moments like this, but Matty was miles away from his reason and the word rang like bells through his whole being no matter how he tried to stop it.

While Warren rummaged in the bedside drawer, Matty went to his hands and knees, shocked when he raised his head to see his own face staring back at him, Warren naked and kneeling behind him, looking like the very wildest of wild dreams.

"What the devil?" he muttered. He must not have noticed when all the pillows were in the way, but there was a bloody *mirror* tacked to the headboard. "You Fox lot are going to hell. Every last one of you."

Warren laughed like a bloke who, Matty remembered, probably didn't believe in quite the same hell, and wasn't about to let it stop him either way. He kissed his way up Matty's back, tailbone to nape, finally resting his chin on Matty's shoulder. They locked eyes in the mirror, and in that moment, that throwaway word, that offhand *sweetheart* rang straight back down Matty's spine, the same way the kisses had come seconds before. He liked the idea of being, not just Warren's friend or his fuck or even his muse. But being his sweetheart. He didn't kid himself that he was any such thing, but he coddled the thought anyway. Sweethearts. He'd never had one of those. Overcome as he was now, he could do nothing but pretend to himself that it was true.

"Ready for me?" Warren whispered.

"Well past," Matty gasped, pressing back. He'd happily take Warren with the least of provisions, but his *sweetheart* was more chivalrous than all that. It was tongue first, then slicked fingers, then...

He could see Warren's face in the mirror as he pushed inside, his rapture perfect and a thing impossible to capture by even the best artist. That expression and the pleasure Matty felt beneath him was all *here and now*, it was all movement and sweat and the living gasps and moans there was no need to stifle in this nest Warren had built for him for no reason but care. Dear God, maybe they weren't anything so sweet as sweethearts, but Warren was still risking so much to be here with him. So bloody much. They both were. But how could they regret it for a second, if the seconds had been even half as perfect as they were right now?

Warren gripped his hips tight and threw his head back as he found his climax in a hard, messy rhythm, eyes squeezed shut and mouth open. There was a hand stroking Matty (whether it was his, Warren's, or some combination would be lost to him by morning next), but it was the sight of Warren in the mirror, mixed with the hot contact, that did him in. Matty dissolved at last in a peak beyond his imagining before his strength or maybe just his will gave out and he collapsed upon the ruined pillows with Warren still on him, still in him, kissing his shoulders and licking his neck until they found it within themselves to disengage.

Face-to-face now, Matty wanted to say something. But Warren found words first.

"Don't leave," he whispered. He was still panting, black strands plastered to his forehead with sweat, gripping Matty's hand and looking far more family-boy than wily bartender all of a sudden. "I'll come up with any excuse you need. But don't leave. Not yet."

That Warren thought for even a moment that Matty would rush out the door made him wonder about the quality of the other lovers he'd taken in this room. Matty knew from club gossip and hints from Warren that there had been plenty of those—indeed, he had a good sense that the illustrator of those notches on the bedpost was right here with him—but the stories were always set as jokes and mishaps. Matty was struck by a chilly notion: Warren wasn't a renter, but he did work here. When he sneaked off from his post for a bit of fun, was he treated as a real companion? Or just another beautiful club amenity? Did his lovers run out the door when they were finished for a fresh gin, leaving sticky pillows and old liqueur glasses for the man whose job it was to deal with them?

A sense of grim comradery hit Matty right in the stomach. There were certain...quirks...when one's visage was the source of his paycheck. It was very hard to be taken seriously. To secure a promotion. To get permission for a guest. To be treated like there was anything going on behind a set of eyes that earned their keep by being seen as much as they did by seeing.

"You're all the excuse I need." Matty kissed Warren's damp forehead. "I'll stay as long as you want. Hours. All day. I'll make Mr. Forester drag me out by the ankle kicking and screaming, if you ask me to, Warren, I swear to God."

Warren smiled at the notion, then rested his head on Matty's chest, swirling a lazy finger through the hair he'd been able to stop obsessively trimming during his stint as an "artist." While he was still a bit ambivalent about the beard, he didn't miss that task one bit, and decided then and there that he was done with it.

"You're dear to me, Matty," Warren whispered. "I don't know when it happened. But you've become very dear to me."

"And you to me," Matty replied without a moment's hesitation.

Warren snorted out a sleepy giggle. "What the devil are we going to do about that, d'you think?"

Matty had no idea. This was terribly inadvisable new territory they were in. Inconvenient. Unwanted.

And absolutely irresistible.

Instead of worrying about it, though, he wrapped his arms around his unlikely lover and kissed the top of his head. "I'm sure we'll figure it out eventually."

Chapter Fifteen

Warren

They lazed in the bed for a slow, stretched-out hour that felt like the perfectly tranquil lifetime neither of them had been granted this time around, talking and touching and laughing—always laughing, the two of them, Matty's dry and occasionally twisted humor tickling Warren like no stage performer had in ages. When practical needs forced them out of the nest and back into clothes, Matty buttoned his jacket for him and playfully wrapped the scarf around Warren's neck, then accompanied him to the alley for a piss and a wander-off in search of something hot to eat—they were too ravenous from their morning for the little pantry lunches Warren usually fixed himself from the Fox's cupboards.

When they got back, Warren expected Matty to start making his excuses. He'd stayed a long time already, longer than anyone had for Warren in ages. Instead, he helped Warren put the bedroom back together without being asked, moving contentedly along to the parlor and the bar to join in the club setup. He followed instructions easily and took to the work very naturally.

Every second of it was so bloody *easy* that Warren considered

Jess Everlee 211

taking Matty up on his offer. He'd stay all day, he'd said. Stay until Forester had to drag him out. Oh, anyone might say something silly like that after a thorough bedding, but as the clock ticked forward and Matty went on dusting picture frames and fluffing pillows, showing not the slightest eagerness to leave, it started to seem like a real possibility. As Matty uncomplainingly cleaned out the grate with well-trained precision, Warren wondered whether Forester could actually look Matty in the eye and still turn him out. Forester's little hero complex could get annoying, but it came from a good place. Maybe they could work things out, if Matty was here as a human being and not an abstract concept...

He didn't have the guts, though. Not because he couldn't take the heat, nor even because he feared how Forester might drag admissions out of Warren that he wasn't ready to put words to yet. All those things were unpleasant enough. But he mostly hated the thought of ending this wonderful day on a piss-poor note. So, since Matty did not even mention leaving once—not once, all day—Warren started the farewells himself late in the afternoon.

"I'll see you in class, won't I?" Warren said, warmed from the horrid scarf still around his neck and a most thorough goodbye kiss. "Or...oh shit." His heart sank. "You're not on the case anymore. You won't be there, will you?"

"I shouldn't be," said Matty slowly. "Though...you know, I've already paid the pup for the whole session, haven't I? And it's not in the way of my work—they won't put me in charge of anything for a while, I don't think. I'm just helping out where I can at the moment. Maybe it's time for—"

"A new hobby?" Warren supplied, tickled that the lie he'd told Forester earlier might wind up true after all.

"Why not?" There were probably a lot of reasons why not, which Matty seemed to wince over as he considered, but eventually shrugged off. "I'll see you in class."

212   *To Sketch a Scandal*

"Then your place," Warren whispered.

"Thought we couldn't make a habit of that."

"We can't. It will be sporadic," Warren explained. He'd been thinking this through all day. The nearer the time of departure got, the more racing his thoughts of what came next. "And we'll just practice our sketching. Mostly."

"Ah yes, *mostly* sketching. Now there's a perfectly innocent pastime."

Warren grinned and kissed his forehead. "Back here again for the rest."

He started to unwind Matty's scarf so he could be on his way, but Matty stopped him.

"Keep it." He kissed the crooked end and tucked it back securely, patting Warren's chest right over his thumping heart. "Love in every stitch, you know."

Where, exactly, the joke ended and the truth began in that particular statement, Warren really had no idea. But after Matty left, he did not take it off all night, in spite of the teasing he got from his friends when all parts of him but that one lumpy object were pressed back into the shape of The Curious Fox's seductive barkeep.

They did just as they said in the weeks that followed. Classes were followed up by pints at the pub and further practice at Matty's house, sometimes upstairs in near-perfect privacy, sometimes down in the common area to deflect any suspicion on the part of the landlady, who came to like Warren well enough. She did comment on the oddness of their sudden friendship, but seemed so amused that quiet, serious Matty had taken on an artistic hobby and companion to match that she very much left them to it, occasionally asking harmless questions and having the kitchen girl bring them tea.

On the weekends, Matty was sneaked into the Fox off-hours. Sometimes, Warren made the bedroom nice for them

Jess Everlee 213

like he had at the first. Other times, he knew perfectly well they weren't going to make it past the parlor and didn't bother. There were blokes who went farther behind the curtained alcoves than they were supposed to per the rules of the place, but he'd bet even most devilish card-shark Noah that he was the first to be brought off right on one of the barstools with all the most garish of the daytime lights on.

It was seeming very sustainable, actually, so long as he didn't pay too much attention to Harry and Anjali's implications that he was in for it with Mother if he didn't come up with an explanation for his absences, and soon. Everyone knew he was not working at White's. Everyone knew he didn't really need to be working anywhere, much less somewhere that was such a hassle. And now that Mother and Anjali were working peaceably together at last to manage the household (which, he began to suspect when he found some odd pickles in the pantry, might be expanding in a few months, and not just from the staff they'd finally hired that the women's social responsibilities were outpacing the domestic ones), he could tell that Mother was losing patience with him.

A faint held him up one particular Friday when he was getting ready to head out to Soho.

He'd not been in the drawing room when it happened, but rather upstairs getting dressed.

His brother had recently floated the idea of hiring Warren a valet of his own, which had inspired a devilish fantasy as he brushed his coat and situated his linen. It would be scandalous indeed to bring Matty on to pretend to fill the role as he'd done in that bygone case for Forester. He couldn't help but think that valeting would be a lot more fun for Matty this time around, and certainly more fun than Scotland Yard was at the moment. An extreme shift occurred in Matty's tone when he discussed the place now that his friend or whatever the devil Barrows had been was retired, from stoic and dutiful to irritated and occasionally even despairing. He did not go into a lot of details,

214 *To Sketch a Scandal*

but Warren didn't need them to know that a building full of bobbies—even "special" ones like the "special investigators" or whatever they were called—had never been much of a picnic in the first place.

"Why don't you leave?" Warren had asked him one afternoon. Autumn was well on its way to winter by now, and they'd lit a fire in the big room's grate, huddled under the same quilt on the couch with a pot of tea before them. Matty had gone melancholy, and was glaring into the flames, so Warren had put a finger under his chin and it tipped toward himself instead until their eyes met. "You got a contract or something keeping you there? If it's shit, get out. You don't belong there anyway."

"Quite the contrary, darling," Matty'd replied with a hint of cynicism. "It's the only place I've ever belonged."

"That's not true. You belong here."

"Here? You mean the place I was literally sneaked into against the owner's explicit wishes?"

"Don't be like that." Warren had tugged the quilt more tightly around their shoulders until their noses were touching. "I meant with me."

The conversation had fizzled then, becoming more about tea-flavored kisses before the fire than anyone's deteriorating employment, but it was on Warren's mind again as he dressed. Maybe it was selfish, maybe it was mere hope that a separation from the law might change Forester's tune about Matty's presence. Either way, he now decided to float the valeting idea to Matty when next they saw each other—not seriously, of course, but the joke might get him thinking. Six months was a long time to pretend to do something, after all. He'd likely walked away with more skills than he thought. In fact, he'd been shadowing Warren during all the Fox's daily upkeep, learning his way around a bar and rented rooms. He had options, if only he could see them...

Those thoughts, though, as well as the tying of his cravat, were interrupted by the unmistakable sound of a faint downstairs. No thump or scream or anything so dramatic, but Warren was so well attuned to such things by now that it took only the sudden ceasing of far-off chatter and the gasp and rustle of guests responding to have him bolting out the door and down the stairs.

He found Mother slumped in her seat, her lemonade glass overturned in a puddle on the floor. The fashionable women she'd been chatting with clucked and fussed uselessly around her like a pack of well-dressed little birds.

"*Excuse me.*" He broke through their cluster and bent over her, checking. She was clammy. "Grab the smelling salts, madam," he said sharply to one of the women. "Under that candy dish."

"The candy...what?"

She was so terribly slow on the uptake—red-faced from an unladylike amount of wine at this hour—that Anjali managed to appear from the other room, trousers and all, and get the strategically hidden salts into Warren's hand without speaking before the lady managed to even get her distressed hand off her own bosom.

Once he'd got Mother to come to, and was supporting her as they went for the bedroom, he paused on the way out to whisper to Anjali, "Occupy the bloody useless nobs for a moment, would you?"

"If you insist, brother," she muttered back with a little wrinkle forming along the bridge of her nose.

He settled Mother into bed with the mix of brandy, hot water, and mysterious droplets her expensive new doctor had prescribed.

"Go on," she said once she was comfortable and looking more alert. "The nurse and Anjali are here for me." She paused with a top-notch sense of drama. "I know you were in a big rush to get to White's before this happened, and I'd hate to hold you up any longer than I already have."

216 *To Sketch a Scandal*

Warren did his very best not to groan. "Mother. It's not White's."

"It's White's until I get some explanation as to what other club in the city of London could inspire such loyalty."

"I'm glad to see you're feeling better so quickly."

"Don't get cheeky with me, Warren."

"I'm sorry," Warren said. He sat heavily in the chair by her bedside, finishing the knot about his neck that he'd had to leave undone. "It's just that I like the work, Mother." *Ever think of that?* he thought but did not add. In fact, he tried not to think it quite so hard either, lest she accuse him of thinking cheekily as well.

"Unless the club is prestigious in the extreme, it's below your station now," she explained. "The women were just asking me where you were off to, you know. Mrs. Applegate wanted to know if we could attend her supper party this evening. And I have to tell her that my son is…what? Serving, that's what. It doesn't reflect well, you know."

God help him.

"You're right, Mother," he sighed. "My mistake. It's White's after all."

She glared again, and nodded, and sipped at her medicine until he took the hint and got on his way.

"I don't know what to bloody tell her!" he told Matty the next day. It was them on pillows now, heaps of them in the biggest bedroom, with cups of brandy not watered down or medicated but there to warm them until they found the motivation to get dressed and fix the fires. The club was even colder today than it had been, a condition of the place much improved by Matty's company. "She knows I'm lying, but what she doesn't understand is that I have to lie. It wouldn't do her any good at all to know 'what other club inspires such loyalty.' My brother already figured it out, but he and his wife are bleeding *pirates* or something now, apparently, and just want me to handle myself in a way Mum can make sense of. No one seems to get that I liked how things were. We were poor, but we were doing pretty well, all things considered, and I liked it. Now...now I have to worry what the *neighbors* think?" He snorted a bit of bitter laughter. "Neighbors who do nothing but drink port and have dinner parties, and can't even be counted on for the least bit of help in an emergency? You know, the neighbors thought pretty highly of me on the other side of the neighborhood, I'll tell you that much. They were fighting each other to get me to marry in."

"Funny." Matty rolled half on top of him and smoothed the hair off his forehead. "For some reason, you don't strike me as the marrying type."

"Wonder where you got that impression." He squeezed Matty's arse and tugged him in tight. "Anyway. Got any brilliant advice for me?"

"Brilliant advice?" Matty raised a brow. "Warren, have I told you about my relationship with my mother?"

"No."

Matty paused. It had clearly been a quip that had been met with more sincerity than he anticipated.

"That's because I don't have one," he said grimly. "There's no advice to give."

It struck Warren that things had been a little one-sided in their conversations. Matty talked a lot about his failing occupation, Detective Barrows, and the others at Scotland Yard. He never went further back into his history than those professional relationships.

"Can I ask what happened, there?" Warren half-expected Matty to balk. He did go quiet for a disconcertingly long time, busying himself with little kisses across Warren's chest. But eventually, he rested his chin on Warren's shoulder and drew breath to speak.

"Not a lot to say," he said. He traced Warren's collarbones

218   *To Sketch a Scandal*

softly as he talked. "She was not married, and I was not wanted. I was probably better off with her than I'd have been at an orphanage, but she paid me little mind beyond keeping me alive. She had more pressing interests of gin and makeshift fathers for me, men who'd come round for a few months before packing up, never to be heard from again. The last of those fellows that I ever met suggested she sell me when they'd drunk their way through all our money—my pretty face would catch a good sum, he thought."

He looked so calm that Warren felt like he was having some prank pulled on him. In his position behind the bar, he'd heard his share of nasty stories, but rarely from anyone he was particularly invested in; certainly not from anyone quite so dear as the one still swirling shapes across his chest like he was practicing in his sketchbook.

"Anyway," Matty went on, "I thought that if my face was worth something, I ought to be the one making the profit off it, not him. So I decided to run away while the choice was still mine to make. And...well, I've already told you the outcome of that debacle. I was caught out practically on day one, fortunately by someone whose capacity for pity had not yet been exhausted." His lips paused, but his finger was still going, tracing hearts above Warren's own. "I don't know what my mother thought about her fellow's idea. I admit, my fear of finding out was not the least of my reasons for running off. We were so distant by then anyway, but a betrayal like that... I couldn't have borne it. I held very fast to my ability to forgive her shortcomings, and I hated the thought she might finally do something I could not excuse. So I just never went back after Barrows put me to work. I told him I was an orphan—he knew it wasn't true, but let me have my story—and he put me up in a spare room until I was able to rent my own. His wife bloody hated me, and it was lonely in its own way too, but Barrows took an interest in my well-being. He expected me to help him on cases where I could be an asset, but otherwise, I was fed and kept warm and even properly educated until I could make it on my own. So. I cannot count it as anything but an extreme improvement in pretty much every way."

Warren had long understood that Matty's attachment to his position as a detective was not entirely rational. He had not, however, quite grasped the depth of that.

"So you grew up with him, then, Barrows," Warren said. "You didn't just work with him. You slept in his house. You shared his table. I admit, I thought it was a bit strange how attached to him you are, but it makes perfect sense, doesn't it?"

He felt Matty nod. "Indeed, though sadly I think it was no more than a pity case. The attachment goes in just the one direction. As most of my attachments have done. Barrows. My mother. Even Mr. Forester—"

"Not me," Warren said, nuzzling at his temple, trying to cheer him. "This one goes in both directions. You know that, right?"

"Hmm," said Matty with a little laugh behind it. "I try to."

Warren held him tighter, as if to prove it for good and all. "So you never went back?" he asked after a moment. "Not even to say goodbye?"

"Well, technically I did return to where she lived, once," Matty admitted. "Made it all the way to the door, in fact. Stood there staring at it for what felt like an hour. But... I knew I wouldn't find anything behind it that would do either of us any good. She didn't want to hear from me. And honestly, I was worried about what her companion might do, if he was still around. Barrows's offer seemed so much better for everyone so... I just turned around and left."

"Matty," he said, snorting with a bit of highly inappropriate nervous laughter. "This is bloody *dreadful*."

"I'm very glad you think so," said Matty earnestly. "It says good things about your own circumstances. But as far as the fate of unwanted, East End children go, I have seen much, much

220 *To Sketch a Scandal*

worse in the course of my work. Worse than I hope you can imagine, my love. I cannot help but count myself very fortunate. Scotland Yard has been complicated, but I've at least gotten some justice for a few of those little ones who weren't so lucky, over the years." He leaned up on his elbows at last, angling that angelic face and those glowing eyes of his in Warren's direction. He gave a little close-lipped smile. "I admit, it's especially hard to have a lot of regrets with a view like this."

Clearly, that was bollocks, but Warren accepted the deflection and the distraction Matty dragged them into for a while. He wanted to know more about Matty, hard as it might be to hear, but...there was time. As he held Matty and let him return the tone of this bedroom into something easy, he felt very sure of that. Matty would be here, because Matty was reliable and devoted and loyal to the point of foolish. That was not unique to his relationship with Warren, but specific to his soul. He'd been loyal to Barrows, to Forester, to his shoddy drawing practice—Warren had little to fear, he knew, now that Matty had attached himself to his side.

But it suddenly occurred to Warren, as he absorbed that certainty, that the structures holding them together were not nearly as reliable. A class that would end. A boardinghouse where a wrong step could spell disaster. And a club that Warren could not explain to his family, where he was lying and sneaking about week after week, risking his place by bringing Matty in while convincing himself that such a scheme could possibly go on forever.

And for what? Because he decided he'd rather break rules than make new ones. Forester was not actually unreasonable. In fact, his attachments were always decidedly reciprocal, including the friendship he had with Warren, no matter how strained the professional aspect of it made things sometimes. If Warren had been brave enough from the beginning to admit just how much Matty mattered to him, Forester might have tried to work something out. But Warren's cowardice and attachment to his image had bungled that pretty badly.

He started to wonder, as he realized how fragile a circumstance he'd created, if he might be able to unbungle it.

He brought it up later, when they were dressed and had begun putting the room back together.

"Matty," he said carefully, as they each took half of the fresh sheet to lay it out smooth upon the bed they'd mussed up that morning. "You know how you said, first time we were here, that you'd be willing to stay so late Forester would have to drag you out by the ankle?"

Matty raised an eyebrow at him from across the bed. "Yes…"

"I was thinking…not today, I'd need to prime things a bit, make sure they land in our favor, but… Do you think that maybe, sometime soon, we could try—"

The first sign that something wasn't right was that Matty—who was always so beautifully attentive—broke eye contact abruptly while Warren was still speaking.

The second sign came when Warren finally heard what Matty must have noticed first.

Bells.

"Shit." Warren dropped the sheet and whipped around. Bells. Not far-off bells, from the front. Close ones. From the hall just outside their open door.

Warren's first impulse was to hide Matty wherever he could. He wanted to make things right, yes. Wanted to admit his feelings for Matty and maybe even what they'd driven him to. But he could not just get caught red-handed, not like this, with the room in shambles and Matty's scarf round his neck. To be ready and waiting for a confrontation looked like a levelheaded decision, made to force the change he wanted on equal terms.

To be busted with a pile of dirty sheets balled at his feet looked like mutiny.

222 *To Sketch a Scandal*

Before he could figure out where to even put Matty, the intruder was in the doorway.

But it wasn't David Forester.

Whether that was for the best or the worst remained to be seen.

"Well, well, well," came a voice pinched with barely-contained amusement. "What have we here?"

Noah Clarke, Forester's dedicated love and longtime best mate, stood with the keys to the club in his hand. He was fashionably suited but rumpled, like he'd come straight from the tailor shop he ran just off Savile Row. He was glancing between Warren (whom he would have expected) and Matty (whom he certainly had not), with no small amount of suspicion.

"H–hullo, Penny," said Warren as innocently as he could, trying to kick the old sheets under the bed like the ass he was and referring to Noah by his drag name to really indicate how *entirely expected and casual this entire moment was, nothing interesting to see here at all, is there?* Certainly nothing to report back to Forester, who would never have trusted that bloody key to anyone but Noah. He almost couldn't believe he hadn't seen this coming. "What brings you so early?"

Noah paused. He didn't look it, with his frill-trimmed clothes and dramatic demeanor, but he had an unexpectedly good mind under his too-long hair and ribbon-wrapped top hat. It made him a real devil at the card table. Warren could see it working at this equally noble task now.

"Annabelle needs my feathered fan for her next show," he said carefully. "David gave me the key so I could stop by for it."

"Oh, well, go ahead." Warren gestured toward the wardrobe where some members stored their drags for safekeeping. He ignored Matty entirely, like he was, perhaps, just a serving lad come a bit early and not worthy of notice. "She does a bang-up job with the properties at that theater. If she says she needs it, I'm sure it's irreplaceably perfect."

"Yes…" Unlike Warren, Noah was not ignoring Matty. He was, in fact, staring right at him, eyes narrowed. "I know you," he said. Matty stood very still under Noah's infamously intense stare. "I do. Why do I know—?"

Warren squeezed his eyes shut tight as the overdramatic gasp washed over him.

"You're that valet!" Noah all but shrieked. "The pretty one. The one who turned out to be a bleeding police officer!"

Matty cleared his throat. "Special Investigations detective," he corrected politely.

Noah clutched his chest like he'd uncovered the scandal of the century. "*Warren!*"

"Will you just get your fan and get out, please?" said Warren through gritted teeth.

"Are you meeting up here off-hours?" When Warren finally opened his eyes, he found Noah was looking all around the room. The sheets Warren hadn't managed to hide. The brandy glasses on the bedside table. The tin of cream left out beside them. He did not have to be a detective or even have a particularly sharp wit to puzzle out exactly what was going on here. "David told me you'd struck up a friendship. He neglected to mention exactly what sort of friendship it was, though."

"That's because he doesn't know," Warren said seriously. "And he can't know. Not like this."

Noah laughed with unbridled delight as he went to the wardrobe. He opened it up and began rifling through dresses and hatboxes for his fan.

"I don't know what's funnier," he said. "That this devastatingly salacious rendezvous happened right under David's nosy little nose, or that cynical slattern Warren Bakshi is rendezvousing at all." Having found the fan, he flicked it open, and then shut again, using it to point at Matty. "You did know that, didn't you?"

"Knew what?" asked Matty. He was standing very still with his hands behind his back.

224   *To Sketch a Scandal*

"That he's cynical?"

"I suppose."

"And a slattern?"

"No doubt."

"Good." Noah stepped in a little closer to Matty, fan held straight before him like a fencing foil. While his voice stayed light, there was a distinct threat in it when he spoke again. "I'd hate to think my dear friend, ah, lured you here under false pretenses. That *anyone*, in fact, might have lured *anyone* here under false pretenses, if you catch my meaning."

Even if Matty suddenly admitted that he was a traitor after all, what exactly Noah thought he was going to do to a genuine lawman with that floppy feathered fan was well beyond Warren's imagination. Fortunately, Matty didn't so much as flinch.

"No false pretenses," said Matty, hanging tight to that professional posture. "Though, if he had, I think you and I would agree it was just, wouldn't we, Mr. Clarke? Considering my own history of falseness?"

"We would," said Noah. He lowered the fan at last. "David doesn't want you here."

"I'm well aware of that."

"And yet, here you are."

"What can I say?" Matty shrugged. "Apparently, I'm a fool for cynical slatterns."

A smile played at the corner of Noah's mouth. "You and everyone else. Sneaking about with our dear barkeep when he's supposed to be working doesn't make you terribly special, *Detective*."

The words stung so badly that Warren almost wished Noah had smacked him with the fan instead. The thought that Matty was no different from any randy bar patron left him with a painful desperation to correct, but without a sense of how to do it. After all, what right did he have to be angry with Noah for seeing him exactly as he'd always wanted to be seen?

Something of this must have shown on his face. Not enough for Noah to notice—he was still smirking—but Matty was nothing if not attuned to details. He stayed quiet for a second, as if waiting for Warren to speak for himself. When that didn't happen, he turned back to Noah. The blankness he'd put on was replaced with something sharper, brighter, and dreadfully hard to argue with.

"Forgive me," Matty went on, more energy in his voice as he stopped trying to blend into the wallpaper and took control of the conversation's energy in one fell swoop. "But I beg to differ with you, Mr. Clarke."

"Do you?" Noah looked surprised, but undeniably pleased to have been issued a challenge.

"Yes. We're not sneaking around for the fun of it, but out of necessity. The situation is special indeed, as far as I'm concerned."

"So you fancy you're in love with him, then?" Noah chuckled, batted his lashes teasingly. "Is that what you're saying?"

Warren watched Matty carefully as he wetted his lips, looked Noah right in the eye, and said, without any hint of Noah's humor, "Yes, actually. That is exactly what I'm saying. I am in love with him. I'm glad to see you understand the situation, Mr. Clarke."

To hear those words aloud, declared to a third party, was so warm and thrilling that Warren could barely keep from scrambling across the bed that separated them and kissing Matty right then and there. It was also, admittedly, very embarrassing. If he ever stopped smiling, he would have to start worrying about how he would ever live it down.

Before his joy could get the better of him, though, Noah turned a look of pity on Matty. "Oh, Detective, you poor thing," he said awkwardly. "And has he…led you to believe that's reciprocated? Because he's been telling us for years that he's incapable of that sort of sentiment."

226 *To Sketch a Scandal*

The very fire in the grate seemed to fizzle and chill as a shadow of possible realization crossed Matty's face.

It was the last thing in the world Warren wanted to admit to Noah right now, that *Warren Bakshi the barkeep* had gone and fallen in love like they'd all said he would. That he was a sap and a lovebird and all the other names he'd called his friends over months and years of watching them pair up and settle in comfortably under each other's wings.

But he'd be a monster if he let Matty think, for even another second, that he'd found himself in a one-sided affair. He'd probably forgive Warren if he let Noah believe what he wanted, and explained himself later. But he'd forgiven enough elsewhere, it seemed.

Warren needed to do the right thing from the start this time around.

Finally, he crossed around the bed so he could slip a hand around Matty's waist and look Noah square in the eye.

"I've let him believe it because it's true," he said. "I love him dearly, Noah, and it's fucking killing me that Forester's making it difficult for us when he's always bending over bloody backwards to enable every other pair of lovers to cross his path."

Noah stared at them, his amusement slowly dissipating as he came to understand that they were serious.

"You two have put me in quite a situation, then, haven't you?" he said at last.

"Are you going to tell Forester you found us here together?" Warren asked.

"I have to," he said, like he was stating a long-held law of the universe. "I've been telling that man everything since sodding eighteen seventy. *You've* gone and betrayed his trust, but I won't. That said..." He sighed. "There's nothing he loves more than a good romance. If I rush off and tell him like I normally would, he might respond poorly to the news. That temper, you know."

"Oh, I know," said Warren.

Jess Everlee

"He might just wind up the villain of a love story. He wouldn't like that, in the long run, because you're right—he'd prefer to enable than hinder."

"So you won't tell him?"

Noah came at Warren with the fan this time, poking him in the center of his chest. "*You* will tell him," he said sternly. "You will tell him tonight."

"Tonight?" Warren balked. "No. You're mad. I'm not telling him tonight."

"Why not? What difference does it make?"

"How bad it looks."

Noah smiled, catlike. "It does look bad."

"I was already of a mind to tell him, alright?" He glanced at Matty, who nodded his testament that the subject had been bought up. "It won't help to have you at our heels, giving us the knobstick wedding treatment with your bloody fan."

Noah looked pleased at Warren's metaphor and tapped said fan against his opposite palm a few times.

"You make a decent point, especially since I have to give the fan to Annabelle," he admitted. "But you know I don't like to keep something like this from David."

"Not even for me?"

"For you? Warren, glad as I am to see a friend find happiness, I will tear apart ten sets of lovers to please my own without a second thought. You know that as well as anyone."

Warren sighed. There was only one person in the world Noah Clarke willingly put before himself, and it was, unfortunately, the bloke in question.

"What if...what if David would be better off for the waiting?" Warren blurted. He had no idea where he was going with that, but Noah looked intrigued, so he tried to dredge something up from the dustiest crevices of his mind. "What if..."

He came up blank. What benefit could waiting possibly offer?

228 *To Sketch a Scandal*

"What if we could promise you," piped up Matty, "that it would be an exceptionally romantic declaration?"

Warren and Noah turned to stare at him. Neither had expected that polite voice to cut in. Particularly not with such an odd idea.

Noah pointed the fan. "Go on."

Matty looked a little blank, like he'd said all he had to say already. He looked pleadingly at Warren, who scooped up the buck.

"Forester responds well to that," Warren said, suddenly understanding where Matty was coming from. "He loves a good, sappy declaration, don't he? Not only will he be more likely to see us favorably, but he'll have a lot more fun with it if we make a production out of it, don't you think?"

The end of the fan was returned to Warren, and one of Noah's brows was reaching for the ceiling. "*You* are going to make an exceptionally romantic declaration in order to convince David to let your little bobby through the doors?"

"Special Investigations detective," Matty interjected. "I've never done street work."

Noah ignored him, still focused on Warren. "You? Of all people. Our resident cynical slattern is going to make an *exceptionally romantic declaration*? Here? In front of *everyone*?"

Noah was right. The notion was completely out of alignment with Warren's reputation. To stand up in the middle of the club and swear devotion after years poking fun at anyone so afflicted by sentiment would be like downing shots while he read the mail with his mother.

But Noah was ruthless. The fact that they'd scraped together a plan to keep him from blabbing immediately was no small feat. And Warren certainly didn't have any better ideas.

"Yes," he said. "I'll do it."

Noah paused, cogs turning again behind his sharp eyes.

"Fine," he said. "You will tell him as publicly as possible, as soon as possible, and with all the sentiment you can muster. I mean it, Warren. I better be *weeping* by the end of this, if I'm going to risk angering David over it, do you understand?"

Warren rolled his eyes, trying to cover his sudden nervous reluctance. "I'll be sure to entertain you, Penny."

"Not just for me," Noah clarified. "It's for your own good as well. I don't want to keep something from him over nothing, and it will take a very convincing love story once he hears you've been sneaking around behind his back."

Warren crossed his arms, indignant. "When you insist on putting it that way—"

"Is it not *that way*?" Noah challenged. "Is there some *other way* that it is, Warren? Because sweet and fun as it may seem from your side, you are going against *explicit* instructions that were put in place for member privacy and safety, putting us all at an enormous security risk. And something tells me today's not the first time you two have done it."

He knew better, by now, than to try to bluff on Noah Clarke's watch.

"Your spin must be proportionate to your betrayals," Noah went on. "If it's not, he will not listen to you. And if he does not listen to you, he's going to be furious with *me* for colluding on it, and he'll have every right to be. If you do not genuinely try to move him—either because you don't actually care for your detective that much, or because you prove too proud to do it right—we will both be in a lot of trouble. And I will make sure, as first lady of The Curious Fox, that if he doesn't sack you immediately, you're going to wish he did. Is that clear?"

Matty looked alarmed, but Warren couldn't help a half-smile.

"You're bloody terrifying, anyone ever tell you that?"

"Why, yes, I get that one regularly," said Noah, adjusting his hat. "Can't thank you enough for noticing, *amore*."

Chapter Sixteen

Matty

"Meddling bitch," Warren muttered with equal parts annoyance and grudging respect once Noah had left. "D'you think he's going to hold us to this ridiculous thing?"

"Absolutely," said Matty without hesitation. Obviously, he didn't know Mr. Clarke as well as Warren did, but he'd seen, toward the end of the Belleville case, the frankly deranged lengths to which the fellow would go for Mr. Forester. He had a decent notion of what they were dealing with. "If anything, I reckon he will grant less time than promised."

They'd not finished making the bed, the sheet smooth but untucked, the counterpane and pillows still heaped on the floor. There was an uncertain silence, half-chill and half-heat like in the Buttersnipes' woozy art room as they quietly completed the task. They'd made this bed up many times together by now. Matty's corner tucks were nearly as tidy as Warren's at this point, and he knew just where each pillow should be stacked for the most pleasing effect. Matty took a little extra time with that, maybe, really making sure the corners' angles and the lay of the fringe were just so…

"Matty."

Eyes fixed, he combed his fingers through an especially ill-used tassel, tucking the fraying strands behind the better ones. "Look, Warren, I'm sor—"

"I meant it, you know."

Matty froze, fingers still tangled in silky threads. He could feel Warren's gaze across the now-tidy bed, so insistent and intense that Matty had no choice but to meet it, even as he felt a competing desire to hide under the counterpane.

"It would be alright if you didn't," said Matty quietly.

"Maybe," said Warren, though he sounded unconvinced. "But I do. I…" He broke off, sheepishly scratching the back of his neck, where that itchy scarf was likely a genuine bother that Warren was forever putting up with simply because Matty had made it. "I'm sorry if I was awkward about it. It's just that I've never felt this way before, like keeping you in my life is more important than…well, more important than most anything, really. Especially something as silly and fleeting as my reputation behind The Curious Fox's bar."

Matty, warmed as he was by the sweet admission, wasn't sure he was following. "What do you mean, your reputation?" Warren sighed heavily through his nose, then slumped onto the edge of the bed. Tentatively, Matty joined him, not coming around but heading straight across the mattress on his hands and knees until they were beside each other, smoothness of the counterpane be damned. "Warren?"

"I lied," Warren said regretfully. "Not to you. But to Mr. Forester. He asked me whether we had something special or if we were just companions. I was too cowardly to admit how I really felt to someone who only knows me as the debauched barkeep. I like being seen as the debauched barkeep—it's so opposite from how I had to be at home, you know, and some days, the escape of getting to be something different was all that kept me showing up strong and doing what I had to do for myself

232 *To Sketch a Scandal*

and my mother. But we're not on our own anymore, and..." He paused, his hand sliding over the brocade to cover Matty's. "There are other things keeping me going. Still, if I'm honest, I don't think I would have admitted it to anyone but you if Mr. Clarke hadn't cornered us. I can't help but think that if I'd just told Forester straight off what this was becoming, it could have saved us all a lot of trouble and stress. And I'm sorry for that, because, Matty, I truly, truly adore you. Now that I've got to face what I did, I hate that I let anyone believe anything else."

Warren's air of confidence and capability did not often waver, but now he could hardly look Matty in the eye. Matty put a careful hand on his cheek and coaxed him until he turned, finding a vulnerability in his eyes that proved a more profound reflection than even the one Matty'd found in the public house mirror.

They were the same, weren't they? Constantly playing at a simple, easy-to-explain character, as if it would save them from a fate they believed would swallow them whole otherwise. But being a debauched barkeep was not really what kept Warren from sliding into the marriage and familial self-sacrifice he felt doomed to—he was far more than a single image and it's opposite. He was a talented artist. A witty companion. A passionate lover. And so much more besides.

And Matty... Matty could see his reflection in Warren's eyes, and knew good and well that such a man would not have fallen in love with a creature who was no more than image and opposite, either. No more than urchin or detective. There was more to Matty too. The trouble was, he wasn't quite sure what that was yet.

"Warren," he said at last. "Can I see the picture you did of me? The first time we came here. Surely, you've finished it by now."

"What's that got to do with anything?"

"I suspect I might learn something from it."

"That's what I was afraid of," Warren muttered. He took Matty's hand from his cheek and kissed the fingers. "But seeing as I've been caught out already, I suppose there's no harm in it now."

Warren fetched the sketchbook and brought it back to the bed. It hadn't been opened today, eagerness overriding any notion of sitting still when they closed the door behind them.

"I've already been told that even the simplest of my sketches of you give something away," he said. "But I've done much more revealing ones."

"The first one you did here," Matty said again, leaning eagerly over the book as Warren began flipping through the many pages he'd filled since they met. "That's the one I want to look at. I want to see what you see, when you look at me. I think it might..." The words were bubbling up and then tumbling over like foam from an overfilled glass before he'd even sensed they were coming. "I don't know if I want to stay at Scotland Yard," he blurted suddenly. "It's been miserable, bloody miserable, and I stay because I can't imagine anything else. But I wonder if..." He trailed off.

"If I had?" Warren finished for him. "Seen something else?"

Matty nodded self-consciously.

Warren grinned as if that were not a foolish or embarrassing thing to say at all. He kissed Matty's cheek warmly, then gathered up a few pages to skip back to what they wanted. "Oh, sweetheart. Of course I do. Here, let me..."

Warren paused his flipping very suddenly and his grin faded. It would have been the right and normal thing to ask him why, but Matty, ever-tuned to a suspicious detail, saw the problem instantly:

Two pages had been torn out of the sketchbook.

Presumably, the emotionally resonant and potentially erotic ones he was looking for in the first place.

"Fuck," Warren whispered. He looked around as if hoping

234   *To Sketch a Scandal*

the missing pages would jump out of the wardrobe and put his mind at ease. "That's…that's not good."

Matty's stomach dropped. He had not seen the pictures, but he certainly remembered posing for them. While Warren had been working on a socially-appropriate version for the showcase, it seemed both versions were missing.

"How not good is it?" he asked.

"Well…not *that* bad." He nodded at the rather salacious painting over the mantel. "But nothing I'm especially keen to find missing, I admit."

"Do you know who might have taken it?"

"I'm hoping it's just the dog again," he joked dryly, then ran a hand down his face. "Fuck." He threw his sketchbook to the ground. "I worked really bloody hard on those."

Matty didn't want to put too fine a point on it, but he'd seen enough dramatic takedowns to realize that, depending on just what those sketches looked like, they had a lot more to worry about than a bit of hard work lost. These might be blackmail-worthy documents they were talking about here.

"Warren, where do you take your sketchbook?"

"I dunno." He ruffled a hand through his hair. "Home. Here. Class. And the pub after class. Oh, and your place."

"Nowhere else?"

"To the bridge once, for a lark. Wanted to try out a cityscape. Found I like drawing people better, though, so I didn't go back…" Warren flipped around in the book again. "Maybe I ripped these ones out by accident, when I meant to rip out the ones I'd done of the river."

"That's…a hopeful notion."

"I don't know who else would do it." He went pensive. "I'll ask my brother. Maybe he did it to protect me? Or to protect our mother from finding it? That sounds the most likely," he concluded, mostly to himself. Not very likely, though, based on the waver in his voice.

Matty went through the locations again in his mind. Home. Here. Class. The pub after class. Matty's place. The bridge.

Here—the Fox—was the least likely location for the theft. The sketchbook was left here only behind locked doors when they went to get luncheon, doors that could only be unlocked by Warren, Mr. Forester and, apparently, Mr. Clarke.

They'd never left an unattended table at the pub—nor had they let the manager hold their sketchbooks for them, thank God—and the bridge seemed doubtful for the same reason, especially once Warren found that he had indeed ripped out those drawings he didn't like.

That left home, class, and Matty's place.

"You should certainly check with your brother," Matty said. "If I'm understanding your relationship correctly, that's the least problematic possibility by far. Otherwise, someone in the boardinghouse or class must have gotten to it when our backs were turned. And if they went to that sort of trouble...well." He took a very deep breath, trying to keep the shudder out of it. "They're not calling that new law 'The Blackmailer's Charter' for nothing, are they? Do you have any idea how inundated Scotland Yard has been with stupid bollocks like this the past few months? A letter here, a photograph there, enemies and desperate men trying to take each other down? We don't even bother trying to keep up with half of it."

Unless the evidence was especially specific or the accused was of particular interest, of course. A lord. A politician. A famous figure. A *detective*. He could not even bloody bear to think what might happen if he was at all recognizable in the picture and it wound up at the Met. If he were recognized, he somehow doubted the drawings would be treated with the same exhausted eye-rolling that most of this sort of sordid evidence was garnering.

"God, that would be miserable business," said Warren with

236   *To Sketch a Scandal*

a sigh and a roll of the eyes that seemed more casual than it should have been. "I've dealt with much closer calls, though."

"Really? You've been blackmailed?"

Warren looked at him like he was very naive, and maybe he was. "This time, at least, I've got money," Warren said. "If someone pops back up with the pictures in the next few days, I can pay."

"We best hope it was a classmate, then, and not one of the boarders," said Matty, mind still racing. "They know who I am, and would know how much their material is worth."

Warren looked at him, and for a split second, Matty saw a flash of something he didn't like at all. Like maybe someone who'd warned him off this affair had a point after all. But it lasted so briefly, Matty might well have imagined it.

They talked through the rest of the details of their case—for of course, that's how Matty was thinking of it already, those grooves carved too deeply in his mind to approach it any other way. Thoughts of leaving Scotland Yard on his own power were overshadowed by all the more dreadful ways his career might come to an end if he did not get out ahead of this.

While Warren promised to check with his brother, Matty doubted anything would come of that. Given what he knew of Harry Bakshi, he had no reason to do such a thing without telling Warren he'd done it. The motivation just wasn't there.

For his own part, Matty examined the boardinghouse parlor, where they often took tea and behaved very innocently. They were sometimes joined by the landlady, served by the kitchen girl, or accompanied by others in the house who read or tinkered on the piano in the evenings. While it seemed unlikely, they'd occasionally been distracted enough that someone might have poked about in the unattended sketchbook. Without any other leads, he could not rule it out.

When Monday morning came, he could think of nowhere

worse to be than his Scotland Yard office, where Barrows was gone forever and it was just him and Ashton and whoever else they wanted him to work with, having been, not just unpromoted, but actively downgraded to filing other detectives' papers and taking their notes.

He got in to find he was still not assigned to a particular case, and yet somehow, *some-fucking-way*, Detective Ashton was on his arse within the first hour and did not let up no matter how calm and accommodating Matty tried to make himself in response.

Handwriting's dreadful on this report, Shaw. I'm going to need it done again.

Why weren't you there to take minutes on the pawnshop murder? I don't care that you had another assignment, Shaw, you should know what comes first.

Shaw, where the devil is that folder? Yes, I gave it to you, don't argue facts with me.

Shaw this. Shaw that. Shaw, you bleeding idiot, why didn't you...? Each one of Ashton's terribly *friendly*, *companionable* demands felt like another box to the ears, until, by midafternoon, Matty could have sworn they were literally ringing. This time, though, there was no escape. Ashton had taken over Barrows's desk, so there was no time to recuperate from the onslaught with a friendly face and a strong cup of tea before the next round. Fortunately, one or the other of them left occasionally, but what the devil was Matty going to do when they eventually had to work a case together? It was bad enough sitting across from Ashton and taking his orders on this scattered basis, but how on earth would they manage to actually get anything done?

"Shaw."

Matty's hand clenched around his pen as he rewrote the offending report from earlier.

"Yes, sir?" he said as pleasantly as possible.

Ashton didn't go on until Matty deigned to look up from his useless work. He finally did, only to find that Ashton was

238 *To Sketch a Scandal*

leaning back in Barrows's old chair like he'd owned it forever, hands clasped comfortably behind his head. He seemed to be surveying Matty—there was no other way to put it. Smirking something dreadful. Eyes narrowed and flicking. Looking for further fault.

"I was just thinking, Shaw," he said lightly, in that oh-so-friendly tone he took when he was about to tell Matty to be grateful for all his unjudging support. "You're off the fraud case."

"Well spotted, Detective," Matty said before he could stop himself. Though his voice was bland as milk, Ashton's face darkened when he caught the unblunted sarcasm behind it.

"Well, given that fact, don't you think it's time you left that raggedy artist look behind?" His tone was light, teasing, one companion giving a bit of advice to the other. But there was steel in his eyes. "That sort of stubbly situation you've got. It's not proper for an officer of the Met. Not even one of your standing. Since you don't need it for the case anymore, it's probably time you got rid of it, don't you think?"

A flare of hot anger flickered to life from the embers that had been slowly smoldering within Matty's belly all day.

"I've grown to like it this way actually," said Matty with an apologetic little smile. "And seeing as no one's trusted me yet with a new plainclothes assignment that might have other requirements, I think I'll leave it as-is until that changes."

Ashton became less casual then, folding his hands on the desk before him. Why the devil he'd chosen this moment to berate Matty for his beard of all things was a mystery. He'd looked too peaceful, he supposed. Ashton could not stand to see him off his toes for even a second. Whatever the case, it had clearly become the most bloody important thing in the world all of a sudden, and there would be no putting him off.

"Tomorrow," he said slowly. "I'd like you to come in looking fit for your office."

"A mustache, then?" said Matty, voice so taut it was a wonder it did not snap.

Ashton laughed. "I mean, if you wanted," he said, as if to want such a thing would be a grievous mistake. "But given the scraggly little thing you've managed so far, I think you'd do better to return to your clean look until you've grown up a bit."

The flare within Matty climbed to a blaze, like someone had thrown a few handfuls of incriminating documents on it.

"I'm twenty-five years old."

Ashton laughed as though it was all good fun. "Old graybeard, are you?"

"I think I'm going to keep it as is," Matty said firmly.

Ashton ignored the finality in his voice entirely. "You are not," he said. "You will come in looking proper for your post tomorrow, Shaw, and that's final."

Something snapped. And not a small something, either, not the mere result of Ashton's poorly-disguised cruelty over the past few hours and days and even weeks. It was not some thread that came apart under the intolerable tension, but a bloody bridge, huge and crumbling, pieces crashing into the water below.

He had given every ounce of his control over to this place for too long. The support and fond-enough feelings of Barrows had made his demands and—yes, though Matty hated to admit it—his exploitation tolerable. But Ashton was a hacksaw to those already-splintering cables. He could not take another second of this. He hadn't gotten to see Warren's picture of him, but he did not need to. What he found reflected in those gorgeous eyes had apparently been enough.

Matty looked Ashton dead in the face and said:

"No."

Ashton blinked at him slowly. "No?"

"That's what I said."

240 *To Sketch a Scandal*

"Awful lot of insolence for someone on such thin ice, don't you think?"

Matty stood up, slamming his pen so hard on the table that ink splattered across the report and clear across to stain the wood of his desk.

"Quit asking me what I *think*," he said, shouted, really, his voice filling the small room and likely carrying out the single window. He was breathing heavily, hand still covering the pen like it was something he'd smashed and feared seeing how thoroughly he'd killed it. "You don't give a damn what I *think*, Ashton. And if you think I'm going to make decisions about what to do with *my own fucking face* based on your opinions, then you're bloody delusional."

"Want to go say all that to Superintendent Frost?" said Ashton in a dangerous voice. "Seems to me you've forgotten, once again, who your friends are—"

"Oh, come off it!" With the way he pushed the mess of pages and pen pieces and ink drops to the ground in a rage-filled sweep of his arm, one might think he had no skill at hiding his feelings at all. But this one would not be hidden. Would not be beaten into submission by his own desperation to be wanted in this stupid place. He *wasn't* wanted here. But he was wanted elsewhere. And that, he found, made all the difference. "You are not my friend. You're a power-hungry arsehole who would sell me out in a *second* if you had the evidence to do it. Which you never will," he added in a hiss. "Never. Because you may have the smarter mouth between us, Ashton, but that's the only thing you come out ahead on. I am the better detective. The better man. And certainly the better schemer between the two of us. That promotion should have been mine, and it would have been if you weren't all so bloody squeamish about what it takes to get justice in this stupid city."

From down the hall, Matty heard a door open, and some

inquisitive mumbling. He'd been heard, clearly. He was too furious, just now, to care.

Not quite furious enough, though, to lose track of what this outburst meant.

But that was alright. In fact, perhaps it was for the best.

Before Superintendent Frost could come in here and make the choice for him, Matty dug his badge out from the pocket of his coat. Detective Ashton was wide-eyed as Matty approached his desk and slammed it down.

"*That*, old friend," Matty spat, quiet now, just for the two of them, "is what I bloody well think."

Matty was, of all things, relieved.

As he'd been unaware of the structures that were keeping him aloft, he'd likewise not noticed how very heavy they were until he was shed of them, going back to his boardinghouse room feeling light to the point of unmoored. It was not as unpleasant as he might have thought, to lose everything. He could see that most of what he'd had was illusion at best.

Oh, there were other feelings too, of course. While his lack of robust social life meant he had plenty of savings, he was clearly not going to be a working portraitist anytime soon, and had no idea what he was going to do for money. While he was not currently being trusted with anything terribly secret, he did worry that some sort of security protocol might lead Superintendent Frost to his doorstep for some unpleasant final threatening. But overall, the joys he'd found outside the Met had grown substantial enough over the past months that he simply could not focus on anything but the peaceful notion that he did not have to go into that dratted office tomorrow.

That is, until he got home. And saw the letter that his landlady handed him on his way up the stairs.

Seeing it was from Barrows, he tore into it while he was still

242 *To Sketch a Scandal*

climbing, pausing to lean on the hallway wall and read before he'd even gone into his room:

Dear Mr. S—
There's something important we should discuss. Please come to see me at your earliest convenience. Wednesday mornings are best.
R.B.

Enclosed was his address on a card, as if Matty had not lived there for nearly two years and did not know it.

Matty took the mysterious thing into his room and looked at it again under the better light of a lamp like it might prove more forthcoming there. But no. It was just as terse. Just as impersonal.

And just as ominous.

Matty threw himself into his desk chair and tipped his head back against it, eyes closed against a nauseous wave of fear as a very dastardly notion came to him all at once.

Regarding the missing sketches, he'd considered Warren's family, the other boarders, and fellow students in their art class.

He had not, however, considered the fact that someone at Scotland Yard might have had something to do with it.

Bloody hell. He turned the lamp up to its very highest setting, the gas hissing and flame blaring, and hunched over the letter. He held it close to the glowing bubble of glass, praying to whoever might be listening to find some hint, some notion that what Barrows wanted to discuss was less than ruinous. He did not think, of course, that Barrows himself meant any harm. He'd done harm, frankly, in his dealings with Matty over the years, and plenty of it—harm Matty suspected he'd be cleaning up after in his psyche for a while yet. But he did not *mean* harm. While Matty did not believe he was particularly special to the old man, he was at least well regarded.

Well-regarded enough that, if Barrows knew something

about the missing drawings, something he could not put in writing, he might very well send Matty a letter just like this to initiate his warning.

Clearly, the letter was bad news.

Bad enough that he should probably let Warren know right away that he might not be dealing with blackmail, but the hand of the law itself.

But unfortunately...well, when Warren came calling to practice their drawing the next day as he usually did, Matty did not say anything about it at all. The more pressing thing seemed to be the update that he'd left Scotland Yard. It would seem dishonest to go more than a minute or two without telling him that.

To which Warren said, "Brilliant, mate," and did not kiss him at all given their location, but clearly would have were they somewhere else. "That might make the rest of the bloody... performance," he said vaguely, referring to their deal with Mr. Clarke to make a romantic declaration, "go a little smoother with Forester. No guarantees—I suppose his worries about your recognizability are still valid enough, but it's better, I think. What do you think?"

After all Detective Ashton's nasty little remarks, it was so refreshing for Matty to be genuinely asked his opinion, that for a while, that was all the talking he could manage.

He could have done it after that, when they got round to sketching together, but he didn't do it then, either. He told himself it was because Warren didn't seem as worried, and he hated to disturb his peace. He still smiled his blindingly beautiful smile in the light of the parlor window, posed Matty at the piano bench, and carried on with his usual tales of the family and neighbors he was so perennially surrounded by, including cheerful speculation that he might become an uncle soon, though no one had confirmed it. What sort of monster would interrupt talk like that with a cloud of fretful gloom?

244 *To Sketch a Scandal*

But even when Warren brought the conversation round to the missing pictures himself once they were alone, mentioning that the conversation with his brother had gone nowhere as expected, Matty *still* couldn't do it. And when he still couldn't do it, it was hard to kid himself any longer about his motivation.

If he admitted how serious he believed the situation was, it would call into question Warren's desire to bring him into the fold at The Curious Fox. It would mean Mr. Forester was right. That Matty was more trouble than he was worth.

Given that Warren was trying to get something drawn that would speak to his friends, wow everyone at the showcase, and keep them both on the right side of trouble, he needed more time with Matty as a model in the week that followed. Which was convenient, since neither of them now had dedicated daily employment, and also meant that Matty had several very good opportunities to bring his fears to Warren.

If he'd had the guts to take advantage of any one of them, perhaps it would have gone better.

They were in Matty's room when it happened, having expressed for anyone who might be listening that the sun wasn't at the right angle in the parlor for their purposes. If any potential picture thief suspected that the second the door was shut behind them, Warren would lean Matty up against it to steal a kiss, they certainly made no sign. Unfortunately. Matty would much rather the perpetrator be someone here than what he was now thinking...

He pulled back from the kiss, guilt riddling his stomach too much to carry on.

"Warren," he said. "I—"

"I know, I know," Warren said with a teasing sort of lilt, squeezing Matty's arse for good measure before disengaging. "I'm the one who said we should keep that to the Fox. But we don't have the Fox for a few more days, and then only if our ridiculous scheme with Noah goes over. Forgive me for being

Jess Everlee 245

a little eager. Let me just sharpen up my pencil, and I can get back to business."

"That's not quite…"

But there was no power behind the protest, and Warren did not seem to notice it. Comfortable here now, and not the sort of chap who deeply overthought his every move and those of the people around him, he went straight to the desk without asking to rummage in the mug for the penknife.

He paused, picking something else up from the desk very casually. Something, Matty realized with a terrible jolt, he'd left out without meaning to.

And this time, it was nothing quite so charming as a way-ward jar of hand cream.

"You've heard from your old mentor," Warren said, all innocence himself as Matty swelled near to bursting with guilt. He flipped the note over to check the back. "Not a chatty chap, is he?"

"N-not especially," Matty said.

"What's he got to tell you, d'you think?"

Matty paused long enough that Warren finally looked over at him. He clearly caught right away that something was amiss; a few days away from the Met and Matty, it seemed, had lost all his well-practiced ability to hide his feelings, at least where Warren was concerned.

"What's he got to tell you," Warren said again, more slowly, each word enunciated with a hint of accusation, "d'you think? Matty? Talk to me."

Matty sat heavily upon the bed. Unable to look Warren in the eye, he let his pillows have him, heels of his hands pressed to his forehead as he spoke to the ceiling.

"Probably nothing good," he admitted at last. Long last. Far too long a last to be considered reasonable at all. His insides curdled terribly. How could he have let it go this far? Bloody hell, he was a monster…

246 *To Sketch a Scandal*

He felt the weight of Warren on the mattress beside him, a hand resting gently on his leg. "What's that supposed to mean? Nothing good?"

"Means he wrote me just after the pictures went missing," Matty mumbled. "And same day I walked out of Scotland Yard. Funny timing, isn't it?"

"How would he even know about the pictures?" Warren asked.

"He wouldn't," said Matty. "Unless someone at the Met had something to do with it. Someone who is now going to be even angrier with me than before, and without worry that my actions might cause a public scandal now that I've left."

The fingers of Warren's hand, still on Matty's leg, unmistakably tightened.

"Is that likely?" he asked.

"I wish I knew."

He dared at last to uncover his eyes. He was surprised to find that Warren did not look especially concerned. "How would they manage it, though?" Warren asked. "It's not like I leave this thing lying around for any old bobby to find, and based on the sort of cases you said your unit is involved in, I can't imagine they'd have anyone sneaking about to catch one detective getting up to a bit of naughty portraiture, love." His hand on Matty's leg relaxed, then squeezed in a decided fashion. "I think it sounds a little paranoid."

Matty turned his head to glare into a pair of very skeptical brown eyes. "Do you have a better explanation at this point?"

Warren gave a decidedly impatient sort of click. "Any of the others, probably," he said. "The dog, even."

"There was no drool or teeth marks on the torn pages," Matty said, a bit impatient himself. "It's not the bloody dog this time. It's also not your brother. Nor do I think it's a blackmailer, from here or anywhere else—I think a simple blackmailer would have come looking for their money by now, there's no sense sitting on something like that."

"The pictures aren't even *that* bad," Warren snapped. "Suggestive, yeah. Bit embarrassing, in the wrong context. But not damning by themselves. Every museum in London houses worse. They're decidedly front-parlor stuff."

"Even worse," Matty explained, this idea really digging its heels in. It was neat. It was tidy. It fit everything he was feeling about the terrible ending to a career he'd thought a done deal for life. "If they're not damning, they're not worth much, are they? We might let a blackmailer keep them and take our chances on reporting *him*, in that case. If not money or family security, what other motivation is there to take such things, unless they back up some more convincing evidence they already have on hand?"

This time, the warmth of Warren's hand left him entirely, his gaze going almost as cold as the absence of his comfort on Matty's leg.

"Evidence on hand?" he repeated. "What evidence would they have on hand?"

Matty squeezed his eyes shut again. It had never seemed a good time to mention the reputational problems that had led to the Met becoming so miserable in the first place.

"I am not," he said slowly, "completely free of all suspicion from some of my former coworkers, alright? There's not... *Evidence* might have been overstating the situation. It's rumors, really, nasty schoolboy name-calling and whatnot because of the sorts of roles I was taking on for my cases. And it just occurred to me that someone might have gone and taken that bollocks to the next step, and that maybe Barrows wants to warn me about it."

He watched miserably as Warren perused the note again. "This notion came to you last Monday," he said. "If you really believe it's what you say it is, why the devil didn't you mention it

248   *To Sketch a Scandal*

before? Why didn't you mention that there were rumors before either, while we're at it? Don't you think I ought to know if I'm caught up in some Scotland Yard scandal as soon as possible?"

"Of course."

"Then why are we just having this conversation now?"

"Because I've lost my ability to practice care and discretion around you," he snapped to the ceiling. "I'm sorry, Warren. I wanted to talk to Barrows first to either confirm or deny that I was right, and I would have done, but I left the note out on the desk because you have turned my brain to utter mush, apparently. I never would have made a mistake like that before. Never."

Warren looked torn between taking that as a compliment or an insult, and frankly, Matty wasn't sure which he'd meant it as himself.

"You should have told me," he said quietly. "Why didn't you?"

"I wanted to talk to Barrows first," Matty repeated.

"That's not a reason, it's a want," said Warren. "Why didn't you tell me, Matty?"

"I…didn't want to drag you in further," Matty said. "If I'm right… Did you sign the pictures? While we're on the subject."

"No, I didn't."

"Then if I'm right, it's the fact that I posed that's the relevant bit of evidence. Since they took it from the sketchbook, and you didn't sign it, they'll have a hard time proving you're the one who did it. And even if they tried, it's not really *you* they want—"

"Why does your tone have me thinking the real reason isn't quite as noble as you're saying?"

Because love is really dreadful if you want to keep anything at all to yourself. Matty thought it so loud, he wouldn't be surprised if Warren had heard it. *I can see why I've never risked it before, can't you?*

Jess Everlee 249

"Matty!"

"Because Mr. Forester is right about me," he snapped, sitting up at last to look Warren in the eye. "There. Are you happy now? He's right. I'm trouble. More trouble than anyone so lovely as you has any reason to put up with, much less speak for to all his friends. I didn't tell you because I didn't want to prove him right. Not..." He faltered under Warren's gaze. "Not yet," he whispered. "I wanted another day before it got complicated."

"Another day?" said Warren accusingly. "Or another weekend?"

"Warren—"

"You were going to wait until I vouched for you at the club," he said sadly. "Until I'd stood up and made a bloody fool of myself in front of everyone who matters to me, saying you were perfectly safe and honest and ought to be given a fair shake."

"I wasn't *planning* to wait any particular amount of—"

"But you would have," he said. "Wouldn't you?"

Matty didn't think he could deny that. Not based on the way the conversation had refused to leave his mouth for days. He wished it weren't true. But it probably was.

"I... I could be wrong about the whole thing," he said shakily. "In fact, you're probably right. They don't use plain clothes for something as small as this, it would hurt public opinion—"

"I have a family, Matty," Warren interrupted. There was a level of hurt in his voice Matty could hardly believe he'd put there. "And that family has a reputation. A very good reputation, which is something a family such as mine doesn't always come by so easily. My lives must be very carefully balanced, now that there are people trying to decide whether to invite my mother to their dinner parties. She likes those sorts of things a lot, you know, and she missed them, when I couldn't afford us an in with that sort of company. Say what you will about whether that's right or wrong—it doesn't matter. I don't want to take it from her now that she's got it back. Staying balanced

250 *To Sketch a Scandal*

is hard enough as it is; I cannot maintain it if I do not know what I'm working with. I thought you understood that."

He paused for a moment, a moment that Matty felt desperate to fill with something, anything that would fix this. "Warren—"

"But you don't, do you?" he went on. His voice was no longer filled with anger, but something much, much worse: pity. "You don't understand it. The family thing. How important it all is. And why would you?"

Never before had Matty really felt like the broken thing he was. He'd seen so many unwanted creatures like himself shattered and smashed beyond all recognition in the course of his work, that the ghastly crack through his own middle had seemed very mild in comparison. But Warren was clearly staring right at that crack now. He obviously did not see it as some scratch to be ignored.

He stood up, leaving the mattress bereft of his weight.

"I have to think," he said, grabbing his coat.

Matty sat bolt upright. "Warren, I'm sorry—"

He came back over. And while he did lean down to kiss Matty on the forehead, it was not an especially warm gesture.

"I need to think," he said again. "I'll see you in class. You can…you can let me know how it went with Barrows then. If it's possible for you."

He shrugged the coat on, took up his hat, and walked out the door.

"Warren!" Matty called. "You forgot—"

But the door clicked shut.

Matty stared at the abandoned scarf, which had been left hanging limp on the peg, its shadow swinging sadly beneath as it swayed with the haste of Warren's departure.

Chapter Seventeen

Warren

Warren realized his mistake when he got home.

"Well, fuck me," he whispered to the cupboard door as he unfastened his coat and found the scarf missing. He was angry with Matty for being a bloody dolt, but he hadn't meant to send quite that harsh a message. He wanted time to think, not to completely reject something that had seemed so certain a few short hours ago.

He hesitated with his coat, considering keeping it on. It would be a bother to go back, but the thought of Matty reading into such a mindless lapse made him sick.

"Warren, is that you?"

Mother came into the foyer. She was in one of the fine new day dresses she'd not had to make herself for the first time in ages, draped over in deep blue fabric with gold stitching along the edges. She was smiling very wide, but looked tired—Warren always fancied the gray streaks in her hair looked grayer when she was overdoing it, perhaps reflecting off some minute change in her complexion. She started trying to help him out of his coat instantly.

252   *To Sketch a Scandal*

"Come on!" she said. "We've been waiting for you. There's *news*."

Mother spent more time with Anjali these days, and certainly knew what the news was by now. Everyone did. While Anjali was clearly of a mind not to announce inauspiciously early, she wasn't very good at hiding it, either. If the odd pickles hadn't given her away, the fact that she'd suddenly started putting inexpertly-draped saris over her trousers last week without any apparent reason was suspicious (and also a little concerning, near the stove…)

"News?" Warren looked over his shoulder at the door he'd been considering heading right back out of. "Now?"

"*Now*." Mother had him out of his coat before he knew it, putting it away. "Mrs. Ahuja and the others from the old place even came by to hear it, isn't that lovely? I know you've missed them so much, you mention it almost every time we have the new neighbors over."

"But…" Could they have picked more dreadful timing? "Are we sure it's a good day for it?" he tried, desperately searching for some reason not to have this happen right fucking now. "She's been waiting for a reason, you know. It should be the right time. The right day. And this sort of news? I mean, we wouldn't want—"

Mother pursed her lips so hard it stopped Warren's own fully in their tracks.

"If my English bachelor son cared in the slightest about such things," she said slowly, arms crossed, "then he would already know it's a perfectly 'good day' for news."

She had him there.

"Can I have an hour?" he asked. "I'm back early as it is. You can't have been expecting me yet—"

"Yes, but you're here now," said Mother. "And so is everyone else. What could you have possibly forgotten out there that's more important than this?"

There was absolutely no way in the world to explain why forgetting a scarf at his art class chum's house was important. On the surface, of course, it was nothing.

And he would have to hope Matty trusted him enough to see it that way. Because he couldn't think of anything that would reasonably allow him to put this off.

"Alright," he said, disheartened but without any reasonable option to resolve these conflicting tensions. "Go on. I'll be right in."

He told himself he'd go back to set things right with Matty once the news was shared, but he must have known deep down how impossible that would be. It wasn't just their old housemates who had come over to celebrate, but what seemed like at least half the Punjabi population of London by the time all was said and done, and plenty of their new neighbors as well. There'd been no wedding for Harry and Anjali, after all. The desire to celebrate them at last was voracious.

The half of Warren that walked this world quite happily congratulated his brother and sister, watched the mother-to-be open gifts of sweets and bangles, caught up with people he hadn't seen in ages, and ate far more food than was frankly reasonable. It was so joyous an occasion, he even tolerated a few introductions to granddaughters. One was so charming that within the context of celebrating his brother's wife and child, some small part of him wondered whether he might not be one of those fellows who could make it all work somehow after all.

That thought, however, faded quickly once the eating and singing did and people started heading home. Natural, he supposed, to get caught up, but his path was his own and being at the center of a day like this was simply never going to be part of it. He was to the side, and as things became quiet, he was comfortable there again—bringing Mother her tonic and a last helping of pudding, tidying up alongside the housekeeper now

254 *To Sketch a Scandal*

that there was no one to judge him for it. He certainly wasn't missing a wife in this peaceful moment.

Though he was, admittedly, missing Matty.

It was stupid. Even as companions, which was all they could ever admit to being, there was hardly a human out there who would have fit in less at his house tonight. And yet Matty was so adaptable, so game, so unshakable when he set his mind to something, that Warren had to wonder if his presence might have made a nice addition. Even if he'd spent the party in a daze of not understanding three-quarters of what was said, it would certainly be nice to have him here now, as a peaceful night settled on the household.

Mother was on the sofa, changed into a warm robe with blanket on top, enjoying the last of her pudding. As Warren returned from dropping the final batch of plates in the kitchen, she patted the seat beside her. His seat, back in the days of opening the mail together.

"So," she said. "What was on your mind earlier? When you thought you might leave all this?"

"I'm glad I didn't," he said quickly. "You were right. It was—"

"I didn't ask if you were glad," she said. "I saw you; I don't doubt you would have hated to miss such an important day. I want to know what could even have tempted you."

Warren took a deep breath and let it out slowly. Harry had warned him a while ago now that Mother would start asking this sort of thing soon.

"I had an argument with a friend," he admitted. "He was in the wrong but… I think I overreacted." As he said it aloud, he felt very certain it was true. He remembered that little note, every detail down to the address on it. While the missing drawings were of concern, there was no indication that Matty was being investigated, and nothing Barrows said really changed that. In fact…

In fact, he had a sinking feeling, now that he was home and his mind was clear, that he might very well know which prat had done it in the first place. And that prat's motivation was likely not as dastardly as Matty was imagining. If Warren had kept his head and had a real conversation rather than fretting once again about what this might do to his reputation at the Fox, he might have figured it out before he went and left Matty with the impression that he wasn't coming back.

"Anyway," he went on, even more regretful than before. "I realized my mistake when I got home. Wanted to set it right before we had to go to sleep with such bitter feelings."

"Is he a friend from your club?"

"Um. Sort of."

"Will you tell me, now?" she asked. It wasn't harsh and was not a demand. Just a real, gentle question. "Where you've been working?"

It was a real tragedy, that he couldn't. He wished there were some way, that she were half-pirate like Harry and able to handle such a truth. She could not, though. At least not now, not under these circumstances. Maybe that would change someday, but in the meantime, lying so extravagantly wasn't serving them, either.

"It's not White's," he said. And she laughed, because of course she knew that. The positive response spurred him on. "It's not Brooks's, either. It's nothing you'll have heard of, actually. No prestige whatsoever. Due to its…location near the theaters," he said, deciding that was about as close as he could get to the reality of the place, "it does very brisk business with a rough crowd, and I was always able to bring in more money there than I might have elsewhere. I'm also quite good, actually. At my job. I get a lot of appreciation. It's not a fancy place, but I know how to make the gentlemen feel like it is."

Mother smiled, and it made him sad. What she thought he was being appreciated for—his helpfulness, his ability to run an

256 *To Sketch a Scandal*

economical ship, his comfort with blending flavors—probably wasn't very accurate most of the time. In fact, he let most of the patrons go on thinking he was lazy. Made them feel all the more special when they got good service and a saucy wink.

"You should have told me from the start," she scolded.

"I wanted you to be able to tell the neighbors something to be proud of," he said. "Squeezing coin out of drunk actors doesn't quite fit the bill."

She grinned even wider. "Well, that's fair enough," she teased. "But you could have told me, and we could have gone in on the fib together."

"I'm sorry. I really believed it was in your best interest to keep the details to myself."

"Why do you stay now, then?" she asked. "If it's as you say, what draw is there?"

"My friends," he said. While there were details that couldn't cross the barrier of his worlds, the honest truth of it was simple and universal. "I have friends there, and so I enjoy myself when I go into work. I didn't want to give it up. Not with everything else changing around me so fast. There may not be a reason to keep it, but there was no reason to quit, either. So, I stayed."

"Is there some reason you cannot see them somewhere else?" she asked. "Can't they come here? I would like to meet them."

"You wouldn't like them," he said. "Trust me."

She paused. For a moment, he figured she'd argue. But then she nodded.

"I see," she said slowly, knowingly. "Are they artist friends, then?"

Warren did a double take. He did not think that his mother was using that term as some sort of euphemism on purpose; she was no sailor with context for the sort of life he and friends kept, after all. But what she said got at something. Got very close to something vital and correct that he'd never been able to broach with her.

"Yes," he said. "I think… I think that's an accurate way to describe them."

She nodded again, pursing her lips. "Your father had his artist friends, too," she said, looking into the distance like she could see that old pack of bohemians at the edge of her vision field. "And you're right." She chuckled. "I didn't like them at all."

Warren laughed too, a sort of nervous burst. "Artist friends?"

"Don't you remember?" she said, squinting like she was hoping to see her memories more clearly. "The ones who smoked, and drank, and dressed oddly."

Once she put it that way, Warren did remember that his father would go out with companions from the school he attended when he was ashore, and that occasionally those fellows would stop by for a drink and closed-door conversations about art and literature. Warren was too young to join in on those, but Harry had done so once or twice, before such visits were ended for good.

"I suppose I didn't think of them that way," Warren said. "I didn't know them well."

"For good reason. You think that was an accident?" she huffed. "But they were always polite to me, and they made him happy, and he didn't become worse for their presence so far as I could tell. He came all the way here to study his passion; it only made sense that he'd find fellows of a like mind eventually, same as I found my companions. So." She shrugged. "What do you do? I loved him as he was, and so did they, so I suppose we had that in common. They didn't even come over that much, since I drew the line at the smoking, you know, and some of them could hardly go an hour without it."

Warren nearly laughed, thinking of some of his own friends. Noah in particular would struggle.

"Mother, are you saying you want me to bring my friends over to annoy you senseless?"

"I'm saying, Warren, that if you did…" She glanced down

258 *To Sketch a Scandal*

the hall. "Your brother has ensured we have a nice parlor for entertaining again. It would be very odd indeed if you didn't have friends this dear over to visit sometimes." She paused, then put a finger up. "But *no* smoking."

"That will certainly limit the crowd, as you say."

"Good."

There was a tipping point, when Warren climbed the ladder and lit each candle in the Fox's chandelier, when the slow, one-by-one creep of the light seemed to finally sweep the room over with its warm glow. The memories he had of the evenings his father went out or huddled with other artists in his study were suddenly brightened just like that, as if what his mother had said was the single candle that made all the difference in his vision. His father's life outside the family might not have been secret or risky, but it had been as interesting and vibrant and vital as Warren's. He hadn't ever thought of his hardworking father as eccentric, but perhaps he had been… Certainly he had been! He'd been born well-off and well educated in India. It took some amount of eccentricity to leave all that to study *painting* of all things, didn't it?

And, to be fair to his mother, it took at least a touch of eccentricity herself to be willing to marry and start a very new life with such a man in the first place. It wasn't an obvious thing about her, but if it weren't there, well, there would be no London and no Curious Fox and English bachelorhood or any of it. They'd be living a very different life, with very different conversations to be had.

"Mother," Warren said. "While I stand by the assertion that you wouldn't like most of my friends, there's one I think you'd get on with rather well. He's very polite, and hardly smokes at all. I'd like to introduce him to you, if I could."

"The one you meet up to draw with?" she asked. "The one in your pictures?"

Warren swallowed hard, but there was no indication she'd

spotted in those pictures quite the same things that Harry and Anjali had. No indication that she ever would, though he supposed he'd cross that bridge if he ever came to it. He nodded.

"The one you argued with?" she said knowingly.

He nodded again.

"Well, patch things up and bring him by, then," she said. She gave a smile that was wistful and even a bit wily around the edges. "Trust me when I say, a polite artist who doesn't smoke much is a rare companion worth keeping around for as long as you can."

Post held a certain gravity for Warren, after years of nearly ritualistic combings over for news of Father or Harry. When he saw an important letter, it tended to leave an impression.

Thus, even when he woke up the next morning, he found he remembered everything about Mr. Barrows's note to Matty. He remembered that Wednesdays were best. That mornings were preferred.

Most importantly, perhaps, he remembered the address.

He didn't expect, with no planning and no warning, to get there at precisely the same time as Matty did. He'd be early, he figured, and have to explain himself. Or else late, which would be easier. But amazingly enough, Matty was just climbing the tidy steps to the front door when he arrived at Mr. Barrows's little house.

Matty wasn't wearing the careworn costume he donned to class, but a tidy gray suit, a black overcoat, and a tall hat. For a second, Warren thought he looked so fine and put together that he must have managed to get his head on straight without any help. But the longer he watched, the less likely that seemed.

Matty wasn't knocking. Wasn't ringing the bell. He was just standing there, staring at the door, completely frozen. Considering his state of mind when last they spoke, it was reasonable to hesitate.

260   *To Sketch a Scandal*

Until, of course, it wasn't.

I stood there staring at it for what felt like an hour.

I turned around and left.

Warren realized what Matty was about to do. He'd done it when he considered going back to his mum. Nearly done it again at the first sketching class, when he and Warren so literally bumped into each other. But he could not do it this time. He was going to have to face whatever he found behind this door, and if he could not do it on his own, well. That was alright.

Warren went up the stairs just as Matty turned with a wild look in his eye, about to bolt. He had a lot of momentum, but this time around, Warren wasn't as blindsided by the attempted escape and avoided the collision.

Matty blinked down at him from a step above.

"I've gone mad at last," he said.

"Pretty much," said Warren with a grin. "That's the conclusion I came to last night, anyway. That you're off your rocker. Scotland Yard's got nothing to do with it, mate. And you know it."

"But what are you doing here?"

"I figured someone off his rocker could use a little help getting back on it," Warren said. "I'm sorry I left in such a hurry. I was more worried about how silly I was going to look if you were right than I was about the fact that what you were saying didn't make sense. You were clearly having a hard time with leaving your work, and I don't think I should have left you in that state. I'm sorry."

"Oh," said Matty, that sort of polite blankness on his features again. "Well. I—I'm sorry I was off my rocker."

"Are you still?"

He nodded, and perfectly calmly said, "Warren, I am in a *state*, believe it or not. A real bloody state."

Warren came to meet him at the top of the steps and took his arm. "I'll face it with you, then. Alright?"

Jess Everlee 261

"It will be very rude to bring a second guest like this, unannounced."

"It was rude of him to send you such a vague note when you've got so much on your mind," Warren countered. "You say you've been working together, what, ten, twelve years? He ought to know better. And if I'm wrong? If it's vague because you're right about the sort of news he's got? In that case, it involves me, don't it? I should hear it myself rather than risk you clamming up again, eh?"

Matty's eyes had never looked clearer or more grateful. Warren wanted to kiss him or at least bring their heads softly together, but neither of those was happening gracefully on a nice little stoop in the middle of the day and both of them in nice hats. So he squeezed Matty's arm and Matty squeezed back, then he knocked on the door at last.

Warren had forgotten until this very moment that he'd once met Detective Barrows.

The same upright, narrow, white-haired man who got up from an easy chair in the sitting room to greet them had posed as a potential buyer of The Curious Fox's property one soggy afternoon last year.

Warren had not, perhaps, been on his very best behavior that day.

"Uh-oh," he said under his breath.

Matty glanced at him. "What?"

But there was no time to explain that, due to circumstances that were really very reasonable at the time, he'd perhaps... sworn a bit at Detective Barrows when they met, and maybe-just-maybe spat on the ground near his feet when the other fellow showing him the property had crossed a line in the way he spoke to Warren. Since Detective Barrows had, apparently, gotten that rude wanker arrested in the end, Warren supposed he got a pass for not curbing the arsehole's speech at the time.

262   *To Sketch a Scandal*

Didn't mean Warren was going to get a pass from Barrows, though, for acting…well…the way he did when home was behind him and it was the expectations of the alleys, rather than his mother, that guided the words he selected in the heat of the moment.

Maybe he wouldn't remember Warren…but no. Even as he was greeting Matty, his sharp eyes—unfairly sharp for his age, really—were taking Warren in.

"And who's this?" he asked Matty, like he already knew.

Matty, blessedly innocent of the awkwardness, patted Warren on the back like he couldn't be prouder to be introducing him. "This is my dearest friend," he said, saying it like Barrows knew and approved of all his vices and would hopefully understand the gravity behind the words. "Mr. Warren Bakshi."

Warren extended a hand because he had to. Barrows took it slowly, appraising him. His recognition was obvious.

"Lovely to meet you," Barrows said, a bit too politely. "Matthew, did you say how you met Mr. Bakshi?"

"In the portrait class I've been taking," he said.

Barrows softened, and next thing Warren knew, a very warm sort of smile crossed his face. "Well, isn't that nice?" he said. "Glad to hear it. That's a very noble pursuit, Mr. Bakshi. Much worse things a bloke could be doing with his time, eh?"

Barrows clearly took it to mean he'd left The Curious Fox behind. Warren let him have it. He'd already come out on top with one former detective nosing into his business—risking full honesty with another might push his luck past the limit.

So he kept that little detail to himself as they got settled into the sitting room with their tea and a warm fire. Barrows's home was a sleepy place, Barrows himself seeming like the sort of bloke with enough energy left in his bones that he'd start to resent his retirement eventually, but who was so new to the slower pace that he was still finding the novelty in it. He talked about the housekeeper's idiosyncrasies and the new grandchild who would be born to him around the same time as Warren's niece or nephew was expected. He told them all about this particular tea they were drinking, looking at Warren a bit too much as he did so, as if being Indian magically meant he knew more about tea leaves than he did about gin.

All the while, Warren felt very strongly the determined retirement around the fellow, and was trying to stay awake, whilst poor Matty sat on the very edge of his seat, hardly moving. He had not even mentioned, yet, that he'd left Scotland Yard, letting Barrows chatter on and clearly waiting for his world to come crashing down.

"Forgive me, Mr. Barrows," said Warren at last, unable to take Matty's tension a second longer. "But what news did you call Mr. Shaw here to discuss? He's been worrying over it, as you might guess, and I think by now we're both very curious as to what it was."

Barrows looked between the two of them, confused. "But I've already told you," he said. "That's what we've been talking about this whole time."

Matty sat up even straighter. "What?"

"The new grandchild, of course," he chuckled. "What did you think?"

Warren nudged Matty. *See? Told you you were off your rocker.*

Chapter Eighteen

Matty

"The grandchild?" Matty repeated. "That's the news?"

Barrows looked taken aback. "Well, I thought it was very good news, myself."

"It is good news," Matty stammered. "But… Then why did your letter sound so grim?"

"Did it?"

"I thought you were bringing me here to tell me…" he stammered, breaking off in confusion. "Some things have gone missing recently, and I… I assumed you knew something."

"Knew something?" said Barrows. "Matthew, I don't think I understand."

"Well, some things went missing, like I said," he repeated, mind spinning. "Things that might not exactly prove, but certainly wouldn't help all the suspicions at the Met, and then… Then I did something that was maybe very stupid, I…" He paused, looking Barrows mournfully in the eye. How could he possibly admit that he'd thrown away all Barrows had done for him? He had not regretted it until this moment, but now…

"Go on, Mr. Shaw," said Warren. Here, it could not be

mate, or love, or certainly not sweetheart. But all three showed through the thin veneer of polite address.

And maybe *Matthew Shaw* was not equipped to have this conversation with Detective Inspector George Barrows, but it did seem that Warren's *mate* and *love* and *sweetheart* could manage it, because that bloke knew he was more than a pretty tool and a charity case. That he was good for something else, even if he wasn't sure what it was yet. And that was alright, because he could be loved for more than what role he could play in someone else's enterprise.

"I left the Met."

Barrows did not mask his surprise. "Why?"

"Because Detective Ashton wanted me to shave," he said. "He ruined my promotion, and then tried to force me right back into the same box that had lost it for me in the first place. I couldn't do it. It was an affront to my spirit, as you said."

It sounded ridiculous, but Barrows nodded slowly and grimly without hesitation. He seemed to understand exactly what Matty meant.

"And what does that have to do with your missing items?" he asked.

"I hadn't considered—therefore hadn't ruled out—that someone at the Met had taken them. So when I left in a...well, a bit of a high temper, I worried that I might have fanned the flames of someone's enmity. And then your letter arrived, and I got it into my head you were trying to warn me of just that sort of thing."

Barrows considered it. "Those are some rather wild logical jumps, Matthew."

"Well, you weren't exactly there to talk me out them this time, were you? What was I supposed to think?"

"You were supposed to think I was inviting you to tea!"

"How, exactly, was I supposed to understand that? The letter was ice-cold, sir, not exactly dripping with friendliness.

266   *To Sketch a Scandal*

Could you not have been a little clearer that this was a bloody social call?"

Barrows looked surprised at Matty's outburst, but Matty was surprised he hadn't sprung right to his feet.

"And if you wanted me for a social call," he went on, "why didn't you ever indicate that social calls were to be part of our relationship going forward? I thought..."

He couldn't say it. It got caught in his throat on the way out. Warren rubbed his arm, but the words didn't budge.

"What is it, Matthew?" Barrows said.

"I have been under the impression," he said finally, taking great care so that his voice did not shake. "That you wouldn't want to see me again. I didn't think you had any reason to contact me if not to tell me some dreadful news. Now that you're retired, I figured you were perfectly happy leaving me behind."

Barrows looked at him like he'd only just remembered where they'd met, why they knew each other in the first place. Like he was just realizing now that he'd not, perhaps, mended Matty quite as thoroughly as he liked to believe. That if he'd wanted to do that, he ought to have put a little more work in.

"Then, ah, I suppose I will be as clear as possible, Matthew," he said. "I would be delighted to continue an acquaintance with you under our new circumstances. If, of course, you would." He took a deep breath. "It's not as if we have the simplest of histories. I asked a lot of you, over the years. A lot that, I'm not too proud to admit, I would not have asked of my own grand-children. I would be disappointed, but not offended, if asking for continued friendship was finally a request too far."

A little "Hmm" from Warren caught Matty's attention.

"What?"

Warren shook his head a little. "Nothing, I just... I'm glad to hear he can admit it," he said. "That he *asked a lot*. Because he did. And it shows. Every day, it shows."

There was a dark sort of undercurrent there that neither

Matty nor Barrows missed. There were more colorful words he wanted to use to describe his understanding of this professional partnership.

"He had every right to ask for whatever he wanted," Matty reminded him. He turned to Barrows, said it again for his benefit. "You could have asked me for anything. I don't resent it. You saved my life."

"Probably," Barrows said. "But you've more than paid that back by now."

"No, I haven't. I couldn't even hang on to the position you got for me."

"Legacy is not necessarily that simple," he said. "Last year, when you risked everything to spare Mr. Forester as I spared you—clumsy as the attempt may have been—you paid it back."

"That doesn't make any sense."

"It will someday. When you're old and retired and thinking through what you're leaving behind. It will make sense then."

Matty wasn't convinced of that. But one thing was very clear: Warren was right. He'd misread this entire situation. Every bit of it, from Barrows's feelings about their friendship to the chances of there actually being more than rumors and gossip among his old coworkers. He'd been wrong about everything, letting small, sad parts of himself take the lead on the case while his reason sat idle and useless. He was just grateful Warren had noticed the spiral he'd gotten sucked into and showed up today. If he hadn't, he might not have even come inside, reeling and worrying until he got himself caught up in a worse situation.

"Well," he said at last. "Th-thank you, I suppose. I... I guess I'll think on it." A particular sadness deep inside him put up a fuss, telling him not to even consider giving up on any scrap of affection he could get. But it was time, at last, to figure out who his friends were. That was easy at the extremes, looking at Warren or Detective Ashton. It was more complicated, though, for the fellow who'd saved him and mentored him, but under

268   *To Sketch a Scandal*

circumstances that were far from straightforward. "I might like to, but… Mr. Bakshi's right. I should think it over."

Barrows nodded. "Mr. Bakshi strikes me as someone who cares for your well-being," he said very seriously. "Whatever you decide, I'll be glad to know you've found that, at the very least."

"Thank you, sir," said Matty. "I'm very glad as well."

"Now that we've settled this," Barrows went on. "Will you take the ring back?"

"For what? The promotion's over."

"To remember me by," he said. "Particularly if you decide that this is our final parting, it would mean a lot for me if you took it. Forget the promotion. It was never really about that in the first place, and I should have told you that to begin with."

"You should have," Matty agreed quietly.

"We weren't working in a place where our feelings could be particularly free."

"Bit of an understatement."

"But we aren't there now," Barrow said. "So will you take it?"

Matty was tempted to turn from this attempt to keep the door open between them. But in the end, he had the courage to nod. To wait, touching Warren's hand gently as Barrows went to get it. And to slip the thing onto his finger at last, now that he knew it had been given out of reciprocation, rather than expectation.

Their departure, after that, was not hasty, but was not put off, either. Some time to absorb the reality of his situation with Barrows was needed in order to decide what made sense going forward. Difficult problems required not just all the information, but a moment to breathe and think and see what it all meant. The better level of himself knew that, and as they left, Warren helped keep him in that space.

"Where to?" Matty asked as they went out onto the street. Warren always had a good idea of the best meeting place for their circumstances.

Warren hesitated, then said, with a determined set to his face, "My place."

Matty felt his brows climb straight up to his hat brim. "*Your* place? As in, your house?"

"That's right."

"But your family—"

"Thinks I ought to bring friends round more often." Warren leaned sheepishly against the black gate to Barrows's house, peering at Matty like he was nervous to broach something. "And I think they might be right. I'd like you to meet them, Matty. I have to be clear with you, though: while my brother and his wife have sort of figured us out, I cannot tell my mother or anyone else what you really mean to me. If you come round, you'll have to be my dear companion. Even if it's months, or years or..." He paused. "Maybe forever. That's how you'd have to be known. But I think I prefer that to the alternative, to having to keep you so separate and secret all the time, particularly if things don't go swimmingly at the Fox. I'm allowed friends, though, and we're hardly the first English bachelors to choose each other over wives. So. Do you think that sort of thing would be too difficult for you? I hate asking someone to pretend like that, but I'm afraid it's what I have to offer at the moment. If you'll have it."

Forever.

It was that word that echoed long past the rest. Matty had never been promised forever in anything. Never even had it floated as a possibility.

"A little pretending," Matty said slowly, feeling a flush creep over his face, "has never been too difficult for me, you know."

"That's why I hate to ask it of you," said Warren. He'd tucked his hands in his pockets now, the wiliness he brought to lovemaking overshadowed by bashfulness in matters of feeling. But he pressed on. "I don't want to be like old Barrows back there, forcing you to be something you're not."

270   *To Sketch a Scandal*

"But I am your companion," Matty said without hesitation. "That's perfectly true. I'm your love and your sweetheart, sure, but I'm your mate as well, aren't I?"

"I suppose…"

"The age we're in…it's proving to be a difficult one, Warren. I don't get the feeling we're at the apex of our difficulties. Neither the law nor the church nor any significant amount of public opinion is on our side in this, and from my vantage, it seems likely to get worse before it gets better. But, Warren, I will be to you whatever this age demands of us. I'll be a back-alley sneak or a pining celibate or anything in between. I don't care what it is, or whether it's easy. I'll have you in any capacity necessary."

He could have sworn he saw Warren's lip quiver, but they were in the street and there was no space for sentiment. He mastered it quickly, along with a lot of other impulses, if he felt anything like Matty did just now, desperate to touch and kiss and celebrate whatever exactly had just happened between them.

Instead, of all things, Warren smiled and tipped his hat.

Matty tipped his back.

And they started off together, arm in arm like the most proper of companions, for Warren's house.

"Something's still bothering me, though," Matty said as they went up the tidy stair that led to Warren's front door. "If my housemates bear me no ill will, and Scotland Yard is prepared to let me go without a fuss, then who stole the pictures?"

Warren gave him a sideways look, half-amusement, half-annoyance as he reached for the handle to let them in without hesitation.

"Have you forgotten, Mr. Detective," he said, as the latch gave way and this new side of his life was revealed to Matty at last, "that *I'm* the one of us who actually went and made an enemy recently?"

Chapter Nineteen

Warren

Mother's manners would have dictated pulling Mr. Sanford Binks quietly aside after class. But between the party, the odd meeting with Barrows, and an evening spent not-smoking with Matty in his home parlor with no less than *a dozen* interruptions from Mother, Harry, and Anjali, even after they'd all had ample time to get to know his new "art friend," Warren's other side—his sex-club-and-alley side—was feeling a little cooped up by the time he got to class and saw the sniveling, black-mailing little thief walking ahead of him toward the building.

"Oy."

He grabbed Binks by the shoulder and spun him round.

"Excuse—"

Warren snatched Binks's sketchbook and took a few steps back. When Binks gasped and came after his precious baby, Warren darted into the alley beside the house. Once in the shadows, he dropped the book near the dustbins and shoved the arsehole up against the wall.

Binks...well, he *squeaked* when his back hit the brick, more mouse than man. Warren squinted into his eyes. He was still

272   *To Sketch a Scandal*

holding Binks's lacy shirt, but his notion of getting rough was deflated by that pathetic sound. Warren didn't fear a scrap, but he didn't go around picking fights with people not itching to fight back. He didn't let go, but he did loosen his grip with an annoying surge of pity.

"You took my pictures," he hissed. The fellow screwed his eyes up and winced like he'd been hit. "You fuck, look at me." Binks opened his eyes the barest possible slit. "You're a bloody thief, aren't you?"

"Please," he said. "I don't—"

"Admit it."

"Yes!" Binks said. "Yes, I took them. Alright? You were busy with Mr. Shaw, and I took them."

"I want them back," Warren said. "Do you understand me? I want them back now. If you think you can squeeze so much as a bloody tuppence out of me for them, you're barking, but I *will* promise not to do *this* again, eh?" He tightened his grip. Didn't even need to jostle the bloke against the wall to get another squeak out of him. "Pretty good deal, if I say so myself."

"Pay me for them?" Binks repeated, high-pitched and panicky. "I don't know what you're talking about. I didn't steal them to *sell* them—last thing I'd do is start driving up more enthusiasm for *your* work, Bakshi."

Warren gave his head a confused shake. "What?"

"Goodness, Warren," came a calm voice from behind him. He turned and saw Matty had arrived, looking all innocence in his patched coat and the familiar scarf that Warren had left behind last time, sketchbook tucked under his arm. Innocent except for his eyes, which were alight with laughter and vindication as he took in the scene before him. "How did I know I'd find you causing trouble in an alley this morning?"

"I was right," Warren said. "He's our thief. He admitted it."

"Oh my." Matty winced. "In that case, Mr. Binks, I suggest you give the pictures back before this escalates. Blackmail

Jess Everlee

remains more illegal than drawing pretty pictures, I'm afraid. As a former officer of the law, I can assure you that you won't come out on top if you pursue your intentions."

"Who the devil said anything about blackmail?" Binks said wildly. "I burned those pictures, Bakshi, so you couldn't bring them to the showcase at the end of the class."

Warren was speechless for so long that Binks began trying to edge out of his grip. Warren tightened it back up to the tune of another squeak.

"You stole my pictures," he said slowly, "because you didn't want me to look good at the Buttersnipes' end-of-class showcase? The bloody showcase where our own mums and a few half-baked amateur artists will ooh and aah and try to get us to buy more classes?"

Binks, at last, drew himself up a smidge. "Some of us take our opportunities seriously, Mr. Bakshi."

Truly shaken by the sheer pettiness of it all, Warren finally let the chap go. Binks gathered up and hushed and shushed his poor dear sketchbook, glaring at Warren for the indignity he'd cast upon the precious thing.

"So, they're really destroyed?" Warren asked.

"Of course they are," muttered Binks as he nursed the sketchbook on his hip, wiping the dust from it with his handkerchief like the specs were dribbled milk. "And look. While you may possess a streak of incidental talent, you're new to this world. A bit of colorful expression won't get you blackmailed by itself. Not yet anyway." His eyes darted, and Warren realized what it seemed Binks had already surmised: that they all had at least one thing in common other than the class. "In any case, if you really want to keep from making enemies, I suggest you stop showing off. Not everyone you meet will have my level of integrity."

With that, he drew himself up, resituated his little darling, and went off to class.

274   *To Sketch a Scandal*

"The showcase," Warren said. "Nearly drove us both to Bedlam and back over the stupid *showcase*."

"At least he has a high level of integrity," said Matty dryly. "Only stealing and destroying your art so as to hobble your career before it even begins. Very dignified stuff." He turned to Warren. "What are you going to display, do you think? Looks like you won't be getting those old ones back."

"Sorry, love. I should have shown you before. I know you wanted to see them."

"That's the life of a muse, I suppose. I am disappointed, but I think I've got the gist. I'll make do with whatever comes next."

"I am working on something new actually," Warren admitted. He'd started it last night, after his worlds had crashed together and not a single thing had been left burning. It was not a scandalous piece, but it was an intimate one. Even thinking about it made heat rush to his cheeks.

"Can I see this one?" Matty asked. "Before your sketchbook is subjected to further integrity?"

"I think, if you're comfortable risking what might happen in the meantime, I'd like to put the finishing touches on it and show you when I show everyone else on Saturday."

Matty looked surprised. "At The Curious Fox?" he said. "You still want to go through with all that, then? After everything that's happened?"

"If you do."

"Why wouldn't I?" said Matty. "As is my usual custom, I mostly get to stand there and look pretty. You're the one who has to make an arse of himself."

"Well, maybe," said Warren. "Something occurred to me, you see, as I was starting out the new sketch last night. Something that might make you change your mind about the whole thing."

"Stop being ridiculous—"

"I'm not. You see, I...recalled something of an idiosyncrasy

Jess Everlee 275

of Mr. Forester's. One I'd forgotten, since I didn't believe it would ever apply to me."

"Something unpleasant? If it doesn't work?"

"Something unpleasant, yes," said Warren. "But it is actually a risk we face if our plan *does* work."

"Oh? And what is that?"

"I don't know if you picked up on this, when you worked for him," said Warren. "But Mr. Forester...well...he likes..."

"Likes what?"

"He likes weddings," Warren concluded. "Really, really likes weddings."

The widening of Matty's eyes showed that he understood the gravity of the situation immediately.

"Oh dear," he said. "So, you think...if he is moved by your confession..."

"I don't think, Matty," said Warren grimly. "I *know*."

Matty thought it through. "So there really is no dignified way to move through this, is there? Either we do it and look like fools, or skip it and look like traitors."

"Correct. I'd say it's a bit more dignified than nicking pictures from your rival's sketchbook," said Warren. "But just barely. Do you still want to go through with it, now that you know what you're in for?"

Much to his surprise, Matty gave the most blinding dimpled grin Warren had seen on him yet.

"Warren," he said, awfully flirty for the hour. "Are you asking for my hand in marriage?"

This narrow spot between the art school and the café next door was shadowed indeed, but no true back alley. A good sliver of sun made it back here, brightening Matty's face, turning his eyes to that dreamlike color they took on when the light hit just so. That joke, though—it would transition very easily to the red-lit parlor where his friends traded in the same sorts of quips and punch lines all night long. Being ignored for fifteen years and then used for another ten had made Matty Shaw a bit odd, cautiously reserved, and more than a little mad. But Warren knew right then that if the others would give him a chance, he'd fit right in with the rest of the crew at The Curious Fox.

"In some sense, Matty," said Warren, "some strange, convoluted, completely ridiculous sense that I couldn't adequately explain if you paid me, I think I am."

Matty was still grinning as he stepped in close. He took the scarf off and finally returned it to its spot around Warren's neck, where they both knew it belonged.

"In that case," he said. "I think I accept."

Chapter Twenty

Matty

On Saturday night, Matty returned to the Gull, the pub he'd stayed at the last time Warren concocted an ill-conceived plan to get him into The Curious Fox. He had a reasonably edible supper, some more of their nice stout, and a friendly chat with that same probable prostitute who reassured him (with evidence, this time) that she really did keep a few fresh toothbrushes handy in her reticule, mostly for her own good, and had never once lied to him nor to anyone else about their history, so-help-her-God.

Hopefully, that was a sign of things to come. Shy of ten o'clock, as agreed, he left his post at the Gull's sticky bar and went to The Curious Fox. Warren handed check-in duties over to the doorman at ten so he could focus on fixing drinks for the theater casts, crews, and audience members who flooded the place after Saturday night's shows. A prompt arrival on Matty's part was vital. A late arrival could put him at the mercy of the doorman, and, worse yet, risked Warren's heartfelt confession being interrupted by a slew of literal clowns.

Faced with the Fox's dingy gray door, Matty took a deep

278   *To Sketch a Scandal*

breath and tried to steady himself. His feet itched to turn back as he had at the Buttersnipes' or Barrows's. But this time, Warren would not be behind him, to talk him back onto his rocker and into his future.

Because it was Warren waiting for him on the other side.

Knock knock.

As promised, it was Warren who greeted him, glittering in that amber waistcoat Matty liked. He leaned in the doorway. A lock of hair fell rakishly into his eyes as he held out a feathered pen and a ledger with a sly smile. The only thing that kept him from being the stuff erotic art pieces were made of was the lumpy scarf around his neck.

"Name?" he asked, as if he'd never once moaned it in any of the rooms behind him.

"Matthew Shaw."

"Occupation?"

"Aspiring artist."

"Aspiring artist," Warren repeated with lush enthusiasm. He dusted Matty's nose playfully with the feathered pen. "Now that's one I haven't heard in at least…twenty minutes."

Matty's face burned at the sight of Warren in his element again for the first time since their original meeting. He was always stunning, but when he turned it on, he was a bloody masterpiece.

"You act like this for everyone who comes in?"

"Sure do," said Warren with a wink. "What do you think?"

"I think I can't believe you've never been arrested."

Warren ushered him inside with a warm hand on his back, laughing. "They've never put me away for anything, but, Matty, sweetheart, who said I've never been arrested?"

They passed through the first layer of curtains, but before they got to the second, Warren pressed him to the wall. He pushed one leg between Matty's and leaned in close.

"I forgot the most important question, Mr. Matthew Shaw,

aspiring artist," he whispered. "No one gets into The Curious Fox without someone to speak for them." He nipped Matty's bottom lip. "Tell me: Who are you here with, tonight?"

Chatter, footfalls, and clinking glasses drifted from the other side of the curtain. While the idea that he might soon be part of it was thrilling, a few bits of Matty were distraught that this wasn't the start of one of their private trysts.

"I'm here with Warren Bakshi," Matty said, a little breathless. "The barkeep."

"Yes, you are." Warren kissed him deep, quick, and dirty. "And don't you forget it."

Still dizzy from that kiss, he said, "How exactly would I forget it?"

"You'd be surprised who forgets what their first night at the Fox." Warren was teasing, but with a thread of very charming seriousness. "Come in with one bloke, next thing you know, they're wandering off with the first pretty face to make eyes at them."

"This isn't technically my first night at the Fox," Matty reminded him. "And I already wandered off with the first pretty face to make eyes at me last time. Wandered so far I met his mum last week." He leaned up to plant a peck on Warren's forehead. "So, I think I've probably got that one out of my system."

"In that case." He glanced nervously at the curtain. "You ready?"

"To be forced into an impromptu marriage ceremony, or get kicked out on my arse?"

"Either. No telling which we're facing."

"I'm ready if you are."

Warren gave him one last kiss, for luck, then brought Matty through the curtains.

No one looked their way at first, but Matty himself could do nothing but stare around in shock. He'd spent many hours here during the day, and had stopped by for a drink that one night

280 To Sketch a Scandal

when all the fun had been going on upstairs. It had looked like a very standard place that night, if a touch overdecorated, but Warren had since told him that was cover for rowdier behavior in the other room.

Now, though, it was populated to its usual extent, and Matty was mesmerized. This was no seedy coffeehouse, but nor did it have the debauched allure of a full-on brothel. Sodomy happened only in the back rooms, of course, but barely a glance around the place showed conspiracy to commit it between blokes flirting at the bar, female impersonation at a questionably-legal betting table, and an embrace that would constitute gross indecency behind a clumsily-pulled alcove curtain. (Probably. No one really knew what constituted gross indecency exactly, not even Matty, who had for a while been expected to know how to spot it.)

But as Warren took him by the hand and led him through the room, that habit of mind that led to a list of crimes went quiet, and he started to see something quite different—groups of friends, pairs of lovers, tables of revelers, all of them finding blessed escape for the moment.

He'd gone back and forth, in the days since leaving the Met. But he knew, right then and there, that he'd made the right choice. To pretend he belonged on the opposite side of all this was far more degrading to his spirit than any other role he'd taken in his years there.

The last table they passed was that of the creatively attired gamblers, interspersed with two more obvious gentlemen, a smiling one with a peacock feather in his hat and a big surly one with spectacles. There was an outright shriek from one of the frocked folks at that table, and for a second, Matty thought the time had come for him to be thrown out on his arse.

The shrieker jumped to her feet. Matty would not have recognized her at all, if not for the way she…he…? (Matty was embarrassingly of his depth on that particular point. He'd have to ask about manners when he got a chance.) In any case, what was unmistakable was how the person pulled a fan out of the folds of a lacy dress like a rapier and waved it in Warren's face.

This was a transformed Noah Clarke, Mr. Forester's lover and the whole reason Matty was here tonight.

"You actually brought him?" Mr. Clarke said, astounded. He looked back at his companions at the table, who were whispering with each other curiously. "B-but... I didn't think..." There was bald shock on his painted face as he gaped at Warren. "You're *Warren Bakshi*. You aren't actually supposed to go through with it! You don't fall in love and make declarations. You've been telling us that for ages."

Matty cocked his head to the side, confused. "But... Mr. Clarke, this was your idea in the first place."

"No, it was your idea, I just allowed you to entertain it," he snapped. He looked oddly panicked. Behind him, the whispers of the others were intensifying, their own pink and red smiles widening mischievously. "But... I didn't think... Th-the *bedpost*..."

"Miss Penelope," said Warren slowly, no less than amazed. "Did you *bet the others* I wouldn't go through with it?" He grabbed the fan just above where Noah's gloved hand clutched the base, grinning wickedly. "Did you bet them, *and lose*?"

The response from the table was all the answer anyone needed, titters and cheers and the fellow with the peacock feather shouting, "Told you so!"

"Not yet!" Mr. Clarke—Miss Penelope, it seemed, as that's how everyone else was referring to her just now—said, snatching her fan back. She narrowed her eyes at Warren. "You brought him," she said. "But you haven't gone through with the rest of it. So I haven't lost yet."

"Penny," Warren said, "do you have any idea how much money I've lost to you at the card table over the years?" She shook her head. "Well, I keep that count on the other bedpost.

282 *To Sketch a Scandal*

Why don't you go look it over and recalculate the odds I'll go through with it now that I know it will hurt your pocket?"

The others loved that. In their celebration, they tried to get Warren to introduce Matty to them right then, but he shook them off. While they knew Warren was due for some sort of uncharacteristic public confession, they did not, it seemed, know exactly who Matty was and why such theatrics were necessary in the first place. Warren clearly wanted to keep it that way for now.

"Later," he said. "Let me secure your win, first, before she finds some way to twist it in her favor. You know how she is."

They *did* know how she was, it was unanimously agreed, and sent Warren and Matty on their way to their final trial.

Mr. Forester was behind the bar, fixing a couple of fizzes and humming to himself. Matty hated the thought that they were about to disturb his peace. He probably shouldn't be so sentimental about the chap, but so it was. He really had liked working for him.

Still, the only way out of this one was through. Warren went behind the bar to relieve Mr. Forester of the glasses and whisper something in his ear. As Warren brought finished drinks to the correct customers, Mr. Forester turned around. There was a sort of incredulous look on his face from whatever Warren had told him, but when his eyes landed on Matty, they became quite wide indeed. Whatever Warren had said, it wasn't Matty he'd expected to find.

"Mr. Shaw," said Mr. Forester, polite but suspicious. "This… is a surprise." He turned to Warren and lowered his voice. "Warren, I thought I made my thoughts pretty clear last time we talked about this. Could you explain—"

"I can." Warren squared his shoulders and stared his manager down. "I can explain. I can explain very well. But not in words."

He disappeared under the bar, and when he came back, it was with his sketchbook in hand. He put it on the bar and beckoned to Matty.

Jess Everlee 283

"Warren," Mr. Forester scolded. "He can't come back here—"

"He's quit Scotland Yard, so just give it a second, would you, guv?" said Warren. Something in his voice made Mr. Forester back down as Matty came around to Warren's other side.

From this vantage, he had a perfect view of the rest of the room. While most were carrying on without much attention, Miss Penelope and some of her friends had sidled closer, and the pair who'd taken the fizzes were watching. Well, one of them was watching, the younger one in the nicer coat. The other was too enamored of his companion to pay attention to anything else.

Warren began flipping the pages of his sketchbook. Matty drew his eyes away from the pair down the bar more reluctantly than he might have liked. Something about them had caught his attention...but there were more important things happening right now than a bit of brazen chatter. He knew who he was here with, so why was he staring at these other chaps all of a sudden? They weren't even particularly attractive, to be sucking up his notice in a moment like this.

Well, one of them wasn't, anyway. The other was, very much so. But Matty had never been drawn to fellows like the ones he played for a case...

Once again, he took charge of his eyes and put them where they belonged: on Warren's drawing.

And he was glad to have done so, because what he saw was...

Well, it was beautiful.

"Warren," Matty said, tracing the page with a finger. "This is..."

"It's Matty," Warren told Mr. Forester, as if the likeness were not half as perfect as it was. "It's Matty and my mother, on the night I introduced them to each other. They were laughing just like this within minutes—they've both got good senses of humor, you know. I didn't think it was a good idea at first, but they got on well in the end." He sighed, and slipped a hand around Matty's waist. "She can't know the extent, of course,

284   *To Sketch a Scandal*

but you can, Forester. You do, I think, now that you're seeing the proof right in front of you."

Mr. Forester examined the drawing, and then Warren and Matty standing live in front of him. "You introduced Mr. Shaw to your *mother*?"

"I tried to tell you we'd become friends," Warren said.

"You've never introduced *me* to your mother, and we're friends," said Mr. Forester. "Just how often do you do that, exactly?"

"Exactly once."

Matty hated himself in this moment. Because it was so sweet, so longed-for, so perfect, and yet his eyes kept drifting to that sodding pair of nobodies with their fizzes and their too-shiny hair…

Well, no. Not both. Just the one with shiny hair. That's the one who kept pulling his gaze, his attention, his sense of…recognition. Because that's what it was. Not the face. He'd never seen the chap before. But he recognized something in his actions, in his outfit, in the clearly false gems that decorated his fingers…

Matty's curiosity coalesced all at once into understanding. An understanding that no one else in the room seemed to have, and for good reason: Matty was probably the only one among them to have intimate knowledge of just what was happening and how to spot it.

He was suddenly glad, very, very glad to have been convinced of coming here. Maybe Mr. Forester was right—maybe he was a risk—but he was something else too. Something that might just balance that risk out in the end.

He was an expert in knowing the enemy.

The slap of a fan on the bar startled him just as he was drawing breath to sound the alarm.

Chapter Twenty-One

Warren

"Sweet as this is, *amore*," said Miss Penelope, hand tight round her fan, "this is not the dramatic and public declaration you promised me."

While it was usually Warren leaning over this bar, Forester had his elbows on it and his eyes trained on Penelope's within a second. She was flanked by Charlie and Miles, but Forester had eyes only for his love—the love he clearly realized had been keeping something from him.

"You knew about this?" he said.

Penelope sighed, and leaned in too, becoming Noah again all at once.

"Yes, *amore*," he whispered. "I found them here together when I came to get that fan for Annie. They've been sneaking around."

"Isn't that *romantic*?" said Charlie, clearly eating every bit of this up.

"That was weeks ago," Forester said to Noah. "Why didn't you say anything?"

"Because this was going to be a lot more fun, wasn't it?" He threw a look over his shoulder. "And...well..."

286   *To Sketch a Scandal*

"Because he turned it into a little wager in the meantime," Warren said. "He bet all the others I wouldn't go through with it."

The look that passed between Forester and Noah was more old-married-couple than ever.

"What the devil am I going to do with you?" Forester asked.

Noah tapped him playfully with the fan. "Share my winnings when Warren doesn't get up the guts to turn this into an event, that's what."

Warren shook his head at his ridiculous friends and turned to Matty, to get a sense for their next action. But Matty seemed distracted, his gaze darting back and forth between Warren and something else on the other side of the bar.

An odd determination filled Warren when he saw that his confession—however backed up by emotional artwork—wasn't even interesting enough to keep *Matty's* attention, much less anyone else's. Maybe Noah, irritating as he was, had a point, here.

In fact, the idea that even Noah, one of his dearest friends, had been so hoodwinked by the image Warren projected here that he'd bet literal money against the notion he could really fall in love...well, he was suddenly sick of it. Warren wasn't two people, living two lives. He was one person. A complicated one, perhaps. Maybe even an odd one. But there was room enough in him for both pieces, and it was time he started acting like it.

"Fine," he said, moving the sketchbook over and putting both hands on the bar to lift himself to sitting on it. "You want a confession? I'll give it."

But as he turned and made to stand up right on the bar, to wave his portrait around and yell out for every bloody wanker in this place that Warren Bakshi the barkeep had found someone worth more to him than a bedpost notch, Matty grabbed him.

He looked blank again. A blankness that Warren hadn't seen in a while.

"Don't," he whispered.

"What?" Warren said, confused. "Don't worry about it, Matty, I can take the ribbing, it's not—"

But then Matty leaned in closer, gripping Warren's arm tightly and whispering so he and the others nearby would all hear him:

"That bloke down there." He jerked his head to the pair with the fizzes. "The one in the coat. I think he's an entrapper."

While the noises of the bar went on behind them, the skipped heartbeat all five of them shared made their corner of the place seem very quiet indeed.

"Do you know him?" Warren whispered.

Matty shook his head. "I haven't been on that low a rung in a long time. But I don't need to know him to know what he is. He's obvious enough, if you know what you're looking for. I absolutely guarantee he's up to no good."

They all looked. And while Warren didn't know what he was looking for as well as Matty did, this fellow wasn't the first to ever sneak in here. He was new blood, here with Mr. Brady, who was always bringing someone or other along, acting like they'd been friends ten years when it had really been ten minutes (or sometimes ten shillings). The fellow certainly fit the profile well enough, something Warren himself might have noticed sooner if he hadn't been fretting about this bloody declaration business.

"What do we do?" Noah hissed.

"We get him out," said Forester, rolling up his sleeves like he expected to do so very literally. He gave Matty a reluctant but distinctly grateful pat on the shoulder. "If you're going to make a habit of saving my arse like this, I'm going to feel like a prick for not letting you in here."

"If you let me in here," said Matty, "I can go on making a habit of saving your arse whenever you like. I'm very invested in this place now, you know, and I've left Scotland Yard to boot.

288   *To Sketch a Scandal*

As well as I got on with Mrs. Bakshi, I think I'd prove a very poor comfort to her if a spot of trouble here took her son away."

"He makes a good point," said Warren. "Better than I did, admittedly. I know you've been thinking of him as a liability, but…"

They all glanced down the bar, where the entrapper in question was smiling and gesturing toward the back to poor, hapless Mr. Brady.

"Yeah. It's a good point indeed. Mr. Shaw, out of curiosity, would it be the end of everyone here," Forester asked, "if they'd made it to the back?"

"Maybe. Maybe not," said Matty seriously. "Depends on the scope of this fellow's orders. I only worked on larger operations myself, but most pretty pieces of bait are only after quick, dirty wins of one or two unlucky fellows. No matter what, it would be the end of the man he's here with."

"Serve him right," Warren muttered.

"Warren." Forester gave a scolding glare, then turned back to Matty. "And you care about that? Not just about Warren, or the club itself. But one little dolt of a patron like Mr. Brady?"

Matty nodded. "I find that I do."

"So you're going to let him in, aren't you?" Warren asked. When Forester still faltered, Warren lowered his voice a bit, but not his intensity. "I love him, mate," he said. It was a whisper, rather than the roar he'd intended, but it didn't matter. He knew he wouldn't be the same after this; would never come off as quite the same barkeep as he was before, whether the patrons all heard the confession or just saw it in his eyes. "I love him enough to risk everything I've built here. If he can save your arse to boot…hell, if he can save Mr. Brady's arse, when Mr. Brady sometimes seems more determined to lose it than to keep it? Come on. Give me this one thing, Forester. Please. I'll take sketching classes and teas with him and my mum if that's all we can have." He glanced warmly at Matty, thinking of what he'd said about being whatever he had to be. "But you know it would be better if we had somewhere it could be easy, you know? Keeping each bloke safe is part of your vision. But there's more to it, and you've got to remember that again."

Forester closed his eyes and gave his head a little shake, and Warren held his breath until his old chum opened his eyes and they were full of his characteristic, horrid, mushy sentiment.

"He's in," said Forester. "I'll want to have a good chat with him about what happened at Scotland Yard. But assuming he's got a good story there, and…well…" He paused. "You know. As long as we can work out an agreement—"

"He means a wedding," Charlie stage-whispered.

"—then he's in."

"Fantastic," said Warren. "Now, go get that traitor out of here, would you?"

"Will do," Forester said, starting off down the bar to handle the mess.

"Hey!" Noah called. "What about my bet?"

Forester might as well have been glaring at his lover out of their matching rockers by the fire.

"Call that bloody thing off entirely, beautiful, and I'll pretend it never happened. Deal?"

"Davy!"

"*Deal?*"

Noah sighed and flipped the fan open so roughly that it turned him straight back into Miss Penelope. "*Fine!*"

Forester raised a brow at Warren. "Don't say you weren't warned," he said. "When you look like us in a few years."

"We'll figure that out if we come to it," Warren said, not as distressed by the idea as he might have been. "Let's just get the unpleasant business over with."

"Right," said Forester. "I'll show that fellow the door, and—"

"Not that unpleasant business," said Warren, rolling his eyes. "I was talking about the wedding."

To Sketch a Scandal

★ ★ ★

"So," said Matty, once Noah and Charlie had vanished to the back to find a dress for him (he'd been dubbed the bride without a moment's debate). Now that the intruder was gone, he and Warren sat on the bar together, awaiting their fate. "Can you explain this wedding thing to me? Forgive me, I've seen a lot of places like this for one reason or another, and as far as I know, this is not…the norm."

It wasn't, not these days anyway. David Forester, Warren had always thought, had perhaps been born a good century too late. How exactly he'd gotten enamored of old stories of "Mother Clap's" and the other old-timey molly houses that made The Curious Fox's paltry number of blokes in dresses look like nothing and had tended to see their owners and patrons hanged in the end, Warren still wasn't quite sure.

Henry Bellville treated me very badly, he'd said once. *But let's just say, he sometimes took me places where I got to talk to people, and those people had sometimes talked to people, and fact is, I got a few stories about those spots passed down right from the source, and you don't hear stories like that from people like that without it leaving an impression, you know?*

"He's always put some of those old-fashioned things into the Fox," said Warren as he finished up the best explanation he could. "His family was like yours, I think, bunch of arseholes. So it's the closest he's got to traditions. It's sort of funny and quaint, really, when it's not, you know, directed at you personally." He already had Matty's hand in his, but now he squeezed it and held it up to examine the lovely link of them together. "That said, there is a perk to being the victims of his particular madness."

"Oh?" said Matty. "And what's that?"

Warren leaned in to whisper, not because he didn't want anyone to hear what he said, but so he could feel Matty shiver when he said it. "Marriages require consummation." He nipped

Matty's lobe, getting the reaction he was after in spades. "Not only do we get to fuck when it's done, we are absolutely *required* to do so."

"Oh dear," said Matty. "What a trial. Please tell me we don't have to produce a bloody sheet; I'm afraid they'll all be disappointed in that case."

"What? You're not a virgin?"

"Afraid not. Will you still have me?"

"No," said Warren, shaking his head without a moment's hesitation. "Definitely not. It's off to the bawdy houses with you, lass. Nothing doing."

Strange blighter Warren had attached himself to, because Matty just beamed like Warren had paid him an extravagant compliment and snuggled in tighter.

After the infamous drag party fainting, it was decided (by one vote) against forcing Matty into a corset against his will when he'd never worn one before (or so he claimed; Warren caught a little sparkle in his eye he'd have to ask about later). The ordeal instead involved outfitting Matty in a white silk robe and Warren in a borrowed tailcoat. They stood in front of the bar together while Forester joined their "hands, hearts, and minds," before reminding them that they would need to handle the joining of the rest of themselves in the back when all was said and done, or it "won't count, and you'll have to do all this again."

There was hooting. Hollering. Drunken singing. Charlie looked very smug at having been right and Noah looked a little sullen at the loss of his ill-fated bet. It felt like a damn age, but having been in the jeering audience of these things plenty of times before, Warren happened to know that Forester's molly ceremony was no English mass (and certainly *nothing* like weddings as Warren knew them best—he really dreaded what ideas Forester might get in his head if he ever learned about *that*). All

292   *To Sketch a Scandal*

in all, it was the usual five to ten minutes of sappy sentiment and sex jokes, and then—

"Kiss your bride, Bakshi," Forester said.

These things, of course, were done mostly for the sake of the show. Forester did get earnest requests for ceremony and celebration from lovers, but most of the time, it was hazing and theatrics, done to build community and lighten a mood that could get heavy sometimes.

So, as Warren looked at Matty in his silly robe, doing this thing that to Warren hardly even looked like a wedding in the first place, he knew his role. He knew what to do to get the cheers and the whistles. He knew that, under this unlikely circumstance in which *Warren Bakshi the barkeep* had consented to a molly house marriage at all, this was his moment to play that card to its fullest. They'd expect him to give a kiss that was dirty and handsy and arguably illegal across the British Empire.

As he hesitated, Matty watched him curiously. He looked very beautiful, as he always did, taking all this nonsense on without question or complaint, giving his all in the circumstances he was in.

And Warren found, as he looked into that face that had become such a comfort to him during this time of immense change, that he really did want to do what he'd not been able to manage earlier. He wanted to make a scene, a confession, a declaration that something in him had changed. The extent of that change remained to be seen—their routines when the class came to an end, what Matty would pursue when it did, whether Warren might take Mother's advice and give up the barkeeping side of his time at the club, the level of closeness he and Matty could reveal to Warren's family, whether Warren had notched his last bedpost or if they'd remain flexible in that capacity. Those things weren't settled.

But he wasn't worried about them. They'd be what they

needed to be for each other. He knew that much, at least, and it was plenty.

"Warren?" Matty said, dimples slowly appearing on his cheeks. "If you ever want this bloody thing to end, you have to kiss me."

There was only one way for a man with Warren's reputation to make the sort of scene he wanted. He slowly and gently took Matty's face in his hands, touching noses first.

"I love you," he whispered. Then, with more honey than heat, he ever-so-softly kissed this uncanny, unlikely, completely unforgettable companion of his to the sound of absolute, stunned silence of everyone else in the room.

He pulled back to find Matty grinning without any trace of blankness or hesitation. The perfect prize he'd been constantly hunting since the first night they met, and hoped to keep winning for a long time to come.

And just as everyone was picking their jaws up off the floor to spur them on to their marital duties, he heard Charlie Price whisper to Noah Clarke, "Feeling lucky you called that bet off right about now, aren't you?"

Epilogue

Since, according to the papers, the art fraud scandal had turned out to be a major Continental operation that completely cleared all English suspects, the Twentieth Semi-Annual Student Showcase of Buttersnipe's School for Artistic Enrichment (Pencil Portraiture, Section One) was held as planned in the pretty and far less turpentine-smelling parlor on the bottom floor of the art school building. Each student had selected his or her best piece to be matted, framed, and displayed on easels and walls for their friends, family, and a rather...particular segment of London's artistic community. One that, like the Buttersnipes themselves, prioritized payment and practicality over things like, well, skill and artistry. To the surprise and dismay of everyone except Matty and Warren, the visiting portraitist "Rex Harris" found himself otherwise engaged, and did not grace the event with his presence.

"Ready for it?" Warren asked, adjusting Matty's tie and smoothing the jacket he'd recently bought to ensure that at least one piece of clothing he owned had been picked out for Matthew Shaw and not some character. They'd stepped into a hallway, not fully out of sight, but they'd mastered the physicality of "inseparable companions" over their last few weeks together. While Matty might have done alright with a more isolated and consistently passionate way of seeing each other, Warren needed that public companion aspect to be happy, as he tried to create careful links between lives that weren't an especially tidy fit. Dishonest though it was around the edges, Matty was determined to be that for him—even if it meant getting his clothes fussed over without revealing how much he enjoyed it.

"Ready, I think." Matty glanced over his shoulder to the gallery beyond. They'd put their pictures beside each other, which made for a very silly-looking corner of the room. Warren had put hours in, perfecting the sketch he'd done of Matty and his mother. He'd shaded it until it moved and breathed, and added an interesting geometric border inspired by a tea tray of his parents' that had nearly the same pattern as a vase at The Curious Fox. It was, without a doubt, the most beautiful thing in that room. Whilst beside it, Matty's sketch was... "I don't know why I wouldn't be ready. It's not like anyone's going to be looking twice at what I've done."

"Oh, stop," said Warren. "I like it, actually."

"Yeah, yeah, something about your wanted poster—"

"No, I mean it," he laughed, and dragged Matty over to the piece, making him look at it. He'd done his picture of Barrows after finally agreeing to talk to the fellow about how they might go forward in each other's acquaintance, after all that had happened. Portrait making had proved a good way to go about it—stuck in the same room, but without having to make consistent eye contact as Matty tried to explain how much Barrows had meant to him, and how little he'd seemed to mean in return as the career that linked them began reaching its end. There were needed confessions, and even-more-needed apologies, and by the end, Matty felt that the relationship was shaping up very similarly to the portrait: shaky and clearly not created by experts, but maybe better than could have been expected, all things considered.

296 *To Sketch a Scandal*

That said, even if the portrait hadn't been hanging beside Warren's masterpiece, it wasn't pretty by any means. It was a little wonky, actually, and complicated; hard to put your finger on where to look or how to feel about the man in the portrait. It was, in the end, a rather perfect representation of Matty's confused feelings about the fellow who'd both saved and exploited him. A man he was planning to take tea with again very soon, to meet each other's eyes and see what came next.

"You're getting at something, I think," Warren went on. "It's not all got to be pretty all the time, eh?"

Matty smiled as Warren gave him a friendly, perfectly appropriate nudge that spoke volumes under the surface. Volumes he was already becoming eager to explore the next time they found themselves safely out of the inseparable-companion sphere.

But in mere moments, they were far from alone. It was a small school, with a small class, but the outpouring of enthusiasm from acquaintances was not small at all.

Especially not for Warren, whose entire family and a handful of family friends came to see where he'd been studying and how he'd progressed.

"You've done wonderfully," his mother said with great affection for him, but a side-eye for the more Buttersnipe-ish portraits. "Though, of course, it's not The Royal Academy..."

Warren put up a finger and said, "In my defense, I never told you it was The Royal Academy. Not this time."

"Maybe next time?" Harry Bakshi teased, sharing a look with Anjali, who was still just shy of having to confine to the house if she wound her sari right.

As much to Matty's surprise as anyone else's, Warren scratched the back of his neck, looking a little sheepish. "Yeah," he said. "Maybe it will be."

Everyone stared at him.

"What's that mean, mate?" said Matty (it was *mate* here, but Warren would hear it for what it was).

Jess Everlee 297

A little yap by their feet startled them all as Miss Martha Buttersnipe inserted herself into the conversation, followed by the gliding form of Mrs. Buttersnipe.

"I do hope," said Mrs. Buttersnipe, "that what dear Mr. Bakshi means is that he's planning to attend our private instruction in the new year?"

"As happy as I am to have taken your class, Mrs. Buttersnipe," said Warren with a brief glance at Matty. "I'm afraid that won't be possible. I actually was accepted into an Academy Class." There was a group gasp, and he held his hand up. "Not full admission. They said I'm not ready for that. But I was offered a chance to sit in and catch up my skills a bit, so I can apply properly next year."

It was all congratulations and proud mums for a moment, a moment that was joined by Miss Martha, who yipped her own approval of Warren's success. Once that all died down, Warren's family began to circle the rest of the parlor out of politeness, and Matty was able to steal a squeeze of his palm.

"Good job, love," he whispered.

"Thanks," Warren said. "There's only one problem. I don't know how to tell Mr. Forester I have to quit the bar. It was a really hard decision. I love it. I do. But there's more to me than who I've become behind it, and I want to see what that is. I'll stay a member, of course, but—" He cut off, staring at something over Matty's shoulder. "Oh, bloody hell."

"What?"

Matty whipped around to see another little crowd coming in and headed right for them. Warren's friends—David Forester, Noah Clarke, Charlie Price, and Miles Montague, along with two women he had not met yet, one in an alarmingly tight bun who looked quite like Mr. Clarke and another that was wearing pin-striped trousers.

"What the devil are you lot doing here?" Warren asked, with an incredulous laugh and shake of his friends' hands.

298   *To Sketch a Scandal*

"We wouldn't miss your showcase, *amore*," said Noah. "What sort of friends do you take us for?"

"Dreadful ones, most of the time," said Warren.

But he was clearly pleased, even when he was subjected to the horror of introducing his family and his friends to each other for the first time. (*"You were right,"* Mrs. Bakshi would say of them later. *"I don't like your art friends much."* To which Anjali would reply with a grin, *"Well, I do."*) Matty was pleased too, and found he enjoyed the showcase much more than he'd expected. His world had expanded very rapidly in the past few months, and for the first time since his career came crashing down, he had a lot of hope for what the future might hold.

"What about you, Mr. Shaw?" Mrs. Buttersnipe asked him quietly, as Warren was fielding questions from some interested amateur artists who'd stopped by. "I'm not sure I can offer you a place in our private instruction—"

"I wouldn't dream—"

"But I do hope you'll be joining us for Pencil Portraiture, Section Two?"

Matty looked demonstrably at his drawing. "I don't know…"

"I think you should," she said kindly. "I have rarely, in all my years of doing this, seen someone make the level of progress you have over the course of our time together. You do not, I think possess any talent," she added bluntly. "But if you chose, you could come to possess skill. And if it is the ability to preserve a face or a moment, rather than a spot at The Royal Academy, that you're after, I think your determination may very well be the ticket."

Matty was flattered by the words, and for the first time, he really considered it.

"If I can find a way to afford it," he said, "perhaps I will."

"Afford what?"

It was Mr. Forester. Who knew how long he'd been listening for, nosy as he was.

Nosy and helpful.

Helpful and sentimental.

Sentimental and pleasant to work for, in Matty's opinion.

Matty glanced at Warren, who was laughing and charming the artists he was speaking to. Beautiful Warren Bakshi, his lover, an artist, and very likely, a barkeep no more.

"Say, Mr. Forester," Matty said carefully, as Mrs. Buttersnipe glided off along her way. "I have a question for you."

"Oh?" Forester said. "What's that?"

Matty felt the smile spread across his face against his will as the next few months took shape in his mind, far better than any he'd had in...ever, probably.

"Hypothetically," Matty said. "If The Curious Fox suddenly found itself in need of a new barkeep..."

★ ★ ★ ★ ★

Acknowledgments

This one was a serious whirlwind! First of all, many thanks to my family and friends for their patience with my deadline drama. Thanks to my agent, Laura Zats, for brainstorming with me when I said I had a fourth Lucky Lovers book in me, but needed a little help getting the details right. Thanks to Stephanie Doig for such spot-on editorial notes and all the other things you did to make this book happen and make it much better (far more than I probably even realize). And, of course, to the rest of the Carina Adores and Harlequin teams—publishing this series with all of you has been a dream come true, and I have been so blessed by your support and expertise. Thanks to my lovely publicist, Leann Schneider-Webb, for handling so much of the non-writing stuff so I could focus on the writing stuff. To my husband, Michael—thank you for reading and loving the early version of this that didn't see the light of day. It wasn't as good as what we ended up with, but it was still nice to have had that version witnessed! And finally, to my readers—THANK YOU for supporting this series. Your enthusiasm and deep care for your queer communities is forever inspiring.